# LIGHTNING STRIKE

Lieutenant Colonel James Dunmore hitched a ride to Land's End, where Patton's First Armored Corps was restaging. The general wasn't surprised to see him. "I figured you'd be around," he said.

"They just yanked my team from the raid on France," Dunmore said angrily. "This is wrong, General. Totally unacceptable."

A tiny smile touched Patton's lips. "Don't fret, James. Simply find them another mission."

"But I need one now, sir. My men have trained hard. They deserve a crack at the enemy. Right now. If I ask them to wait, they'll go stale and demoralize."

Patton rose and moved to a large wall map of Europe and Africa. He stood gazing at it, then looked at Dunmore over his shoulder. "Roosevelt and Churchill have decided to hit North Africa," he said bluntly. He took a drag on his cigar. "The assault will be in three separate invasion groups. One against French Morocco, the other two against Algeria. I'll be commanding the Morocco landings."

Dunmore watched the general closely. "Sir, I would like to ask your—"

Patton cut him off. "I've already done it. I'm assigning your strike team a crucial mission." He stared hard at Dunmore. "They're to neutralize a battery of seven mobile field guns." Patton pointed at the map, at the ancient caravan city of Marrakesh in southern French Morocco. "Right there."

# BOOK YOUR PLACE ON OUR WEBSITE AND MAKE THE READING CONNECTION!

We've created a customized website just for our very special readers, where you can get the inside scoop on everything that's going on with Zebra, Pinnacle and Kensington books.

When you come online, you'll have the exciting opportunity to:

- View covers of upcoming books
- Read sample chapters
- Learn about our future publishing schedule (listed by publication month *and author*)
- Find out when your favorite authors will be visiting a city near you
- Search for and order backlist books from our online catalog
- Check out author bios and background information
- Send e-mail to your favorite authors
- Meet the Kensington staff online
- Join us in weekly chats with authors, readers and other guests
- Get writing guidelines
- AND MUCH MORE!

Visit our website at
http://www.kensingtonbooks.com

# RECON FORCE

# LIGHTNING STRIKE

## CHARLES RYAN

PINNACLE BOOKS
Kensington Publishing Corp.
http://www.kensingtonbooks.com

PINNACLE BOOKS are published by

Kensington Publishing Corp.
850 Third Avenue
New York, NY 10022

All Kensington Titles, Imprints and Distributed Lines are
available at special quantity discounts for bulk purchases for
sales promotions, premiums, fund-raising, educational or
institutional use. Special book excerpts or customized print-
ings can also be created to fit specific needs. For details,
write or phone the office of the Kensington special sales man-
ager: Kensington Publishing Corp., 850 Third Avenue, New
York, NY 10022, attn: Special Sales Department, Phone: 1-
800-221-2647.

Pinnacle and the P logo Reg. U.S. Pat. & TM Off.

First Pinnacle Printing: October 2003

10 9 8 7 6 5 4 3 2 1

Printed in the United States of America

*With love and respect to my brother, N. Pat Ryan,
who was also there at the beginning.*

The measure of our torment is
  the measure of our youth.
God help us, for we knew the
  worst too young!
—Rudyard Kipling, *Gentlemen Rankers*

# Part One
# The Beginning

*Cobbett Hall*
*Chester, England*
*12 February 1942*

General George S. Patton Jr. silently watched his staff intelligence officer, Lieutenant Colonel James Dunmore, study the silver-edged chessboard. It was silent in the room, only the faint whisper of rain on the window. Dunmore picked up his queen, frowned, made a move. Patton chuckled. In two moves, he put Dunmore's king in check.

They were in the study of the general's temporary residence at Cobbett Hall, an eighteenth-century manor a mile from the town of Chester. Patton had been there a month while the men, material, and armor of his I Corps arrived at relocation depots along the estuary of the river Dee.

"Your mind's not focused tonight, Sticks," Patton said. Sticks was Dunmore's nickname from when he played hockey at Princeton.

"Sorry, sir. I guess I'm a bit tired."

"Bullshit," Patton snapped amiably. He had gray eyes that could snake-stare. He leaned back, hooked a thumb under one gray suspender, and blew cigar smoke at the medieval ceiling. "Okay, let's have it."

"It's about my recon unit, General."

"I thought so."

"Damn it, I know the concept's workable. A small, independent force striking behind enemy lines? Every conquering army in history used them. Greece, Rome, even during our own Revolutionary and Civil Wars."

"I agree, James, I agree. Unfortunately the army doesn't. The shortsighted bastards dislike independent units. Too far outside the wire."

Dunmore hissed, distractedly pushed his glasses back up his slender nose. "It's utter stupidity."

"Not really. They're just afraid of soldiers with too much initiative. Tends to fuck up the neat balance of sand-table tactics."

"But why can't they understand the value of such a unit? A small force in the right place at the right time could change the entire profile of a battle."

Patton stared at him. "Passionate son of a bitch, aren't you? Good, that's one reason why you're on my staff." He flicked ash from his cigar. "How much time would you need to get such a unit operational?"

Dunmore glanced up, shot right back, "Six months, sir."

Patton's gaze swung to the window. He thoughtfully scanned the sculptured landscape of lawn and yew trees, the long, rainy-gray Cheshire plain beyond. "Make it five months. Get your TO and requisition drafts worked up. I'll authorize them."

"I—Jesus, sir, I don't know what to say."

"Don't say a goddamned thing. Just get it done."

"Yes, sir." Dunmore came to his feet, braced. "With your leave, General?"

Patton nodded. As the colonel reached the door, he said, "Pick good men and push the bastards hard, James. I want soldiers mad enough to *enjoy* killing Nazis."

"Yes, sir," Dunmore said. He went out, closing the heavy oak door quietly behind him.

# One

*Fort Nathan Allen*
*Chaolin, Connecticut*
*20 May 1942*

Blue Team leader Lieutenant Parnell's six-foot-three, two-hundred-thirty-pound body commanded him to stop. Instead, he merely blinked and lifted his head. Sweat stung his eyes. He glared at the sky, the evening overcast as gray as melting pewter. He willed his mind to override his body's commands, shifted mental pictures, imagined a soft Caribbean beach, waves like cellophane. . . .

*Go! Go!*

He lowered his gaze to the hill's summit, way up there. The Beast, waiting. A cluster of blue pines darkened by the slanting light were etched across the ridgeline. He struggled to hear the whisper of Caribbean surf above the ringing, pounding adrenaline of his blood. . . .

*Go! Go!*

He forced his senses to his mental surf. *Feel it, become it.* A mantra to focus on. As on those other days of gut-wrenching workouts when he played for the Detroit Lions. Wind sprints until you wanted to drop, endless hit-and-drive lunges against that godforsaken lineman's sled that you pushed up and down Briggs Stadium Field, lungs gasping for air, assholes sucking cleat dust.

Slowly he settled, his body momentarily recaptured. He shifted the straps of his seventy-pound field pack, adjusted his Thompson submachine gun against his back, and ran on.

His full name was First Lieutenant John "Red" Parnell. Twenty-seven years old with brush-cut hair the color of fall wheat and a broad-featured face dominated by deep, mischievous brown eyes. As a graduate of the University of Colorado with a degree in mine engineering he had twice been voted an All-American and had eventually played professional football as a tight end.

Now he was a Recon Force officer, running up to kiss the ass of the Beast, Mount Hope, the two-thousand-foot hill of granite and dirt with its two-mile road of continuous thirty-degree inclines. The thing was a symbol, a metaphor for the continuous physical and mental stress of training, the pushing beyond barriers of exhaustion to teach a man that he possessed more than he knew he had.

Red glanced over his shoulder. His team came doggedly on, strung out in single file with their heads down, their field ODs and pack straps black with sweat and Springfield 03s at high port. He smiled. Tough boys, he thought, the ones who had gotten this far, seven weeks into the training cycle.

In the beginning, there had been 105 volunteers for the newly organized Recon Force unit. Now only sixty-three were left, the others having dropped out through the simple act of turning in their helmet liners, the signal that indicated they wanted to return to their previous units.

Eventually Recon Force's Table of Organization would consist of fifty-six men, seven teams of seven men each with six staff officers and Colonel Dunmore as commanding officer. Each team was given a color designation: blue, red, green, yellow, white, orange, and purple. Parnell's team had been assigned the color blue. In order to establish that intimate cohesion of action essential in combat, each team functioned independently of the others, even having its own cadre of instructors.

He slowed, easing to the side of the road to let his men jog on past him. The road seemed terribly lonely now as evening softened the edges of things, drew silence from the sky. Cicadas hummed in the brush. The air smelled of warm stone dust.

The man directly behind him moved past. It was Buck Sergeant Solomon "Horse" Kaamanui, a huge Samoan with a tiki-god face and a ponderous body as strong and hard as a curved cement wall. Known for his voracious appetite for beer and food, he was also famous for the stallion size of his penis, which explained his nickname. Although normally soft-spoken and ponderously serene, he could achieve stunning speed and focused retaliation when insulted. A transfer from the Corps of Engineers, he was an experienced hard-hat diver and underwater demolitions expert.

Behind him came Corporal Billy "Cowboy" Fountain, a twenty-one-year-old from Estacado, New Mexico, down there on the Texas border near Bronco and Denver City. He was easygoing, a third generation mustang wrangler and rodeo bronc rider with the artless boyish look and speech pattern of a medium-sized Gary Cooper. He grinned at Parnell as he passed.

The Beast run was a daily challenge, although no one was required to take it. Its tradition had started in the late 1920s when a bored, half-drunk lieutenant named Gilliland first tried it, carrying a forty-pound field pack just to make it interesting. On that initial occasion, he didn't get very far before he vomited and dropped to his knees.

But the hill taunted him, became a matter of pride.

Every day in the early evening he'd take another crack at it, run until his body simply refused to obey and he'd fall down. He always marked that day's point of failure with a pebble. The next day he'd force himself to run past that pebble, by a few feet, sometimes a hundred yards. It took him three and a half weeks to reach the top of the hill.

Since then, many recruit-trainees who had been processed through Fort Allen had given the Beast a try. Some conquered it, others said, "Screw it!" Hundreds of pebbles still neatly lined the road, artifacts of their daily failures. When Blue Team was told of the tradition, to a man they accepted its challenge without comment. With men of this type, none was needed. They were now on their eighth attempt and still a half mile short. . . .

The third man moved past Parnell, Pfc Rafael "Weesay" Laguna. Short, stocky, he was a fast-talking L.A. street matador and ex-pachuco gang boss who always carried a knife in his boot, a needle-bladed stilleto he could maneuver with a sweet, floating grace. When in the field, he always wrapped a bandanna around his head under his helmet like his hero, Zorro, El Digno, from those black-and-white movies that had entranced him during those childhood Saturday afternoons at the Dreamland Theater in Willowbrook.

Next came Pfc Harrison Travis Kimball, the "Virginian." Descended from a governor of Virginia and numerous senators, he had twice been expelled from the Citadel military academy for accumulating astounding numbers of demerits. With the clean-cut good looks of a frat brother, he possessed an impressively creative cunning along with a cold, cynical disregard for authority in any form.

The lieutenant watched him. Kimball had his eyes closed, dreaming, far away. Of all the men on the team, Parnell considered Kimball the weakest link. He was too intelligent and he had a certain rich-boy condescension hidden down under the charm. Red figured him to be the type who could at any given moment decide this whole volunteer thing was bullshit and walk away from it.

He moved up beside Kimball. "How you doing, Harvard?"

Kimball turned, looked at him. His face was blotchy with a distant strain. "Couldn't be better, Lieutenant."

"Yeah? Looks to me like you're lagging."

"Just enjoying the scenery."

Parnell bobbed his chin, indicated Laguna. "You gonna let that little south L.A. chihuahua beat your ass to the top?" He watched Kimball's reaction to that remark closely. Football had taught him something profound: if you needle a man when he's physically exhausted, vulnerable, you can get a good look at his real self. Kimball spat a ball of cotton saliva and looked at Parnell, his blue-gray eyes gone suddenly opaque. He gave Red a fierce grin. "Fuck you, Lieutenant," he said. He picked up speed, passed Laguna.

Parnell nodded. *Okay.*

One of the first things he had encountered when he came to Recon Force was the difficulty of handling volunteers. Such men were too individualistic, too independent. That was why they had volunteered in the first place. That and a restlessness engendered by the boredom of military routine. Guys like these preferred stimulation, any stimulation, which they usually found in unorthodox ways, legal or illegal. The only common denominator they had at all was a strong contempt for anyone who preferred the safety of a lockstep existence.

His primary challenge had been to form such a group of discordant notes into a team, a single-thinking and -moving unit. But he had had no idea how he was supposed to do that. Now they were several weeks into the cycle and he still hadn't worked out a successful means to gain that cohesion.

Still, he'd come up with a theory, at least. If he could somehow discover the main thing that made each man what he was, he might be able to use it to direct him into the team concept. So far, however, it wasn't panning out. There were simply too many egos involved. And all of them were generally on edge at being suddenly thrust together in way-too-close quarters.

There had already been two fistfights within the team, vicious things, fought in dead silence. As an officer, he was obliged to stop such combats. But he didn't, not right away. Instead, he'd let the men fight it out until one seemed about to win. Only then did he step in. To allow any man to be whipped completely in front of the others would break his spirit.

The next team member, gleefully sucking air through his clenched teeth like a steam engine, was Pfc Joe "Smoker" Wineberg. His body was made of lean, taut wires, his nose and ears molded from wounded cartilage. Before the army he'd been a drifter, a roustabout, and an itinerant boxer, slightly crazy-eyed but with a surprisingly receptive sense of his immediate surroundings.

Parnell slapped his shoulder. He liked Wineberg, a bit touchy to handle but an easy read and a man you'd have to beat to death to stop. "How's it hanging, Smoker?"

Wineberg chortled, drawing lips against his teeth. "Love it, Lieutenant. Fuckin' love it."

The last man was top-kick Sergeant Wyatt Bird, the most solid member of the team and a quintessential infantryman. An old hand at twenty-six, he came from the Twenty-fifth, the Tropic Lightning Division, a natural-born soldier on his second hitch. Like Wineberg, he was spare, rawboned, a Depression man, used to little from life. He had a wry, deadpan way of speaking, a heavy southern drawl, and a steady look in the eye that made men think twice.

Parnell said, "How goes it, Wyatt?"

The sergeant gave him an impassive glance. "Can't wait to get off the top and do her again."

Parnell chuckled. "Like a kid with his first piece of ass, huh?"

"You got her, Lieutenant."

The deep-throated staccato slam of a Browning Automatic Rifle suddenly shattered the evening stillness, and a line of dust bursts stitched themselves across the road ahead.

Everyone hurled themselves to the side of the road and went to ground. Parnell crashed into heavy weeds and grass. Columbine and lupine pressed against his face, the sudden weight of his body releasing their Valentine-candy smell of peppermint. He shrugged out of his pack harness, swung the Thompson off his back, jacked a blank round into the chamber, and clicked off the safety.

He tilted his head, hollering, "Ambush! Ambush! Live fire!" He heard scattered voices shouting the same. He tried to recall the shape of the bullet impacts he'd seen in a fleeting glance. Did they cast to the left or right? He thought to the left.

He shouted again, "On the right. They're on the right." But where on the right? High, low, or flank? It must be high, he thought. You never ambushed from low ground. Still, could it be a decoy?

He heard the grass rustle, and Sergeant Bird came up beside him. Except for a slight frown, Wyatt was as calm and watchful as always. "They're right and downslope, Lieutenant."

Parnell nodded, absently noted a bug crawling on his

hand. It was black and red. He ignored it. "Take the left. Don't let the bastards get us in a cross fire."

Bird moved away, disappeared. Directly behind him came Wineberg, his eyes bright and joyous. He, too, was soon swallowed by the grass as he followed the sergeant.

There was a flash and a hard *thrump* in the earth. A smoke grenade, somewhere forward. Another went off, this one far back down the road. He saw a drift of white smoke seep across the sky, noted its direction. The ambushers *were* below them.

Now there was firing from his left, the hollow cracks of two Springfields. Bird and Smoker were engaging. Parnell lifted his head. It was time to move. The correct reaction to an ambush, he knew, must be swift and coordinated. First locate the enemy's firebase, lay in heavy countering fire, then attack it head-on so as to neutralize their advantage of surprise and thus regain the initiative.

"Move, move," he yelled. "Lay in cover fire. Right and down." Almost instantly, Springfields opened up from across the road. He shoved to his feet. Running hunched over at the waist, he dashed across the road and dove into weeds, instantly slid into a boot sole, leggings. He looked up the man's leg. It was Sergeant Kaamanui.

"Downslope," Parnell shouted. "Fan out and close with them."

"We already doin' that, Lieutenant." Sol's face was coated with sweat.

"Watch out, don't bunch."

Kaamanui moved off.

There was more firing, the BAR again, its muzzle flashes like shorting wires in the deepening dusk. They came from a fold of ground downslope sixty or seventy yards away. Parnell paused a moment, then lifted his head to see, trying to pinpoint the positions of his men.

He spotted Laguna to his left, shifting forward on his

belly in perfect manual fashion, knees and hips sidewinding, the Springfield cradled on his elbows. Then he saw Fountain to Laguna's left, up on one knee behind a rock formation, leaning out, looking downslope. As he watched, Cowboy fired his rifle, pulled back to jack out the spent round, and rammed in another. He fired again.

*Where the hell is Kimball?* Parnell wondered. He scanned left, right. There, a tiny glint from the Virginian's silver watch band. "Goddammit," Red hissed loudly. *Just like that arrogant son of a bitch. He's too far forward, breaking the team's frontal integrity.*

He lifted higher and fired two bursts with his Thompson, toward the trees, the weapon jolting back and up. The sharp smell of cordite lifted around him. He saw Kimball immediately make a lunge downslope toward a small ravine. Half-grown Douglas firs were on one end, rocks and grass on the lower side. Kimball threw himself over the lip and disappeared. Parnell fired again until his clip was empty, the barrel scorching hot above the wooden guard.

There was an answering burst from the BAR, sustained, traversing, the rounds coming in four feet above the ground. He heard them go zipping-cracking close overhead and ducked his face into the dirt. The firing stopped abruptly into a wild, ear-ringing, humming silence.

He eased up and saw Fountain and Laguna running down toward Kimball's ravine, hunched way over, skittering, sliding, fanning to the sides to cover the Virginian's flanks. In a moment, they too disappeared into the gully.

"Damn it, they're bunching," Parnell growled. Well, at least they were thinking alike. He listened. Why weren't they firing? He yanked his spare clip from his pack, reloaded. As he opened up again, twin bursts, he saw Kaamuanui fire once, twice, then lumber off toward the ravine and quickly drop down into it.

Once more Parnell threw a pair of bursts downslope. As the echoes died, he thrust himself up and headed down, running hard, the slope accelerating his plunge. He vaulted a rock, distractedly noticed the lacy grain of it, like fat streaks in a slab of beef. He reached the ravine, hurled himself down into it, rolled once, and came to one knee.

His four men were sitting on the ground, their Springfields lying across their ankles. An instructor with his starched campaign hat pulled low on his forehead, the brim casting his eyes into shadow, stood at one end of the ravine. Another instructor was at the other end. Both were grinning at him.

"Shit!" he said.

No one spoke for a whole minute. Then they heard the scrape of boots. A moment later, Bird and Wineberg glumly came over the edge of the ravine, their weapons slung across their backs. Up on the lip, two more instructors appeared. One had a Thompson, the other the BAR, its muzzle resting on the tip of his boot.

"Looks like you boys miscalculated some," the BAR man said. "Got a little overaggressive, din't ya?" He lifted his gaze to look at the dusky sky, came back. "I guess y'all gonna have to start your run all over again."

They silently glared back at him. Parnell felt disgusted, bettered. They'd sure as hell been careless, bunching, overextending their front. Later these same instructors would meticulously go over this incident with them, point out their mistakes. No smiles then, just teaching. But for now they were the victors.

Still, he saw something else in their eyes. Respect. To a man, Blue Team had acted correctly, without panic, no freezing with their noses in the dirt. Instead, they had responded with directed aggression, focused and unified. And essentially without orders, moving by instinct.

*You bet your fucking ass,* he thought with defiant triumph.

He turned his head aside, spat, then shoved himself to his feet. He climbed up the side of the ravine and wordlessly headed upslope to retrieve his pack. One by one, his men followed him.

That night, two hours after dark, Blue Team conquered the Beast.

After chow, Colonel Dunmore called his cadre instructors and team leaders together and quietly informed them he had just received orders from army headquarters in Washington to disband Recon Force. . . .

# Two

It was 1:00 in the morning. In the old stone barracks of the fort's headquarters company, the quad duty officer, a spit-and-polish lieutenant, shook Corporal Jerome Fechner awake. The long barracks room was dimly lit, two men down at the other end just coming off duty and quietly talking.

Fechner jerked his head up, sleepy-eyed. "What is it?"

"Hit the boards, Corporal. Colonel Dunmore wants you. Now!"

Fort Allen had originally been a training facility for military police companies. Three months earlier, it was converted into a truck-head and redistribution depot attached to ATS, the army's transportation service. Now it operated twenty-four hours a day, endless convoys of trucks coming and going as they hauled Class 1 and Class 3 supplies. When Dunmore's unit arrived, they'd been given the fort's old obstacle course situated in a remote, wooded section of the post. Permanent tent sites and quansets had been quickly constructed there.

Dunmore had assembled a superb cadre of instructors to run the unit through its training cycle. All were from the best outfits in the army, experts in all phases of combat: demolitions, weaponry, hand-to-hand fighting, communications, small-unit tactics, infiltration and exfiltration, field medicine, sabotage, code skills. Anything and everything a soldier needed to know in order to survive and accomplish his mission.

To fill out his operational TO, he had also drawn from the fort's regular personnel complement of cooks and clerical staff. Corporal Fechner, a slender, slightly balding young man, he had chosen to be his chief clerk.

Three minutes later, Fechner braced before the colonel's desk in his office quanset, the place still smelling of new wood and sheet iron. "Corporal Fechner reporting as ordered, sir."

Dunmore was pouring a cup of coffee. "At ease, son. Coffee?"

"Thank you, sir."

Dunmore handed him the cup, poured another. The colonel had the look of a scholarly man, an academic. He studied Fechner for a moment. "How good are you at making telephone connections?"

"Fairly good, sir."

"I'll need better than that. I want you to locate General Patton and get him on the horn."

"Yes, sir."

"Okay, let's get to it."

Parnell lifted the half-empty fifth of Jack Daniel's whiskey and took a long pull. The liquor burned nicely down his throat, sent warm fumes into his belly. He handed the bottle to Sergeant Bird.

They were seated at the small makeshift table in Parnell's tent, which he shared with another Recon Force officer, Second Lieutenant Richard Mellow, leader of White Team. Above the table hung a Coleman lantern while back in the shadows Lieutenant Mellow snored. An hour earlier, Red had invited Bird to share a farewell drink with him.

"I gotta tell you, Lieutenant, this ain't good," Wyatt said. "They've flat gut-shot us and left us hangin' like wolves on a fence."

Parnell hissed with disgust. "I know, it stinks. And just when we were beginning to come together."

They fell into momentary silence. Through the open tent flap they could see brilliant lights beyond the trees, hear the surge-and-fade of machinery. The night air was cool and held the scent of pines and wildflowers, which mingled with the Cosmoline odor of the tent canvas.

Finally, Wyatt said, "You all think they'll send me back to Bliss, Lieutenant?"

Six months before Pearl Harbor, Bird had been temporarily detached from the Twenty-fifth Division's permanent station at Schofield Barracks in Hawaii and sent to Fort Bliss, Texas, for advanced infantry tactical training. Yet after Pearl he hadn't been returned to his home division. Instead, he'd been upgraded to a T-5 and assigned as an instructor in the Bliss Basic Training Infantry School.

Parnell shook his head. "I don't know. Where do you want to go?"

"Back to the Twenty-fifth." He took another quick drink, lowered the bottle. "I know she ain't in Hawaii no more. I guess them boys is long gone down in the southern islands by now." His eyes went hard, like a man who'd just been told his wife was cheating on him. "What's left of 'em, anyways."

Parnell retrieved the bottle, drank. He wiped his mouth with his sleeve. "Tell me something, how'd you come to be in this outfit?"

The sergeant shrugged. "Me and the colonel served together at Benning. With the ole Thirty-sixth. He was a major then. When I heard he was startin' a new unit I wrote him a letter. A month later my orders come through. Where you figure they'll send you, Lieutenant?"

Red snorted. "Back to that goddamned construction battalion in Washington, most likely." At the University of Colorado, Parnell had been in the ROTC program and had graduated with a second lieutenant's commission. When he was signed by the Lions, he'd been allowed to go into inactive reserve.

Then the day after Pearl Harbor he reactivated his commission and requested immediate assignment to the Advanced Combat Officer's School at Fort Benning, Georgia. Afterward, instead of combat, the army had sent him to build quansets and civilian housing in Washington, D.C.

In early March he heard the scuttlebutt about Dunmore forming an elite commando-type force. The prospect appealed to him, a chance to get into it, kick some Jap ass. He immediately requested permission to volunteer. Twice he was denied. On his third try he managed to wrangle an interview with Dunmore personally, who instantly chose him. Soon after, his reassignment clearance came through.

"You know the colonel," he said. "Is he as good a man as he seems?"

Bird nodded. "Yeah, he is."

Parnell handed back the whiskey. Bird drank. For a moment, he seemed pensive. Then he asked, "You suppose we might get us another crack at this, Lieutenant?"

"Could be. What do you think?"

On his bunk, Lieutenant Mellow mewed in his sleep and the Coleman lantern hissed hollowly, like someone blowing over the top of a bottle. "Well, I'll say this," Bird responded. "The colonel's one determined sumbuck. If they's a way it can be done, he'll sure as hell find it."

Parnell took back the bottle, held it up. "Then I say we toast to that possibility."

"I'll by God do it," Bird said.

It didn't take Dunmore long to locate Patton through one of his friends on the general's staff at Land's End, England, I Corps's present headquarters. He was told the general was in Gibraltar meeting Lieutenant General Mark Clark, Eisenhower's deputy commander. The real problem was getting a line through to him. All I Corps's radio and telephone traffic was on strict priority assignment and it could take days to get through. By then, Patton would most certainly be elsewhere.

But Corporal Fechner now proved a wizard at making low-echelon phone connections, using the universal comradeship between army company clerks. By 4:15, he'd worked out a complicated hookup from Canada to the U.K. to Gibraltar and the Catalan Bay Hotel where the general was staying.

On the Rock it was now ten o'clock in the morning. Patton had just finished a breakfast meeting and was in a particularly sour mood. "All right, Dunmore," he rumbled through the phone. "What the hell's the goddamned problem?"

The colonel quickly explained, ending with, "Can you offer come advice, General?"

"What you mean is, do I have enough juice to pull your ass out of a goddamned hole?"

"Precisely, sir."

"I'm disappointed, Dunmore. You should have known something like this was coming. Why in hell didn't you have a contingency plan in place?"

Dunmore distractedly shifted a pencil from one side

of his desk to the other. "You *are* my contingency plan, General."

Someone with Patton murmured something. He snapped, "No, goddammit, no more coffee." There was the sound of puffing. Finally he said, "All right, James. I've got some chits in the General Staff I can call in. For now, you keep your men in the cycle."

"Thank you, sir." He sat back. Recon Force was still alive. For now. "I'm afraid the men's morale took a hefty jolt," he said. "This news will certainly boost them."

Patton came right back. "Don't be too sure about that."

"Do you have any estimate of how long things will take, sir? I mean, I'll have to do some fancy stalling here."

"You'll know when I know."

"Of course, sir."

There was a long silence, the general deliberately waiting for him to ask it. *How do I do it?* After all, playing dip-and-dodge with a direct order from Army Ground Forces Command, Washington, could prove fatal. At last, Patton snorted loudly. "Jesus Christ, Colonel. Use your goddamned imagination. Like any son of a bitch with balls would do."

Dunmore flushed. "Yes, sir," he said.


At 0510 hours, he gathered his officers and senior noncoms and told them the dispersal order had been completely rescinded. They seemed relieved but still wary. He hated fudging the truth with them. But, damn it, he had to have his men remain focused, especially now, and not worried about the possibility all their work could be for nothing in the end.

He estimated he had at least a solid two-week respite. Whatever the army did, it always moved with infuriating, constipated slowness. Fortunately, this time that would

work in his favor. Before any implementation of the
AGFC order could be officially processed, Patton would
certainly be able to come up with something. At least, he
hoped so.

Recon Force continued with its training cycle. Yet it
was immediately apparent that things were different.
Something inside the men had dissipated, their fire and
drive, which now dulled the edge they had begun to
hone. Despite Dunmore's assurances, everyone knew
the real score. It was only a matter of time before the dispersal order was reissued.

The trainees became sluggish, poutful, ran through
the training schedules halfheartedly. In response, Parnell, Bird, and the other team leaders and instructors
became tyrants. They lashed out at the men, drove them
harder. The result was that they grew even more sullen.
Their tempers heated up, began running on quick trig-
gers. Hand-to-hand combat drills particularly became
brutal as the men worked off their frustrations. Soon the
personal fistfights broke out again.

Late one afternoon during a shallow river crossing,
Kimball and Laguna got into it. For several days, they'd
been ragging at each other, insults and hard eyes. Now,
up to their waists in water, they began throwing solid
punches. Laguna's boot stiletto quickly came out, the
short Mexican crouched, the tip of his knife drifting back
and forth, catching light. Kimball pulled his bayonet.

Roaring curses, Parnell and Bird went after them. The
lieutenant reached Kimball first. He bodily lifted him
into the air by his pack straps and hurled him fifteen feet
away. Then he swung to face Laguna, his eyes hot, tight.
"Sheath that goddamned blade, you little bastard," he
bellowed. "Or I'll take it away from you and shove it up
your ass."

Weesay blinked, jolted by the sudden change in opponent. For a moment, he seemed confused. Then he dipped his shoulders, bent, and slipped the stiletto back into his boot. The other men eased back. A few yards away, Wyatt waded to the bank and stood watching, his Thompson across his shoulders.

Parnell was trembling. He glared at them, everybody except Bird looking sheepish. "All right, you sons a bitches, listen up." His voice was low now, menacingly quiet. "I've had enough of your childish bullshit. From here on in when I say move, you're gonna move. And you're gonna do it fast and full-out." He slowly scanned their faces. "Or so help me Christ Almighty, I'll personally beat the holy crap out of every fucking one of you."

The men stared silently at him. From far off came the sound of trucks pulling grade. A hawk squealed high up in a sky as blue as porcelain. "Anybody doesn't like it, you want out, say so," Red went on. "Right here, right now."

He waited. They continued looking at him. But he saw something in their eyes, a subdued look of embarassment. He'd made them feel foolish. One by one, their gazes slipped away from him, focused on the ground, the river. One tugged distractedly at his pack strap.

"All right," he said. "We got a goddamned river to cross. Let's get to it." The men instantly moved back toward the water, fanning out in proper dispersion technique. He and Bird exchanged a look. Wyatt shrugged the Thompson off his shoulder and followed, chuckling.


The days ground past with still no word from Patton. Then, on the seventh day following his conversation with the general, Dunmore received a call from a captain in the Personnel Section of AGFC. His name was Carpenato. He had a jolly tone.

"Sorry to bother you with this, Colonel," he said brightly. "But it seems we haven't yet received your personnel reassignment requests yet. That would be persuant to Field Order . . . let's see here . . . yes, FO dash 19655 dash TT dash 10045, I believe."

"Really?" Dunmore said.

"I'm afraid so, sir."

"Those requests went out at least five days ago," Dunmore lied.

"Ah, well, sir, I suppose they just got sidetracked in transit. Easily done. As you can imagine, we're ungodly swamped here."

"Of course."

"Not to worry, sir. I'll track them down. Thank you, Colonel."

"Yes," he said.

Another call from AGFC came five days after that, this time from a full bird colonel named McMurtrey in the Operations and Training Department. He got right to the point. "What the hell's going on up there, Dunmore?"

"Sir?"

"We haven't received anything from you. No acknowledgement of receipt of our FO of nineteen May or any implementation report. G-One hasn't gotten your PRRs, either."

Dunmore inhaled, let the breath out slowly. *Here we go,* he thought. "I have no explanation, sir. Those data were sent through channels some time ago."

"Some time ago?"

"Yes, sir."

"I see."

"I'll certainly recheck our files."

"Tell you what, Dunmore. If that material isn't on my desk in the next three days, I'll personally come out and pay you a visit." Without another word, McMurtrey hung up.

Dunmore looked up to find Fechner furtively watching him. The colonel's eyebrows lifted. "Well," he said, "the shit's about to hit the fan."

Forty-eight hours later, a new field order came through from Washington. Patton's recall of his chits had finally taken hold. Unfortunately, it wasn't what Dunmore had expected. The order read:

From: Commanding General
Army Ground Forces Command
Fort McNair, Washington, D.C.
1 June 1942: 0367 Z/EWT
Field Order: 19656-TT-10045

1) By specific and authorized order of the Com Gen: AGFC, you are hereby notified of the partial rescinding of Field Order 19654-TT-10045.
2) In accordance, you will designate by aptitude choice a single (1) squad-team from your unit to participate in completion of present training cycle.
3) All remaining squad-teams within your unit will immediately be reclassified for reassignment.
4) Only those instructors and cadre personnel necessary to complete the single squad-team cycle will remain on detached duty. All others will immediately be returned to their original units.
5) You will officially notify OT/AGFC at the termination of your training cycle so as to implement duty assignment for operational status of the processed squad-team.
6) All communications (to/from) will follow

standing operating procedure as per this order code.

A-Code: R014Q2Q
Annex: XX-1B
IR: Lieutenant Colonel James Dunmore
SO 311
Fort Allen, CT
Des: 1

Dunmore read it twice, laid it on the desk, and looked at it. Then he lifted his arm and slammed a fist down onto it. "Unacceptable," he shouted.

# Three

It took Dunmore a half hour to work out the details of his new plan. The thing was dangerous as hell. This time he'd be risking a definite court-martial. But what choice did he have? He suspected Patton knew precisely what his reaction to the updated order would be, the sly dog undoubtedly keeping a weather eye to see how he, Dunmore, worked out a scheme whereby he would get his entire Recon Force unit through the cycle and into operational status.

*Okay, George old boy, just watch.*

First, he chose one man out of each team, a total of eight troopers in all: seven working, one standby. These he officially listed as the designated squad-team. Next, he picked twice the number of instructors the team would need to complete its full training course. The remaining cadre he temporarily assigned to deconstruction duty, dismantling the training facility itself. By doing this, he could keep the entire complement of instructors on base.

Third, he issued false six-week passes to the rest of the Recon Force trainees. Since such leaves were always given at the discretion of the commanding officer, they were never reviewed by senior commanders. He also transmitted the notices to AGFC in small groups so the sudden rash of leaves wouldn't be noticed.

Then he sat back and waited.

The training cycle went on without interruption. As expected, news of the colonel's shell game swiftly worked its way through the barrack's telegraph. A strange thing happened. The trainees' attitudes changed immediately. They liked what he was attempting, even respected him for it. It wasn't every day a commanding officer put his career on the line for his men.

They also responded to the gamble of Dunmore's fast shuffle. Could he really get away with it, actually lay a con on the top brass in Washington? Every ordinary soldier loves to stick it to an officer, any officer. When that particular officer's either a general or a colonel, the stakes are simply too good to resist.

So everybody climbed on the bandwagon. The earlier lethargy disappeared and was replaced by a new energy, everyone moving with a sharper, quicker intensity. Routine drills became snappier, training sessions more efficient. The men even began challenging each other with a new, fierce glee.

Two weeks passed in this gung-ho mode. Then, late one blisteringly hot morning, two inspectors from Fort McNair showed up to look over the single squad-team now in cycle. Dunmore was caught completely off guard. His first warning of the coming disaster was a call from the main gate. He had fifteen minutes before the inspectors got to the training grounds.

He instantly hustled Fechner off to notify all team leaders to temporarily break off training. Then the senior instructor was to choose any team, truck it to the infiltration course, and wait there. The moment his jeep was spotted, the instructor would start his team through the course. And he'd better look goddamn sharp doing it.

Meanwhile, he ordered the rest of the teams to vanish into the scenery, appear to be working fake details. The leftover instructors were then hauled over to the bivouac area to begin a hurried disassembly of tents and staff buildings.

The inspectors appeared, picking their way to Dunmore's quanset through hastily set up stacks of gear and tent canvas. Both were captains, young, looking like new Officer Training School graduates in their polished brass and chocolate-and-tans. Dunmore greeted them expansively. He drove them around the facility himself. Except for the bivouac area, the whole site was quiet now, a few details apathetically policing the grounds. The last stop on the tour was the infiltration course. He parked his jeep under a blue gum tree and handed out binoculars. Below them was a meadow where the working team was executing an attack exercise on a machine-gun bunker at the edge of a small wood, the men scattered and hidden in deep grass.

Suddenly, rifles began banging away. Two smoke bombs went off. The team, laying covering fire as it advanced, executed a frontal assault in manual-perfect, fire-and-dash movement. The bunker opened up. Fifty-caliber tracers zinged white-hot lines just over their heads. In less than four minutes, the assault team had neutralized the MG position and disappeared into the trees.

The inspectors were impressed. Splendid, they said, absolutely splendid. HQ would be very pleased. Dunmore drove them to the fort's officers' mess, where they shared a pleasant chicken-and-dumpling lunch. Afterward, he returned them to their staff car and, smiling happily, they drove away.


Another three weeks sped past, all the teams sharp, combat skills beveled to a fine edge. The men were a different breed now, cool and sure of themselves.

Still, Parnell wasn't quite satisfied with Blue Team. He still detected too much independence in his men, which continued to lessen the team's overall unity of action. He was even aware that he himself retained a residual vanity that prevented a complete adjustment to the team concept.

By now every one of his men had become a solid combat soldier, each possessing, beyond a soldier's basic skills, natural abilities in specific areas. Bird was the quintessential infantryman, the best right-hand man any officer could have. He and Kimball were also the best demolition men. Kaamanui was cool and steady and could handle any water obstacle or submerged charges. Laguna was a tiger in close combat, fast and decisive, and Fountain had magic fingers with any weapon he was given. Wineberg was inexhaustable and as unbreakable as a steel bar.

But they weren't yet a team. The soul of a team was something else, something unspoken. He couldn't have defined it in words, but he was certain he'd recognize it when it came. So far, it hadn't, not completely.

He knew he was dealing with a delicate balance here. To become completely part of a unit, each member had to surrender himself to the whole, everybody thinking and moving alike. At the same time, this particular kind of unit would often throw these men into situations where they'd be alone and behind enemy lines, isolated from any command or help. Their survival would then have to depend on how well each man could think, react, and improvise on his own.

Thus far, Parnell hadn't seen the total absorption of both of these two countering qualities in them. They could perform combat duties at an extremely high level of aggression, focus, and efficiency. But they were still acting as little more than a group of good men.

On 26 July 1942, the training cycle finally ended. Under the smoky scarlet light of evening, Colonel Dunmore assembled the unit for a short, congratulatory speech. He apologized for not having a parade, for not even awarding an official unit insignia.

"Such things will come in the future," he said. "But for now, I at least have some good news. General Patton's come to our rescue once more. He's designated us a special reconnaissance unit temporarily detatched for training from his First Armored Corps. So, tomorrow morning, this entire unit—I repeat, entire unit—will begin transition to the British Commando Training Depot at Achnacarry Castle, Scotland."

Men exchanged smiles, a pleased murmur riffled through the formation. Dunmore nodded to Fechner. The corporal unloaded three wooden cases from the colonel's jeep, lifted the tops off, and stepped back. Inside were thirty-six bottles of Jack Daniel's whiskey.

"Tonight, gentlemen, enjoy youselves," Dunmore said, "This one's on me."


Sergeant Kaamanui was the closest to the control cabin of the C-47, right at the door, the pilots just a few feet away. For the past twenty minutes, he'd been watching out the windshield, to the left. There were mean-looking headlands out there, five hundred feet high, straight down, as if the earth had split and the broken part had disappeared into deep ocean. It was the coastline of the northwestern tip of Scotland.

Behind him, sitting on metal benches along the bulkhead, were three Recon Force teams: Blue, Red, and Green. Most of the men were asleep. In the center of the aisle under tight freight netting and heavy straps were

their gear and weapons. The aircraft carried the odor of
wiring insulation and altitude coolness.

It had been a long, boring trip in a flight of four C-47s,
twenty-five hours from the States with refueling stops at
Sydproven, Newfoundland, and Reykjavik, Iceland. For
the last twenty minutes, the aircraft had been descending imperceptibly and was now at about a thousand feet.

They were low enough for Sol to easily see the small
towns that began appearing. Just ahead now was a fishing
village with jetties and moored boats. Beyond the harbor
were clusters of white, thatch-roofed houses and shops and
a church steeple. Farther in, the land was a deep green,
gently rolling hills and dark upland forest. Several small
lochs, or lakes, shone gray white in the distance.

He watched the shoreline drift past, noting the colors
of the current, darker near the land, whitecapped farther out. The water looked gray, nut-cracking cold. It
brought back an image: laying underwater charges for
the Melones Waterway in Selwik, Alaska, when he was
with the Corps of Engineers.

The thought of Alaska drew up another memory, a
sharper one, of Ginny Techek, the half-Aluet Eskimo,
half-Tillamook Indian girlfriend he'd had back then. A
woman as pretty as a doll and one who could fuck a man
into oblivion or scourge him with a temper as sudden
and ferocious as a stick of sweating TNT.

He grinned quietly, remembering.

Someone pressed against his shoulder. It was Cowboy
Fountain, leaning down to look out as the plane banked
again. Bursts of radio noise came faintly over the changing roar of the engines. Gradually, the aircraft leveled
and headed east, over land.

"By God, Horse," Fountain said. "Yonder's Scotland."

"I guess."

Fifteen minutes later, there was a jolting screel of tires,

the engines surging for a moment, then dropping into a rapping whirr as the plane lost momentum, and they were down. The aircraft eased up beside a huge maintenance hangar. The door was pulled open and the men began unloading their gear.

The field was newly made of Marsden matting. Several British Lancaster bombers were lined in echelon on the grassy taxiways. A British sergeant major in a short brown battle tunic with trousers bloused over the tops of his boots appeared in a green lorry. He spoke with the team leaders and then drove off.

They waited. Finally, a convoy of lorries arrived. The men loaded gear again and climbed aboard. The trucks turned north along a narrow dirt road with low stone walls on both sides.

Cowboy watched out the back of the lorry, the countryside solid grass now, hilly with scattered farmsteads and stone-marked fields containing stacks of peat bricks. There were herds of shaggy, blackfaced-sheep, too, their coats the color of oatmeal, and cows and horses, black as ink.

He studied the horses, wondering if they had spirit. He didn't think so. They looked as fat and docile as the sheep. They wouldn't make a goddamned pimple on a decent mustang's ass. Still, the country was pretty enough, especially where the land rose into foothill forest. It reminded him some of the high meadows in the Pinos Altos Mountains of southeastern New Mexico.

For an aching moment he felt a longing to be mounted a-horse again, heading out of a line camp on an early winter morning, the air so clear and cold it would have chimed if flicked with his finger. Or working a bucking, twisting bronc in the old hot, dusty Roswell rodeo arena, feeling the full, hurtling power of the animal each time it leaped, feeling the deep surge of its lung blood between his legs. . . .

"Wot chu smilin' at, vaquero?" Laguna asked. He was seated across the lorry.

"What?" Fountain opened his eyes, hadn't realized he'd closed them.

"Chu was smilin' like a shit-eatin' bird, *meng.*"

Cowboy nodded toward a pair of horses grazing a quarter mile away. "I was jes' thinking I'd like to ride one of them ole boys."

Sergeant Bird, seated beside Laguna, chuckled derisively. "Who couldn't? A gawdamn old lady with a broke leg could ride them sumbitches."

"Yeah," Cowboy said.

The commando training school was set up inside Achnacarry Castle, a tall, forebidding-looking structure of ancient granite built during the time of Robert the Bruce in the fourteenth century. It sat in high moorland of heather and golden broom at the *ceann* or head of Loch Claise-Carnaich.

Its eastern ramparts lay in ruin, covered with blankets of ivy. But the western portion with its grand gatehouse and watchtower and a wide bailey, or courtyard, fronting on the main living quarters of the castle were being used for the school's staff and commando trainees.

The Recon Force lorries pulled through the high arch of the gatehouse and into the bailey. There were several other lorries, a pair of American jeeps, and a British Humber Mark II armored car parked there. Everybody off-loaded and formed up in their respective teams. Above them, the sky was overcast, the air dank and cold and heavy with the smell of moss and loch water like spawning fish.

Another sergeant major and two lance corporals came quick, stepping through an arched doorway in the tower. The Brit senior noncom was ramrod straight and carried a short baton with a .30-caliber slug on its tip. As he faced the formation, he snapped it smartly up under his left armpit.

"Welcome to Achnacarry Castle, gents," he barked. "All team leaders will hang back a bit, if you please. The rest will follow the corporals to your assigned kits. All right, lads, off you go."

All the officers were being quartered in the barbican, the ancient guard keep next to the grand gatehouse. But the rest of the team members were split between the great and lesser halls of the main inner building. Blue Team, along with the Red and Yellow Teams, were marched into the great hall. One of the lance corporals told them they would be sharing kit space with a double platoon of commando instructors.

The hall was 150 feet long and nearly two stories high with heavy, dark timbers bracing the roof. The floor was flagstone. The only windows were narrow, slit apertures, which allowed in very little light. Instead, huge flare lights had been affixed to the overhead timbers. There were folding bunks and foot lockers lined along each wall and a wooden gun rack down the full length of the vast room.

The men began unpacking and stowing their gear. It was nearly noon. The place was dungeon cold. After a half hour, a dozen commando instructors came in, their combat jumpers covered with mud and sweat. The Brits and Americans eyed each other. No words were exchanged. The commandos racked their weapons and moved to their bunks at the opposite end of the hall where they sat quietly talking and smoking.

Wyatt watched them curiously. All were young, yet they carried about them a silent, iron-cold watchfulness. Occasionally, one would turn and look at the Americans, and Bird would see how the man's eyes seemed closed off, void of emotion.

He'd seen that kind of masking before, in the faces of combat vets, old hands still in harness, back in the States. They were guys who had fought in the trenches of Europe in World War I and still had that peculiar, guarded stare, mostly when the booze or the talk drew up old, terrible memories.

From the next bunk, Smoker Wineberg said, "Them guys ain't very talkative, are they?"

"What the hell you want 'em to say?"

"They could at least say hello, for chrisesake. The bastards act like they're pissed at us. And we're over here to help the sons a bitches."

Bird didn't answer. He knew it wasn't anger in their faces but something much deeper. He concluded these men had probably faced German armor and crack infantry units in northern France. And then got themselves humiliated by getting shoved into the Channel at Dunkirk. Some may even had taken on Rommel and his panzers in North Africa. Any way you looked at it, it was obvious these boys had already seen the *real* face of war. . . .


The training was grim and hard. Interminable days and six-hour nights, always pushing, forcing themselves to move faster, quieter, farther. First there were amphibious operations, learning the skills of surf broaching and beach and reef landings in inflatable boats. Then came the mountain work, maneuvering in landscapes as stony-barren as the moon's, and crossing wild, icy, whitewater rivers, rappelling down cliffs and rock steeples with nor'westers slamming at them.

They were left in deep, brooding glens of Caledonian forest for days with nothing but their portable gear.

And twice they crossed the Minch Channel by sub to run mock insertion raids along the coasts of the Hebrides and Orkney Islands, moving swiftly at night, living off the land until they could strike with maximum force and then withdraw back into the darkness.

Three and a half weeks after they started, they were flown aboard Lancaster bombers to a base at Swansea on Carmathern Bay in the southwest of England. There they went into jump training with the U.S. 509th Parachute Battalion. High-altitude free falls and then quick insertion jumps from five hundred feet, the sticks going out on static lines with the ground right down there and coming up fast before the chutes finally popped and snapped and ballooned overhead. They made night drops to develop the instincts for moving through strange country, and jumps over water.

Back to Achnacarry Castle and a final two weeks in the snow-streaked Grampian Mountains on combined maneuvers. At last, on 9 September, their training was completed. At formation in the main bailey, Colonel F.W. Alistair Storry, CB, DSM, the school's commandant, awarded commando badges to the seven Recon Force teams and sixty-one new Brit commandos.

Each man was also presented with a new fighting knife, a Sykes-Fairbairn, the standard commando blade weapon. Colonel Storry gave a short speech and then dismissed them with the news that each was to be given a thirty-hour pass.

It took Blue Team precisely three hours and sixteen minutes to get into trouble. . . .

# Four

It started over a woman.

The alehouse was called the Cock and the Hat, on the cobbled dockside of the fishing town of Kinlochberrie, twenty-five miles from Achnacarry Castle. Out in the harbor were double-ended seiners and flat-bottomed cobles, all camouflaged to escape the German L-boat patrols off Point Wrath. Gulls swooped and screamed.

Kaamanui, Fountain, and Kimball had been in the pub for twenty minutes. Earlier, they had visited two other alehouses with Wineberg. Smoker had remained at the last one, flirting with a young woman he'd met. This place was dark and smoky and stank of urine and mutton. A dozen fishermen sat about in their scruffy oil-skin jackets and crew caps and thick rubber boots, each big- shouldered and ruddy faced. They sullenly eyed the three Americans. The barmaid's name was Maggie. She had huge breasts stuffed into a red-and-blue bodice and her hair was the color of new rope. She flirted with the three Yanks. Cowboy and Kimball, both a little drunk, teased and flirted back.

"By damn, darlin'," Fountain said, grinning boyishly. "I'll bet y'all could make a man twist and paw."

"Go awn wi' ya, Yank," Maggie said and slid her chubby face to the side with a saucy look.

"True, true," Cowboy said. "Just flat-heel and head the poor ole boy." Maggie turned away.

The fishermen watched in dead silence. "Hey, hold on now," he called after her.

She returned. "Aye?" Fountain reached up and poked a pound note into her cleavage. Maggie instantly drew back, shocked. "'Ere now, wot's this?" she cried angrily. "I don' gather gear na more, Yank." She extracted the note and tossed it onto the table, twisted away.

Cowboy frowned. "Now what the hell's the matter with her?"

Kimball leaned forward, chuckling. "I think she thought you were wanting to purchase some pussy. Sounds like she doesn't whore anymore." He jerked up suddenly, his gaze over Fountain's shoulder. "Uh-oh," he said slowly.

One of the fishermen had pushed away from the bar and was moving toward their table. The others had also stepped back, watching, dark-faced. The fisherman stopped behind Cowboy and tapped him on the shoulder. He was tall and heavy-chested and had a thick red beard.

"I thaink yu'd best tak ya bluddy brass and git oot, Yank," he said. "Ya've insulted our Maggie."

Cowboy turned and smiled lopsidedly at him. "Don't sweat it, cousin. I didn't mean no harm. The money was a tip."

Across the table, Kaamanui finished his eighth pint and gently set the glass down. His eyes held on the fisherman. Kimball shifted slightly, turning his chair out.

"Maks na mind," the man growled. "We dinna' care for Yanks here aboots." He leaned down and viciously swept the change to the floor. The coins tinkled loudly.

Fountain came swiftly to his feet, his chair sliding back, squealing. His eyes had gone solid, like ice the moment just before it freezes. "Whoa there, bud," he said slowly. "I think you all better pick up that money. And do it right quick."

"You pick it oop." The Scotsman jerked his head toward Kaamanui. "An' win ya lave, ya can tak the bluddy black caird wi' ya."

Sol's steady gaze didn't change but his lips drew back, showing teeth. He rose slowly, as did Kimball. The entire room went utterly still, the air suddenly compacted.

Cowboy moved. His arm came up fast, fisted, the full weight of his shoulder and body behind it. It smashed into the fisherman's jaw and the man went down like a sack of potatoes. There was a pause, two breaths long. Into it, the squeal of a seagull drifted. Then the other fishermen, en mass, charged across the room.

Before the two groups collided, the barman was between them, waving a thick tap handle. "Utside, ya bluddy bastads," he yelled. "Tak this utside."

They fought in the alley behind the alehouse, eleven against three. Kaamanui braced himself against the wall and hurled incoming bodies away from him. Kimball, high on the balls of his feet, dodged and weaved and threw pinpoint combinations as Cowboy hammered away at whoever was in front of him, crouched low, arms going like pistons, down-home, honky-tonk fighting.

A crowd quickly formed. The men yelled Scottish obscenities at the Yanks and somebody tossed a mug. It hit Kaamanui on the neck. Suddenly, a distant clanging sounded. A moment later a police van swung into the alley, the crowd scattering out of its way. The van was boxy, black with wire windows. As it skidded to a stop, five constables leaped out carrying yard-long black truncheons and waded into the battle.

Cowboy went down first, struck in the neck by a billy club. Sol and Kimball stood over him for several more minutes, fighting both the fishermen and the constables. Eventually they were overwhelmed. All three were handcuffed, tossed into the van, and hauled away.

The girl's fingers played suggestively along Smoker's inner thigh. Her name was Clarise. She was twenty-eight, English, and married to a Scotsman in the Royal Argyll Highlanders. She was plain as a scrub-board but had nice legs and a pretty smile.

Wineberg had already loaned her five quid. For necessaries, she said, fags and such, since her bleedin' mother-in-law never shared her allotment. "Oh, a bossy boots an' a real witch, that one," she sneered.

People began running along the sidewalk outside. Clarise looked up. "Aye, wot's this?" She went out to inquire. In a moment, she was back. "It's your mates," she said.

"What?"

"Those other soldiers was with you? They've been copped off by constab'lary. They was in a big punch up at the Cock and the Hat."

Before she finished, Smoker was up and running toward the door. "Aye, wait, luv," she called frantically after him. "When are you comin' back?"

The salmon hit like a small rocket, Red Parnell's line singing as it flashed out. The fish cleared water for a second, silver sides flashing like polished chrome. On the bank, the two girls and Lieutenant Willy Rogers watched. Willy shouted, "Stick wi' the bugga, Reddo. He's runnin' like a bloody baramundi."

He and Rogers, on detached duty from the Ninth Australian Division to learn commando tactics, had rented fishing gear from an old Scotsman in a bookstore in Kinlochberrie. The rods were ancient, exceptionally long, and made of stained bamboo.

Across from the bookstore was a tea shop run by two sisters, Pamela and Abigail Fergerson. They were both in their twenties with bright round faces and rosy cheeks. They had seemed genuinely excited to be asked to go fishing by two such good-looking commando officers.

The men bought Banbury cakes and strips of heather-seasoned mutton and bottles of dark ale. In Red's jeep, they drove to a narrow, swift stream called the Bealach Bo outside town and next to an old stone church. The girls wore snood nets and had large pompadors and summer dresses.

Pamela sat beside Parnell. The breeze blew sensuously against her breasts. He studied her, caught the drift of rose perfume. In a warm rush he pictured her naked. Desire sweltered through him. *God,* he wondered, *how long's it been?*

Driving slowly along the narrow streets between cottages with bright red doors, he mentally explored Pamela's nakedness. Skin like warm milk, the sounds of frantic arousal, air thick with the wondrous scent of female heat and pubis. At that moment, she turned and smiled at him with her pretty Scottish lips, almost as if she were giving consent to his fantasy. He smiled back. Her eyes went lazy for a second, a hand distractedly brushing a strand of hair from her forehead.

*Oh, sweet Jesus,* he thought happily.

He quickly landed the salmon, a ten-pounder topped with blue, which indicated it was fresh from the sea. They drank a toast to it, the girls slightly tipsy now, and then Willy tried his hand, casting out and riffling the fly back across a deep pool, the water clear as gin.

The Aussie glanced around, laughing. Then he

frowned. "Aye, Reddo, here come your mates. An they're lookin' fair snarky." Sergeant Bird and Laguna were double-timing toward them, faces somber. Parnell bent and placed his ale bottle in the grass, straightened as they came up. "What's the matter?" he called.

"We need your jeep, Lieutenant," Bird said.

"Why?"

"I'd rather not say."

Red's eyes narrowed. "Cut the bullshit, Wyatt. Why?"

"They got some of our boys in the jailhouse."

Lieutenant Rogers came up, reeling in his line. "Wot's the problem?"

Parnell ignored him. "Arrested? For what?"

"They took to shit-kickin' some locals."

Red looked toward the town, came back, nodded. "Okay, let's go." He glanced at the two women. "Sorry, ladies, I've got something to do." The girls pouted. Willy said something to them, tossed down his pole, and followed Parnell.

Red glanced around at him. "Where you think you're going?"

"To give you blokes a bleedin' hand, of course."

"Thanks but we'll take care of it."

"You can always use another cobber, Reddo."

"This is team business, Willy. You just keep an eye on the girls."

"Aye. Well, good luck, mates."

They drove off.


Back in Kinlochberrie, they searched for the jail but finally had to stop and ask an old lady where it was. Two minutes later, Red pulled the jeep up in front of a building made of pink and black stone with a slate roof. It had flower beds and a white picket fence and looked like a parson's house. They got out, carrying their Thompsons down along their legs.

Parnell paused at the front step. "Weesay, around to the back. Anybody comes out, herd 'em back in."

"Right, Lieutenant." Laguna sprinted off.

"Wyatt, you and me. The rest of you hang tight. Nobody in."

The main room of the jail was whitewashed with a dark brown wainscoting. A screened counter ran across part of the room. It had a window in it behind which a constable in a green-visor hat was writing in a large, leather-bound book. In the back were two doors, both painted forest green.

On the other side of the room were several chairs and a long table with a checkerboard and tea mugs where three other constables were seated. Their uniforms were scruffed and torn. One had a puffy right eye and a bandage on his fist, the other a swollen cheek. Everybody froze when Parnell and Bird came through the door, moving swiftly to the center of the room.

Red put his weapon on them. "Stay right where you're at, gentlemen," he snapped. "Which one of you birds has the keys?"

The policeman behind the screen said, "Wot th' bluddy Jaisus do ya thank ya're doin', Yank?" He had a florid face and blue eyes so light they were almost white.

"The keys, goddammit."

"Ya won't get thim from me, mahn."

Bird instantly stepped to the counter and pressed the muzzle of his Thompson against the screen. "Scotty, y'all got five seconds. Let's have them fuckin' keys."

The man stared, then hissed loudly and reached for a large ring of keys from a board on the wall beside him. He skidded them through the screen window. "Tak thim and go ta the deevil."

"Get 'em out," Parnell said. Bird rounded the counter and opened one of the doors, looked out, shut it, and went through the other. One of the seated constables said to Red, "Ach, Yank, you're in soome deep shait now, ay'll till ya."

Red nodded calmly.

A moment later, Bird returned with Kaamanui, Kimball, Fountain, and Wineberg. They were laughing. Cowboy had his arm around Smoker. The prisoners were all dirty with bloodstained uniforms and various bruises and scrapes.

Parnell studied Wineberg. "Can he walk?"

"Yeah, he's okay, Lieutenant," Cowboy said. "The crazy bastard. He come in here swingin', took on the whole police force by hisself."

"Let's go," Red said. They started out, all except Wineberg. He had shrugged off Fountain's arm and now stood staring balefully at one of the seated constables, a big man with a face shaped like a pear.

"Move it, Smoker," Red shouted.

Instead, Wineberg walked around the table and stopped in front of the policeman. "Stand up," he ordered. The constable rose. "You're the son of a bitch who kicked me in the head, ain't you?" Before the man could respond, Wineberg hit him, twice, both blows crashing violently against his thick jowls. The constable slammed back against the wall and then slid down, his eyes blinking rapidly.

They left the jail in single file, Bird covering their rear. Parnell whistled. Laguna came running around the side of the building, everybody shouting happily now, giving out whoops. The constables came to the door and peered out as the Americans piled into the jeep.

Weesay stood up and grabbed at his crotch. "Eat this, *pandejos*. Don' nobody fuck with Blue Team, *meng*."

As he accelerated away, a wide grin creased up into Parnell's face. The last piece of the picture had just been put into place. Now they were a team.

Colonel Storry had a birthmark, a dark triangle under his left earlobe. It was the only blemish on him, the man in his mid-forties but lean and tight with hair cut close to the scalp, and gray, penetrating eyes. He sat behind his desk in the castle barbican, the room filled with radio gear and cabinets that looked out of place in the ancient stone room. Colonel Dunmore sat at one end of the desk. Parnell stood before them, braced, eyes straight ahead.

"I just received a call from the District Lord Advocate," Storry began evenly. "Seems you and your men got into a bit of a cock-up in Kinlochberrie. Care to explain?"

Parnell did so, quickly, concisely. The officers listened. When Red finished, Colonel Dunmore leaned forward. "May I, Colonel?" he asked. Storry nodded. Dunmore turned back to Parnell. "Lieutenant, have you any idea how many military and civilian regulations you broke when you went into that police station under arms?"

"I'd say quite a few, sir."

"That's what you'd say, huh? Then why in hell did you do it?"

"They had my men, sir."

"Which justified such precipitous actions?"

"I would say so, sir." Colonel Storry glanced at his desktop, touched a finger to his nose.

"Did you intend to actually use your weapons?" Dunmore said. "Against civilians?"

"No, sir. I figured just carrying them in would be adequate."

"What if it hadn't been?"

"Then we would have gotten physical, sir."

Both officers stared at Parnell. The silence in the room was as cold and still as its stone walls. Finally, Storry glanced at Dunmore. "You have anything else, Colonel?"

"No."

"Dismissed," Storry said.

"Thank you, sir," Parnell said. He executed a snappy about-face and left, closing the door softly.

Storry chuckled. "Bloody cheeky fellow, isn't he?"

"Yes."

"I like him."

"Frankly, so do I," Dunmore said. Both officers shared a laugh. "Will there be repercussions with the civilian authorities over this?"

"Undoubtedly. A bit of a flurry. But it won't amount to much. It never has."

"You've had problems before?"

"Now and again. These Highlanders are a touchy and ill-tempered bunch, the lot of them. My men've had their share of incidents. Frankly, an occasional bounce tends to keep these bloody kilters in line for a bit."

Storry grew thoughtful for a moment. "D'you know, James, I think this Parnell and his men would make the perfect team for that test your GHQ wants you to run. Their don't-give-a-bloody-damn-for-consequences sense of loyalty to each other is quite splendid."

"Yes, I agree."

"In fact, I might have just the test for you. I was speaking with Brigadier Wainsborough recently. Seems Second Commando's planning a small strike on the French coast. A few weeks down the line. Perhaps your people could go along."

Dunmore's eyes lit up. "That sounds perfect."

"Good, good. I'll set the gears in motion." He smiled.

"Actually, I'm rather curious myself to see how this Blue Team of yours reacts under fire."

"You won't be disappointed, Colonel."

It was called a "butcher and bolt" raid: go in quick, take out anybody you found, blow up as much equipment as possible, then fade back into the night. Afterward, the raiders would scatter, make contact with the French underground, and eventually be picked up by a sub farther south.

One week after the fight in Kinlochberrie, Blue Team boarded a Lancaster bomber and was flown to an airfield outside the town of Folkestone on the Dover coast. There they were quartered with a ten-man team from the Second Commando.

Each night the combined force made dry-run insertion jumps onto the rolling ocean bluffs of Dover, terrain that was similiar to that which they'd find near their mission target, a small German radar station outside the fishing town of Isigny-sur-Mer on the Normandy coast. This particular station had been jamming British naval radio traffic for several months. The strike was code-named Operation Hunter.

In early September, Parnell, the commando lead officer, a Lieutenant Spackle, and three of their senior NCOs were briefed by the Second Commando's tactical officer, Major J.J. Cobb. He went over the entire mission sheet, issued time sequences, code references, underground contacts, and submarine pickup points and times. The jump-off date was set for 2300 hours, 8 September, three days away.

Twenty-four hours later, Colonel Dunmore appeared at Folkestone. He was livid. Angrily drawing Parnell aside, he informed him that AGFC had just scrapped Blue Teams' part in Operation Hunter.

"Goddammit," Red cursed. "Why, for Christ's sake?"

"Dieppe," Dunmore answered. "That bloody mess hit Washington hard." He was referring to a massed raid by a combined force of British commandos and Canadian troops on the coastal town of Dieppe, France, on 19 August 1941. Code-named Jubilee, it turned out to be a disastrous mistake, ill planned and badly executed. Most of the six thousand men involved were either killed or captured. Among them were fifty troopers from the U.S. First Ranger Battalion.

"Well, my men're gonna shit a brick over this," Red said.

"I already have. Still, it's not over yet, Red. You sit tight till I get back."

That night Dunmore hitched a ride to Land's End where Patton's First Armored Corps was restaging. The general wasn't surprised to see him. "I figured you'd be around, Sticks," he said.

"They've just yanked my team from the Isigny-sur-Mer raid."

"I know."

"This is wrong, General. Totally unacceptable."

A tiny smile touched Patton's lips. "Don't fret, James. Simply find another mission."

"But I need one now, sir. My men have trained hard. They deserve a crack at the enemy. Right now. If I ask them to wait, they'll go stale and demoralize."

Patton remained silent. Then he rose and moved to a large wall map of Europe and Africa. He stood gazing at it. Finally, he turned and looked at Dunmore over his shoulder. "Roosevelt and Churchill have decided to hit North Africa," he said bluntly.

Dunmore grunted, nodded. "I expected something of the sort. To relieve Russia?"

Patton took a slow drag on his cigar. "Partially. Those poor Ruskie bastards are up to their assholes in Nazis." He turned back to the map. "The assault will be in three separate invasion groups. One against French Morocco, the other two against Algeria. I'll be commanding the Morocco landings."

Dunmore watched the general closely. He sensed Patton was leading up to something. "When's it start, sir?"

"Eight November."

"General, I would like to ask your—"

Patton cut him off. "I've already done it. I'm assigning your strike team a crucial mission." He stared hard at Dunmore. "They'd by God better not fuck it up."

"They won't, sir. That's a promise. What's the mission?"

"They're to neutralize a battery of seven mobile field guns." Patton pointed at the map, at the ancient caravan city of Marrakesh in southern French Morocco. "Right there."

# Part Two
# Operation Torch

It was a long time coming.

All over the world the Axis had been soundly whipping the Allies. Throughout Europe, deep in the Pacific, in Burma, and down south in the Indonesian Corridor, German and Japanese forces were spreading like a dark stain.

In North Africa there had been victories and defeats for the British since 1940, fighting against the Italians and then the Germans, back and forth across the Great Western Desert of Libya and Egypt, and on the Mediterranean littoral. Bloody, vicious offensives and counteroffensives that slammed Italian tank brigades and Rommel's Afrika Korps against generals like Wadell, Alexander, and Montgomery with his redoubtable British Eighth Army.

Now the Americans were in it, full bore, itching to hit back. Their generals wanted to go at the European continent right off, but cooler, more battle-tested heads prevailed. An alternative was agreed upon, a combined invasion of North Africa along a thousand miles of coastline. It was set for 8 November 1942, code-named Operation Torch.

On 4 November, as U.S. First Marine Division troopers fought for their lives on the beaches of faraway Guadalcanal, as the defenders of Stalingrad held on with unbreakable tenacity, and just four days after Montgomery's crushing defeat of Rommel at El Alamein, a huge armada of 675 British and American ships rendezvoused at two points off the North African coast. One was southwest of the Strait of Gibraltar, the other off Algeria.

The Torch invasion would be three-pronged. A western task force would go ashore at the four French Moroccan ports of Lyautey, Fedala, Casablanca, and Safi on the Atlantic. Within minutes, a central task force would strike at Oran, Algeria, while an eastern task force would hit Algiers.

All the assault sites were French protectorates, controlled by the pro-Axis Vichy government of Marshal Henri Petain. Therefore, the main question for the Allies was whether or not the French would fight. Depending on the answer, the invasion could be bloody or a walk-in.

For Blue Team, the war began at precisely 2134 hours of 7 November 1942 as the American submarine USS *Skidder*, TG–34, rose out of the depths of the Atlantic two miles off the southern Moroccan town of Safi and surfaced onto a storm-lashed sea. . . .

# Five

Parnell, squatted with his back against the bulkhead of the officers' wardroom, surveyed his team. All were dressed alike in black-dyed battle fatigues, woolen watch caps, and greased faces. The room was dim in red light so as to increase their night vision. The men were quiet, motionless, like dark ghosts in an ink sketch by Durer.

Two minutes earlier the sub's diving alarm had sounded, three raucous blasts. Then came the relayed call, "Stand by to surface." Safety tanks blew, sending the high-pitched whistle of rushing air throughout the ship. The deck tilted slightly by the bow as the vessel slid out of depth toward the surface of the Atlantic.

A sailor poked his head through the hatchway, his white hat glowing as red as a flare. "Captain wants you forward, sir," he told Parnell. The entire team rose. Red stood beside the hatchway as each man passed, ducking, pulling himself through. Each carried oilcloth-wrapped weapons and musette bags containing demolitons and extra ammunition.

They moved along the passageway and through the forward battery room. The air stank of diesel fuel, eletrical wiring, moistured metal. At the hatch to the control room, Parnell and Wineberg halted while the others continued on to the forward torpedo room where their rubber foldboats were stowed. The sub was rolling now, responding to surface turbulence.

In the red-lit control space, the boat's captain, Lieutenant Jerry Daum, was hunched over the periscope, swinging it in slow 360s. Sweat made dark patches on his shirt. A few feet away, the dive officer called out, "Eighteen feet, holding steady." From the conning tower came the muffled voice of the quartermaster, "Visual in the eye ports, sir."

The captain made one last turn of the periscope, ordered it down. He moved to the conning tower ladder, glanced at Parnell, motioned to him to follow. Red and Wineberg went up with him into a tiny room with a desk and stowed signaling gear. The ladder continued up. They could hear the officer-of-the-deck snapping orders below. The red lights went out and everything was plunged into a sudden blackness. Two lookouts joined them, everybody tight in there now.

"Crack the hatch," Daum said. Instantly, the soft squeak of metal and a whistling hiss as the higher pressure of the sub began venting through the hatch seals. Then a sharp rush of cold, wet air came flooding down. "Lookouts to the bridge."

A moment later, Parnell and Wineberg emerged beside Daum onto the bridge, into stinging rain and wind gusts freighted with cold and the thick salty scent of the sea. Parnell looked eastward over the parapet. Far off lay a cluster of lights, winking and distorted by the rain. It was the coastal town of Safi. Beside him, Daum scanned with night binoculars as the *Skidder* rolled back and forth, waves lashing up and over its starboard hull.

Parnell squinted at the lights, feeling good, the storm infusing itself into him and releasing adrenaline. It was like those moments just before a football game, the players coming along the corridor under the stands, their cleats cracking loudly, everybody ready to go.

"There they are," the captain shouted over the wind. Parnell looked, spotted a pinpoint of light south of the town. It held for a few seconds, disappeared, then came again in three faint bursts. Daum leaned down and called back through the hatch, "Down by eight. Standby to deploy boats."

Escaping air came as the submarine settled, the deck awash now so Blue Team could launch their rubber boats with greater ease. Parnell turned to Daum, held out his hand. "Thanks for the ride, Jerry." They shook.

"Good luck, Red," the captain said.

They inflated the two foldboats beside the forward torpedo hatch. As they filled out, the wind caught them, swung them up like kites, luffing, the men fighting to hold them down by their painter lines. At last, they got them deployed. The men dropped in one by one, stepping awkwardly on the rubber bottoms. They were in a momentary stretch of smooth lee water. But then the wind caught them and swept them into storm chop, the boats bobbing and jerking sharply.

For a few seconds, they heard the faint sound of venting air. Massive bubbles erupted up through the turbulent surface. They could still vaguely make out the *Skidder*'s sail out there, a square of darker dark against the night. Then it was gone.

Bending to their paddles, they made for shore.


It was difficult coming in through the heavy shore surf, twelve-foot combers crashing in shallows. Ahead, the beach was misty with rain as it curved southward, empty now save for night plovers darting and squealing along the high-water line. Above the beach were thick growths of eucalyptus. Safi lay two miles to the north.

The team waded the last hundred yards through waist-high water, pulling the plunging boats. As they reached the beach, a tiny light flashed a quarter mile away, among the trees. Everyone hit the sand. Parnell snapped an order. Instantly, weapons were unsheathed, charged: Thompsons and M3 submachine guns. Laguna and Fountain, the swiftest, rose and sprinted up the beach toward the light, running low, slanting toward the trees.

Several minutes later, they returned with Francois Ecrin. He was their main contact, a member of the CNLF, de Gaulle's Free French resistance party. He and another agent would be the team's guides as they worked their way deeper inland. Ecrin was short and stocky in a hooded jellaba that made him look like a monk.

They hid the boats under eycalyptus debris and Francois led them through the trees and up a narrow dirt road. Across the road were orange groves, the trees heavy with fruit. They reached a small whitewashed building, a country schoolhouse. Beside it were two dilapidated Peugeot lorries, flatbeds with curved turtle cabs without windshields or windows. Stacks of straw crates were on the beds, covered with canvas tarps. They smelled strongly of fish.

The second CNLF agent appeared from the trees. Ecrin introduced him to Parnell. His name was Felix Martier, tall, balding, the rain beading across his head. Red and Sergeant Bird went with the two Frenchmen into the schoolhouse. It was a single room with pillows for the students instead of desks. The floor was hard-packed mud and smelled of chalk and incense.

Parnell unrolled his waterproof tactical map on the floor and he and Ecrin quickly went over the mission, Parnell hunkered down beside the Frenchman whose

English was throaty and heavily accented. His hair was black, shiny-wet, and faintly scented with jasmine.

The team's mission field order was clear-cut and time-critical. They were to prevent seven mobile 205mm rail-mounted artillery pieces from reaching Casablanca in support of coastal batteries once the invasion started. The train that contained the guns was now in the military garrison in Marrakesh, eighty miles southeast of Safi.

Their big problem hinged on the degree of resistance the Vichy French would give. If they retaliated forcefully, the guns would have to be destroyed before they could be railed to a point on the Marrakesh/Casablanca line within range of the coast. But if the French chose not to oppose the landings, the big guns were to be spared. To carry out either possibility, Parnell's Tactical Task Plan specified that the team would split up once it was beyond Safi, three accompanying Parnell and Ecrin, while two went with Bird and Martier.

Parnell's squad would head straight for Ben Guerir, a junction town sixty-four miles due east. There they'd board the Marrakesh train as it approached the junction and, once it had passed beyond the town, commandeer its locomotive and uncouple the rest of the string of cars. This particular locomotive was the only standard-gauge engine south of Rabat so the French would be unable to retrieve any of the stranded artillery cars.

Meanwhile, Bird's group were to head for the bridge at Boulaoune, which spanned the Oum River northeast of Safi. Once across, they'd use motorcycles hidden in a farmhouse to race the four miles across country to the Marrakesh/Casablanca track south of the town of Settat. If Parnell failed to isolate the guns and the train continued on toward the coast, Bird's mission was to blow up the entire train before it reached Settat. . . .

* * *

The harbor city of Safi lay on marshland, now mostly cultivated into fruit and nut orchards and fields of winter wheat. The town itself was completely surrounded by an ancient twenty-foot-high wall made of red pise brick topped with crenellated parapets and rounded towers like Norman keeps.

As the two trucks approached the city, Parnell spotted a massive stone structure on the southern side of it. Ecrin told him it was a *skala*, a fortress, built by the Portuguese in the sixteenth century. Both men were in the rain-soaked front seat of the leading truck, Francois driving. All the team members were now also dressed in jellabas. Kaamanui, Wineberg, and Fountain were under the tarps in back of Parnell's vehicle. Bird and his men followed in the other.

Francois said, "The fortress has two batteries of one-five-five-millimeter coastal guns. Batterie railleuse, on tracks."

"How good are the crews?"

"Well trained."

Beside the fort was the town's south gate, the Bab bou Zhanib. Shaped like an upside-down horseshoe, it bore intricate friezes of brilliantly colored tile. Quickly, they passed through. Inside the wall were palm-lined streets, crowded despite the hour or the rain with old European-built cars, donkey carts, and carriages with big red wheels and horse trains loaded with firewood. The street lamps were umbrellaed and there were outdoor cafés under awnings. Farther down, near the harbor, were modern homes, stark white and square-shaped, resembling Italian villas on the Mediterranean.

Francois turned east, into the medina, the oldest quarter of the town, once its main fortification. At first it was a labyrinth of dark, narrow alleyways between steppes of ancient wooden apartments. But soon they reached the main *souq* or marketplace, a dense warren of tiny, candlelit shops and tradesmen's atelier.

The entire *souq* was covered with huge panels of filthy canvas that trembled and hummed from the rain. The air stank of cooking smoke and spices and fish and butchered meat and dung. People milled everywhere, mostly men in their colorful jallabas and desert kaffiyeh turbans. The few women present, Francois explained, were either prostitutes or Berbers in *bakhnoug* shawls and *assaba* headbands. Their hands and naked feet were delicately tattooed with henna designs to ward off the Evil Eye.

The trucks inched forward, both drivers hissing and cursing at the pedestrians. They finally cleared through the market area into a clutter of tanneries and goat and sheep pens. Nearby was a small train yard, its tracks running beside the road through the Bab el Sherk, the east gate.

A hundred yards beyond the gate, the road forked. Parnell leaned out and looked back. The second truck blinked its lights, then turned to the left, northward, its headlamps curving from view, leaving only the beams glowing against the rain.

The two foreign legionnaires stood in the middle of the road in the rain just ahead of the bridge that crossed the Qehwi River a quarter mile outside Safi—arrogant in their white kepis and *seroual* drill trousers and khaki greatcoats.

*"Putain!"* Ecrin swore. "Be careful, *mon ami.* Legionnaires." He eased the truck to a stop a few feet from the men. They stood squinting into the headlights, their faces starkly illuminated, glossy wet. One had a long scar on the left side of his face, from the outer tip of his eye to his chin.

Parnell felt himself tighten, his body dropping subtly, getting ready. Beneath the jallaba, his right hand moved downward, slipped out his boot knife. He rested the blade on his thigh.

The legionnaires came forward with a rolling, insolent gait. They were nearly as big as Parnell. One went to the driver's side, the other, Scarface, to Parnell's. They stared in at the two men.

"Where the fuck are you going?" one growled at Ecrin in gutter French.

Francois laughed lightly. "To Ben Guerir, my friend. A load of bream fish."

On the other side, Scarface put his forearm up on the top of the cab. His greatcoat was drenched, and rain dripped from the brim of his kepi. He leaned forward and stared sullenly at Parnell. His face was shadowed now from the back glare of the headlights, the scar forming a dark, indented stripe across his cheek. Red stared back, felt blood ticking in his ear, energy gathering in his arms. "I think you have contraband," the other said to Ecrin.

"Oh, no, sir." Francois laughed again. "Come, I show you."

The one with Parnell said to him, "Why do you look so hard at my face?"

Parnell didn't understand the French. He remained silent. The legionnaire thrust his face closer, reached over, and pressed his fingers against the scar. "You like this? You like to see cut flesh, eh?"

Parnell caught the sweet-sour odor of *majaun*, hashish, on the man's breath and thought, *Here we go*. He shifted the knife in his hand, blade up, his other hand also moving now, crossing over to flick off the holster strap of his Colt .45 pistol. He silently thumbed the hammer off half-cock.

With his mind's eye, he watched himself moving, calculating the precision of it, his blade coming up, just over a foot, straight up into the man's Adam's apple while in the same lunging reaction, his pistol coming up and out and firing, past Francois's front. . . .

He jumped at the touch of Ecrin's hand on his shoulder, Francois talking quickly now, anxiously. "Forgive him, my friend. My brother, he is . . . you know?" He made pointing movements at his own forehead, indicating that Parnell was insane. "You know? Sometimes he cannot speak. When he is frightened. You know?"

The legionnaire continued staring at Parnell. Then he snorted with contempt and leaned back. The other one said to Ecrin, "Give me your money."

"Yes, of course." Francois fumbled under his robe, brought out several dirham, crumpled blue-and-white bills. He handed them over. The legionnaire studied them in his palm.

"This is not enough," he said.

"But I have no more."

The man jerked his chin up, indicating Parnell. "What about him?"

"He never has money. He is too stupid to have money."

Scarface snorted again. "Cunts," he said and walked away, toward the town. The other legionnaire spat and said, *"Va te faire foutre!"* It meant "Fuck off!" He turned and followed his companion.

Parnell took a deep breath, gave Francois a grin. They moved ahead, crossed the bridge, the truck wheels banging over the worn planks between the rail tracks. Below, the river was swollen, hissing against the bridge pilings.

Ecrin pointed at the main struts. "Right there will be the charges," he said. "Four or five sticks of nitrate d'ammonium."

According to the established plan, the bridge would be destroyed precisely three hours after the start of the invasion, at 7:00 in the morning. This was to prevent reinforcements from entering Safi and also to trap any French soldiers attempting to flee the town and regroup beyond the river.

It began to rain again as they cleared over. Parnell glanced at his watch: 11:03. Damn it, they were already an hour behind schedule. He held up his hand, pointed at the watch. Francois accelerated and the truck struggled ahead through the mud and pools of standing water, lumbering and clanking loudly as they headed for Ben Guerir.

# Six

Red hunkered down and studied the landscape out there in the wet darkness. Now and then everything was illuminated for a few seconds by lightning flashes: flooded fields and olive groves and scattered stands of cork oak and date palms. They were now thirty miles east of Safi, the land steadily rising toward the foothills of the Middle Atlas Mountains. Beside the road was a rail embankment.

Neither he nor Francois had spoken since crossing the Qehwi Bridge, both just staring ahead as the rain blew back into them, cold as ice showers. Fortunately, their soaked jallabas trapped enough body heat to keep off hypothermia.

Actually, Parnell liked cold. Born and raised in Leadville, Colorado, he knew what real cold could be. As a boy he'd loved snow, the exhilaration of the mountains, skiing. Nearly as much as he had loved football.

At the University of Colorado, he'd been an outstanding ball player, fast, strong, and smart. So good, in fact, three pro teams had offered him contracts while he was still in his junior year. Although tempted, he'd gone on to receive his degree first, a promise he'd made to his mother, who had possessed a deep love of learning. Both his parents were dead now, his father killed in an avalanche in Afghanistan where he was supervising construction of a rail line near Khandabad in 1937.

Eventually, Red chose to play for the Detroit Lions with such pro greats as Dutch Clarke, Ernie Cadell, and Alex "The Woj" Wojciechowicz. . . .

Francois interrupted his thoughts, saying, "We turn here." He did so, hurling the Peugeot hard over onto a partially mired dirt road. Soon they were among leafless vineyards and scattered, dimly lit farmhouses where the air stank of sulfur dioxide and wet manure.

The rain came in waves now. Abruptly, a large opening in the clouds appeared and the landscape was washed in brilliant blue-white moonlight. It only lasted a few minutes. The cloud break moved on toward the northeast, passing over Lake El Barouj and the Oum River fifteen miles away and casting little pools of white on the water's surface.

Parnell saw something suddenly loom up at the edge of the headlights. It was a fallen tree. He shouted a warning. Francois had also seen it and was already twisting the wheel. The truck fishtailed to the left and a rear wheel caught the road edge. In a drifting slide, the vehicle went completely over the side and came to a jolting stop, canted sharply.

Francois cursed and rammed down on the accelerator. The tires spun, hurling mud. It was no use. Parnell slapped his arm. "Ease up, ease up," he yelled. "You're just digging us in deeper."

Ecrin killed the engine. Parnell slid off his seat, stepped down, and instantly sank into mud halfway to his knees. The others climbed down onto the road. Red squatted to examine the wheels. The tires on the right side and part of the axle were deep in the mud. It started to rain again, the downpour slamming through the orange trees on both sides of the road.

\* \* \*

Felix Martier turned out to be a talker, jabbering away
to Bird as he drove the second crew north. A half hour
earlier, they'd left the coastal road and were now going
toward the Boulaoune Bridge four miles ahead. The rain
had stopped but the wind off the Atlantic was very cold.

Once they had to stop to retie the tarp covering the
straw bales. As Bird lifted the edge, he caught a blast of
fish stench. "Good Christ," he cried. "One a you boys
crap back here?"

"It's the goddamn fish, *meng,*" Laguna grumbled.
"They stink like dirty *cocha.*" He and Kimball were
stretched out beside the bales, their weapons and explosive musettes on their chests. Wyatt had specifically
picked the Virginian because he had a fine-tuned touch
with explosives. Laguna was stealthy and fast, a good
demo cover man.

Bird chuckled. "Hey, make you homesick for south
L.A., Weesay?"

"Shit," Laguna scoffed. "L.A. pussy don' smell like
that. That's like roses, baby."

Now Felix was rambling on about the difficulties of
being a Moroccan farmer. He grew table and wine
grapes, he said, Alexandrian muscats and *aligotes.* But
the goddamned weather and soil never cooperated with
him. His wine always turned out *gout de terrior,* not fit to
drink. Such fates made an honest farmer poor.

Bird nodded in a partial doze, not really listening. Although only twenty-six years old, he'd been a soldier for
nine years and knew enough to rest when and where he
could. Originally from Galbraith, Louisiana, he was the
middle child of twelve of a sharecropper on the Texas
border. When he was fourteen, he left home, his parents
glad to see him go since it was one less mouth to feed.

For the next two years he wandered throughout the
South, riding the rails, picking up odd jobs where he

could, living in hobo camps. Then one day, on impulse, he walked into an army recruiting office, lied about his age, and enlisted as an infantryman. He soon discovered that he was a born leader, a natural soldier with a deep instinct for the field. He quickly moved through the ranks. . . .

Lights appeared ahead, cars and trucks backed up. Bird felt the Peugeot slow and was instantly alert. Felix growled, *"Zit!* There are soldiers on the bridge."

It was two hundred yards away, lit by tall construction lights. The bridge was built as a Roman circula arch with timbering and mason foundations on each bank. Soldiers were working in a makeshift cofferdam on the opposite shore. Under the lights, the Oum River looked swollen and fast-moving.

The Frenchman glanced at him. "So, what we do? Continue?"

Bird considered the odds. The soldiers could be checking loads for weight. Too risky. "Turn around," he snapped.

"Where we go?"

"Ain't there no other roads down to the river?"

*"Oui.* Many irrigation roads."

"Grab one."

Felix frowned. "You mean we are to ford the water?"

"Yes."

"But I can not swim!"

"Don't worry about it."

There was the squeal of brakes. A truck had just pulled up behind them. It was filled with soldiers. Felix went pale. *"Merde!"* he gasped.

"Relax," Bird said quietly. "Jes' tell the bastards to back off so y'all can turn around." Under his jallaba, his fingers slid smoothly to the trigger guard of his Thompson. Felix was staring at him. "Do it," he ordered.

The Frenchman leaned out and waved at the army driver, pointed backward. The driver honked his horn and shouted something. Bird gently reached back and knocked his fist against the flatbed, three times, and rested his right foot onto the running board.

Martier finally got out and walked back to the other truck. He stood there waving his arms around and yelling. The soldier driver got out, too. At that moment, a policeman on a motorcycle came racing up, dodging between the pools of rain. He wore a white kepi and a long leather overcoat and gauntlets. The rain made the leather glisten like polished ebony.

He talked with Felix and the soldier a moment, then made the army truck back up enough to allow Martier to swing the Peugeot around. As they passed the soldiers going in the opposite direction, Felix made an obscene gesture at them.

The man stood motionless in the road, just beyond the glow of their flashlights. "Stand fast," Fountain challenged. Everybody's head jerked up, and then they grabbed for their weapons. "Advance and be recognized." Cowboy's flashlight pinioned the man. He was old, dressed in baggy breeches, a yellow doublet, and a peaked straw hat. He stared into the light with watery eyes.

"It is a farmer," Francois whispered to Parnell. To the old man, he shouted in French, "Who are you, friend?"

The man poked his chin forward. "Who the crap are *you?*"

"Merely travelers passing through your grove."

The old man snorted. "You broke my tree. So now you pass motionlessly."

Francois laughed. "No, we did not do it. It was the wind." To Parnell, he said: "He's all right."

The men relaxed. They had been unsuccessfully trying to extricate the Peugeot for the past twenty minutes,
using tree branches down under the wheels and finally
the straw from the fish bales. But the mud was so sticky
and clayish it wouldn't release. It simply compacted itself
until it was slick as oiled glass.

Parnell had already decided to leave the vehicle since
it was 2:13 now. He told Francois his decision. The
Frenchman seemed doubtful. "We do not have enough
time to reach the line before the train comes."

"How far is it to the track?"

"About thirty kilometers."

"We'll run it."

Francois shook his head warily.

The old man had now come down into the mud and
was studying the truck's wheels. He ignored the men
and their weapons. At last, he nodded, mumbled something to Francois, and returned to the road. He started
walking away.

"Where the hell's he going?" Parnell shouted. "Stop
him."

"No," Francois said. "He merely goes for his donkeys.
To get us out."

Parnell jerked his head at Fountain. "Go with him."
The young man sprinted off into the darkness. Ten minutes later, he and the old Frenchman were back, leading
two donkeys. They were small with sleek, dark gray coats.
Each had a leather yoke and harness. Wordlessly, the old
man got them into position in front of the truck, then
wound the harness straps around the bumper. When
he was done, he waited patiently for the others to help
him.

With the added pull of the animals, they quickly got
the Peugeot moving, inch by inch, until the tires and
axle finally pulled free of the mud with a great sucking

sound. The truck rolled easily back onto the road. The old man silently unwound his harness straps, recoiled them, and laid them neatly back across his animal's yolks. He started off, the donkeys following.

Francois shot Parnell an anxious glance. "So, we go now, *mon ami?*"

Red watched the old man's bowed, receding figure, his face tight. A rush of rain swept past and the donkeys ducked their heads. He withdrew his side arm. Holding it along his right leg, he started after the old Frenchman.

"No, *mon ami,*" Francois cried. "It is truly not necessary."

"We can't leave him alive. He might talk."

"He won't."

The others had climbed back onto the flatbed. They exchanged looks, turned away. The old man stopped. He stood there looking off into his orchard. Suddenly, he turned and shouted, addressing Parnell, "You are *Americaine, non?*"

"What's that?" Parnell said.

*"Americaine.* You. And you and you."

"Yes."

"Why you are here?"

"To fight Germans."

"But there are no Germans here."

"There will be."

The old man thought about that. He nodded. "Yes," he said. "Yes."

Francois walked up to him, stood close, talking in rapid French. The man said something. Then he spat to the side and wiped his mouth with the edge of his sleeve. Francois returned to Parnell. "He hates the Vichy," he said.

"Can we believe him?"

"He would not have helped us if it were otherwise."

Parnell studied the old man, who had again started walking away. A slash of lightning flickered high among

the peaks of the Middle Atlas. It resembled the flashes of
a short circuit along distant power lines. Abruptly, he
slipped the Colt back under his jellaba, stepped to the
truck, and pulled himself aboard. "All right," he
shouted. "Let's get the fuck out of here."

The old man didn't even look up as they went by.


They were down below the level of the main road now,
down in flood ground. Bird watched the fields move past
as the truck rumbled along a levee road, the river to the
left beyond thickets of gallery trees and dense brush.

The earth was loamy, newly plowed, black where it
protruded above the water. Good land, Bird thought.
Wheat, most likely, maybe sugar beets, too. Ever since
childhood, watching his father kill himself in the dry,
scrabble country of Sabine County, he had developed a
deep appreciation for good cropland.

They passed a field of newly mown hay, the crop
bound into big rolls like huge cinnamon pastries. He ordered Felix to stop. They pulled up beside an irrigation
weir. Water hissed through the gate, sending up a cloud
of spray that formed tiny moon rainbows. Wyatt got out
and went down into the field. The mud was thick and
deep. He crossed to one of the hay rolls and cut the
binding line, coiled it around his arm, and came back.
They continued on.

A mile upstream from the bridge, Felix parked in a
small grassy spot at the edge of the gallery of trees and
switched off the engine. It was wind-silent down here,
only the treetops soughing softly. Then a loud chorus of
crickets started up.

Bird posted Kimball upstream, Laguna down. He and
the Frenchman searched in the alfalfa grass along the
river's edge for fallen logs and loose brush. With these,

they fashioned a small raft, using the hay bindings to hold it together. Wyatt anchored it to a thick cork oak with his rappelling line, eased it out into the river, and climbed on.

The main current caught it and swung it out into midstream. Using his legs as keels, he let the vector force of the current and the line keep the raft moving toward the opposite bank. The surface of the river was smooth and shiny with flow pressure and moonlight. Dark objects and drifting debris swirled past. He spotted a movement upstream, a widening V ripple on the surface. Something was swimming toward the raft. He watched as a snake soon slithered up onto it, three feet from him.

"Gawd *damn*," he murmured angrily. Bird hated snakes. A cold shiver fluttered up his spine. Very slowly, he took out his handgun, a Browning Hi-Power 9mm. In the moonlight, the snake appeared black, about five feet long. It was coiled tightly as if from the cold, its head lifted, tongue testing the air.

Bird stared at it and gently thumbed back the hammer of his pistol. He knew a shot could rouse the countryside. But he'd already decided that no damned snake was going to nail his ass, poisonous or not. The snake made no sound but watched him steadily.

"All right, fella," he whispered to it. "Y'all jes' set there yonder, an' me and you'll get on by God fine." The raft's leaves trembled in the current and the raft itself lifted and dropped rythmically as if the river were breathing.

It seemed an endless crossing. Finally, Bird's boots touched sloping ground, lifted, touched again. He slid off the raft and went down neck-deep into the water. Its coldness against his chest jolted him, sucked his breath away for a moment. Backing slowly, he crab-crawled up the bank slope, his feet slipping and sliding clumsily on the muddy bottom.

He saw a quick, dark flash as the snake propelled itself
from the raft and into the water. It made for the bank,
head still up, eyes glinting like black agates. It passed a
foot from Bird's face. He felt the turbulence of its body.
It reached the bank and disappeared into a laurel
thicket.

Bird pulled himself out of the water, squatted there
blowing on his hands. He could still hear the snake moving through the laurel twigs and wheat grass. He turned
his head and spat. Then he gave a long, low whistle, signaling the others to retrieve the raft and send another
man across.

There were four motorcycles, old 180cc Griffon-
Buchets with twin cylinders. Their frames and fenders
were scratched and dented and each had two box-
shaped saddlebags on the back. Martier said they had
been used in the Tangier-Tripoli road races during the
early thirties.

They were hidden in an underground storage shed
with stone steps and a hurricane door. Inside were fer-
mentation tanks and coils of brace wire and harvest
utensils, the air compacted and cold and smelling of
grape rot and old stone chips and chain oil.

They had made good time from the river, a mile back,
quick-jogging it all the way in single file on a levee road,
Felix struggling to keep up. Now it was nearly 3:00 in the
morning.

They heaved the bikes up the steps. A flat-roofed
farmhouse stood nearby. It was made of large stones
with wide, white mortaring. There were no lights on but
a man came to the porch and stood watching, saying
nothing.

They mounted the cycles and started the engines,

gunning them up into operating heat. The engines had a clean, solid rap. The Frenchman glanced over his shoulder at Bird, who gave him the go sign. In unison, the four motorcycles leaped forward, went flashing past the farmhouse and up onto the levee road. Skidding into a turn, they headed east in echelon. . . .

# Seven

Alain Valais's sexual prowess was phenomenal but mechanical. He could make a woman writhe and moan in abandoned ecstacy, reach orgasm repeatedly as he thrust with pistonlike, authoritative power into her body. Yet to him it was more a matter of vanquishment than lust.

This particular woman's name was Zim, Madame Zim Rossiniere, a French Moroccan. She was thirty-five, eight years older than Alain, and married to Eric Rossiniere, a Swiss diplomat to Morocco. She had been Valais's mistress for two weeks. He was growing bored with her.

Now he reached his own release with images of sunlit, snow-capped peaks. *"Finchen!"* he growled in German. The image peaks faded, were replaced by others, dim forest glens buzzing with silence. Ah, yes. He rolled away, lay staring lazily at the ceiling of blue *zelliz* tilework.

Zim panted helplessly at his side. He reached for a cigarette, lit it, lay back. It gave off cinnamon-scented smoke. For a moment, it overpowered the cloying reek of pudenda and jasmine that invested the room. He hated jasmine. All Moroccans seemed to douse themselves in the stuff, men and women. He considered it an effeminate business.

"God!" Zim croaked in French. "You are magnificent." He smiled. She shifted, cast a leg over his. He pushed it back. She sighed, girlishly petulant. "You bit my breast when you came."

"You enjoy pain."

"Yes," she said. "Yes, it enflames me sometimes."

He rose from the sleeping couch, moved to the window. The room beyond the covers was cold. He felt the sweat on his neat, muscular pale frame turn chilly. He stood at the window, looked out. They were in the Hotel Sahara on Rue Riad Zitoan el-Quidim. Directly across the boulevard stretched the Djemaa el-Fna, the central square of old Marrakesh where for centuries caravans out of the Sahara and the Grand Erg Deserts to the east had brought gold and spices and slaves.

It was a vast, raucous, open-air marketplace of food stalls, musicians, storytellers, snake charmers, magicians, animals, acrobats, sneak thieves, and prostitutes, which never closed. A frenetic jumble of color and noise and smoke from bonfires and cressets of burning oil and tall watchtower flares. Its wild pageantry and exotic smells poured through the windows.

"Come back, *mon cher,*" Zim called throatily. "I want you again." Her husband was nearly sixty. In Alain Valais, she had discovered an exhilarating excursion into youthful force. She would do anything for him.

"Go to sleep."

"Please, just once more?"

"Later."

"You're cruel."

Cruel, he thought, a fitting word for a man. Cruelty was the mark of strength. Like Nietzsche's *Ubermensch,* the superman, who possessed the eternal will to power by forever resisting compassion.

He drew on the cigarette, hummed softly to himself a snippet from the Horst Wessel song. He'd always treasured its thunderous drama. Sometimes he even sang it aloud in his strong voice. Especially the final verse, *Marschieren mit uns in ihrem Geiste mit,* his icy-blue eyes glaring in challenge and insolent arrogance.

Zim said, "You hum that tune often. What is it called?"

He snorted contemptuously. "You wouldn't recognize it."

"I might."

He turned, looked across the shadows at her. "Madame, you have neither the intelligence nor the courage to understand its beauty."

"Why do you say such things to me?"

In the half darkness, a smile touched the edges of Alain's finely shaped lips. He crossed the room, reached down, and grabbed her hair. It was thick and rich brown. She cried out. He pulled her up. "Lick the sweat off my body," he commanded.

She did. Lowering, she took his flaccid penis into her mouth. Disdainfully, he shoved her away, returned to the window. A rush of rain rattled against the *mashrabiyya* latticework. He idly wondered if he would find anything this day.

In truth, Alain Valais's real name was Gerd von Bekker. He was a captain in the Second Fliegerkorps of the Luftwaffe, currently on detached duty as agent C-32 for Abwehr, the Secret Intelligence Service of Germany's armed forces.

Born of Prussian barons, he was a nephew of General Wilhelm Keitel, head of the Oberkommando der Wehrmacht, the German General Staff. His assignment to Abwehr had come directly through the Air Ministry. Although he preferred being at the controls of his beloved Stuka, he knew that this was all part of being groomed for higher command.

The false passport he carried identified him as an executive with a Swiss machine tool company, in Morocco to do business with the Vichy government. His true mission, however, was to verify that Vichy was abiding by the 1940 armistice, which required the French to dismantle all their heavy and medium guns except shore batteries and their heavy tanks and fighter aircraft. He was in Marrakesh specifically to check out a rumor that had surfaced among field agents that the French were hiding seven mobile, train-mounted 205mm field guns inside the town's military garrison. . . .

The rain ceased abruptly. Above the high glow of the Djemma el-Fna, the moon looked like a white-hot steel plate. It illuminated the three beautiful minarets of the Kontoubia Mosque, which rose on the high rim of the city. He returned to the couch. Zim lay stiff and silent. He pulled up the covers and went to sleep.


Six hours earlier, the three invasion fleets of Operation Torch had arrived at their designated assault points off the coasts of French Morocco and Algeria. Although many of the ships of this huge armada had crossed over 4,500 miles of ocean during sixteen days, each force had arrived on station within fifteen minutes of the others.

To deceive the Germans about the real target of such a large armed fleet, false war plans had been deliberately leaked to Axis intelligence agents over the last thirty days. They indicated that simultaneous invasions were to take place against eastern France and Crete. Thus far, the Germans had swallowed the bait.

On 5 November, Patton's western assault force had

separated from the others near the Strait of Gibraltar
and steamed due south off Africa's Atlantic coast. At
dawn on 7 November, it split again into three assault
groups. The northern group would go in at Port Lyautey;
the central force with Patton aboard the flagship cruiser
*Augusta* at Casablanca-Fedala; and the southern into Safi.

The Safi force comprised twenty-two ships, including
the carrier *Santee,* the battleship *New York,* and the heavy
cruiser *Philadelphia,* along with eight destroyers to pro-
vide covering fire and screening and barrage support.
Within the convoy were six troop transports. Two carried
men of the Forty-seventh Regimental Combat Team of
the Ninth Infantry Division and the Sixty-seventh Armored Regiment of the Second Armored Division, I
Corps. The remaining transports bore the corps's combat service battalions.

Two other destroyers, old, stripped-down four-stackers
named *Bernadou* and *Cole,* were to act as assault ships,
moving directly into the narrow harbor entrance ahead
of the main invasion to land three hundred assault
troops directly onto the main jetties. In addition, 108
light and medium tanks were aboard two old ferry boats
from Havana, Cuba. This armored force would be put
ashore at Safi Harbor, the only Moroccan port where
tanks could be off-loaded.

At 0012 hours the order to lower and load assault
boats came, the ships twelve miles from shore and
formed into screening position. In pitch-blackness and
under strong winds and a heavy Atlantic swell, the LCMs,
LCPs, and LCVs were let go on their davits and invasion
nets were unfurled.

By 0321 hours, thirty-nine minutes to H-hour, everything was set to go, the loaded assault boats circling their
mother ships like ducklings struggling through surf.
Everyone was on tense hold, awaiting the final order

from Eisenhower's Allied Force Headquarters, Gibraltar, to commence the invasion.

Two additional code orders would be used, depending on the Vichy French reaction to the invasion. If they decided to retaliate, the phrase "batter up" would be flashed throughout the three invasion forces. It immediately authorized all local commanders to then issue the second phrase, "play ball," which meant "return fire for maximum effect. . . ."

Parnell checked his watch, cupping his hand against the bright moonlight. Twelve minutes to four. He glanced toward the south, down the rail line, the thing glowing in the moonlight like twin shafts of acetylene flame.

Earlier, they had passed through a eucalyptus plantation, the trees dripping with rain runoff, the air sharp with the turpentine odor of tree bark. Occasionally the wind shifted sharply, bringing the smell of snow and alpine coldness.

To the east, the high black precipices of the Atlas Mountains were partially visible whenever the moon burst free. There were thick masses of clouds filling the high, deep gorges like motionless dam breaks of glowing foam. Sixty miles to the southeast, the lights of Marrakesh threw an amber wash up against the undersides of the storm clouds.

Leaving the truck in a small gully beyond the plantation, the men had jogged the last few hundred yards to the rail line, up a steep incline among scattered stands of juniper and cedar. They struck the rails a mile from Ben Guerir on the upper side of a long, rising curve. Halfway to the town, the ground plateaued out. Here, Francois said, the train would be going only eight or ten miles an hour as it pulled the steep grade.

In Marrakesh, a Free French *gardien* or watch-agent was already set up to monitor the city's military garrison where the mobile guns were located. If and when the gun train departed, he would immediately radio Parnell in Morse code.

Both Red and Bird carried SCR-511 portable cavalry guidon radio sets. These particular radios were known to be undependable in bad weather and carried a limited signal range. So they had been slightly altered to take a Morse code key. With it, they could send out a continuous wave transmission, which would carry farther in stormy conditions. Each radio had been preset to guard the international emergency CW frequency of five hundred kilohertz.

Their attack plan called for them to board the train as it came slowly up the slope. Once they'd taken over the locomotive and detatched the rest of the train, they'd highball it to a rendezvous with Bird and his crew outside Settat. There, they'd destroy the locomotive and rail line. Then, while Francois and Felix lost themselves in the Settat medina, the team would double up on the motorcycles and head southwest to link up with the forward elements of the invasion force as it moved inland.

Now they waited on their bellies in deep alfalfa grass, the closer rail fifty feet away. It started to rain, lightly, the moon still shining. Parnell rested his arm under his chin. The ground smelled oddly of cloves. There was a tiny movement on the rail, a Berber skink. It paused, lifted its lizard head to sniff the rain. Its scales glinted like tiny shards of glass. The moon vanished. Red checked his watch. Seven minutes to four.

He turned to look out at the sea fifty miles away. Dense blackness out there save for the scattered light blooms of the coastal towns of Safi and Qualidia and Essaouira. He grinned. *Get set, Morocco,* he said to himself, *you're about to get one helluva surprise.* He was calm, quiet, confident that this, Blue Team's first blooding, would go off with clocklike precision.

He was wrong. . . .

# Eight

Pfc Kimball knelt beside the left rail and quickly bound his first charge, four sticks of TNT with a core stick containing a blasting cap and three sticks wrapped around it. He was two hundred yards downline from Bird, Laguna between them, all laying demo charges. Each bundle would be connected by detonating cord to a single DK-11 twist-plunger exploder so they would all go off simultaneously.

He moved to the next site, two cross-ties down, and taped the second charge, then spooled out about thirty feet of detonating cord off his main reel. He cut off two pigtails, hooked them into the blasting caps, and tied their other ends to the main trunk line.

He worked rapidly, his hands sure. He liked handling explosives, liked the constant sense of risk. Just a single sheet of cardboard between him and a stray electrical charge that could set everything off. It was an adrenalating pleasure: the story of his life.

While he worked, his mind drifted back to the wild ride from the Boulaoune Bridge, the four cycles racing through the rain and moonlight over strange ground. Damn, it had been a good, clean high. Made you want to lift your face and howl. It reminded him of another ride, one just like it, that night they ran out of booze at a frat party at La Crosse, Virginia. . . .

He'd told everyone he would solve the problem. Borrowing somebody's Harley, he crossed the North Carolina line to purchase fifteen quart jars of ninety-proof white lightning from an old peckerwood in Norlina. Heading back half drunk, he switched off the headlight, just for the crazy hell of it, have a blast, and went rocketing through moonlight bright as a blue explosion with the shimmering, snaky Roanoke River off there on his right.

But he missed a turn and hurtled off into icy water. A passing Lunenburg County deputy had dragged him and his cycle out and immediately slapped cuffs on him. But then the man realized Harrison Travis was actually kin to Governor William "Big Buck" Kimball. He commenced to stammer and sweat. Apologizing profusely, he took off the cuffs, helped Kimball get the Harley running, and watched in silence as he roared away, his clothes soaking wet and stinking of charcoal-spiced alcohol. . . .

Kimball double-checked all his clove-hitch connections, then jogged back to Laguna, paying out cord behind him. As Weesay hooked up his charges to the master line, Kimball glanced at his watch. It was 3:59.

Laguna looked up. "What's the time?"

"One minute to four."

Weesay cackled happily. *"Ay, ellos van a cortar los cojones!"* He shook his fingers as if flicking off moisture, a gesture of excited pleasure. "Here we go, *hermano.*"

They headed back toward Bird, paying out cord, both men looking westward to the sea. Here and there the lights of small towns threw the trees into silhouette.


Four A.M.

Through Parnell's binoculars, the ocean was total blackness. Moving toward shore, he picked up the lights of Safi, flares on his glass. He scanned right, left, the flares smearing softly.

Beside him, Francois said quietly, "I think I hear engines."

Parnell lowered the glasses, tilted his head. Wind noise, up high. Then *there*, a distant surge of machinery that instantly vanished, only to return again and once more fade off. He looked down the track, saw Sol and Smoker and Cowboy sitting up in the grass gazing seaward. He glassed the shoreline again. Everything was still motionless, dozing.

A movement in the harbor to the right of the main part of town caught his attention. There were strings of tiny lights marking the water break. They looked like the footlights along a darkened movie-house aisle. But large shadows were slipping past them. Suddenly, silent gunfire started from the shoreline of the harbor, muzzle bursts and tracer rounds sundering the darkness.

*Batter up.*

Francois hissed, *"Ce foutu!* The idiot Vichy are opposing."

Red quickly unzipped his radio musette, pulled out the set, and extended its antenna. He flicked on the power swtich. A crackle of static blew from the speaker. He momentarily returned to his binoculars.

Several star shell bursts appeared above the harbor entrance, hung motionlessly. In their day-bright, shimmering light, he saw two warships moving slowly between the water break and the harbor shoreline, destroyers, old four-stackers. Both ships now opened on the shore guns, their three-inchers and automatic weapons slamming away.

*Play ball.*

Then another section of town entered the battle, the *batterie railleuse* inside the Safi fort. Its muzzle blasts blew triangles of smoky orange light for a few brief seconds before being swallowed by the darkness.

Almost immediately, counter-battery fire erupted from the invasion ships, huge fourteen-inch salvos from the *New York* and the *Philadelphia*. They cast ovals of illumination onto the sea ten miles offshore. Closer in, smaller barrages were let loose from destroyers and corvettes, their combined bursts of light momentarily exposing the lines of assault boats streaming shoreward.

The sound of the guns drifted faintly up to Parnell on the wind, a gentle roaring like thunder beyond distant hills. He scanned across Safi, saw explosions geyser among the city lights. The lights began going out, in blocks, until there were only scattered patches left.

He swung his glasses north, toward Casablanca. There was total darkness in that direction. He winced. Had something gone wrong there? He scanned back, fixed on Safi again, felt his heart blood ringing.


Gerd von Bekker opened his eyes and stared at the semidarkened ceiling. The air was cold. Something seemed wrong, out of place. What? He listened intently. The night was silent save for Zim's soft snoring. Absolutely no sounds came from the Djemma el-Fna.

He frowned, reached over to look at his watch: 4:38. He felt the bed tremble gently. A second later came a distant, rolling roar, thunderlike yet not thunder. It went on for several seconds before fading. Almost instantly another, larger roar came, from farther away, heavier, fuller. He sat bolt upright.

*Barrage!*

The phone rang. Before it could ring again, he scooped it up. Beside him, Zim rolled and sleepily asked, "What's the matter?" He ignored her. Into the phone he shouted, "Yes?"

"There is serious trouble," a man replied calmly in German. He instantly recognized the voice of Gerhart Dengler, his control agent and plant within the headquarters of General Auguste Nogues, resident commissioner for Morocco. "We are being invaded."

Gerd felt a thrill pass through his loins. *"Britisch?"*

*"Americkanisch."*

*A new enemy.* "Where are they striking?"

"So far, at Casablanca-Fedala, Port Lyautey, and Safi."

"Are the French fighting?"

"General Nogues has ordered full retaliation. But there's still much confusion among the local commanders. Everyone seems to be waiting for precise orders from Darlan or Juin." Admiral Jean Darlan was commander-in-chief of all French forces in North Africa with headquarters in Algeria. General Alphonse Juin was CinC of all French ground forces.

"Will any units retaliate on their own?"

Zim Rossiniere pressed against his back, whispering insistently: "Who is it? What's wrong?" He viciously shrugged her back. She fell off the couch.

"Certainly Lascroux and Michelier," Dengler said. These generals commanded naval and ground forces at Casablanca. "The only one we're certain will not retaliate is Bethouart. Nogues has already ordered his arrest."

"What about the air force?"

"Yes, General Lahoulle can be trusted."

"I'm returning to Rabat."

"No, not yet. Nogues has ordered the Marrakesh guns brought in to support Casablanca. You must come down with them."

"Then they *are* here."

"Yes."

"What about General Martin? Can he be trusted?" Major General Henri Martin was commandant of the Marrakesh-Meknes district.

"He claims loyalty to Vichy but is known to vacillate. His deputy commander, Colonel Paul Pineau, is strongly pro-Vichy. He also has distinct sympathies toward us. You are to get with Pineau. If Martin balks, he must take control of the guns."

"Do I identify myself?"

"Only if absolutely necessary." Without farewell, Dengler was gone.

Gerd began to dress. Zim tugged at him. "Where are you going? *Mon Dieu*, what's wrong, Alain?" He back-handed her. She tumbled back to the floor and began to cry. He fumbled in his case, pulled out a black 9mm Beretta automatic, tucked it into his belt. He stood over her. "Give me your diplomatic card."

She stared at the gun in his belt, shook her head silently. According to international law, all senior embassy officers were issued diplomatic cards following their accreditation by their host country so as to be protected from arrest or seizure under the laws of that country. Similiar cards were also given to members of the diplomat's family.

Bekker seized her arm, wrenched her up. "Give me your card."

Whimpering, Zim moved to her overnight bag, produced the card, and handed it to him. "When will you be back, Alain?"

He didn't answer and left the door open as he rushed out.


At precisely 0459 hours, Parnell's radio crackled with something out of the ordinary. Over the last forty-five minutes, he'd been picking up a lot of Morse signal traffic, most of it concealed in code language. Undoubtedly it was coming from ships relaying battle reports. And perhaps a few ham operators jumping in. Now a specific single call was coming through, slow dots and dashes going out over open air. It was strong, from somewhere close by: *CQ . . . CQ . . . CQ . . .*

That was the standard code for all stations to listen.

He leaned closer to the radio and placed his Morse key on his thigh. Francois noticed him and crawled over. "Is it Georges?" Georges Trulett was the Marrakesh *gardien* agent.

Red waved him off. The radio hummed softly; then the dots and dashes started again: *QRA . . . QRA . . . DELTA . . . DELTA . . .* "It's him," he said. He waited for a break and tapped out his own code ID: *ZULU . . . K . . . K . . . Zulu, go ahead.*

The following message said: *TRN 2 DPRT . . . GNS ABRD . . . SQ7 . . . ZOUV ES FL ABRD . . . AR . . .* Translated, it read: *train to depart . . . guns aboard . . . gun cars seventh in line . . . Zouaves (Moroccan-born troops) and foreign legionairres also aboard . . . end of message.* Trulett sent it twice. After the second time, Parnell tapped out: *CPY . . . CPY . . . I copy.* Trulett's signal disappeared, the speaker filling with general static once more.

Red glanced at Francois's anxious face. He whistled in the others. They squatted around him, a fresh rain squall tapping softly against their clothing. The sound of the shore barrage hung in the air. "She's headed our way, boys," he said quietly. "And she's carrying troops."

# Nine

The light was orange yellow, small, out about a half mile down the track. It disappeared, then was there again. Bird frowned. He'd just received a message from Parnell informing him the Marrakesh gun train was headed north, with troops aboard. He knew there was only one narrow-gauge locomotive on this line. So, what in Christ was that out there?

He glassed the light. Dawn was close, about an hour away. The temperature had dropped and there was fog on the ground. He finally caught and held the light. It was more yellowish through the binoculars. Again it disappeared and quickly reappeared, turned slightly as it moved across his line of sight. The reflection off the fog cast a glow back onto the vehicle. He saw it was a small road master's jitney with a pumper car hooked on.

"What is it?" Felix asked.

"A line crew." Wyatt settled onto his haunches, thinking. Should he simply let them pass? But what if they spotted the detonating cord? Still, they'd probably miss it in the fog. He turned his head, spat. At least it was damn good they hadn't used pressure detonators on their charges, he thought. Even the weight of that little shit wagon would have set them off, alerting the people in Settat. Then again so would a firefight.

He made a decision, whistled Kimball and Laguna to

his side. "That's a road gang car comin'. If they spot our cord, we'll hafta hit 'em. Then we'll pull charges and set up again farther south. Weesay, go north about a hunnert yards and lay a small charge. They get past me and Kimball, blow the bastards."

Without a word, Laguna ran off.

Bird looked at Kimball. "Cross the tracks and set up so we ain't shootin' at each other. If they stop, open up. Take 'em out fast, there could be soljers aboard."

Kimball nodded. He crossed the tracks and went into the grass on the other side.

Wyatt tapped Felix with the back of his hand. "Frenchy, you carryin' heat?"

"*Quel?*"

"You got a weapon?"

"*Oui.*" He pulled a German Luger from his pants, jacked a round into the chamber, the toggle-joint breech cranking up and back like a spider's leg.

Wyatt looked at it appreciatively. "Where in hail y'all get that thing?"

"I stole it."

"Good man. All right, you follow my lead. If I fire, you fire. And shoot to kill. Understood?"

"*Oui.*" Felix nodded rapidly.

It took the jitney four minutes to reach them. The vehicle was like a pickup truck fitted with flanged wheels. Its bed was stacked with toolboxes and there was a metal canopy under which six workmen huddled. A dim red lantern hung from one of the arms of the trailing pumper car.

It reached the first charge but didn't slow. The iron wheels made a soft humming sound and the back glow of the single headlight lit up the driver. He wore a red-and-white-striped Hindu *pagri* headpiece. The jitney quickly passed over the second charge without slowing. A moment later, it flashed past Bird's position.

He watched it move off toward Settat. Soon its dim red lantern disappeared into the fog. Kimball came walking back over the tracks, grinning. "Those're some lucky sons of bitches," he said. "Blind as fucking bats, though."

Although the men of Blue Team couldn't know it, the three attack groups of Patton's western invasion force were having problems.

The fort batteries at Safi, although initially firing with surprising accuracy, had been finally silenced by the big fourteen-inchers of *New York* and *Philadelphia*. Inside the harbor, the two old attack destroyers had also knocked out four 75mm dock guns. But the *Bernadou* was unable to approach the main jetty and had to off-load her assault troops out of position.

Of the four Safi assault forces, only two had managed to come ashore. Heavy surf off Yellow Beach in the south had pushed A Force up into B Force's Red Beach sector. Now both were still in the water and under heavy small-arms fire. Luckily, troopers of C and D Forces on the northern Blue and Green Beaches got ashore without opposition and were now slowly regrouping and moving inland.

In Casablanca and Fedala, the central assault group had run into major difficulties. First, there was massive confusion during the loading of the assault waves because of the darkness and the extremely heavy sea. The force commander had had to move H-hour forward to 4:30.

Navigation errors by the boat coxwains had also worsened the situation, landing assault waves all along the coast. Numerous boats had capsized against stretches of rocky shoreline, drowning many of the heavily loaded troopers. Others had barely made it to ground where they ended up hundreds of yards from their assigned landing points. Beach masters were now frantically trying to reassemble units in the darkness under heavy fire from French shore batteries and anchored warships.

The northern assault group at Port Lyautey and Mehdia was also coming up against stiffening resistance. The Vichy shore battery commanders had hesitated at first but finally ordered their gunners to open fire. Meanwhile, the American thrust toward the major airfield at Mehdia eight miles up the Oued Sobou River had been totally stalled.

The attack destroyer, USS *Dallas,* carrying the Sixtieth Regimental Combat Team, had tried to dash upriver. It was immediately pinned down by French infantry and armored vehicles. Now French fighters out of Mehdia were starting to strafe the beaches. Added to this was a recon report that said a column of eighteen Renault R-35 light tanks was headed toward Port Lyautey from Rabat. . . .

The captain of the guard at the Marrakesh garrison gate closely studied Bekker's diplomatic card. He was tall and had a delicate mustache that made his face look ferretlike.

Bekker turned to glance back down the slope to the town. Many lights were still on. As his taxi had passed through its narrow streets, he'd been struck by the lack of fear. Groups of townspeople stood on street corners watching the guns and explosions along the coast as casually as if they were witnessing a fireworks display. What imbeciles.

"I'm sorry, Monsieur Rossiniere," the captain said finally

and handed back the card. "This is not a valid military pass. I have no authority to admit a diplomat."

Bekker glared at him. Such a ridiculous asshole in his red-and-blue chocolate-soldier uniform, he thought angrily. God, how he despised all things French. During the battle for France, he had felt great exhilaration as he bombed their pathetic little towns and strafed the lines of fleeing refugees. They were all sheep, fit only for slaughter.

"It's a diplomatic pass, Captain," he said tightly. "It thus permits me to enter any facility of your government. I assume this is a government facility?"

The captain frowned, thought a moment. "Perhaps I can clarify this. Remain here, please." He disappeared into an office constructed within the high garrison wall.

Bekker looked through the gate. Although most of the fort's lights had been extinguished, he could see and hear hurried activity, shadows with tiny flashlights running across the large inner quadrangle, the impatient revving of military vehicles. Farther back were the steam bursts of a locomotive as its engine surged and faded amid the jolting slam of couplings.

The captain reappeared. "Follow me, monsieur," he said. He led him through a small door in the larger gate and across the parade ground. It was under several inches of rainwater. The French captain held the scabbard of his sword against his leg to keep it dry. The air reeked of coal smoke and engine exhaust.

Bekker spotted the train a hundred yards inside the fort. It was lit by tall stanchion lights that cast its shadow sharply onto the tracks. Steam blew sideways from the locomotive and was quickly dissipated by the cold air. A double line of Zouave soldiers, weighted down with field equipment and weapons, stood restlessly waiting to board its passenger cars.

General Martin's operations van was directly behind the tender. Unlike the dull green of the other cars, it was painted red. Next in line were three passenger cars, then the seven-gun flatbeds with their mounted 205mms.

The long barrels of the artillery pieces were resting horizontally and had muzzle brakes attached. Their huge breech blocks were snugged under canvas tarps, which were then tied to the firing turntables. Beneath the car chassis were heavy retractable outriggers that, when swung outward, would absorb the powerful recoil when the weapons were fired.

Behind the gun flats was another passenger car, then an oversize ammunition van, and finally one more passenger wagon, which had not yet been coupled. Next to it was a company of foreign legionairres in battle dress and harness. Unlike the Zouaves, these men waited in motionless silence.

The locomotive's engine roared and its huge driver wheels skidded for a moment. Then the entire train shifted back slightly, couplings slamming together in a rapid sequence, all the way back to the legionairres' car, where the jaws of its coupler shank quickly and loudly locked into place.

Gerd swung his gaze back to the locomotive. It was a faded black in color, its boiler, steam boxes, and smoke-box facing streaked with blue and scarlet from heat tempering. It was what was known as a four-eight-four rig with eight huge driver wheels and two smaller fore-and-aft truck sets. Stamped into the cab bulkhead was a coat of arms. It bore a red cross and the words NORD–CHAPELON.

The captain led Bekker past the Zouave troops in their blue tunics and white havelock hats to the operations carriage. The sides were decorated with polished brass swagging, the windows curtained. The officer went up onto the rear platform and knocked lightly at the door. It opened. He spoke for a moment, then signaled Gerd to come up.

Four officers and a radio operator were in the van's main room. It was thick with cigarette smoke and held the sweet odor of cognac. The car was partitioned into two sections, this one a formal lounge. Against the forward wall was a bank of radios, and a large field table had been set up in the middle, the thing now covered with maps and parallel rulers. Four partially empty bottles of cognac held down corners.

General Martin was hunched over the table, supporting himself on his palms. He was heavyset and elderly with wispy white hair. He wore no coat and had bright yellow suspenders and large sweat rings under his armpits. He blinked several times at Bekker before growling, "You are a Swiss diplomat?"

"Yes, General."

"Why are you here? This is neither the time nor the place for diplomacy."

Gerd smiled graciously. "I don't come as a diplomat."

"Ah? Then why are you here?"

"As an observer, sir. My country has been negotiating with your government about the purchase of heavy field pieces. I'm here to observe how well your two-oh-fives function when they go into action in support of Casablanca. I will then be—"

One of the other officers, a colonel, cut him off sharply: "How do you know we intend to support Casablanca?" This man was paunchy but had a hard eye.

Gerd figured he was Pineau. "Simple logic, Colonel," he answered. "I assume that during this ridiculous attempt to invade your country, you would want to protect your main naval base. Is that not true?"

The officers silently studied him. In back, the radio

operator tilted his head suddenly, held his headset
tightly against his ear, and began scribbling on a telepad.

Bekker returned the officers' tight gaze, calmly moving his eyes from one face to another. Martin seemed
inebriated, obviously distraught. He kept blinking. In
contrast, Pineau squinted, as if peering at a bright light.
The third officer, a major, possessed absurdly chubby
jowls and a confused, childlike look. Gerd dismissed
him.

But the fourth officer drew his studied attention. He
was a Foreign Legion captain of medium height with muscular shoulders. He was dressed in sharply creased khaki
battle dress with *seroual* trousers bloused into glistening
black boots. His face was Tartar-like, copper-skinned, with
canted eyes that were cold and black.

General Martin snorted suddenly, waved his hand.
"You may observe, Swiss. But stay out of the way."

"Thank you, General. Might I inspect the guns before
we leave?"

Martin ignored the question. Colonel Pineau stepped
forward. "I'll escort you, Monsieur Rossiniere."

They walked along the cars without speaking, their
boots scraping on the ballast gravel. They reached the
gun cars and Pineau stopped at the first one. Bekker
moved past him, walked along the flatbed, and intently
examined the I-beam foundations, the grease-scummed
outriggers. He returned, nodding. As he looked up, he
stopped abruptly. Pineau was holding a Lebel .32-caliber
revolver on him.

"Who are you?" the colonel asked quietly.

"I've already told you, sir," Bekker answered pleasantly.

*"Non.* I know Monsieur Rossiniere. Who are you and
why are you here?"

Gerd straightened, his smile gone. "I'm Luftwaffe
Captain Gerd von Bekker."

"Ah, a Nazi," Pineau hissed.

Bekker's eyes narrowed. "Colonel, it would be advisable to walk softly with me. I represent the full power of the Third Reich." His smile returned, changed now, haughty. "It would be expedient of you and also beneficial to court me and such power."

Pineau stared and stared, his mind obviously weighing options. Finally, with a quick flip, he reholstered his weapon, turned, and strode back to the operations van. Bekker followed.

As they entered, General Martin informed Pineau he had just received new orders from Rabat. The guns were not to go to Casablanca. Instead, the train would switch rails at Ben Guerir and proceed directly toward the coast to support Safi since the Americans were expected to land tanks there.

# Ten

The train seemed to be coming straight at them, the light from its headlamp smeared by a new deluge of rain. The ground shuddered under the motion of its great weight. Parnell glanced at his watch: 5:51.

Francois lay beside him in the grass. On the other side of the tracks was Wineberg, lying prone. Fifty feet to his right was Kaamanui. He couldn't see Fountain farther down and across.

The train came on, pulling hard on the grade. Bursts of smoke, black and roiling as volcanic ash, blew out of the stack with a slow spacing, a deliberate struggling. Seventy-five yards off, fifty . . .

At last it was there, the rumble of its leader wheels, the earsplitting expulsion of steam from the cylinder drums and the clanging, clattering din of moving rods and crossheads and heavy metal. The headlamp snapped past, leaving only the copper-orange glow of the firebox reflected off the cab's header. Now the tender rumbled past, then the operations van, red as a faded circus car, and the lighted windows of the troop cars, one, two, three . . .

Francois shouted close to his ear, "Look, there are guards on the gun cars."

He saw the white cap of a soldier sitting on the forward end of the first flatcar. The third troop car moved past with a thump of rails, its back coupling now opposite him. Parnell braced his muscles, dug his boot tips into the wet ground, and shoved up.

He ran bent over, the flatcar moving slowly away. Six strides and then he took hold of the stirrup step, lifted his weight to it, and snapped his right boot onto the bottom rung. Quickly he was up and over the side of the car, rolling to the edge of the canvas gun cover. A moment later, Felix came aboard and scurried up beside him.

Red inched forward. The air was dense with coal smoke and the gun canvas smelled of Cosmoline and big-bore grease. He peered around its forward edge. The French soldier was sitting with his back to him, shoulders hunched, hat pulled low against the rain.

Parnell pulled his belt knife. It felt solid, very cold. His fingers tingled, his head buzzed with blood. When he moved, he went swiftly, silently, his senses aware of everything around him. As he closed with the soldier, he caught the odor of pomade: jasmine, distinct.

His blade went into the soldier's liver with unexpected ease, as if he had just plunged it into slightly hardened lard. With his other arm, he jerked the man's head sharply back, arching his spine. There was the slightest exhalation of breath, screamless, and then the man went totally limp, heavy in his arms.

Energy scattered chaotically through him for a brief moment. He had just killed a man at close quarters. *Jesus God Almighty.* But no time to think about it. *Move, move!* He pulled the guard's body and his rifle back against the side of the canvas. The weapon was a long-barreled bolt-action rifle like an old Springfield '06. Francois peered at him from under the canvas. The Frenchman crossed himself. Parnell glanced aft, saw Smoker back there. Wineberg had already made his kill and was now shrugging into his victim's tunic, the dead man heaped in a pile at his feet.

Red searched the next flatbed for Kaamanui, finally spotted him. The big Samoan was pulling the coat off his guard. Sol looked up, flashed two times with his tiny harness light: *thumbs-up*. He tried to locate Cowboy but couldn't see beyond the high hump of the gun breech block.

He began unbuttoning his dead man's tunic, pulling hard at the polished metal brads.

Hiding behind the edge of the canvas on the second gun car, Cowboy cursed hotly. His guard was talking to the one on the next car, both men shouting back and forth. He waited anxiously. A sudden wash of rain swept in and the guards ducked their heads. Fountain became aware of his breath coming hard, as if he'd been running a long way. The rain increased. *Go now,* he told himself. He held back. A full minute passed. The train was speeding up now, its stack bursts coming closer and closer as it cleared over the grade. He turned. The distant dim lights of Guerir shone out there in the rain.

Suddenly, the guard on the third car stood up. Fountain tensed. The man laid down his weapon and moved to the upslope side of the car. He turned his back to the wind, fumbled with his pants, and began to urinate.

Cowboy was already moving before he even realized his brain had ordered him to do so. As he neared his guard, the man must have sensed something. He turned. At that moment, Fountain's knife blade entered the soldier's Adam's apple. A thin but forceful stream of blood spurted back onto Cowboy's forearm. He pulled the blade to the right, back, slicing. More blood. The man's head lolled forward.

He felt a violent surge of nausea coalesce in his belly. He fought it as vomit welled up, his hands frantically tearing at the dead soldier's tunic buttons. At last, he got the jacket open. It was sticky with blood.

*Goddamn, how hot it feels!*

He dragged the dead man backward, shoved him under the canvas, pausing long enough to flick his penlight, twice. Then he ran back, pulling on the tunic, searching for the man's cap. He found it, jammed it onto his head, and sat down, the soldier's rifle across his knees, just as the other guard came back, buttoning his trousers.

Guerir was a desert town, structured of mud walls and adobelike flat-roofed houses that were stacked up the slope like layers of a snake's scales. Everything was as brown as the semidesert belt in which it sat, the land rocky with low brush and prickly pear cactus. Stands of acacia and eucalyptus trees lay two miles higher.

The train passed a young boy shivering in a blanket and driving four camels. Parnell and his men hunkered down in the cold up on the gun cars in their Zouave jackets. It was one minute after six and the cloud cover over the mountains was beginning to lighten now, a soft, indistinct gray wash as dawn approached.

The train rolled slowly through a doorless gate with crumbling sides. It continued on at a walking speed down what seemed the central avenue of the town. The hiss of its steam, the scream of its whistle richocheted off the low houses as people hustled out of its way, everybody bundled in dark bernooses like Bedouins. Nothing was bright-colored here either. Even the lights were dim, mostly kerosene lanterns. The town had once been an outpost for a tenth-century sultanate, isolated out here to guard against the desert raiders who came through the high passes of the Atlas Mountains.

They reached a small train yard with a deep turntable pit. There were several empty boxcars and gondolas on a siding. Ahead, a man stood swinging a red lantern.

The train's wheels click-clicked as they switched from the main track onto a secondary line that curved gently to the left.

Hearing the wheels, Parnell sat up, puzzled. He took a quick glance forward, the locomotive visible to him now as it continued into the turn. The engineer repeatedly blew his whistle as they passed diagonally across the northern side of the town.

Five minutes later, they exited through another gate and began picking up speed. Now Red had no doubt, the train was heading west, straight for the coast. As soon as his car cleared the gate, he ducked back under the canvas.

The dead soldier lay on his face. His blood had gathered into a dark coagulated pool beside him. It had a raw, cold stench, like that from a slaughterhouse. "Goddammit," Red said to Francois. "We're heading for the goddamned coast."

Francois nodded sadly. "I thought so. This could be disastrous. The orders must have been changed at the last moment."

"How far is it on this line?"

"About eighty kilometers."

"Not in kilometers, in miles."

"I don't know. Perhaps fifty, sixty."

Parnell mentally did a rough calculation. "These two-oh-fives have a range of fifteen or sixteen miles, right? If this train holds at sixty, we'll be in range of the coast in about twenty minutes."

"It is downhill all the way. We'll be traveling quite fast."

Red dragged his musette to him, pulled out the radio and Morse key. "I'm ordering Bird to head for the coast. As soon as we're fully clear of Guerir, we take the engine."

"Yes."

He tapped out a quick message: *blu 2, blu 2, rainout,*

*rainout, coast, coast, sk.* It meant: *blue two, abort mission . . .
head for coast immediately . . . out.*

Leaving the radio for Francois to rebag, Parnell slid
out from under the canvas. He looked back toward the
town, its lights falling away as the engine continued increasing speed. He glanced at the mountains. Dawn
was coming fast, the high cloud layers glowing now and
the lower Atlas peaks beginning to silhouette against
them.

He moved to the edge of the car, gave a sharp whistle. On the next car, Smoker turned around. Red gave
him the closed-fist pump sign. Wineberg instantly rose,
as did Sol beyond. Francois crawled out from under the
canvas, carrying the soldier's rifle slung across his back.

Red looked into his face. "You ready?"

The Frenchman nodded. "Yes."

"Let's go."

The message to Bird had been garbled, Parnell's radio
too close to all that gunmetal. But Wyatt figured it out
anyway. He felt disappointment. He'd gotten his mind
all narrowed down to carrying out the mission, all set to
test the plan, snap-snap, see if it would fall into place.
Now they had to back off.

They retrieved their charges, leaving the detonating
cord behind, and went down for the motorcycles, everybody constantly checking the increasing light in the sky.
It was like a gray bleach seeping into the surrounding
clouds.

Parnell moved forward atop the passenger van directly in front of his gun car. Its roof was domed slightly,
the paint peeling and warped from the sun. A beam ran
down its center and he kept his boots on it, letting its
thickness take up the sound of his passing. The air

around him was saturated with the stench of coal smoke, the wind whipping it past as he leaned his body into it.

Distractedly he was remembering how easily his knife had gone into the French soldier's body, so softly, so gently. It seemed somehow inappropriate, the thing as simple as a hand wave. It should be harder to kill a man, he felt. And an absurd thought came to him. The killing instrument, his commando knife, wasn't even an American weapon. Wasn't that a slight hypocrisy, if nothing else?

He reached the end of the car, timed his steps, and leaped across to the roof of the next one without breaking stride, keeping to his crouched, high-legged lope.

His gaze momentarily fixed on the coast. Far out was a faint line now, thin and gray, the demarkation between sky and sea. Beyond it was a soft glow. Suddenly two ship salvos appeared deep in the black velvet of the sea, tongues of orange within a bloom of smoke, everything visible for only the blink of an eye.

He finally reached the operations van, paused to glance back. Francois and Wineberg were directly behind him, both carrying musettes. Farther back, he saw Kaamanui clear over the top of the third car and start forward.

The operations van had a viewing window shaped like a dormer. He stepped over it. The smoke was thicker now, cinders hitting his face still hot from the firebox. He held up the radio bag to protect his eyes and studied the tender car, next in line. It was a combination rig with a huge coal bin on top and a water tank below. The after part was flat but had steel flanges radiating from the bin.

He braced his legs and jumped, landing between the flanges. Coming up instantly, he rolled over the edge of the bin and down onto the load of coal. It was like large gravel with knife-sharp edges. Francois came right behind him, then Smoker. They huddled inside the bin, the air resounding with transferred sound off the engine and wheels. Using hand signals, Red indicated to them what he planned to do.

Leaving their bags, the three men crawled to the forward end of the bin. Red lifted his head. He could see the engineer leaning out his window on the right side of the cab. Across the platform, the fireman was hurling shovelfuls of coal into the open firebox, which roared with a rushing sound.

He inhaled, gripped the bin's bulkhead, and pulled himself over it. A French soldier's head suddenly rose over the edge, less than two feet from him. It was sharply silhouetted against the red-yellow hole of the firebox. The man froze, open-eyed.

In a single movement, Parnell twisted his body to the left, brought up the butt of his Thompson and slashed it in a semicircle against the soldier's jaw. The man fell down. Red heaved himself past the edge of the bin and onto the engine's platform.

As he did, he caught a glimpse of the soldier down on the coupling between the locomotive and tender. He was desperately clawing for a handhold. Parnell knelt down and grabbed for him but missed. The soldier screamed once and slid off the coupling. He vanished beneath the forward wheel truck.

Red groaned, swung around. The engineer and fireman were staring at him, terrified. The engineer was fat with a walrus mustache while the fireman was naked from the waist up, his body muscular and reddened by the heat of the firebox.

Abruptly, through the pounding, pulsing noise of the locomotive, came the sound of two rifle shots.

* * *

Horse Kaamanui, who had just climbed onto the operations van, was squatting, waiting for Cowboy to jump across and follow him up. Above them, the sky was lightening rapidly, sheets of gray and objects beginning to emerge out of the dark landscape.

He heard the two rifle shots and bullets zipped over his head. He dropped flat just as Fountain appeared at the top of the van's ladder. Sol waved him past. "Keep moving," he shouted. "I'll cover." Cowboy dodged around him and headed forward, crouched very low.

As the Samoan started to turn and follow, he spotted the two guards who were firing, back on the first gun car. They were standing on the weapon's high breech block. Again they fired. He instantly raked them with his Thompson, holding it shoulder high, the weapon jolting slightly as its muzzle pulled it upward. Both guards dropped out of sight.

He again started forward, cutting his head back and forth to make certain French soldiers weren't at the windows of the passenger cars. Suddenly, a hand holding a pistol appeared over the after edge of the van. A moment later, a legionnaire officer in battle harness pulled himself up onto the roof.

Sol swung his Thompson and fired, heard a round hit. The officer scrambled back down the ladder. Watching his position, Sol began backing away. He stumbled against a corner of the van's viewing window, tried to recover, but went down hard on top of it.

Instinctively, he tucked his weapon and tried to roll back to his feet. As he came up, he saw the legionnaire officer lunge back onto the roof and come lumbering toward him. He saw it was a captain, the man's right shoulder covered with blood. He had a bayonet in his left hand. His face showed no pain, only a black rage as he came on, the bayonet held straight out, aimed at Kaamanui's stomach.

Sol recoiled, drew himself in, still moving up. The bayonet sliced through his tunic and cut hotly across his stomach. Then the Frenchman slammed into him. They went down again, grappling. The captain growled against his cheek, tried to clamp his teeth into the thick flesh of it. Bellowing, Kaamanui hurled him away.

Instantly both sprang to their feet and closed once more, punching and slashing at each other. Horse took hold of the legionnaire's ear and twisted it violently. The pain forced the captain's face back, which exposed his throat. Kaamanui punched him in the Adam's apple, felt something hard go soft inside. The captain's eyes clamped shut. He began gagging, falling back, slipping, and finally disappeared over the side of the van.

Several more bullets went past. Then came the familiar, deep tone of Thompsons firing. Sol scurried to the forward end of the van and jumped onto the tender. Cowboy and Smoker were standing on it, braced against the flanges and throwing bursts of covering fire over his head.

Up in the locomotive's cab, Parnell glanced at his watch: 6:18. Damn it, ten minutes more and they'd reach the outer range of those 205mms. He turned to Francois to shout, "We've gotta cut those guns loose now."

He leaned over the railing and squinted down at the coupling mount. It was steel-thick, black with grease and roadbed scum. He slipped under the railing and gingerly stepped onto the coupling.

Instantly, the engineer began yelling at Francois, frantically waving his arms. Red paused, looked back. Ecrin and the engineer were shouting back and forth. Finally, Francois moved to the railing. "He says we can not uncouple the tender. It would force us to stop or the boiler sheets would melt down and explode without a water feed."

Parnell pulled himself back onto the platform. "Then we'll have to uncouple between the tender and the operations van. Tell that son of a bitch to slow down so I can do it."

"No, no, *Leftenant,*" Francois protested vehemently. "You forget the Qehwi Bridge and the planted charges. They will go off at seven o'clock. If we slow down and fail to cross, we'll be trapped on this side of the river."

Red cursed aloud. He stood there, his mind working, his eyes glaring into Ecrin's face. Then, decided, he twisted, vaulted the platform railing, and disappeared down into the coal bin.

# Eleven

They emerged out of a stand of cork oak and acacia trees a quarter mile ahead, a six-man patrol of Zouaves mounted on horseback and coming up onto the road into the grainy dawn light.

Bird instantly braked his cycle and stopped, the others pulling up behind him. He glanced right, left. The landscape out there was a study in black and gray: flooded fields on both sides like sheets of buffed steel with scattered islands of orchard trees.

He turned in his seat. "Ever'body stay in tight. We're takin' these sickles straight through 'em. The noise'll spook the horses and we'll be long gone before they know what happened."

The three Americans unshouldered their weapons and laid them across the handlebars. Felix pulled his Luger and held it in his right hand. Bird nodded. The four engines roared and the bikes leaped ahead, hurling mud.

Down the road, the horsemen drew up as they saw them roaring straight toward them. The horses, sensing something, tossed their heads and skittered sideways. The Zouaves just stared, puzzled, then began pulling rifles from their saddle scabbards. One soldier fired, the bullet going wild.

The four cycles were very close now, boring in with full

power. The roar of their engines threw the animals into panic. They were small horses, their manes knotted like circus ponies'. They swerved and backed and twisted as the soldiers fought to stay mounted and fire their weapons at the same time.

Two Zouaves were thrown and their mounts fled down the slope of the road and out into the flooded ground. One immediately sank into the mud, causing it to tumble over its own head. It thrashed back to its feet and dashed off again, following the other deeper into the field.

Wyatt reached the first horseman and flew right past him. He caught a fleeting look at a face, a gun barrel. Another horse loomed ahead, but then veered aside. A rifle cracked. Several more. The two thrown soldiers were on their knees now, firing. He swung his Thompson around and cut them down.

He glanced back. As if in slow motion, he saw Felix fall to the side, a feathering of blood floating off his face. His motorcycle went catapulting out, arching, and then plunged into the water. Directly behind the French agent, Laguna frantically fought his cycle to keep from hitting him, dropping it to the side, skidding.

Ten yards back, Kimball also stopped. Straddling his machine, he began firing over Weesay's head. Gun smoke fumed in the air. Two more soldiers were hit, then a horse. This one was black as ebony. It reared, screaming, and fell onto its neck on the sloping side of the road and then slid down into the water. The other three animals galloped off wildly toward the trees.

Laguna and a Zouave engaged each other, the French soldier firing first. He missed and began frantically trying to ram another round into the breech. Weesay shot him in the chest. The force of the round blew him back off his feet. The single remaining soldier jumped off his horse and ran down the road bank and out into the flooded field. He fell several times but continued going. They ignored him.

The bullet had struck Felix in the left eye. The back of his head was blown out, the blood black in the colorless light. Bird cut his engine and walked back. Kimball was already squatted down beside the Frenchman, shaking his head. "Aw, shit," he said softly.

Four of the Zouave soldiers were also dead. The fourth was shot in the thigh. Without a word, Laguna knelt and cut the man's trousers away, exposing the wound. It formed a puckered hole, red as cherry meat with loops of fatty tissue in it. He sprinkled sulfa powder from his med kit onto it and bandaged it up, the entire time the French soldier staring at the wound, at Weesay's hands, saying nothing.

Wyatt walked back to the downed horse. It was still screaming, panting heavily. Bloody foam blew from its nostrils. It couldn't lift its head. There was a huge wound in its neck and its eyes were wide and hot-bright, rolling and showing iris and rolling again. Bird gently placed the muzzle of his Thompson against the animal's forehead and fired.

They dressed in the bloody French uniforms over their own and rubbed mud into the fabric to cover the bloodstains. Then they field-stripped their Thompsons and hid the parts in their musettes. With each now carrying a French Lebel-Berthier rifle, they remounted the motorcycles and once more headed for the coast.


Parnell hunched down on the coupling mount between the tender and the op van to study its mechanism. From above and behind him came sporadic fire as Sol, Smoker, and Cowboy continued throwing bursts back along the train each time they went into a curve, which exposed the trailing cars. Their fire was instantly answered by French soldiers, who were now moving forward on top of the passenger cars. Most of the enemy fire was high, yet an occasional round would slam into the side of the tender.

Red quickly figured out the coupling mechanism. It was an old double-knuckle rig with heavy shank jaws like opposing fingers held in place by a friction pin. Beneath the pin was a disconnect bar with a loop handle that ran past the car frame to a coupling box next to the upper mount.

He braced himself, took hold of the handle with both hands, and tried to lift it. It refused to move. He inhaled, tried again. Still, nothing. The high speed of the train was causing the knuckle jaws to freeze the friction pin inside its sheath. To loosen it, they'd have to slow down until the train was barely moving.

He studied it a moment longer, then stood up and tapped Sol's boot. "Light up a stick with a sixty-second fuse and some tape," he hollered. Kaamanui disappeared. Another fusillade came from the passenger cars. The bullets sounded like sticks being snapped through water as they passed.

Cowboy and Smoker opened up again just as Horse returned with a stick of TNT. Its short fuze was already lit. It sizzled and sparked. He leaned down and slapped it into Red's hand like a sprinter passing the baton in a quarter-mile relay.

Parnell squatted again and quickly jammed the charge between the bottom of the friction pin and the disconnect bar and taped it tightly. "Fire in the hole," he bellowed and quickly pulled himself back onto the top of the tender. The others were already lying flat.

The explosion was muffled down between the two cars. Metal fragments ripped up against the tender and the back of the operations van. Red peered over the edge. The blast had torn the disconnect bar out of its bracing. Its end was dragging on the gravel ballast and cross-ties flashing past. The friction pin had been blown partially out of its sheath and now wobbled back and forth in the surge-and-fade of the engine's pull.

There was a loud snapping sound and the pin shot out of its bore like a bullet and struck the back of the tender. Instantly, the upper knuckle jaw jerked up heavily, rode over the curved hump of the opposing jaw, and pulled out.

At first, the disconnect was hardly noticeable, the string of cars keeping pace with the locomotive on momentum alone. But slowly they began to fall back, the distance widening faster and faster.


Bird and his men continued southwest. Beyond the flooded fields, they cut through olive groves of ancient trees, gnarly-trunked. Soon they could smell the ocean and crossed through what must have been a copra plantation. The coconut trees were planted in rows and the ground was flat and sandy and hardened by the rain.

They reached the coast road at a point eight miles north of Safi. The ocean was wind-scoured into whitecaps and erratic wave action, the shoreline along here rocky and indented with small bays and narrow beaches filled with driftwood.

Out in the ocean to the southwest, the invasion ships were clearly visible and seemed much closer than they actually were. Salvos were still erupting from the heavy cruisers. Each time, the huge shells made long slurring trills before they struck inland, and even at this distance, their impact concussions shuddered faintly through the ground. Beneath these heavier sounds came the sporadic crackle of small-arms fire.

Lying out beyond the heavy cruisers was the carrier *Santee.* Rays of yellow-gray sunlight came down on it through the thinning clouds, which made the ocean glow softly. The carrier was launching its first-light strikes now and its aircraft, like tiny gnats, hovered above the ship's great bulk.

Five minutes later, the three cyclists caught up to a military convoy, nine gray trucks filled with soldiers in khaki battle dress and old World War I soup-bowl helmets. Wyatt slowed, then accelerated again, and they pulled up to within twenty yards of the trailing truck. The soldiers inside waved at them as they attatched themselves to the convoy.

A half hour later the trucks reached a small, hastily set up roadblock. Just beyond it was a fork in the road. Four French policemen in dark blue uniforms and white gauntlets stood beside two Lars lorries. The convoy stopped and one of the policemen began conversing with a French officer in the lead vehicle, gesturing southward.

Straddling his cycle, Bird studied the surrounding ground. On the inland side of the road were eucalyptus trees planted as a windbreak for orange orchards beyond. He turned slightly. "If we break, head for the trees," he whispered softly. Both Kimball and Laguna nodded.

The gunfire from Safi was close now. American troops and more incoming assault boats were clearly visible. Huge stacks of equipment were scattered along the beaches. Out in the surf were overturned boats and scattered bodies. Yet the scene seemed oddly lethargic to Bird, little more than a training exercise that was about ready to wind down.

The convoy finally started forward again and turned inland at the fork. Soon, they reached the road to Boulaoune. Four miles due south were the outskirts of

Safi. One by one the trucks turned onto the road headed toward the city. The three Americans followed close behind.

The rail marker looked like a gravestone, four feet high. The rain had melted the bird guano on its top, which streaked the leeward side with white lines. French and Arabic words were chiseled into the stone and painted yellow.

Minutes earlier, Parnell had watched as the gun train finally came to a complete stop far behind them. French soldiers poured out of the cars and began moving forward along both sides of the track. Then the company of legionnaires came up. The Zouaves respectfully got out of their way as the legionnaires, running in two steady, straight lines, weapons at high port and boots striking the ground in precise double time, took the lead.

The marker snapped past. He glanced at Francois. The Frenchman was scowling down at his wristwatch. Close by, heat fumed off the locomotive's boiler head and rolled back over them like surf. The cab held the cloying, hot stench of tar and burnt steel plating and coal smoke. To escape the fumes, Sol, Cowboy, and Smoker had crawled back onto the tender.

"What'd that marker say?" Red yelled at Francois.

"We are thirty-two kilometers from Safi."

"How fast are we going?"

Francois spoke to the engineer. He pointed to a large dial high up on the back head of the boiler, which was covered with crisscrossing pipes and valves and brass dials with filthy glass faces and water tubes holding liquid red as diluted blood. The speed indicator showed 110 kilometers an hour.

"We should reach Safi in about eighteen minutes," Francois shouted.

"Can he make more speed?"

"I have asked. He says no. We're pushing red limits now."

Red glanced at his own watch: 6:40. Twenty minutes before the Safi Bridge blew itself apart. If everybody's calculations were correct, that gave them at least a two-minute cushion.

He felt better.


Their names were Pascin and Charle Monnier, twins born six minutes apart forty-four years before. Both belonged to an active Free French cell in Agadir, a small port town down the coast.

In the predawn darkness thirty minutes after the invasion began, they had launched a small pirogue onto the swollen Qehwi River and floated down to the bridge outside Safi. Hooking a dragline to its center piling, they snugged the boat in tight against the swift current. Then Pascin, a canvas bag around his shoulders, climbed the rungs of the piling to the underside of the span deck. The wind down there was strong and stank of starling and turnstone shit.

As the fighting had intensified, townspeople had begun to flee across the bridge. First they came alone or in scattered pairs, then in groups: women and children and old men and automobiles and donkey carts. The sounds of their frantic passage directly over Pascin's head sounded like gentle thunder.

He ignored it. Taking a bundle of four sticks of nitrate d'ammonium from his bag, he quickly affixed it to a main deck girder. Inside the bundle was a cardboard cigar tube stuffed with guncotton along with a four-foot length of burn wire. This was the charge primer.

He signaled his brother. Charle handed up a small object. He took great care handling it and keeping it upright. It was made of two small lengths of two-inch steel pipe fitted together with a sleeve. The ends of the pipes were corked. Tightly fitted between them under the sleeve was a thin copper disk that separated the contents of both sections.

The bottom section contained sulfuric acid, the upper a three-to-one mixture of potash and commercial sugar. Once the acid came into contact with the copper disk, it would begin dissolving it until it ate completely through to the sugar-potash mixture. An immediate incendiary reaction would follow, which in turn would ignite the burn wire to the guncotton primer, and that would then detonate the main explosive.

According to the data from ordnance manuals smuggled into Morocco, coupled with their own tests, the twins knew that it would take the sulfuric acid precisely one hour and thirty minutes to completely dissolve the copper and reach the potash mixture.

The setup was makeshift but had proven exceedingly effective.

Using a small flashlight, Pascin checked his wristwatch. It read 5:28. He flicked off the light, waited, again checked: 5:29. At precisely 5:30, he turned the pipe incendiary upside down, taped it to the piling, and inserted the tip of the burn wire through the upper cork. It was complete.

At exactly seven o'clock, the main charge would explode.

The two men released the tie-in line and swiftly drifted away from the bridge. Since the Qehwi River drained directly into the main harbor, the brothers intended to float right down into the Allied lines.

Five minutes later, a fuse-timed round from a 37mm aboard one of the American destroyers exploded thirty feet over their heads. Both twins were killed by shrapnel.

Although Pascin Monnier had not known it, his watch had been one minute fast. . . .

# Twelve

A mile from the outskirts of Safi, the French military convoy stopped again and the soldiers now began to dismount. All were young men, their anxious faces turned to look toward the town and out at the harbor. Noncoms came along the truck line shouting and shoving at them.

A stream of refugees was also on the road, donkey carts and camel strings, men and women and children. The sound of muffled explosions could be heard from the town and the periodic rattle of small arms. A few fires sent up a blurry haze of yellow-brown smoke over the town.

In and around the harbor there was a great deal of activity. Assault troops were spreading out and vehicles lumbered up onto flat ground. Behind them came a second wave of assault boats. Among these were two odd and incongruous vessels, the ferries *Lakehurst* and *Titiania*. Both were stern wheelers. On every deck were dozens of light and medium tanks, M-3 Grants and Stuarts, part of Patton's First Armored Corps. Ahead of them, an American destroyer was cutting loose with point-blank fire at enemy positions just beyond the docks.

The French troops dispersed down into the inland side of the road among the orchards where they would set up a defensive line. One of the sergeants shouted something at Bird, who had been scanning the beach, estimating its distance from the road.

He figured it was about a mile. But the ground was completely flooded, showing only mudflats and grass islands. For a moment he considered making a dash for the beach but canceled that. The motorcycles would bog down the moment they left the road.

The French sergeant approached, angrily shouting at the three cyclists and pointing down at the orchards. Wyatt said, "We're moving. Stay on the road and head straight for the town."

He gunned his cycle and shot forward, heard the others coming close behind. The French sergeant stopped, shocked. Then he lunged out to grab Bird's tunic as he sped past, missed, and fell down. A second later, Weesay and Kimbal shot by him.

They all hugged the edge of the road, dodging refugees. Wyatt nearly slammed into a camel but swerved just in time. Hearing the roar of the engines, people began scrambling out of their way. Finally they were beyond the crowd and all three put on full throttle, rocketing toward Safi.

They reached the outer medina, the ancient fortified part of Safi, within a minute and hurtled through the northeast gate. They were immediately in a maze of deep, narrow streets lined with dank, multistoried *partee* apartments. Close beyond were groups of town houses called *riads*. Each was hidden behind a high brick wall with a single door painted blue.

There was house-to-house fighting going on here, skirmishing and the isolated reports of snipers. Drifts of cordite smoke lingered just above the ground. The streets were empty. Muzzle flashes winked in dark recesses and bullets *whanged* and screamed overhead. Suddenly, an American Browning Automatic Rifle opened up from nearby and its slugs chewed up a wall to their right.

Bird instantly threw his cycle hard over and went flying into a tiny side alley between *riads*. Kimball and Laguna roared in after him. Skidding to a stop, they dismounted and began tearing off their French uniforms. More rounds came in, higher this time. Brick fragments showered down. From somewhere over their heads came the periodic, slow-sequenced rap of a French St. Etienne 07/16 machine gun.

Crouched low, they gathered beside the first door they reached. Its blue panels were covered with symbols and stylized hands of Fatima. Weapons ready, they kicked it open. Inside was a *dar* garden, which contained a central fountain with tinkling water bells and a large laurel tree that had bright yellow cages of canaries hanging in its branches. Despite the gunfire, the birds were singing and the air was cool and perfumed with the scent of roses and jasmine.

Again the French machine gun above them fired a burst. They ducked under an arched doorway and entered the house, each man moving and covering. The interior walls were pure white, made of stucco *muquarna,* and the floors were blue and white tile. Pillows and eating rugs were strewn about. The building seemed to have many rooms, some mere cubicles. The sweet, cloying reek of *majoun* or marijuana and opium smoke saturated the air.

Several young, dark-skinned women peered fearfully at them from behind a latticed *mashrabiyya* screen. They were all naked, their hands, feet, and faces covered with delicate henna tattoos.

Laguna spotted them and a broad grin creased across his Hispanic face. "Hubba, hubba, baby," he cooed lasciviously. "Hey, chu know what? We in a goddamn cathouse."

The clear *thrump-whoosh* of an American 60mm mortar came hollowly into the room, high-arching a round in. It was somewhere close by. All three men hit the floor with Bird bellowing back at the women, "Get down! Get down!"

A click of time later, the front of the house blew in.

It was astounding how quickly the two American F4F fighters appeared. One second the western sky was empty and then they were there, coming in at treetop level, hunting. They flashed close overhead, their Pratt and Whitney TO-2000-J engines screaming as they went into a sharp pull-up and then a slow, wide turn to the left, side by side, their fuselages gray on top and cream beneath.

"Oh, shit," Parnell yelled. "They're gonna make a run on us. Take cover!" Everybody went flat onto the cab deck and down behind the tender's bulkhead. Even the engineer left his seat and squatted beside Francois, his face flame red. The fireman, still holding his shovel, dropped onto the tender coupling.

The two aircraft came around, bright for a second against the Atlas peaks and the rain clouds. Obviously, the pilots were studying this lone locomotive, a decent target, yet figuring out if they wanted to waste ammunition on it. Something bigger might be farther up the rail line. They rocketed past a second time, paralleling the tracks. They were so close to the ground, their prop washes lifted a misty spray of rainwater.

Parnell tried to focus his thoughts. If they didn't identify themselves as American soldiers, American .50-caliber rounds would soon be slamming into them. He didn't relish the irony. But how could he let them know? He lifted his head, saw the others staring at him, eyes squinting. He grabbed at an idea.

Turning to the engineer, he yelled, "Do you have paint?"

The engineer shook his head, unable to understand. Francois quickly translated. The engineer grinned suddenly. "Ah, *oui,*" he said. *"Chauffe au rouge."* He crawled to a large metal box on the left side of the cab, jerked it open.

Inside were red lanterns and marker spools and heavy wrenches. He brought out a paint can. The sides were streaked with hardened red lead used to prevent rust on steel. He hunted further for a brush but couldn't find one.

Smoker leaned down and pulled at Francois's sleeve. "Tell him we can use his light-off rods."

"What?"

"His light-off rods. Tell him."

The enginneer's eyebrows went up as Francois translated. "Ah, *oui, oui,*" he said. He brought up two three-foot metal rods with oily burlap strips wrapped around their ends, which were normally used to ignite the boiler fires.

Carrying the paint can and light-off rods, Red and Smoker climbed onto the roof of the cab. Parnell paused a moment to look westward, trying to relocate the fighters. There they were, coming in from the right in strafing formation, the leader slightly higher than his wingman.

"Watch out," he hollered. "Here they come again." He dropped to the roof, hugged its dirty, heated curvature.

The first burst was high, the .50-caliber rounds cracking the air and passing over to hurl up double lines of mud and water on the other side of the engine. The second aircraft's burst did the same thing. Both fighters went into a sharp, climbing turn.

The instant they were gone, Red and Smoker rose and moved forward, their bodies and legs braced against the wind and the thick, hot roil of stack smoke. Parnell chose a flat area for the message. They opened the paint can with Wineberg's boot knife and rammed the light-off rods sloppily down into the red lead.

"What're we gonna write, Lieutenant?" Smoker hollered.

Parnell thought. "Torch. Use the word *torch*. You make the t, o, and r, I'll do the rest."

They frantically slapped on red lead, printing four-foot-long letters. The oiliness of the burlap made the paint streak and run down the curve of the roof. Then someone began pounding on the edge of the cab and yelling. They both dropped flat again.

The rising roar of the first F4F came up in a sudden burst of sound. Its guns had a slow, pulsing rhythm that merged into the jolting clang and rush of steam from the locomotive. Then there was the hot, sundering crack of the incoming rounds. Some struck the boiler with the explosive shock of grenades. A shrill, ear-piercing blowout of steam came as the planes flashed overhead and disappeared back into the sky.

Parnell and Wineberg returned to the letters, the things coming together now to form TORCH. Finished, they hurled the paint can and light-off rods over the side and scrambled back across the roof. Steam poured out from under the cab's eves, white and thick as a snow avalanche, and the cab roof was scorching hot. Gingerly, they hurried to the rear and jumped onto the coal bin.

The inside of the cab was chaotic with shooting steam from a ruptured line across the boiler face. Everyone lay on the deck under the steam cloud that lifted and then began whipping off in the wind. The engineer crawled forward, reached over his seat, and tried to shut off a large valve. Its metal handle burned his hand but he kept at it and finally got it down and locked. The loud hiss of steam stopped abruptly.

Now a spray of oil near the fire door burst into flame, blue, then red orange. The fireman grabbed an extinguisher and shot a thick stream of foam at it. The foam stank of acid. It splashed off the boiler head and sprayed onto the deck, smoking. The fire quickly died.

Cowboy shouted, "The sons a bitches are back."

But this time the pilots didn't fire, both aircraft hurtling close overhead. Red caught a glimpse of them rising back into the sky, turning slightly, wagging their wings in apology. Soon they were lost against the background of the Atlas Mountains.

Everybody relaxed.

Parnell moved to the side ladder and looked down the track. He could see Safi in morning light, about four miles ahead. There were streams of people and vehicles pouring through the eastern gate, bunching on the Qehwi Bridge. *Oh, Christ!* If the locomotive went highballing across, it would slaughter hundreds of civilians.

His first reaction was to stop the engine immediately, on this side of the river. No, he couldn't do that. Those trailing legionnaires would quickly catch up to them, retake the engine, and go back for the guns. There had to be another way. Okay, what if they ran the locomotive into the river? No, they couldn't do that either. The moment water hit the boiler, they'd all get blown to hell.

He glanced at his watch. Seven minutes to seven. . . .

*Well, at least we can slow down,* he thought, *blow the whistle, warn those civilians off the bridge.* Figuring on that two-minute cushion, they could spare a few minutes and still make it across before the bridge went up.

He shouted at Francois, "Tell him to slow down. There are people on the bridge. Keep blowing the—"

There was a sudden lurch and everyone was thrown forward. The engineer had also seen the crowd and had sharply yanked off the throttle. Now he was struggling with the tall brake lever next to his seat. From below the deck,

the huge steel brake flanges screeched like banshees as
they came up hard against the wheel drums. A white-hot
shower of sparks and smoke blew off the linings.

"Stop that bastard," Parnell bellowed.

Francois, the closest to the engineer, leaped forward.
He pulled his pistol, shoved it against the man's head,
and hauled him away from the brake lever. Red darted
around them both and dropped onto the engineer's
seat. He shoved the throttle back up and released the
brake. There was a momentary stall and then another
jerk and the rushing expulsion of smoke from the stack
rose back into speed rhythm.

He sat there staring stupidly at the maze of pipes and
valves and hand switches across the boiler head, and the
realization struck him that now *he* was controlling this
huge mass of power and momentum. What the hell was
he supposed to do?

Someone appeared at his side, the fireman. He said
something in Arabic, then grabbed a greasy rope that
hung above the seat. Above them, the whistle went off,
stopped, went off again, rolling out in a long, continuous blast.

Parnell checked his watch: Six minutes, fifteen seconds
to seven. . . .


Beneath the Qehwi Bridge, the pipe incendiary device
smoked gently. The smoke was a greasy blue that seeped
from between the burn wire and the edge of its drill
hole. Inside the pipe, the sulfuric acid had already eaten
away most of the copper disk. Only a thin filament remained. In precisely four minutes and fifteen seconds, it
too would dissolve completely. . . .

* * *

The river was coming up fast, five hundred yards away now. The bridge was still crowded with people and animals. Beyond it, more came, their colorful clothing stark against the backdrop of the Safi wall, which loomed like a reddish-colored bluff.

Standing on the cab roof, Sol and Cowboy shouted and waved wildly at the poeple on the bridge and fired their weapons into the air. It did no good. The crowd was in a panic, seemingly unaware of the locomotive's high-speed approach. Red had finally begun bleeding off speed but the indicator still showed they were traveling at eighty kilometers an hour.

Three hundred fifty yards to the river. Absently, Parnell rechecked his watch. One minute, twenty-three seconds to seven.

He smiled icily. *We got her whipped.* . .

The copper disk had been cold-worked so its crystals would elongate and form a tight, cubic density that increased its tensile strength. Now as the sulfuric acid entered the last stratas of copper, these began to shatter like plate glass, layer by layer, releasing explosions of cuprite ions as smoke and blue vitriol salts. In twenty-three seconds, the sulfuric acid would eat through these final layers. . . .

They crossed the bridgehead with the resounding thunder of a storm cloud, beams and planking echoing their hurtling weight, intensifying it. People screamed and frantically scattered, some jumping into the river. The edge of the engine's pilot catcher crashed into the back of a donkey cart, hurled it and the animal off into the water.

The locomotive and then the tender cleared the other side of the bridge in a flashing blur. Parnell immediately hauled the throttle lever full back. Instantly the engine sound changed, dropped out of rythmn. He grabbed for the brake lever but the engineer beat him to it. Wrenching it out of Francois's grip, he had flung himself onto the six-foot lever and was hauling it back. The big driver wheels locked up with a vicious scream of steel on steel.

There was a flash from under the Qehwi Bridge, as blue white as an acetelyene torch. A nanosecond later, the entire structure lifted in a violent explosion, steel beams, planking, river water, all going up inside a column of black smoke. The concussion wave swept past them, made their ears pop.

Parnell slid off the seat, let the engineer take over. Cursing, the Frenchman shoved valves, jammed levers. Seconds sped past. Then the wheels shifted in sound as the engineer spun them in reverse. The entire locomotive shuddered and rolled from side to side like a small boat in a rough sea.

Sol and Smoker and Cowboy came tumbling down off the tender and onto the cabin deck. Kaamanui grinned lopsidedly at Parnell. "Cut that close, didn't you, Lieutenant?"

Red leaned out to look back at the river. Debris was still falling, the water black brown and coated with an oily foam. He looked at his watch. It was still forty-five seconds to seven. He hissed with disgust. "Those dumb fucking Frenchmen," he growled. "They set their goddamn charge too early."

The eastern gate and city wall were still cannonballing toward them despite the engineer's frantic efforts to stop the locomotive. A dozen soldiers rushed through the gate. Several stopped long enough to fire back into the marketplace. Red emptied his pistol at them. Two went down.

The engine tore through the gate. Immediately inside was a small French officer's car on the tracks. It was empty. They smashed into it, cleaving it in two. Each side flew up into the air.

They reached the end of the track. The leader wheels slammed and bounced over the big timber-stop at the end and then the locomotive plowed on through several empty sheep and goat pens, hurling mud and manure sludge up through the catcher tines onto the forward smoke box and railing.

Still carrying momentum, it smashed into the tannery's stacks of huge wooden vats. Tannic acid and wood bark and soaking animal skins flew everywhere as the huge engine finally came to a stop amid a vicious cloud of steam.

Slowly everybody got up. Parnell counted heads. No one had been hurt. Cautiously they dismounted onto the muck-soaked, foul-smelling ground. The area was deserted. Then a bullet came whining through the gate followed by several more. Up in the cab, the engineer was still cursing.

Forming up, the Americans and Francois moved off into the marketplace along a main alley. It was dead silent suddenly, as if all power had been cut off. They felt the ground tremble. A distant metallic clanking came from far back in the *souq*.

*Tanks!*

They dove for concealment among the deserted food stalls and artists' kiosks. The clanking increased and the ground began to shake violently. An American M-3 Grant tank appeared, barreling and lunging up through an alleyway, crashing through stalls and awnings and scattering vegetables and merchandise. It was painted in desert camouflage and looked massive and lethal and incongruous amid the medieval bazaar shops and piles of food. Directly behind it was another Grant.

Squatted down behind the turret of the second vehicle, Thompsons at the ready and eyes scanning, were Bird, Laguna, and Kimball. . . .

# Part Three
# Algeria

Despite scattered French opposition, Operation Torch was a major success. All resistance in Algeria was quickly overcome and the port city of Algiers and its main airfields at Maison Blanche and Blida taken on 9 November. The following day, Oran and the La Siena and Tafaraoui Airfields fell to elements of the Sixteenth and Eighteenth Regimental Combat Teams from the First Infantry Division.

Casablanca and Fedala in Morocco were the lone holdouts. Patton, growing more frustrated by the hour, finally ordered an intense naval and air bombardment against Casablanca. But before it could be mounted, Admiral Jean Darlan, CinC of all Vichy military forces in North Africa, ordered his men to cease all resistance at precisely noon of 10 November.

On that same day, the German First and Italian Fourth Armies struck across the 1940 demarcation line into Vichy-occupied southern France. Also on that day, Hitler, finally realizing the value of North Africa as an Allied stepping stone to Sicily and southern Italy, ordered massive reinforcments into northern Tunisia. The country was still technically independent. Yet, despite the fuhrer's duplicity in invading Vichy territory on the continent, the Tunisian French gave him tacit consent.

Now Tunisia became a prize in a desperate race. Could the Allies reach Tunis before the Germans solidified their positions? Eisenhower decided to go on the offensive immediately. But continued attacks on Gibraltar and Algeria by Luftwaffe bombers out of Spain deeply worried him. So he left the western and central invasion forces in place to protect against these attacks and sent only units from the eastern group into Tunisia.

Although already fatigued, undersupplied, and lacking air support, this assault group quickly occupied the coastal towns of Bougie, Djidjelli, Phillippeville, and Bone. Meanwhile, a strong contingent called Blade Force managed to drive deep into the Tunisian plain.

But the Allied thrusts soon lost their steam and were finally stopped completely by the newly arrived panzer divisions of the Fifth *Panzerarmee* under *Generalleutnant* Jurgen von Arnim at the crucial battle of Souk el Arba, a railhead eighty miles southwest of Tunis.

Now the conflict entered a partial lull, a time of scattered but indecisive skirmishes. Eisenhower called off all major operations in Tunisia until the winter weather cleared, and both sides settled into holding positions to consolidate and replenish.

In Libya and Tripolitania, Rommel's *Deutsches Afrika Korps,* the vaunted DAK, were executing a continuous fighting retreat against Montgomery and his Eighth Army. The Desert Fox intended to link with von Arnim's panzers and thereby establish a powerful front along the old French Mareth Line in south central Tunisia. From there, the combined German forces could launch a coordinated Axis counteroffensive in early spring.

Meanwhile, the Americans and British hurriedly began shoving men and material into Oran and Algiers aboard thousands of ships that ran the deadly gauntlet of German U-boats in the Atlantic. Montgomery also started restrengthening his desert force, which had been badly depleted during the bloody fighting at El Alamein.

For Blue Team, however, it was a time of exile. . . .

# Thirteen

*Oran, Algeria*
*22 December 1942*

The French soldier was strong and had a stinging right hook. His name was Aumoitte, a Tirailleurs corporal in the French 2eRM-VI *Regiment de Marche* stationed in Oran. He had a hawkish nose, yellow-green eyes, and a body that smelled like wet cement. Wineberg was having a hard time with the lanky Frenchman, bobbing and weaving under his good left jab. But Smoker noticed his opponent's thin legs and was sure he could take him out by the fifth round.

They were now in the fourth of a six-rounder, the ring in an open field inside a mobile evac hospital-tent camp two miles from Oran. It had rained earlier and a frigid winter wind swept in off the sea. Both men fought barefooted so as to maintain traction on the soaked canvas.

Since Blue Team was not officially attached to I Corps, all the men were now reassigned as floaters. Colonel Dunmore had returned to Patton's staff at Allied HQ in the St. George Hotel outside Algiers and from there had managed to get good jobs for them while they waited for their next mission.

Wineberg and Laguna had been placed with a military police company at the hospital camp. Kaamanui and Parnell were posted to an engineering battalion raising sunken ships and equipment from Oran Harbor. Bird, Kimball, and Fountain had overseer duty, supervising hired Arab stevedores for the unloading of cargo ships.

The bell rang. Smoker sat down in his corner and squinted across at the Frenchman. Weesay swabbed him down, rubbed on Vasoline. He looked worried. This was Wineberg's third fight. He'd won the first two by knockouts. Before each battle, Laguna hustled the crowd, proffering bets. So far, they'd won eight hundred dollars, U.S.

"Goddamn, baby," Weesay croaked. "When you gonna take this *bicho* out?"

Smoker winked at him. "Don't sweat it, amigo."

"Don' sweat it? He's workin' you, *meng.*"

The fifth round went badly. Aumoitte still had fire, boring in hard with jabs and then slamming Wineberg's ribs with jolting body punches. Smoker covered and backpedaled. Then he got dirty, laced the Frenchie's face, slammed a shoulder into his chin at the breaks. These were tricks he'd learned the hard way in numerous dust-bowl shit towns and honky-tonks back in the States, where he'd fought while on the bum.

The Frenchman didn't reciprocate. That angered the hell out of Smoker so he quit doing it himself. *Goddamn Frog,* he thought fiercely, *I'll whip your son-of-a-bitching ass legit.* By the end of the fifth, he had a bad cut over his left eye and there were red blotches under his ribs.

Laguna said, "Aw, shit, we gon' lose our whole goddamn stash, *meng.*" Then he noticed the raw look in Smoker's eyes. That elicited a big grin. "Okay, baby, okay." He slapped Wineberg's shoulders. "Go stomp this fucking *broche.*"

The Frenchman came out fast. This time Smoker met him head-on, down low, throwing punches into his belly like a buzz saw, lifting just long enough to slam in quick combinations before returning to the man's stomach. Aumoitte had apparently underestimated Wineberg's ability to recover from the fifth round and was caught off balance. He tried desperately to duck and back off. Smoker went right after him, got him into a corner, and hammered away.

Two minutes into the sixth round, the Frenchie's legs buckled. He held on for a few seconds more until Smoker caught him with a stinging right that came off no lead, all shoulder-weight heaving forth. Aumoitte went down and stayed there.

Wineberg and Laguna had just doubled their winnings.


Earlier that morning, Colonel Dunmore had run into Colonel Dodson Tedder, British military intelligence chief-of-station in the lobby of the St. George Hotel. "Hello, James," Tedder called cheerily. A vicar in civilian life, the Britisher was a slender, jovial man with a thin, Clark Gable mustache. "How goes it this morning?"

"Fair, fair. You?"

"Overworked, as usual." The hotel lobby was filled with officers and staff personnel from French, American, and British units. Sequestered on a lushly gardened hill a mile from downtown Algiers, it had been Admiral Darlan's center of operations for North Africa for years. It was still being used for that, but now it also housed the general headquarters command of Eisenhower's Allied Expeditionary Force, Mediterranean.

Tedder studied him. "Have breakfast yet, old boy?"

"No. Why?"

"What say we take it in my office?"

"Sounds good."

The St. George had been completely renovated, every

bit of space utilized. Admirals and generals worked over strategic war plans in what had once been sculleries, cupboards, and pantries. Tedder's own intelligence and encryption unit was housed in a onetime men's room. Where once had been urinals and toilets, there were now wireless sets, coding machines, and teletypes. The colonel's personal office was in the old lounge.

Tedder nodded Dunmore to a chair. He smiled ruefully, indicating the surroundings. "Ironic, isn't it? Operating in a loo? Intelligence and defecation. A rather appropriate philosophical comment, what?" Dunmore chuckled politely while Tedder dispatched one of his wireless operators to fetch croissants and tea.

Under normal staff operations, the on-site British and American intelligence chiefs met daily to exchange and coordinate data. It was almost always in the late afternoon. So Tedder's invitation to breakfast, Dunmore realized, had been a deliberate change of protocol.

They chatted casually until the food arrived, creamfilled croissants and strong Mauritanian tea. The Britisher spiced their cups with *boukha,* a fiery, gin-clear liqueur made from dates. Dunmore took a long pull, rested his cup on the corner of Tedder's desk, and appraised his host. "Dod, as pleasant as this is, I've a feeling you've got something to tell me."

Tedder laughed. "Jolly good instincts, James." He sipped his tea before going on. "Tell me, how's that team of yours? I understand the chaps did a bang-up job in Morocco."

"They did a helluva job, actually."

"Indeed, indeed. Is it still operational?"

"Not at the moment. The men are now on detached duty in Oran. Is that important?"

"Rather unfortunate about your brass, isn't it?" Tedder mused. "I mean, such a stiff attitude toward independent units and all. I'll admit our elite lads've botched things a bit lately. But I still say it's blasted narrow thinking on the part of your superiors. All things considered."

"I'd call it stupid thinking."

"Yes." The Englisman's eyes twinkled. "But we must all suffer fools, mustn't we? I say, could your team be assembled quickly?"

"Of course." Dunmore stopped eating.

"Here's the thing. I recently received an op summary from LRDG headquarters in Cairo. Thought it might interest you." The LRDG stood for the Long Range Desert Group, an elite British unit composed of small mobile patrols. Using Ford and Chevrolet trucks, they operated behind enemy lines in the Egyptian and Libyan Deserts.

"The LRDG? That's a damned fine outfit."

"Yes, splendid fellows. In fact, at the moment two LRDG patrols are here in Algeria. They just crossed through Libya's northern Hamadat al Hamrah Desert. Target's some Foreign Legion outpost at Ghoraffa. Bloody beastly place, that. Smack in the middle of the Grand Oriental Erg. Here, let me show you."

Using a wall map, he located Ghoraffa. It was two hundred miles due east of Quargla, Algeria. On the map, the entire area was colored a butter yellow, which indicated dune desert.

"Our recce photos show the outpost is currently under siege by an Italian force," Tedder explained. "Battalion strength, at least. Unfortunately, the Frenchies can't send help. And we've certainly got more pressing things to attend to than a contingent of trapped legionnaires."

He took another sip of tea. "Still, General Staff thinks Ghoraffa would make a dandy emergency refueling field for our Malta bombers returning from their runs against Tunisia and northern Libya. So they gave LRDG the green for a foray."

"Where's the patrol now?"

"It replenished at a secret designated air drop east of the Tunisian frontier and then crossed into Algeria yesterday at dawn. That should place them at Ghoraffa about midmorning today."

"How would my team be used?"

"Well, our lads could certainly use some added firepower. And your chaps would get a crack at real desert. Learn from experts."

Dunmore grinned. "Dod, old boy, you're on."

"Good show, James. When can you have your people ready?"

Dunmore glanced at his watch: 8:51. "By 1600 today."

"I'll clear arrangements on my side and coordinate with LRDG for a drop zone. Can you arrange air transport out of, say, Tarafaoui?"

"No problem."

Tedder smiled craftily. "There's one other aspect to this. Bit of romantic adventure, actually. Very Beau Geste. D'you ever hear the stories of large shipments of gold bullion that were supposedly smuggled out of Paris just before the Jerries took over?"

"Yes. As I recall, the shipments were split up and hidden in various secret places for safekeeping."

Tedder nodded. "Right. Primarily in North Africa and Tahiti."

"Then there really *was* gold."

"Oh, yes. Actually, most of it was eventually shipped to America and England. All except one cache. Value was several million pounds, I believe. But the French records of that particular shipment mysteriously disappeared. We're fairly certain it's still at Ghoraffa."

"Really?"

"Indeed."

Dunmore chuckled. He lifted his cup in a toast. "So, let's go prospecting."

It was four minutes after noon when Dunmore's order reached Parnell. He was instructed to assemble Blue Team in full battle gear and report to Tafaraoui Airfield no later than 1600 hours that day.

At the moment, he and Kaamanui were on a recovery crew working on a sandbar at the mouth of Oran Harbor. Several American LCVs had mistakenly offloaded their cargos of armored vehicles and jeeps onto the sandbar, and then had promptly been driven off into forty-five feet of water. The recovery crew was from the Forty-first Combat Engineers Battalion, most of the men hard-drinking ex-oil-field workers from southern Texas.

Both Red and Horse had found recovery work boring and uncomfortable, out there in the freezing winds with periodic air raids by German Ju-88s from fields in the Balearic Islands. Still, it had had its pleasant distractions. Parnell was billeted with other battalion officers at an Oran hotel named the Baudelier, while Kaamanui was bunked at a larger hotel for enlisted men, where he had quickly developed a deep affection for Algerian beer.

During off-duty hours, amid the exotic trappings, the white-suited French colonials, and the tall, red-robed Saphis, Parnell and the other Americans usually got doggedly drunk on good French cognac and gambled away their pay. Occasionally they took the hotel's coffee-colored dancing girls upstairs to luxurious red boudoirs. The women were beautiful and lithely sensuous and their bodies always smelled of balsam-sweetened turpentine.

Ten minutes after Dunmore's order arrived, the two caught a feeder tug back to shore. They quickly cleared their reassignment through the battalion's headquarters and Red requisitioned a jeep. After retrieving their combat gear, they headed out to round up the rest of the team. . . .

Colonel Dunmore squatted under the wing of the C-47 and unrolled a map of the Grand Oriental Erg. He had come into Tafaraoui Airfield aboard the aircraft. Planes were parked everywhere, C-47s and Curtis P-40s, British Spitfire IXs, a few Vickers Wellington IIs. All were under hastily constructed and desert-camouflaged revetments.

Sitting in on the briefing with Dunmore and Parnell were Sergeant Bird and the two Transport Command pilots, who looked like movie stars in their leather jackets and dark glasses. The edges of the map were brown and crisp as dead leaves. It contained few landmarks and the ink was faded. In one corner was a notation by the mapmaker, a Captain Claud Williams, MC, of the First Pembroke Yeomanry. It was dated 14 March 1905.

Dunmore pointed out the Foreign Legion fort at Ghoraffa. "Sorry this map's so out of date," he said. "It was the only one I could scrounge up from Darlan's archives." He looked up at Red and Wyatt. "This is real desert you're going into, gentlemen. So watch yourselves. And watch the LRDGers. They know desert."

He had brought additional gear for the team with him: rations for eight days, extra canteens of water, digging tools, desert goggles, and grenade packs. Since they'd be armed with British ammo, he had included British Sten MK II submachine guns and Webley/Scott pistols to replace their Thompsons and personal U.S. side arms. There were also extra ammo clips, flashlights, walkie-talkies, and reserve chutes, small CUC-114 chest packs.

He ticked his finger against one of the chute packs. "I couldn't find any AT-Five's. With these, your weight'll make you hit hard. Be set for it. The drop zone's seven miles due north of the fort, out in the dunes. You'll jump along an east-west line, so regroup accordingly. Here are your drop-zone coordinates."

He handed Parnell a small logbook and nodded to one of the pilots. "This is Captain Hicks. He'll fly you straight to the DZ using star fixes. The Brits'll signal when you're directly overhead. They're four hundred miles south of the coast. I've already checked the weather. There shouldn't be any storms." He smiled. "But it's going to be monkey-balls cold at night."

A Wellington landed nearby, its wheels squealing for a second, and then the engines roared up as the pilot reversed props. A thin dust cloud from its passage blew over them, smelling of hot engine oil and rubber.

Dunmore looked around. "Anybody got any questions? All right, let's get it under way." He rose, shook hands all around. He then accompanied Parnell and Bird to the other side of the plane and shook hands with the rest of the team, wishing them all godspeed.

At twelve minutes after five, the C-47 with Blue Team aboard lifted off the Tafaraoui Runway and turned southeast, skimming over the ground at a hundred feet.

# Fourteen

The port town of La Goulette lies ten kilometers north of Tunis. Once part of the Ottoman Empire, its perfect harbor was home to the pirates of the Barbary Coast who ravished Christian shipping during the sixteenth century. A huge fortress, the Borj el-Karrak, still stands above the harbor.

Now it and its vast grounds were being used as the headquarters and main staging area for the German Tenth Panzer Division. Hundreds of armored vehicles and the newer, gray-colored Mark VI Tiger tanks were scattered under camouflage netting in the sand hills surrounding the fortress.

At 2:31 that afternoon, Captain Gerd von Bekker, well tanned and immaculate in his dark gray Luftwaffe tropical field uniform, presented himself before Lieutenant General von Arnim. Snapping to attention, he gave the senior officer a precise, brisk salute.

Arnim returned it, then smiled graciously. "Stand easy, Gerd." He rose and moved around his desk to take Bekker's hand. "What a pleasant surprise to see you again."

"As it is to see you, Herr General."

"Come, come, sit. Share a drink with me."

The general was forty-seven years old, lean, nearly six feet four. He had dark blue eyes that constantly scanned in what seemed a casual manner but wasn't. His voice was low and, like his tactics, bold and quick.

He and Bekker were both descended from baronial families, his from the Unterfranken region of Bavaria, and they both possessed that inborn Germanic arrogance and contempt for all things non-Teutonic. An outstanding tactician, Arnim had befriended Gerd Bekker when he was a lecturer in military theory at the Technische Hockschule in Frankfurt.

He poured two glasses of schnapps, handed one to his old student. His office was well appointed, the furniture expensive and stylish with a European flair. Dressed in a sandy-colored desert tunic with semibreeches and high canvas-and-leather desert boots, the general sported a *ritterkreuz*, a knight's cross with oak leaves, swords, and diamonds, at his throat.

They talked of the Frankfurt days, of mutual friends, of Germany's glorious destiny. Standing, they toasted the fuhrer. Then Gerd recounted his escape from Morocco. Pro-Axis French officers had smuggled him first to the Algerian town of Ain-Sefra, then across the Saharan Atlas to Leghouat. There he had stolen an Italian Savoia-Marchetti light bomber and flown unmolested to Kairouan, Tunisia.

"Quite an adventure," Arnim said, impressed. He studied Bekker's uniform. "I see you're now attached to a Luftwaffe field division."

"Yes, sir. Until Air Ministry decides to send me back to my old *Jagdkorps Kommand*. I'm most anxious to get back. Still, I've grown rather fond of North Africa."

Arnim grunted with cold amusement. "Don't grow too fond of it, dear Gerd. Our time here is limited. Hitler wants us merely to delay the enemy until stores and troop units can be built up in Sicily and southern Italy. We can't let the Allies establish a foothold on the continent. As for North Africa?" He sneered. "It's already lost. Thankfully along with these imbecilic pimps Mussolini strapped us with."

"Italians *are* rather useless as fighters, aren't they?"

"They're shit. All bombast and no steel."

The conversation went on for several more minutes. Then Arnim asked, "Tell me, would you fancy another little adventure before you leave us?"

"Ah?"

The general explained. He had recently received a fascinating bit of intelligence about a cache of French gold ingots believed to be stored in a small Foreign Legion fort in the Algerian Desert. "An Italian force now has it under seige. They've been at it for more than a week, actually. As usual, the baffoons are unable to invest it."

He lit a long black cigarette and smiled at Gerd. "A personal gift of French gold would be deeply appreciated by the fuhrer. I'm certain a good German officer with a small patrol of my armor would be adequate to get the job done. Wouldn't you agree?"

Bekker returned the smile. "When can I start, Herr General?"

"Immediately."

"What if the Italians have already seized the cache?"

"An unlikely possibility. But if so, you'll simply commandeer it."

"And if they oppose?"

"Then slaughter the bastards."

Gerd's smile gleamed, his eyes danced. "Splendid," he said.


Weesay Laguna stood in the doorway of the C-47, his hands on the sills getting numb in the cold. *Jesus Christo,* he thought, *how can a fucking desert be so goddamned cold?*

Eight hundred feet below him, the desert glowed like a vast silvery sea. The sky was a different shade, not quite as pale along the horizon but then deepening despite the light of a moon gone past half. Millions of stars glittered across the heavens, bright enough to be visible despite the moon. Forward of the aircraft, two tiny lights were visible on the ground, the desert patrol marking its drop zone.

Lined behind Laguna was the team, each man's gear already checked by the man behind him, each close to the next, foot to foot, braced, and ready. Since they were using the CUC chutes, there were no static lines.

He felt adrenaline pulse through his body. With only this reserve rig, he knew there would be no backup in case of a blown panel or a streamer. It would just be tough shit, baby. He'd never quite gotten used to jumping out of a plane. It was a stupid goddamn thing for a man to do. Still, it always gave him a rushing sensation of power whenever he did it.

Just like that sense of personal potency he had possessed back home in south central L.A., down there in the barrio around Washington and 110th, snazzy in his zoot suit with the choke pants and golden chains and the big, cool hat as he headed out to tangle with those punk-ass *lambiosos* from Van Nuys or the gringo sailors out of Pedro down in the quarter looking for Mexican pussy. *Aye, mio Dios,* them were the days.

As the jump master, Parnell was kneeling to his left, watching forward for the green JUMP light above the pilot's cabin. The air rumbled and hissed frigidly past the door. Inside the aircraft, it was nearly as cold and held the sharp odor of electrical wiring and cargo belting.

Laguna felt Red's hand slap his left leg and heard him shout: "Go!" He went, shoving out, legs set, turning himself to face the tail so as to avoid the prop wash and the hard snap to the left. The great bulk of the aircraft flashed past, the air vibrating all around him and himself falling but not feeling like falling, everything glowing around him now as if he drifted over a make-believe landscape.

One thousand two . . . one thousand three . . . He yanked the D-ring, felt the chute pack blow open close to his face, a slithery, clothy sound, the flap slapping against his cheek. Then the solid jerk and *whomp* of the chute as it deployed above him and the instant deceleration and bounce. He tilted his head to listen to the panels filling and the gentle humm of the risers and shrouds. The underside of the chute glowed as brightly as the desert.

He hit the ground hard. But the sand was soft, slanted. He rolled downhill, the chute collapsing and dragging behind him. He shrugged out of his harness, squatted, listening. Total silence. No wind, the deep, singular feeling of total aloneness.

He quickly assembled his Sten gun and turned on his marker light, pinned it to his jump blouse, its tiny beam shining straight up. He took out his compass and took a directional reading.

Since the aircraft had been on an east-to-west heading, the team members were now strung along a similiar line covering about a mile and a half. Their linkup would be simple. The first five men would simply head due west. Meanwhile, Parnell and Bird, the last to leave the C-47, would head east. Eventually the two sections would come together with their marker lights preventing them from passing each other in the darkness.

Headed due west, he started off. Up and down the sand dunes he went. Some were at least a hundred feet high, appearing like great ocean combers that never broke. All around him, the night was utterly silent and cold. The sand sucked at his boots with a soft hissing sound and smelled oddly like charred paper.

A sound began infiltrating the night. There was no direction to it, just the faint, periodic surge-and-fade of an engine. Weesay stopped and unshouldered his Sten. The sound grew louder. Suddenly a hulking shadow thrust itself over the top of a dune directly behind him, the thing silhouetted against the stars. A bright light pinioned him. He actually felt the heat of its beam. His heart leaped as he lifted the muzzle of his weapon.

"Aye, easy there, Yank," a voice called out cheerily. "It's only us Diggers come to collect ya."

Captain Archie Carr, commanding officer of the Long Range Desert Group patrols T-1 and T-2, opened the big thermos and passed it to Parnell on his right. "Here you go, gents," he said. "Have a plow of this. A welcome to the desert."

Red took a pull. The liquor was thick and smelled of cloves and had a hot sting to it. The New Zealanders called it Devil's Brew and told them it was made of Woods rum from their daily ration, lime juice, a can of sugared fruit, toothpaste powder, and chips of acacia bark, which was then allowed to ferment. He passed it on.

They were all seated in a circle in a dune valley, nineteen men in all now, the LRDG troopers bearded, in garrison sweaters and British Tropal long-coats or Arab goatskin jackets. Some wore native *kaffiyeh* headdresses like Bedouin sheiks.

A few yards beyond the group were the patrol's vehicles strung along the base of the dune. They formed big, nonangular shadows with peculiar protuberances that were antennas, clothed machine guns on pivot columns, stacks of petrol cans and spare tires, boxed gear stowed and strapped onto every inch of space.

This particular LRDG force was made up of two six-man patrols, all volunteers from the First New Zealand Divisional Cavalry. They referred to themselves as Diggers or Kiwis. Their vehicles included a Willys jeep, four Chevrolet 3300X2 one-and-a-half-ton trucks, and two Ford 3300X2 V-8s. One was a fitter's rig with spare parts and medical supplies. All were loaded with ordnance: swivel-mounted Browning and Vickers machine guns, two Boys six-pounder antitank rifles, a Bofors 37mm reach-out gun, and a Breda 20mm cannon.

Such patrols could remain in the deep desert for weeks at a time, running surveillance missions or strike-and-flee raids against enemy depots and airfields far behind the lines. Afterward, they'd disappear into the remoteness of the sands and could travel three thousand kilometers without replenishment.

The thermos came around again. Parnell took another shot. It made his belly warm. As he passed it, Carr tapped his shoulder. Together they walked up the side of the dune to the crest. The captain pointed southwest. In the infinite expanse of luminous silver and blue black, Red saw a tiny smear of light.

Carr said, "That's the Italian encampment, about twelve kilometers out. They've set up west of the Frenchie outpost on a bit of gravel plain to the northeast."

"What's their strength?"

"A full battalion, primarily motorized infantry. Eight Lancia Light Armored Personnel Carriers and five old Marchetti half-tracks." He chuckled pleasantly. "I expect the Eyeties got their noses bloodied, though. It looks like they tried a frontal attack, straight across open ground. Left some dead bodies and three burned-out APCs on the approaches."

"How about their artillery?"

Carr idly scratched his short beard with the back of his fingers. It, like his close-cropped hair, appeared sandy.

He was tall and angular like a long-distance runner. "Only thirty-sevens and light mortars, all bunched in the center of the encampment."

A distant flash of white light appeared from the direction of the Italians. Another. Then a brilliant chute flare went off. It hung in the air like a distant star. Two more flares appeared, all trailing smoke.

Carr pointed with his chin. "They've been sending the Frenchies sporadic harassing fire and flares every couple of hours. Two, three rounds at most. I've got a hunch they can't barrage. Too low on ammunition."

"They're not getting resupplied?"

"No. Which means they'll also be low on water and petrol. The only water between here and the oasis at Quargla is a deep well inside the fort."

"I'd say they're hurting."

Carr nodded. "Aye. The condition of their bivouac shows it. Damned sloppy and fart-assed. I don't think they even send out recce patrols. So they won't have a bloody clue anybody's close." He turned to Red, smiling. His teeth were very white in the moonlight. "Are your jockos ready to have a go at them?"

"Locked and loaded."

"Jolly good. Then let's give the dagos a surprise."

It was two hours before dawn, the moon low, casting crest shadows on the dunes. They came in along the ancient caravan track from Quargla, Carr and Parnell in the pilot jeep with two one-and-a-halfs following. The rest of the force was scattered out in the sand east of the Italians, lying in wait to give covering fire.

In order to mislead the Eyeties, the three approach vehicles had been hastily altered, plywood disks with painted swastikas tacked to their hoods and German *beutezeiche* stripes taped on their bumpers. These would indicate that they were captured British vehicles in German service.

The Italian encampment was surrounded by a barbed-wire fence, the accordian rolls on the outside, and guard pickets along the perimeter. Two men were at the gate in gray greatcoats with the orange and black collar stripes of the Venezia Mobile Infantry Division. Each carried a 9mm Beretta submachine gun.

One came forward, waving for Carr to stop. He was a *capo squadra,* a corporal. He peered at Carr and asked in Italian for his papers.

The New Zealander angrily barked back in Italian. Parnell, wearing a Hebron goat coat over his battle dress, didn't get too much of what he said. But Carr's tone indicated he was actually dressing down the corporal, saying something about them being Germans in need of petrol and that the man better damn well see that they got it.

The *capo squadra* instantly braced and saluted smartly. Then he waved them on through the gate, mumbling something and pointing at a collection of four tents inside the compound near several parked Lancia ACs.

Instead of moving on, Carr continued berating the corporal. He angrily whipped out a small notepad, asked the man's name and serial number, and scribbled it down. The Italian looked frightened. At last, Carr gave one last, hard stare, geared the jeep, and drove on into the encampment while the other guard held the gate open.

Carr glanced over at Red and grinned. "By the time that bloody dill realizes my accent isn't German," he said, "he'll be dead."

Inside the encampment it was mostly dark save for interlocking post lights along the fence. "See that furrow outside the wire?" Carr pointed out. "That's personnel mines. The Frenchies must have been sending out sapper teams at night." At that moment, two Italian officers stepped from one of the tents, buttoning their tunics.

It happened very quickly. The instant the last truck cleared the gate, Carr slam-shifted and jammed down on the accelerator. They sped forward on the hard roadway between the field tents and parked vehicles. Beyond these were low pallets of tins of high-octane gasoline and diesel fuel stacked under canvas canopies.

Red brought the Sten from the folds of his coat and opened up on the two officers, hurling them back into their tent. He then fired at the fuel stacks. The bullets slammed through the thin metal cans. Gasoline began flooding down onto the wooden pallets. Behind, the other LRDG troopers were firing their Brownings, Vickers, and Stens, the lighter guns going off with quicker, choppier rattles.

Both gate guards were killed instantly. Italian soldiers began running everywhere, dodging, diving. Muzzle blasts came out of the darkness and bullets whanged against the sides of the charging vehicles. A stockpile of gasoline went up in a whooshing, whomping blast.

They reached the end of the road. Carr swung the jeep around in a doughnut and tore back, the heat and concussion of the fuel blast sweeping over them. Flaming debris and smoke lifted up against the stars, making everything shimmer and waver in the heat.

Covering fire started from the desert, the incoming rounds tightly grouped, focusing on the lines of tents and other storage piles on the south side of the bivouac. The jeep flew past the other two trucks just as the first one lumbered around in its own turn. Thick smoke drifted across the road.

Soldiers rose into the light, some half dressed, fumbling with their weapons. Several went down, hurled into grotesque postures by the impacts of the bullets. An Italian Fiat-Revelli machine gun started firing near a mortar nest. It had a peculiar hollow sound. Its rounds tore up the ground to the right of the jeep, and then the gunner began traversing toward it. But he overled the vehicle and his rounds began to go wild again.

As they headed through the gate, the right front wheel of the jeep ran over the leg of one of the dead guards. It spun the corpse up and around in a half circle and made the little vehicle rock. At last they were through and racing back up the Quargla caravan track, back into the moon-shadowed night.

# Fifteen

Just after dawn the patrol went to ground ten miles northeast of the Italian encampment, smoke still rising from it into the new morning light. They parked the trucks on the lee slope of a crescent dune under camouflage netting.

They'd taken one casualty, Corporal Tug Westlake. A tiny piece of shrapnel had punctured his right buttock. Now the medical orderly, Lance Corporal Quinn "Doc" Bindle, was taking it out and sewing up the wound with Westlake draped over a fender.

Meanwhile, the others ate their breakfast, porridge, tinned sausage, and biscuits hard as tree boles, and Indian tea to wash it all down. They cooked the porridge in an iron billy over a hole in sand drenched with gasoline.

The Italians had continued their harassment shelling of the fort. But around eight o'clock a full firefight developed. Its faint chatter drifted across the desert, sounding like the soft crackling of burning twigs.

The day's heat increased rapidly. All the Diggers stripped off their night clothing and went around in desert shorts and sandals. In the dazzling light, they were even more motley looking than they'd appeared last night. Their skin was sunburnt to the color of old leather and their bodies reeked of sweat and weapon oil and citronella they used to keep off the desert fleas.

The trucks had the same look of hard use, dusty and dun-colored with huge radiator condensers on the running boards and thick-treaded tires. There were sand mats and steel channel plates strapped to their sides, everything dented and bullet-riddled. Each truck bore a native Maori name like Te Rangi or Te Hai stenciled on the bonnet beside its unit number.

After breakfast, the two signalmen, McKinnen and Barbett, began transmitting the patrol's daily report, which was sent to a secret listening post in Libya. The messages went out in Morse code using field cyphers and continually changing frequencies. The radios were heavy-duty Wyndom No. 11 HPs, and the two operators were wizards at utilizing the peculiar atmospherics of the desert in order to transmit for several hundred kilometers, far beyond normal range.

A sky sentry was set out while the others settled under the nets to clean their weapons. Would the Italians send out a tracking patrol? one of the Americans asked. No way, the Diggers answered, these Wogs were spooked. Quivering shit, they was. Even if their commander did sortie a patrol, the fools'd just sit out in the dunes until night came and then return to safety.

Bird listened, then turned and spat in the sand. He looked over at Senior Sergeant Jocko Johns, the square-shouldered, bleach-bearded leader of T-2 Patrol, and asked, "What in hail's duty like out in this damn desert?"

"Well, mate, I'd say it's like shackin' with a snarky sheilah," Johns answered. "You know wot I'm sayin'? She'll suck your cob dry as a beer fart, then like as not turn around and shove a *qibli* up your arse."

"A what?"

"A *qibli*. That's a bleedin' hot wind wot comes straight off the southern Sahara. During wintertime, mostly. Christ, hot it is, I tell ya. The bloody thing can put the thermo over a hunnert fifty degrees Fahrenheit in ten minutes."

"Aye, it's bad shit and no muckin' about," Private Maggie Gifford put in. He had black hair and girlish eyes. "Blows in like a flamin' Bondi tram and bakes yer brain till ya think it'll explode. Remember that one hit us east of Kufra a year back, Jocko? Jesus, like to karked us all."

"You mean it actually gets *hotter* than now?" Cowboy said skeptically.

The Kiwis grinned at each other. "Today?" Corporal Rufus Murphy said. "Why, mate, this here's bleedin' balmy."

On into the late heat-glittering morning the talk continued, the Diggers giving advice on the finer points of desert life and combat. Like the proper way to crest a dune with a truck and use the downslope to regain traction or how to forecast the direction of a coming sandstorm by watching the flight of a painted lady butterfly.

They warned them to keep a sharp eye for peculiar purple patches in the desert, which meant quicksand bogs. Murphy, T-2's navigator, showed them how to shoot a daylight bearing with a sun compass while still on the move. They taught the Yanks how to rig a delayed-action bomb and where to place it on a tank's bogie wheels, and Gifford imitated the high-velocity sound of a German taper-barrel PzB41 "Squeeze Gun" so they'd know when to get the hell out of its way.

Then they fell into silence for a bit. Finally, Gifford looked over at Laguna and pointed at Weesay's bandanna. "Aye, mate, wot's with the bloody kerchief?"

Fountain interrupted, saying, "He thinks he's Zorro."

"He thinks he's who?"

"Zorro. You know, the guy in the movie? Fights everybody with a sword?"

"Oh, aye. Tyrone Power."

"Yeah, that's the one."

Kaamanui snorted playfully. "Shit, this little chicano wouldn't make a pimple on Tyrone Power's ass."

"Y'all got that right," Cowboy agreed.

"Hey, don' fuck with me, gringos," Weesay growled with mock anger. "I cut goddamn Zs in your *cajones.*"

Murphy was nodding seriously. "You know, he does look a bit like Tyrone." Then he pointed at his own crotch. "But has he got the bleedin' snagger to go along with it?"

Weesay snorted. "Listen, *meng,* if I fuck Power's women, they throw rocks at his ass."

Everyone laughed.

Suddenly, the sky sentry shouted, "Aircraft! Aircraft!" Everybody grabbed weapons and hit the sand. It was a single, multiengine plane, up high and moving southwest. They watched it until it disappeared into the distant sun haze. Casually, they returned to cleaning weapons. But the intrusion had destroyed the flow of the conversation. One by one the men wandered off to find soft sleeping places in the shade under the trucks.

Parnell had gone over and was squatted down beside Carr, the captain smoking a pipe next to the fitter truck. Overhead, the camo netting hung limply and smelled of heated rubber.

"You figure they spotted us?" Red asked.

Carr shook his head. "Not likely. Day glare keeps us fairly invisible. Dawn and sunset's when it's dangerous. The long shadows expose objects." He tapped out his pipe. "Either way, we'll know soon enough."

"How's that?"

"If they did see us, we'll have visitors pretty quick. Probably a pair of one-oh-nines. They handle most of the strafing strikes."

Red was surprised at the matter-of-fact way Carr spoke

of the possibility of being strafed. Every combat vet he'd ever met had always told him to look out for strafing and artillery barrages. These were the worst things troops came up against, especially in open country.

"Just remember a few simple rules and you'll be fine," Carr went on. "They'll always make one high pass to pinpoint a target. Don't fire on them yet. Wait till the bastards drop low, then open on 'em. And concentrate your fire. Listen to my men, they'll be calling out the killing spot. Also, you'll be firing nearly head-on, so don't lead them. Just offset for distance."

*Head-on,* Red thought. *Jumping Jesus, fully exposed in the sand and looking down the barrels of a goddamn Messerschmidt.*

Carr stretched and sighed. "Well, Parnell, I think I'll crash for a bit. I advise you to do the same." He crawled under the fitter truck, brushed out a shallow hole in the sand for his hips, and stretched out. Within a minute, he was sound asleep.

Parnell studied him, glanced around to look at the other New Zealand men, everybody sleeping now except the sky sentry up on his dune. Strange men, he thought, so callous in the face of death, even their own.

Last night the Diggers had headed into battle singing dirty Maori songs and the tune from *The Wizard of Oz,* just as if they were heading to a damned beach picnic. Then when the fighting got hot, he'd noticed that their faces revealed nothing. They seemed totally emotionless, detached, without expression. As if the killing had become no more intense than any other craft they had practiced into perfection.

It struck him suddenly that he too had felt a strange distancing during the fight in the Italian bivouac. But where was the shock and nausea he'd experienced during the killings in Morocco? Had these solid, humane groundings simply vanished?

He thought about that, disturbed.


Leutnant Hans Stracher gently shook Gerd Bekker awake, the captain's eyes instantly opening behind his dark glasses. He sat up. He was beneath a patch of camo netting draped over one of the half-tracks. His tan desert tunic was spotted with sweat.

"It's four o'clock, Herr Kapitan," Stracher said. "The men have already messed. Would you care for some food, sir?" The lieutenant seemed slightly older than Bekker, deeply tanned with wide features, blue-green eyes, and a crooked nose.

Gerd adjusted his cap, a pair of tinted desert goggles resting above the brim, and took a drink from his field flask. The water was hot and tasted oily. "Yes, I would like that. Prepare the men to mount up. We'll move out in thirty minutes."

"Yes, sir." Stracher walked off.

Bekker ate his *feldportionen* slowly, bland tinned beef and cheese with black Zweiback biscuits. In the scorched stillness, he watched the soldiers preparing to move, their vehicles parked in a night-camp circle.

Arnim had given him a small but well-armed force, nine vehicles in all. There were two Pz. Wg. 2 half-tracks, two four-wheeled Leichter Pz. Wg. 2 armored cars, one swift Sd. Kfz. 250 light-armored fighting vehicle, two Pz. Kpfw. III tractored 75mm assault howitzers, and two Opel "Blitz" three-ton trucks to carry troops, spare parts, and extra fuel. Including the mounted infantry, his force totaled sixty-seven men.

Starting from a Tenth Panzer Division's secondary assembly depot at Sfax, a hundred miles south of Tunis, they had made good time, following the coast and then turning inland at El-Hamma. Here was a desolate expanse of *chotts,* or salt lakes, and alkaline flats located at the southern end of the juncture of the Western and Eastern Dorsal Mountains. They had finally reached the medieval town of Douz, where they entered the true Erg, 195 kilometers northeast of the French fort at Ghoraffa.

At exactly 4:30 in the afternoon, the force headed out, moving in travel formation: a single echelon to the left, the half-tracks out front, with one armored car four miles ahead as scout. Already, the slant of the sun cast long shadows across the dunes.

Bekker and Stracher rode in the open leading half-track, Gerd in the commander's seat wearing a harness with clip pouches for his MP-40 machine-pistol and binoculars around his neck. The vehicle's gun deck was cramped: the two officers, the driver's pit, a two-man gun crew and stacked ammo, barrel racks and belt troughs for the twin machine guns.

Gerd felt exhilarated up there with the hot wind in his face. Arrayed behind him, despite its diminutive size, was the invincible power and beauty of a German armored strike force in motion. He felt the pride of Teutonic superiority rise in him like a shout and grip his throat with powerful emotion.

It evoked the same sense of glorious destiny he had felt as a younger man when he and his comrades lifted their voices in the rousing drinking songs of soldiers. Or, when he and the other young *schwertmien,* swordsmen, at the Akademie, dueled without jackets, exalting in their bloody wounds, which bore proof of German valor and virility. . . .

The two aircraft suddenly appeared out of the north, approaching at five hundred feet in lead-and-wingman formation. Stracher instantly signaled the column to scatter, everybody going off at angles to make separate targets. The planes passed close overhead, twin Focke-Wulf FW-190s, their 2,100-horsepower radials screaming. Stracher quickly fired off an identification flare, which created a pinkish purple smoke line in the windless air. The Focke-Wulfs made one more pass, then turned and headed southwest.

Bekker watched them go, then turned to Stracher. "Work up an ETA for the fort."

Stracher leaned down to tell the driver to stop and signaled the rest of the column to do the same. Not having anything comparable to British sun compasses, the Germans and Italians always had to be stationary to take a bearing. The lieutenant shot the sun angle and then consulted a book of logarithms.

"At our present rate of movement," he said a minute later, "we'll reach Ghoraffa at oh-four-hundred hours tomorrow, sir."

"Excellent," Bekker said.


There was a sudden great roaring that burst over them, the two German 190s coming in at two hundred feet. Red caught a flashing look at them. They were painted a soft green and brown camouflage pattern, odd for desert, more like jungle. They hurtled past.

Red was already flat on the sand, his Sten ready. The sand was dappled by sunlight through the netting. The sound of the fighters disappeared as suddenly as it had come, leaving only the turbulence from their prop wash gently shaking the net.

He heard truck engines start up and the tinny crank of the jeep. He glanced to his right. Bird was over there with two Diggers, their hands shading their eyes against the harsh light, searching the sky.

Someone shouted, "Here they come."

He caught sight of the two fighters again, banking in perfect unison far out. Then they were gone for a moment. His finger tightened on the trigger. Then he remembered the safety and clicked it off just as the 190s appeared once more, two hundred yards out, lifting over the rim of the dunes, coming dead-on, their blunt round snouts looking large and dark and the blades of their props catching the sun, shimmering.

Calls came from different positions, yelling out the aircrafts' killing spot. "Engines, engines," and "Go for the props." Then a full, sweeping fusillade began as everybody opened on the planes, concentrating their fire. Tracers cut white-hot lines.

The first Focke-Wulf fired, staccato muzzle bursts from its 20mms and 50mms. Smoke flew back over its wings and spent cartridges tumbled wildly away under it. The rounds slammed overhead and into the dunes beyond the men, the air jolted as the fighter hurtled by at fifty feet.

The next one was right behind it, lower, adjusting fire from its leader's misses. Twin geysers of sand exploded into the air forty yards in front of the men, cannon rounds, and then lines of machine-gun bullets blowing through the upswept sand. As the fighter pulled up and away, fire was visible inside its engine cowling. A fine mist of oil drifted down onto the sand.

Three of the trucks were already moving, their netting pulling off as their machine gunners fed new ammo belts into their Brownings and Vickers. Each vehicle was headed in a different direction. The sound of the fighters had vanished but a thin trail of black smoke hovered over the dunes.

Then they saw the damaged 190, its engine running irregularly, sputtering. It hugged the earth and seemed to strain to lift over the crests. A moment later, it smashed into the ground and exploded.

The remaining fighter made two more strafing runs, coming in so close they could see the pilot's goggles and his tan flying suit. The men blasted away each time, most of them kneeling in the open now, firing right up the blade hub line of the incoming aircraft. Suddenly, there was another explosion and a huge ball of fire-laced smoke lifted into the sky. One of the trucks had been hit and its petrol cans and stored ammo went up. The vehicle and the two New Zealanders aboard were blown into smoking bits of debris that scattered across the dunes. At last, spent of ammunition, the German pilot broke off the attack and was soon out of sight, headed north.

Everyone quietly gathered around what was left of the truck. They didn't say anthing, just stood there looking. The smoke smelled of burning rubber and cordite. Sergeant Johns moved about, counting heads. As it turned out, the dead men were Signals Corpral McKinnen and Gunner Private Pongo Shepherd, their truck the *Te Rangi*.

Carr, seated in his jeep, waved Parnell and Johns over to him. They stood beside the vehicle. To Johns he said quietly, "We'll be heading due west, Jocko."

"Yes, sir." Johns hurried away, signaling the others.

Carr looked at Parnell. His face was stiff but his eyes gave nothing, only the tight squint against the steeply slanted sunlight. "You ride with me. We've got to vacate this area fast."

Red hesitated. "But aren't we going to gather their remains?"

"There aren't any remains, Lieutenant," Carr said in a flat, toneless voice. He turned and stared through the windshield. "Tonight we'll hit the dagos again. They'll figure the fighters wounded us. They won't be expecting an attack."

He remained motionless for a long moment. At last, very softly, he murmured, "Oo'roo, mates." *Good-bye, mates.* He quickly geared, waited for Parnell to climb aboard, and then swung away. Behind them, the smoke from the *Te Rangi* and the Focke-Wulf drew thin black columns in the evening sky.

# Sixteen

Sergeant Bird's blade touched metal. He froze. Then, gently, he began testing the contours of the buried metallic object, feeling suddenly completely exposed out there under the compound lights, an Italian picket only fifty feet away standing with his head down in the collars of his greatcoat.

The object in the sand was a picket mine. Ahead and to his right was Gunner Corporal Titch Crichton. He too had discovered another mine. Behind them both lay Gunner Private Geordy Greenhill, at the edge of the light, ready to take out the picket if he looked up. . . .

Earlier, Carr and Parnell and one Chevy truck had headed due west from the strafing site, crossed the Quargla camel track, continued in that direction for another five miles, and then turned south so they could approach the Italian camp from the southwest. They kept hidden in the dune gullies, which also muffled the sounds of their engines. Meanwhile, the rest of the patrol went directly south to take up firing positions a mile north of the Italian compound.

It was nearly two o'clock in the morning when Carr's crew came up through the gravel plain and scattered acacia scrub a mile from the Italian bivouac, their engines idling. The small trees gave good cover in the moonlight. Four hundred yards out, they stopped so the captain could glass the enemy compound.

Fifteen minutes before, the Italians had sent a few salvos of harassing fire into the French fort, this time using mortars. Now Carr swept his glasses across the fence and quickly spotted a weak point in the picket line. An LACP was parked too close to the wire on the eastern side and obscured the sentry at that position from the other two farther along the wire.

Bird, Crichton, and Greenhill had been chosen to act as sappers. Wyatt, the most experienced demo man on the American team, had the steady, delicate touch it took to defuse ordnance. Carr had gone over their instructions and synchronized watches. Then the three headed across the acacia scrub to a sand berm, which would give them cover all the way to a series of shallow dunes near the encampment. They darted and crawled in the moonlight, loaded with sticky bombs and grenade DABs and three two-kilo-weight thermite bombs. . . .

Bird poked his finger gently down into the sandy gravel, felt the mine's round plunger cap. *Careful,* he reminded himself, *don't touch the damn pressure plate.* He was sweating in the sharp night air, his lean face clamped tight. *There!* He'd found the narrow barrel that housed the mine's safety pin. Then something occurred to him: What if that Wop mine-layer had left the pin in? He gritted his teeth, gently shoved at it, and felt it snap agianst his finger. He relaxed. The mine was defused.

Ahead, Crichton had also deactivated his mine. From the positions of the devices, it was obvious they had been laid down in an arrowhead pattern. Deactivating these two thus allowed them a clear five-foot-wide pathway to the fence. Crichton now rose and scooted to it. By the time Wyatt came up, Titch was already moving along the wire, hunched down, walking toe-to-heel toward the nearest sentry.

Bird checked the fence, hunting for alarm wires. Sure enough, one ran along the bottom coil. He quickly rigged a bypass shunt by placing two clips onto the alarm wire three feet apart and then cutting the center. He listened for any hum of a warning bell. Nothing. Using the heavier cutters, he rapidly severed the fence wires and pulled them back to form a hole.

Down the fence, Crichton was coming back. Behind him, the sentry lay in a heap against the bottom of the coil wire. Bird signaled Greenhill. A few seconds later, the gunnery private came running in.

The three entered the compound. Five Lancias were backed against the fence. They knelt beside the first one. It was where one of the stacks of fuel drums had exploded during the first raid and the ground around it was badly scorched. Farther along the fence was a pile of wooden boxes and a wooden building, probably an ordnance shed. From somewhere deeper in the camp, they could hear soft talking from the on-duty mortar crew.

Stealthily, they moved off to their separate targets. Bird's was the parked LACPs, Greenhill's the supply stack, and Crichton's the ordnance shed. Each man's charges were armed with time pencils that could be activated by pinching their middles to break a tiny glass vial of acid on the inside. The acid would then eat through a lock wire and release a spring-looped plunger into the main firing cap.

The time pencils were set to explode in a staggered sequence. Wyatt's would go off precisely three minutes after he broke the acid vial. Greenhill's would detonate three minutes later and finally Crichton's three minutes after that. This would allow them to regroup before any charges blew. The sequenced firing would also draw the enemy soldiers into the open, exposing them to the next explosions.

Bird laid his sticky bombs and DABs on the first two Lancias, down on their four-wheel-drive transfer cases, the vehicles sitting high off the ground with their undersides faintly lit by moon reflection. He placed the charges so he could activate all the igniters within three seconds.

Finishing, he crawled to the last LAPC in line and pulled himself up to peer over the cowling into the gun deck. The thing was littered with empty ration cartons and tins. There were two Fiat-Revelli 6.5mm machine guns mounted on pedestals and metal benches along both sides. Everything stank of dirty metal and dried wine.

Carr's plan was for them to remain hidden until all the charges went off. At that moment the rest of the patrol out in the dunes would open up with suppression fire and give them the chance to escape out through the main gate using one of the LACPs. In the confusion, the Italians would think they were their own men simply moving the vehicle out of harm's way.

Bird returned to the first two Lancias, squinted at his watch. The luminous hands indicated 0300 hours on the button. He immediately began activating his time pencils, moving quickly. Done, he ran back to the last Lancia and waited beside its left front wheel. Soon, Greenhill soundlessly appeared beside him. Then Chrichton. One by one, they climbed up the side of the vehicle and dropped down into the gun deck to wait.

Bird's bombs went off with a sharp, metallic crack, like ice breaking up on a river, and were followed by a peculiar thrumming. A surge of scorching hot air and orange light crossed over the vehicle. Objects slammed against its side. There was a pause and then voices started yelling, officers screaming orders.

Wyatt pulled up the hatch to the driver's seat and slipped down inside. It was tight, the edges of things knocking painfully against his arms. There were two viewing slits in the forward armored sheet. Light came in from the open hatch, dim and flickering, but enough for him to see the controls. There was a double gearshift and four floor pedals against the firewall along with a small dial panel and a left-handed throttle.

There was a loud metallic slam behind him. He jerked his head around. The Lancia's rear hatch had just fallen back onto its lock as an Italian soldier in an undershirt and a garrison cap came climbing through. Crichton loomed up, blocking him. The two men merged for an instant. There were two muffled shots. Bird saw both rounds blow out through the Italian's upper back, the man slumping until Titch caught and hauled him inside the vehicle, then reached back to close the hatch. The Italian moaned for a few seconds, then stopped.

Bird started the engine, a diesel. Its tappets clacked loudly, warming. Fifteen seconds later, Greenhill's charges went off, boosted by his two kilos of thermite. The ground shook under the armored car. Larger objects went hurtling overhead, cutting the air. Black smoke lifted above the fence lights and turned them amber.

Seconds flew past. A minute. Another. The sound of tractor motors came, the clank and rattle of tracks moving. There were three long bursts of machine-gun fire from somewhere beyond the fence, the sound of the weapons peculiar. Bird instantly realized it was coming from the French fort as the legionnaires jumped into the fight. Bullets *whanged* against the Lancia. Crichton and Greenhill crawled back, pressing tightly against the rear armor plating.

When the ordnance shed went up, there was a double explosion, the first Crichton's charges, the second the shed's stored munitions. Together they sucked the air back and sent up a dome of orange like a rising autumn moon, which broke apart thirty feet above the ground and hurled upward a boiling black fire-charged cloud of smoke. Bullets and mortar rounds began exploding, sending shrapnel and debris across the compound. Three seconds later, the rest of the LRDG patrol out in the desert opened up with their concentrated fire.

Through the viewing slits, Wyatt saw men crossing through his field of vision, a half-track, another LAPC. Parts of bodies were visible out there, too. He heard Greenhill abruptly shout, "Damn bluddy hell." He jerked around and saw, far out over the desert, a bright pink and purple flare. It shimmered through the explosive smoke.

Crichton slid closer and slapped Wyatt's shoulder. "Gun 'er hard, Birdie, we got comp'ny," he yelled through the roaring din. "We'd best get our arses the fuck outta here."

Wyatt engaged the clutch and rammed the throttle full forward. The vehicle leaped ahead. He hauled it into a hard left, all four wheels turning at the same time. It was a crazy feeling, side-slipping, but he finally got it straightened out. They surged forward, soldiers diving out of their way. Within twenty seconds, the Lancia hurtled through the main gate and headed up the old camel road.

* * *

Standing on his jeep's seat, Captain Carr glassed the flare. It glistened and twinkled out there against the moon-washed sky, its small chute and shroud lines clearly visible. Cursing softly, he lowered the binoculars to the dim horizon, scanned it for a moment. The black bulk of a vehicle appeared on the top of a dune. Still studying it, he said to Parnell, "That's a German ID flare. Looks like there's an armored car out in the sand. A pence on a bikkie it's a recon from a German armored patrol."

He swung the glasses back to the Italian encampment. It was chaos down there with the legionnaires still hammering away from the fort with their *fusils-mitraailleuse* or long-barreled machine guns, and the Bofors, Lewis guns, and Vickers 303s sending in rounds from out in the sand, their muzzle blasts looking like distant flashbulbs.

He caught sight of an LAPC racing toward the main gate. As he watched, it crashed through and headed up the old camel track. "There they are," he shouted. He noticed another Lancia and a half-track following the first one out. "Goddammit. The bloody Eyeties're trailing 'em out. . . . Stand ready."

The men in the Chevy truck had already uncased their Lewis antitank gun and the Browning MG. Out there, the three Italian armored vehicles raced beyond the fire-lit area of the compound. Carr felt his scalp tighten. Which one were his men in? Christ, he might fire on the wrong vehicle! But if he didn't engage, they'd all disappear far up the track and his men would have to take on the other two alone.

The headlights of the leading Lancia suddenly began blinking on and off. He leaned forward, squinting, and saw that the lights were coming in a definite pattern, long-long-short-short, the sequence repeating over and over. Carr suddenly realized what it was. The driver was using Morse code for the letter Z, which was often used as a nickname for a New Zealander.

"They're in the lead," he shouted. "Take out the other two fast."

The half-track was struck by the second Lewis round, a burst of flame shooting out from its undercarriage. It fishtailed off the track and immediately smashed into a low rock outcropping. The fire spread.

Up the road, the lead Lancia stopped, swung around to face the other LAPC coming up behind it, and opened fire. Like a mongrel dog cutting back, the Italian hurled around in a sharp left turn, lost the road for a moment, regained it, and sped back toward the encampment. As it passed the burning half-track, it slowed only long enough for the crippled crew to clamber aboard.

Gradually the compound explosions tapered off although the fires continued to rage. The French machine guns also stopped, as had those from the rest of the patrol out in the dunes. Into this comparative quiet came the clear, feathering whistle of a German 37mm recoiless antitank round.

It struck north of the Italian camp, out in the dunes, the Germans in the scout AC homing to the muzzle flashes of the LRDG's guns. A moment later, another round came, then a third and a fourth, the Kraut gun crew working rapidly, expertly, trying to saturate the area.

Carr dropped into his seat. "Time to leave," he said simply.

The jeep and Chevy headed out, tearing through the acacia scrub and angling toward the old Quargla camel track. A few minutes later, they linked with Bird, Greenhill, and Crichton. Moving in a line, they gradually disappeared into the moon glow, leaving a faint haze of desert dust hanging in the air.

# Seventeen

Carr stood on a thirty-foot-high dome of basalt rock black as coal and studied the three tiny dots coming across the dunes, humping into view as they topped crests, disappearing for a moment only to reappear a few moments later. It was a German hunter patrol following the LRDG's tracks.

Just before sunup they'd destroyed the stolen Lancia. It was nearly empty of diesel fuel and had only a few 20mm rounds in its ordnance case. They stripped the breech blocks and then set it on fire. It was still smoking gently in the distance.

Now the Germans were close enough for him to identify individual vehicles through the glasses, the three of them moving in single file. The lead was a German SD-KF2 251 half-track with a mounted 75mm gun behind a tall armor shield. The second was a German four-wheel, open-topped Grenadier armored car, which was followed by another Italian Lancia.

It was a few minutes after 10:30 in the morning. The Digger patrol had made camp twelve miles northeast of the Italian bivouac, on the edge of a rock field of sandstone and basalt outcroppings that looked like castles on a plain. The ground was red-brown gravel with patches of date palm and tamarisk brush. Carr ordered a dry camp, no fires, only rations and British campo kits with the men remaining on their vehicles. Then he, Parnell, and Johns had climbed onto the rock dome for a better view.

Johns said, "I think that Kraut commander's made hisself a mistake. Wouldn't you say, Cap'n?"

"Aye," Carr agreed.

"Mistake? Why?" Parnell asked.

"He's split his force," Carr answered. "And foolishly sent one of his big guns out after us. What he should've done was either come at us in full strength or stayed where he bloody well was." He tapped delicately on the binocular's adjuster ring. "Yellow and purple, Jocko?"

"Yah."

"That sews it. These aren't DAK." The incoming Kraut vehicles had yellow and purple stripes on their gun barrels, he explained to Parnell. Rommel's *Deutsch Afrika Korps* divisions, on the other hand, always used blue and green striping. "These brumbies must be a fresh outfit in from the continent."

Parnell shaded his eyes and looked out at the desert, trying to spot the Germans, the vehicles out about five miles now. Even with dark glasses the hot glare made him squint too tightly to see. A slight breeze had started. Freighted with solid heat, it made the palm fronds below them rustle gently.

Carr lowered his binoculars and gave a short, sharp whistle. He extended his right arm, twirled it in a circle twice, and pointed east. Two of the patrol trucks parked a hundred yards away under palm canopies immediately started up and headed off into the desert.

Twenty minutes later they returned. One pulled up beside the rock dome. Its driver, Private Maggie Gifford, climbed up. "There's a whole barchan field out there, Cap'n," he reported. "An' they've got bloody deep wadis runnin' northeast to southwest."

Carr grunted and turned his binoculars east, scanning.

"What's a barchan field?" Parnell asked nobody in particular.

"An area with a special kind of dune system," Jocko told him. "When there're rock hills like these here, they cause the wind to get all choppy kind of. When it does, it always forms crescent-shaped dunes with steep wadis or gullies. They have hooked ends, which make bluddy good natural traps. If a truck or an AC gets down in there, the bahstad can't climb out again. Has to backtrack. That's when he's vulnerable."

Carr was still gazing thoughtfully out at the barchan field. Finally, he glanced over his shoulder at Sergeant Johns, nodded. "All right, let's give her a go, then."

They all climbed down off the rock. Walking back to the jeep, Red asked the captain, "I take it we're engaging?"

"Aye. We'll set up an ambush. I figure these boys aren't desert savvy yet. If I'm right, we can maybe draw the bastards into a wadi and then high-road 'em."

It took thirty minutes to deploy the patrol vehicles into ambush positions. The two Chevys were hidden among the rocks while the rest of the force moved out into the barchan dunes. The men hurriedly prepared saddle charges and gasoline bottles for close-in fighting.

Carr had chosen a particularly steep wadi for their killing zone. He ran a false trail into it with his jeep using spare truck tires bolted to its bumper to make the tracks appear as if several vehicles had passed. Retracing himself, he planted two Hawkins grenade charges on a trip wire at a point where the wadi formed a sharp curve.

It was past eleven o'clock now and the sun made a merciless, blistering hole in the sky as it neared noon. The breeze had shifted slightly, increasing in strength and coming from the south. They waited.

\* \* \*

Cowboy absently leaned his back against the tire rim of the Chevy one-and-a-half and instantly let out a cry as the sun-hot metal seared through his blouse. Seated beside him, Private Gifford grinned and tossed him a pack of Egyptian cigarettes called Salomes.

The two were with Kimball and Signalman Barbett in one of the trucks, positioned among the rocks at a point that was well protected and had a clear field of fire. Kimball was now off somewhere and Barbett dozed under the Chevy.

Fountain lit a cigarette, let the smoke seep through his dry, cracked lips. It smelled like honeysuckle. He took another drag and asked, "What y'all think, Gif? Is them Krauts gonna bite?"

"Bite? Ya mean like into a bikkie?"

"No. I mean, are they gonna be dumb enough to get trapped in that goddamned wadi?"

"Oh, yah. Krauts ain't good in small-unit operations. Like them out there, separated from their mates? Makes the buggahs nervous. The bleedin' Germans are trained to act in big field maneuvers, ya know? When they get busted outta familiar ground, they get spooked, start makin' mistakes."

"Really?"

"Yah. Besides, these here ain't learned the desert yet. Prob'ly don't even know what a bleedin' wadi is."

"But the dagos do."

Gifford snorted derisively. "Shit, it'll be a frosty day in hell when a Nazi *oberfuhrer* pays any mind to a bleedin' Eyetie on battle tactics."

Cowboy started to say something, then stopped abruptly and jerked backward. "Holy Christ, watch out!"

"Wot the . . . ?" Gifford glanced at him, then down at his own trousers. A jet-black scorpion nearly six inches long had crawled up onto his pant leg.

He chuckled and reached for the huge insect. "Got a visitor, ain't we?" He nudged it gently up onto his knuckles and returned it to the ground. The scorpion scurried away, its body plates shining like enameled metal in the sun. "Don't fret them little buggahs, mate," Gifford said. "They won't hurt ya. You're too bloody big to be prey."

Fountain stared at the scorpion as it disappeared under a rock, the damned thing actually leaving tracks. His skin got prickly. He'd seen big scorps back home, but nothing like this one. He shook his head, peered out at the small grove of withered palms a few yards away. There were no shadows under them, the light coming straight down out of a vast, white, pulsing sky.

How in hell did people live in such a place? he wondered. Coming from New Mexico, he'd known a fair amount about desert country. At least what he thought of as desert country. But all that was nothing compared to this wasteland. Back home deserts had *some* green, things growing and snow in the winter and not *everything* so deadly and venomous. Out here the whole goddamned place and everything in it seemed designed solely to kill. Heat that fried you, wind that dried out your brain, and scorpions tall enough to piss on a fence post without even raising up.

For a moment, he thought about the coming battle and felt a little streak of fear. But it didn't linger, flashing through his mind just for a second. He'd already disciplined himself not to allow such thoughts to grab hold. They could make you loco.

He found that he preferred to think about what he'd do after the war, form up mental pictures to swing his focus away from the here-and-now. Like for instance him riding up through a high piñon forest just at dusk. Or running coyotes out on the rock plains. Or tasting an icy long-neck in a smoke-filled honky-tonk with some pretty rodeo baby whispering in his ear, saying, "Billy, hon, you all jes' been gone so long," and later, in her small, dirty-sheeted trailer bed, urging him on in frenzied, hissing arousal: "God Jesus, do it to me . . . don't stop . . . Oh, I'll kill you if you stop. . . ."

He caught a sudden movement, saw Kimball running back toward them. His boots slapped loudly in the hot stillness. "Look alive, guys," he called out. "The bastards're here."

Smoker Wineberg had also been thinking about the desert, lying out there on the upwind side of the ambush wadi. Two LRDG trucks were nearby, downslope with their nets on tight and guns charged. Two Digger troopers were resting near it. Up on the crest with him were Horse Kaamanui and two New Zealanders.

What he'd been thinking was how much he liked the desert. The heat was a bitch, but he'd been in hot places before: roughnecking on oil rigs in the gulf where the tools and grip chains got so hot they burned through to bone if you forgot to use gloves; working on prison road-gangs in west Texas around Lubbock and Big Spring in mid-August with a week's hangover hammering at his brain.

There was something special about this desert. He tried to pinpoint exactly what it was and the word *deadly* came to him. That was it, the place was goddamned deadly. It was also plain, up-front with you, no bullshit. There was nothing about it a man had to think about or piece out because it came right at you, let you know up-front that if you fucked up, Jack, you were gone.

That sort of simplicity always pleased Smoker. He preferred an uncomplicated world. Most of his life had been lived in such artlessness, everything black and white: steal or starve, fight or get whipped. In a large sense this desert was symbolic. Big word, that, but smack on the button. Yeah, symbolic. Basic. It also made one damn fine place to fight a war in.

Now he looked challengingly toward the south and said aloud, "Come on, you Kraut cocksuckers. Let's get this goddamn bout on the road."

As if in immediate answer, a German 75mm opened on them. It came from the half-track out about eight hundred yards, beyond the accurate range of the Digger's reach-out guns. The round willowed like a giant whispering and then the ground shook as it struck thirty yards beyond the trucks.

A few seconds later another round came in, then another, six in all, the Germans laying a fan pattern, trying to drive the raiders out of the sand and into the rocks where that big mounted howitzer could take them out one by one.

The shelling stopped abruptly. It left a ringing in the air and the dry, antiseptic stench of explosive. After a few moments, it started again. These new rounds landed closer in, the Germans moving their target base west a few clicks. The first shell hit twenty yards from one of the Ford trucks, hurled sand down through its netting. Smoker glanced downslope and watched as a New Zealander crawled toward it, scrambled aboard, and began backing the vehicle downhill. Its net pegs went popping out of the sand.

Five seconds later, a round struck the truck dead center. The explosion sounded oddly muffled. Debris crossed up into the sunlight, the Ford heaving up and then down again, landing on its side. Flames leaped from its bed.

Smoker jumped up and ran down to it, down onto the harder-packed sand at the bottom. The driver was slumped over the edge of the running board and the fire was extremely hot. Shielding his face, he darted in and grabbed the Aussie's arm. The man's head lolled, empty-eyed. Did he make a sound?

Suddenly Smoker was falling backward, off balance, the New Zealander's weight too light. He caught himself and looked back. The lower part of the man's body had been blown away. Tendrils of clothing, skin, blood, and other liquids left a wet line in the sand, on top of his pants and boots. His throat gripped up.

Then came sudden, furious machine-gun bursts. Shouts and bullets sundered the air overhead. He twisted away from the half corpse and lunged forward into a run. Behind him, the truck exploded in a jolting blast. Concussion and heat rolled over him and the ground lifted upward. He went sailing through the air, his hearing suddenly gone, leaving only a roaring inside his head. He struck the ground twenty yards away.

His body pulsed with electricity. He struggled to his knees and then to his feet. Over the crest of the dune, tracer bullets were going in both directions. Kaamanui and a Digger were firing, their spent cartridges hurling off their weapons.

*Firefight!* he thought giddily. *Gotta find my weapon.* He started forward but immediately fell down. Everything tilted. He got up, fell down again. The ground continued shifting. He crawled around on it, confused, like a drunk trying to find the edge of things.

Rage poured through him. *Get up, you son of a bitch,* he shouted at himself and heard it only in his head. Goddammit! He concentrated his will, forced himself to his feet. There. A moment of dizziness. He took a step, another, then staggered up the slope and dove for the crest.

Two hundred yards away, the German Grenadier armored car was on the top of the opposite crest, burning, its gray paint peeling off in huge ribbons. Two German soldiers jumped free and started to run off. They were instantly cut down, curling over tightly on the ground like gut-shot snakes.

Across the wadi, the Italian Lancia was dueling furiously with the New Zealanders and Americans. A 20mm round suddenly blew a hole in its left side, big as a watermelon. A sizzling explosion of phosphorous went off. Its cannon stopped firing but then started again and finally stopped completely.

Wineberg searched the sand around him: *Weapon, gotta get a fucking weapon.* He spotted the Sten, scooped it up, instinctively clicking it onto automatic fire. He began blazing away at the Lancia.

Something appeared suddenly to his left. The German half-track had just burst into view, rounding a curve in the wadi. Its treads churned up the hard-pack. Behind its tall armor shield, the gun crew banged away with its 75mm howitzer, the shots coming with even, precise-fire discipline.

The Allied fire swung away from the Lancia and concentrated on the half-track. But their rounds merely bounced off its heavy armor. Only two shells from the recoiless 57mm bored holes through the corner of the armor shield.

The vehicle rumbled past directly below Smoker and continued up the wadi. He tried to fire down into the open-topped deck but the two German machine gunners were raking both crest lines. Ducking, he pressed his body tightly against the sand and felt the bullets hitting close by.

At last, the Germans' firing passed on. Cautiously, he slid to the crest and looked over. There it was, its huge ventilator plates sweating and wire loops and field bags hanging off its stern. He bellowed at it.

Afterward, when anybody asked him why he had done

it, he said simply, "How the hell should I know?" It was true. Yet in that sudden, muted moment, he simply rose from the sand and ran down the inside wall of the wadi, his legs still rubbery, slipping and sliding as he headed after the half-track.

Heat radiated off the steep gully walls and bullets slammed into the sand all around him with peculiar sucking sounds. Gun smoke and engine exhaust drifted and curled, enclosed. He neared the German half-track, its stern massive, its treads tearing up hard-pack. He could see the tops of the machine gunners who were still blazing away, weapon heat fuming back over their olive-khaki shirts and black, sweat-drenched *feldmutze* caps.

Ten feet from it, he threw his Sten ahead of him and wrenched a grenade from his combat harness. Jerking out the cotter pin, he hurled it, heard the spoon lever snap through the safety tape as it triggered its three-second fuse. It went sailing over the sand-dusted gray curve of the half-track's rear bulkhead. He grabbed another grenade, yanked the pin, and threw it, then dropped to the ground and covered his head with his arms.

One of the Kraut gunners turned in time to see the first grenade coming in. Frantically he tried to throw himself back and down. It was too late. As the second grenade tumbled in, the first exploded in a blurred flash of white. Two heartbeats later the second went off. The body of one of the gunners went hurling up into the air like a broken doll and smoke instantly began pouring up over the armor shield.

The half-track careened up the side of the wadi quarterwise, its tracks hurling loose sand. It began straining and finally came to a stop near the crest, the tracks still going. It was fully afire now. Germans began jumping out, weapons in their hands. A furious burst from the crest instantly killed them.

Several yards back, Wineberg got to his feet. He reached for his Sten, picked it up. He felt oddly petulant now, broody even. He couldn't understand why. He looked at the half-track just as its forward tires exploded. A shirtless German soldier crawled out from behind the shield cradling an MP-40 machine pistol. He raised it. Smoker shot him.

Then he turned and moved back down the wadi in a shambling run. His thoughts were still fuzzy as he looked up at the white-hot sky. He tilted his head to listen, heard absolutely nothing. Something caught his eye, in the air, an out-of-sync movement. A dune hawk, brown orange, was making gentle, slow circles, its wing feathers trembling. He watched it, fascinated.

# Eighteen

They buried the dead New Zealander, medical orderly Corporal "Doc" Bindle, among the rocks. It was tough digging down into the hard, red gravel and harder still to look at the pathetically short canvas bag that contained all that was left of his body. Two other men had been slightly wounded.

Later, while the men searched through the burnt-out Axis vehicles and the exploded Ford, Carr, with Parnell listening, interviewed the only enemy soldiers still alive, two Italians from the Lancia.

Both were young and frightened, their gray-green tunics dusty and stained with phosphorous powder. Carr squatted in front of them. "You have a choice," he said quietly in Italian. "Cooperate and I will give you enough food and water to walk to Quargla. If you refuse, I will shoot you."

The men exchanged terrified glances. One looked no more than sixteen and was quite handsome. The other, a *capo squadra*, said, "We do not wish to die, *Capitano.*"

"Very well. How many Germans are there?"

"Perhaps sixty or seventy in all. Vehicle crews and dismounted infantry. They have nine vehicles . . . no, seven, now. Another half-track and armored cars and two mobile field guns."

"Seventy-five milllimeters?"

"*Sí.*"

"What is your battalion?"

"The fourth of the Third Armored Regiment, First Bersaglieri."

"What's your strength now?"

"Many are wounded and dead," the handsome young one piped up earnestly. "Some are even rotting unburied in the sand."

"How many are able to fight?"

The two men thought a moment; then the *capo squadra* said, "Perhaps seventy."

Carr shifted his legs. Far across the rock-strewn landscape a dust devil curled thinly up into the sky like a red wraith, slanted northeastward by the freshening breeze. "How is your water?"

"Almost gone."

"Petrol and diesel?"

"About a quarter. You destroyed the remainder. Diesel, perhaps a thousand liters."

"These Germans are not Rommel's men. Who are they?"

"They are of the Eighty-sixth Grenadier Regiment of the Tenth Panzer Division. They were before on the Russian front."

"Who is in command now, your commandant or the German?"

The Italians looked at each other again, then at the ground. Carr waited. Finally, the *capo squadra* said, "It is the German *capitano.*" He spat. "He humiliated our *tenente colonnel.* A filthy *capitano* who talks as if he owns the world. *Un cretino.*"

"Do you know what he intends to do about the fort?"

"We are told he will attack this night. First with bombardment, then a ground attack. We are to assist."

Carr nodded. He stood, took a water flask from his jeep, and handed it to the men. He looked at Parnell and walked off to stand beside a date palm. When Red joined him, he said, "He claims the Germans are going to assault the fort tonight. Probably just after dusk. They've got field guns." He shook his head. "They'll rout the Frenchies by midnight."

"Then let's hit the bastards before they start it."

"Aye, we've no choice. They'll be after us as soon as they finish with the Frogs. Only this time they'll come in full strength with air strikes." He shrugged. "In any case, we need some of their petrol. With two of our loads gone, we haven't got half enough to reach our DAD in Libya."

"So, how do we do it?"

"There's but one way, mate. Right up their bleedin' bunghole."


The French fort was dead silent, appearing ancient, a medieval stronghold out there in the evening light. Its walls were shell-pocked, made of dusky mud and sandstone with *ghaf* poles protruding from it. There were no windows nor viewing holes of any kind. Makeshift scaffolding was visible over the parapets and the sentry turrets at the four corners were shell-torn. The main or western gate contained twin *skifa* doors of black iron.

Bekker studied it with his binoculars. The sun had dipped beyond the western horizon and now the day's shadows were dissolving into the soft orange glow of dusk. It was fifteen minutes to six.

His force was five hundred meters east of the fort. Farther back another hundred meters were his two mobile field guns, their crews ready and awaiting his signal whistle to begin shelling. He swung the glasses over to the Italian encampment. Armored cars and LAPCs, the few that were left, were lined along the compound fence with soldiers milling about.

"*Dummheit,*" Bekker grunted, disgusted. *Look at those fools, giving away their intentions.* Ah, well, it wouldn't make any difference. He knew his battle plan would unfold too swiftly for the enemy to break its thrust even if they knew precisely what was coming.

He, Lieutenant Stracher, and the Italian commander, a scowling, shaven-headed lieteunant colonel named Pietro Guzzoni, had worked on the plan through the long afternoon. It was a modified version of the Box and Spearpoint attack, straight from the German tech manual on battle doctrine, Section XXIII: *armored attack against a fixed defensive position in open country.*

First there would be a bombardment, twenty minutes of barrage fire from the field guns and the half-track's own 75mm. Three rounds per minute of high-explosive and hollow-charge shells, the guns firing in staggered twenty-second intervals. Then a pause of five minutes followed by another short shelling using smoke rounds to screen the main assault. With the wind now blowing quite hard, these shells would be placed to the south of the fort so the smoke would drift back across the eastern wall.

While the smoke barrage continued, the Italians, signaled by Bekker with flares, would quickly assemble two hundred meters from the fort. The moment the shelling stopped, with the fort obscured by a smoke barrier, they would move into assault positions across Bekker's front.

The Germans would then come up in support while the Italians dismounted and set their attack into motion behind their own armor. Once they had fully engaged the French, Bekker's force could then dash through their lines, dismount infantry, and penetrate the fort's eastern wall through breaches made by the artillery.

Guzzoni, completely cowed, had listened to Bekker's plan without comment. After he had gone back to his battalion, however, Stracher pointed out three concerns he had.

First, he said, the Italians were too badly demoralized to keep from bolting if enemy fire grew too intense. "That would leave our troops exposed on open ground."

Bekker scoffed. "These idiots are merely there to hold French attention until our own men get under their guns. Beyond that, they're expendable."

Stracher's second point was his uneasiness over the failure of the hunter patrol to return. The last radio contact with it had been a position fix. Even more ominous had been those smoke trails in the north.

Again Gerd dismissed the lieutenant's point. The smoke was from the raider vehicles, he said. Did he really think a ragged group of desert rats could best an armored German patrol? Absurd. And the reason there had been no further radio contact with it was simply another malfunctioning wireless unit. Since there had been no time to install the new, desert-adaptable crystals in their radios before leaving Sfax, the force's radios had been operating badly ever since leaving the coast.

Stracher hesitated before voicing his last item. "Might I suggest, *Herr Kapitan,* that we leave a watch outpost and double mine belts in our rear."

This time Bekker lost his patience. "*Ach du Seheisse, Leutnant!* You are exhibiting womanish timidity. Is there anything out there? Do you see anything out there?"

"No, sir."

"Then return to your duties and cease your whining."

"Yes, *Herr Kapitan,* " Stracher said, his sunburnt face flushing as he turned away.

Once more Bekker checked his watch. Five to six. He looked eastward. The light was rapidly fading along the horizon, turning to a gray indigo. Above it, the brighter stars were becoming visible, the already-risen moon looking like a pale, lopsided plate hanging just over the desert's rim.

Six o'clock.

He blew his signal whistle, its shrill sound traveling clear and sharp into the silence. A few seconds later, one of the field guns fired off with a throaty, cracking discharge that split that same stillness. This single round was a high-ranging burst used to set up a target base. It exploded thirty feet in the air near the fort's eastern wall, its white marker smoke quickly disappearing in the wind.

Next came a probing round, then several creeping rounds, each one twenty-five yards nearer the fort than the one before it. These were placed directly in front of the wall in order to create assault lanes through any French mines that might be there. The concussions set off buried charges all across the fort's approaches.

The gun stopped. There was a drawn-out moment of stillness. Then all the German guns opened up at once, laying in solid direct fire. Their shells made sluicing, rushing sounds through the air and their muzzle blasts came in clean, precise spacings.

All afternoon the LRDG force had worked its way behind the Germans, first going due east until they passed beyond the barchan field into regular sand dunes, then following in their valleys toward the southwest. The increasing wind aided their stealth. It was blowing quite hard now, lifting sand swirls off the crests, which hid the dust from their wheels.

Now they were in a shallow sand gully about four hundred yards behind the German mobile guns, the trucks strung out. Carr had divided his force: three men in the jeep, three in each of the Ford V-8s, and the rest in the Chevys.

During their passage, everyone prepared for the coming combat. Guns were cleaned, ammo belts filled, and MG boxes loaded along with with the making up of satchel charges and blasting slabs. The Diggers took time to explain to the Americans the basic tactics for close-in fighting against tanks and armored vehicles. It had a specific sequence of action that they referred to as BSD. That stood for Blind, Stop, Destroy.

To blind a tank or an AV, they used Very flares, smoke grenades, or focused fire into its viewing slits. Once the vehicle began moving erratically, they threw concentrated charges or blasting slabs under its tracks to bring it to a complete halt. They could then board it and, using the blasting slabs on its turret or gun deck, create deadly concussion waves on the inside, which would kill the enemy crew. If the concussions didn't kill them all, they could still disable the armored vehicle's guns by draping saddle charges over the barrels.

Carr gathered everyone together for a final talk, sixteen men squatted down on the hard-pack. "It looks like they're using a modified B and S assault formation," he said. "AC and APV on echelon point, troop tractors and trucks in support. The halfer's acting as command car, inside the V crotch." He chuckled mirthlessly. "Apparently, they're throwin' in the bloody dagos as gun fodder."

As the main barrage started, he was forced to shout over the constant roar of the guns. "We'll hit 'em in two attacks. Undoubtedly, they'll lay in smoke just before the main assault. We can't let their armor reach it. If it does, they'll merge point and be able to cover each other's dead space."

He paused as the hard thunder of a particularly loud series of explosions rolled over them. When it passed, he said, "The jeep and the Fords are the quickest, so we'll take on the armor. Geordy, you and your blokes hit the

APV. Tug, Lieutenant Parnell goes with you against the AC. Maggie, you and—you"—he pointed at Kimball— "come with me. We'll handle the halfer."

He glanced over at Sergeant Jones. "Jocko, you bring up your Chevys and rip those mobile guns as soon as we engage. Once you neutralize them, come up in support. When you do, concentrate your fire on those troop trucks."

Johns nodded.

Carr looked around at the shadowed faces. Above them the dune crests were washed in faint red light now. "Anyone have anything to add?"

No one spoke.

Carr retrieved the thermos of Devil's Brew from his jeep. He passed it to Parnell, watched as every man took a long, silent drink. When it came back to him, he drank, lowered it. "All right, gents," he said brusquely. "Crank 'em up and stand to your weapons."

# Nineteen

Darkness came quickly, a sudden vanishing of light: one minute there, the next gone. Only the stars and the glow from the moon, which wasn't yet high enough to illuminate anything but large objects, like the fort that appeared as old ruins on a plain.

The LRDG vehicles were now lined along the crest of their dune, their engines idling. The German barrage had stopped, leaving a hollow silence broken only by the sound of other, faraway engines revving as the Italians prepared for their assault.

Then the 75mms started up again with the same paced sequencing. Parnell could hear the slam of their breech blocks, the tinny ring of empty shell casings on their gun decks. This time it was smoke shells, the bursts appearing like sudden, snow-covered trees in the moon's glow.

A white signal flare abruptly arched into the sky. It was small and left a streak of sparks before bursting. Red felt his insides tighten as adrenaline began spewing into his bloodstream. The distant engines came up into full power as the Italians keyed on the signal and began moving into position across the German front, their vehicles merely vague dark objects in the smoke, seen but not quite seen.

Beside Red, Lance Corporal Tug Westlake lightly

tapped his fingers on the truck's steering wheel and softly hummed four notes of a song, over and over. Up on the swiveled Browning was Titch Crichton. Red's own fingers nervously rubbed against the smooth metal of his Very pistol. The guns stopped again, this time an extended pause. From beneath him, Parnell felt the Ford's V-8 breathing easily through its chassis.

A blue flare popped into view. And then the night exploded, everything going off: mobile howitzers, machine guns, tracers from the German half-track as it laid in guiding fire, engines howling, tracks clanking.

The Ford rolled forward, Tug letting gravity pull it down the sand slope. As it rolled onto the bottom, he hit the throttle and they went roaring up the next dune slope, crested, and started down again. Thus they went, up, down, up, down, the V-8 screaming with Red getting lifted out of his seat only to be slammed down again.

They passed the mobile howitzers, fifty yards to their left, the muzzle flashes like huge horizontal candle flames. Soon the dunes began to shallow out as they neared the outer perimeter of the gravel plain. Parnell saw a truck to his right, caught it only in light bursts. Ahead of it was another, filled with mounted German infantry. He saw flickering reflections off their battle helmets and gun barrels.

Now the dark hulk of the German armored car loomed ahead, silhouetted against the tracer fire and bursting shells inside the smoke screen that illuminated it like sheet lightning. Red focused his mind on the AC, tried to recall its nomenclature, form a mental picture: s*onderkraftfahrseug . . . boxy, four-wheeled, no tracks, closed deck, 44mm plating, weapons . . . what? what?*

They closed rapidly with it and then it was directly in front of them, hurling sand dust into their faces and heat off its ventilators. Its guns were firing rapidly, a 20mm antitank cannon and a 7.92mm machine gun.

Westlake hollered, "Get set, Lieutenant."

Parnell picked up a C-charge from under his seat. It consisted of seven stick grenades tied together. It felt heavy in his lap. Tug drifted the truck to the left and they raced beside the Germans, a loping up-down dash, the armored car trailing a stench of cordite and exhaust fumes.

For a fleeting second he took his eyes from it, squinted at the flashing, thundering wildness ahead, the smoke almost gone now and the Italian troopers screaming, charging forward in full assault. He thought, *The dumb bastards're going in without cover.*

A shell exploded thirty yards off their left fender, jolting him. *Where in hell did that come from?* A short round? Another shell hit close to the first and he realized what was happening. They were now coming under fire from the fort, from French antitank guns.

Seconds hurtled past in the wind. The German AC's tires tossed up small stones that pinged against the Ford like pellets, both vehicles onto the gravel plain now, four hundred yards from the fort's walls. He noticed that the French machine guns were raking the advancing Italians, traversing wildly back and forth. Gaps began showing in the Italian ranks as soldiers went down.

They were past the German AC's left front. Its guns continued punching out rounds. A soft red glow from its interior battle lights showed through the viewing slits looking like devil's eyes. Tug yelled something and cut sharply to the right. They crossed directly in front of the Germans. Above Parnell came the slamming, heavy rap of the Browning as Crichton opened on its fore plating.

Holding the Very pistol with both hands, he twisted in his seat and fired at the viewing slits as the Ford cleared away to the side. The pistol jerked back powerfully and Red felt the heavy charge go out with a metallic ring. The flare hit the front of the armored car and exploded in a brilliant spray of white light that sizzled like water dropped onto a skillet.

The German AC began to fishtail, lunging from side to side. White fire crackled inside it. Westlake, double-handing the steering wheel, hurled the Ford around in a half circle and they bore in at the Germans from the side.

Abruptly, the AC stopped. Tug skidded to a halt beside it. Before they lost momentum, Red leaped from his seat, his C-charge pack under his arm. The ground felt rock-hard. He shoved a boot onto the back edge of the armored car's left fender and heaved himself up onto it. His hand touched the edge of a slit panel, then the barrel of a machine gun, the thing scalding hot. It was still swiveling back and forth but not firing.

He stretched himself out and slammed the C-charge onto the top of the turret, yanked the ring on the center grenade, and threw himself backward and off the vehicle. When he hit the ground, he rolled and came up running.

Seconds later, the Ford pulled up beside him, slowing enough for him to take hold of the back of his seat and jump aboard. Tug poured on the gas and they roared away as Crichton give the Germans one last burst.

Red took a look around. The air smelled of fire, the kind that burns in city dumps long after the main inferno has settled. Back in the direction of their wadi, he saw a sudden flash of blue light, then orange flame. A moment later another flash and more flame. Sergeant Johns and his crew were taking out the German mobile guns.

\* \* \*

Kimball, with Captain Carr and Maggie Gifford in the jeep, absorbed the jolting, lunging ride with his legs. Hunkered down behind the Vickers machine gun, he watched the ground battle rage ahead of them and realized the French legionnaires were laying in heavy counterfire, antitank cannons and MGs whacking the crap out of the dagos. But he couldn't spot the muzzle flashes of their reach-out guns. Smart Frenchies, he thought, using blast mats so they couldn't be targetted.

For the last several minutes, Carr had gone slowly a hundred yards behind the German half-track, staying back there until the two Fords engaged. They finally saw Parnell's truck commit to the attack on the armored car and a moment later Greenhill immediately struck at the armed fighting vehicle. Instantly, Carr sped up and they went sailing over dunes, the half-track ahead and slightly to the right, dimly visible.

They rapidly caught up to and passed it, several yards out. The German machine gunners were firing continuous guiding fire at the fort so the other units had a target base to home to. The gunners were so intent on their work, they didn't notice the jeep as Carr started a long, slow turn back toward them.

They were on flat surface now and as they curved back, Kimball got a last glimpse of the infantry battle, the Italians still advancing but starting to seriously falter in the face of the fierce French fire. Men were starting to bolt toward their right flank.

Carr straightened out the little vehicle. Kimball peered ahead and heard the intermittent surge and fade of the half-track's treads as it came on. Carr pointed the jeep directly at it, going for its dead space, the area close around it that was below the deflection arc of its guns.

His intention was to maintain a head-on course until the half-track was nearly on them. Then he'd veer slightly and flash past it close enough so Gifford could hurl gasoline bottles up onto its firing deck. The spreading fuel would then be ignited by a flare. Once that was completed, he'd snap-spin and come right up the half-track's rear end to lay in a concussion mat.

Closer and closer thundered the German half-track, its viewing slits glowing, the tall armor shield catching flash reflections. Kimball felt his testicles grip up. He opened fire, aiming at the long slant of the halfer's fore hood as he tried to angle in his bullets, going for the driver's viewing mirrors. The Vickers jerked and kicked back against its mount, spewing cordite smoke and metal slivers. His rounds threw off sparks as they smashed into the thick fore armor and richocheted away.

Forty yards . . . thirty . . .

Carr cut the jeep to the left and they flashed past the side of the half-track. A spent German machine-gun casing struck him in the forehead, stinging, shocking him, making him acutely aware of split-second images: bore fire and a black German helmet, the smell of gear oil, the dying-bird squeal of tracks right beside him, and then the slow-motion-seeming movement of Gifford hurling his two gasoline bottles over the cowling of the gun deck.

The half-track turned sharply to its left, the tracks locking down. As it did, its rear end swung wide. Carr tried to cut away from it but the right side of the jeep slammed against the German's rear bogie wheel and was instantly shoved around in a half circle.

Kimball felt himself in the air, tumbling. He hit the ground on his chest, his breath rushing out of him with a loud grunt. He began gagging, desperately trying to pull in air. A few yards beyond him, he saw the jeep rolling over and over.

Through frantic eyes, he saw Gifford's dim figure, the man on his hands and knees slapping at the ground as if he were trying to extinguish a fire. Then he picked something up and came to his feet. There was a sharp crack and a streak of yellow-white light shot from the end of his arm. It was a flare gun. The flaming missile struck the German half-track on the edge of the deck. Three ticks later, the vehicle blew up with a rushing, whoosing blue explosion just as Kimball managed to get his first complete lungful of air.

They found Carr under the turned-over jeep. Both men heaved, struggling with its weight, and finally got it up and back onto its wheels. The captain was jammed down between the seats. He said angrily, "Sweet bloody Jesus hell," as they lifted him out. His right ankle was broken.

Two hundred yards away, Sergeant Jones's trucks were now laying heavy fire into the German vehicles bearing the mobile infantry, and the Kraut troopers were returning it with equal intensity. Since no one was using tracers, the exchange created a solid storm of invisible lead crossing out there in the moonlight.

Kimball tried to start the jeep's engine. It turned over slowly and finally caught. They loaded Carr back into it. "Where's the halfer?" he growled. "Where the hell did it go?"

"She's left the field, Cap'n," Maggie said. There was blood on his forehead. "We blew her deck and she flanked out."

"Good, good," Carr said between clenched teeth. "We've jammed their attack."

"Aye, that we have."

The firing from the fort had slackened somewhat over the last few minutes, only antitank rounds and short bursts of machine-gun fire still coming. Even the exchange between Jones and the German infantrymen gradually lost its fierceness as the Krauts, outgunned now, were being forced back across the main assault area.

Carr shifted his leg, his agonized face grimacing up at the sky. As tall as he was, he had it crunched up against the firewall. He finally got it resettled and, panting heavily, looked at Kimball. "Get that bloody Vickers workin', Yank," he barked.

"I can't, sir. It's jammed solid."

The captain swore, closed his eyes, opened them. "All right. We'll fall back to the dune line."

Two shadows suddenly approached in the moonlight. Kimball and Gifford dropped to the ground, bringing up their weapons. A voice called out, "Diggers comin' in, mates."

They came up. One was carrying a third man over his shoulders. The two were Geordy Greenhill and Fountain with Gunner Private Rufus Murphy, who was wounded. They gently laid him down beside the jeep. His right pant leg was drenched in blood and he kept sucking spittle loudly through his teeth.

Carr leaned over the edge of the vehicle and looked down at him. "How bad, Rufus?"

"A through-and-through in the thigh," Greenhill answered for him. He shook his head, his kaffiyeh snapping in the wind. "But we lost the bloody truck, sir. That Kraut mongrel of a driver rammed us before we took him out."

"Where's Lieutenant Parnell and Tug?"

"Somewheres on our right flank." He laughed. "Lord, they karked that AC good."

They loaded Murphy aboard and then everyone climbed on, two out on the hood. Gifford drove. The front wheels wobbled badly as they went slowly back and into the desert. Behind them, several vehicles were still burning fiercely as were parts of the fort. Dead and wounded lay all over the approaches to its eastern wall.

Maggie took them into the dunes and then north down in a wadi for several hundred yards. A partial silence had now descended on the killing ground, disturbed only by the faint growl of engines moving off in the moonlight as the LRDGers, Germans, and Italians disengaged from each other, going off in separate directions to regroup and lick their wounds like stealthy animals.

At last even the engines faded away and the desert went completely still, a deep hush in which only the vast distance made a delicate whisper. Even the wind subsided. They splinted Carr's ankle and got the blood stopped from Murphy's wound. He was in shock. They wrapped him in a blanket on the ground with a plasma bottle beside him.

Eventually, the other trucks came in, the men using their tiny vest lights to identify themselves. First Parnell, Westlake, and Crichton, and then Jones's Chevys. Two of his men were slightly wounded.

Jocko posted a guard and the rest of the men climbed out and dropped to the sand beside the others. They lay there without speaking. After a while they gradually began to murmur softly to each other. Someone brought out another flask of Devil's Brew and they drank it and felt themselves slowly coming down from that peculiar, deadly, mystical elation that always comes with combat.

Hours seemed to pass. Then a strange and beautiful thing happened. From the fort came the sound of a bugle. It drifted out into the moonlit night filled with a deep melancholy, each note true and complete and unwavering.

The men listened to it, silent, afraid to disturb such fragile beauty. The bugler repeated his refrain. It seemed vaguely familiar. At last, it faded gently away and the desert was quiet again. Yet, still no one spoke, each caught up in the bugle's memory.

Finally, Maggie Gifford said, "I think that tune was a bonny carol. I remember it from when I was a sprout. . . .

Aye, by Jesus, ya know wot tonight is, mates? This 'ere's Christmas Eve."

By dawn both the Germans and Italians were gone, the Krauts to the east, their tiny dust trails in the far distance, the Italians in full flight up the old Quargla camel track. As the sun broke over the horizon, Carr took his men down to the fort, staying out about three hundred yards just in case the legionnaires intended to continue the battle. They sat out there and waited, not really knowing what to expect.

At precisely 0600 hours, the two flags over the fort were suddenly lowered. One was the French national standard, the other the black-and-white French Foreign Legion battle banner. They came down very slowly.

"What the hell does that mean?" Parnell asked Carr. "Are they surrendering to us?"

"Not likely."

Fifteen minutes later the fort's main gate swung open. Fourteen legionnaires marched out, coming forth two abreast, all of them ragged and dirty and bandaged yet striding with that clean, upright marching style of the Legion, each man fully armed, their guidon and battle streamers fluttering gently in the morning breeze.

Carr and Parnell walked out to meet them, the New Zealander hobbling on a makeshift crutch. The leader of the small legionnaire contingent was a sergeant. He had a thick beard and dark skin and there were dirty bandages at his throat and on his left arm.

He halted his men. They stared straight ahead, their eyes dark, defiant. The sergeant quick-stepped up to the two officers, came to rigid attention, and saluted sharply.

Carr returned it. "You speak English or Italian, Sergeant?" he asked.

"English, *Capitaine.*" The sergeant had an Egyptian accent.

Carr looked at the legionnaires. "Are these men all that's left of your command?"

"Yes, sir."

"From how many?"

"Forty-one, sir."

Carr glanced at Parnell, returned to the sergeant. "Are you declaring your garrison abandoned?"

"No, *Capitaine.* It is only temporarily inactive."

"What are your intentions, then?"

"We will return to Quargla, sir. Temporarily."

"But, in effect, that leaves your position unprotected."

"Not quite, sir. Our dead still stand guard mount."

Carr glanced at Parnell again. What? He searched for another question but couldn't think of one. Finally, he said, "You and your men can ride with us."

"That is not necessary, *Capitaine.*"

"But you have wounded and—"

He was interrupted by a sudden series of violent explosions inside the fort. Rock and strut poles and dust erupted into the morning sky. A powerful concussion wave swept past them. Coils of fire began flaring among the shattered buildings.

"Bloody hell." Carr sighed softly. The legionnaire sergeant was not looking at the fort. Instead, he watched the two officers with an expression of sly delight. Carr turned back to him. "Where is it, Sergeant?" he demanded brusquely.

"Where is what, sir?"

"You know bloody well what."

"But there is nothing in the fort, *Capitaine.*" A faint smile played across the legionnaire's lips. Was it contemptuous? "There never was," he said.

Carr stared at him. The sound of the fire increased,

roaring like high surf as the building remnants began blazing powerfully. White and brown smoke boiled skyward. Finally, the New Zealander shook his head with a sardonic chortle. "So it's all been a great waste of time, has it?"

"Yes, sir," the sergeant agreed. "But a bloody bit of fun, what?"

# Part Four
# Tunisia

By December's end, Mediterranean storms had turned the coastal plain of Tunisia into a sea of knee-deep mud. On both sides of the Allied-Axis front, even minor skirmishes got bogged down before they could really get started. The Germans still controlled the air and despite the heavy influx of American material, supplies reaching the forward units were far less than was needed. Eisenhower decided to break off all enemy contact in northern Tunisia until spring.

Attention now turned to the central part of the country where the weather was generally clearer and allowed operations to continue. It was a land of barren mountains and harsh, treeless valley-plains two hundred miles south of the coast.

The area was dominated by a range of mountains that rose out of the sea on the Cape Bon Peninsula and then split inland into two separate ranges, both running north-south. One was the Western or Gran Dorsal, the other the Eastern Dorsal.

Each was about 150 miles long and cut by numerous passes. A sixty-mile-wide plain lay between the two ranges, which eventually came together again in the south at the Great Chott El Jerid, a vast salt flat that lay a hundred miles due west of the Gulf of Gabes.

As the year 1943 opened, the Allied front had solidified

itself along the Eastern Dorsal. In order to create a single, unified control over the diverse Allied forces scattered along this main defense line, Ike had appointed British Lieutenant General Sir Kenneth Anderson as overall commander of all the units in Tunisia.

The northern sector just south of the coast was occupied by the British First Army; the center by the French XIX Corps; and the entire southern region of the mountains was guarded by the American II Corps under Major General Lloyd Fredendall.

General Anderson proved to be a stubborn, officious martinet who ruled with an iron hand, even issuing orders for his American troops down to company level. Fredendall and his deputy officers were outraged. U.S. Army policy had always left local tactical dispositions and decisions to local commanders. Friction between the British and American commands steadily increased until Eisenhower was forced to intercede. He finally decided to personally review his Dorsal Mountain units on 13 February.

Meanwhile, the Germans were experiencing similiar ego-driven dissension. Rommel and von Arnim, the two cocommanders in North Africa, were constantly questioning the orders of Feldmarschall Albrecht Kesselring, CinC of all German operations in and around the Mediterranean, and the Italian Commando Supremo in Rome. In addition, they were also engaged in a bitter personal tug-of-war over the placements of their own troops.

For two months, Rommel, suffering mounting ailments, had successfully brought his Afrika Korps across Libya and Cyrenaica ahead of Montgomery's Eighth Army. By early February, he had actually crossed the Tunisian frontier and set up strong defenses along the old French Mareth Line, anchoring his inland flanks on the southern Dorsal passes of El Guettar and Maknassy in the west and his ocean flank along the Gulf of Gabes to the east.

He was well aware he was facing American units in the southern Easterns. Still, he considered Montgomery the greater threat. As a result, he pressed Kesselring to order von Arnim to reassign large elements of his Tenth and Twenty-first Panzer Divisions to strengthen the Mareth perimeter. But the arrogant von Arnim, always jealous of the Desert Fox's fame, had other intentions. . . .

# Twenty

*Sbeitla, Tunisia*
*12 February 1943*

The Siliana Restaurant was housed in an eighty-year-old sandstone building that resembled a bordello in Navajo country with its whitewashed walls and red tile roof. Colonel Dunmore parked his jeep beside one already there in the rear of the building and he and Parnell got out and walked around to the front entrance.

After the icy rain, the interior felt uncomfortably warm. There was a large fire going in a hearth fashioned of Roman marble. The dining room had red-and-white curtains and picnic benches and French prints of the twenties on dark green walls. It was empty except for seven French officers sitting near the fireplace.

Colonel Monk Dikkson, chief intelligence officer for Lieutenant General Fredendall, sat alone near the front window. He waved them over. The owner nodded pleasantly to them. He was a fat, sweaty Frenchman with pommaded black hair parted down the middle. It made him look like the bass singer in a barbershop quartet. His wife was a complete contrast, thin as a stalk of winter corn with washed-out gray hair who dashed about the place with the stealthy swiftness of a mouse.

Dikkson was eyeing the French officers across the

room, a look of distaste on his face. He was six-six with a horsey shape to his features and peculiar orange-red hair. The Frenchmen were all quite drunk, repeatedly making loud toasts accompanied by Gallic marching songs and an occassional hurling of glasses against the back wall of the fireplace.

"You know something?" Dikkson said as Dunmore and Parnell sat down. "I do believe I've come to dislike the French. Always claiming to be so gracefully romantic. It's a batch of hog shit. They're damned near as patronizing as the fucking Limeys." His equine eyes now fixed on Parnell. "I hear you and your team are hotshots, Lieutenant. True?"

"Yes, sir, it is."

"Good answer. What are you boys drinking?"

Earlier, Dunmore had searched out Red at a huge supply depot on the outskirts of Sbeitla. Nearby were Roman ruins, marble pillars, and the remnants of amphitheaters among cactus and olive trees. He had come in from Algiers to liaison with Dikkson, who was visiting Sbeitla for a few days from Fredendall's HQ in Tebessa eighty miles away.

Dunmore said, "Make mine a beer, Monk."

"Lieutenant?"

"The same for me, sir."

It turned out to be rather pleasant, the three Americans chatting about home. Despite his scowly expression, Dikkson possessed a dry but bawdy wit. The food was excellant: omelets and goat meat with sweet potatoes and orange marmalade sauce.

Four days after the battle at the Ghorafa, Blue Team had been flown from Quargla to Algiers while Captain Carr and the remnants of his LRDG patrol turned east to reprovision at a desert drop zone and then head back across the Erg to join up with Montgomery's Eighth Army.

All through late December and early January, endless convoys of equipment and supplies had been coming into central Tunisia to replenish the American and British units manning the Allied defense line there. Dunmore was able to place Parnell and his men with the 178th Transport Battalion of the U.S. First Infantry Division as truck drivers, running from coastal depots to Sbeitla and Gafsa.

It was still raining when the three Americans left the Siliana, the air wet and sharply cold with fog lying between the buildings and feathering the olive trees. Dikkson nodded for Parnell to get into the backseat of his jeep. He and Dunmore followed him in.

The colonel took a moment to light a cigarette, then turned in his seat. "Okay, Lieutenant, here's the skinny. I want an area Priority Intelligence Requirement of the terrain east of Faid Pass. The Krauts're gonna hit us within the next ten days. I want some idea as to where."

He leaned out and spat onto the ground as a fresh deluge of rain came. Mist blew into the jeep. He returned to Red. "That imbecile Anderson's got our line stretched so thin out here a chicken could shoot shit through it. Now his goddamned Y Section tells him Enigma intercepts indicate the German strike's coming at Fondouk. They're wrong. It's going to come through the Faid Pass and Maizila. What I need is recon proof the Germans are massing east of us, not fifty miles to the north."

Parnell nodded.

"Understand this is strictly outside channels, Lieutenant. Anderson has his staff people stuck so far up our asses we can't bunk-fart without him requesting an indepth report on the stink."

"I see, Colonel."

"You and your men will report to a Captain Frank Theile at Sidi bou Zid by twenty-two hundred hours

tonight. He's McQuillin's G-Two. He'll requisition
whatever you need. Keep radio silence unless there's
something we *have* to know pronto. Remember, all your
reports go to Theile and *only* him. Your PSG gives you
five days for the operation with a limit of advance of
fifteen miles. If you think you can penetrate deeper,
do it." He pulled a brown envelope from his jacket and
handed it to Red. "As of now, your team's attatched to
Combat Command A. Welcome to Second Corps."

Moments later, standing beside the jeep, Parnell
snapped a brisk salute. "We'll get the job done for you, sir."

"I'm certain you will."

"You can use my vehicle," Dunmore told Red. He held
out his hand. "Good luck."

"Just don't get your ass overrun, Lieutenant," Dikkson
said. He started the jeep and roared off.

Captain Frank Theile turned out to be a handsome
devil, curly black hair, eyes the blue white of glacier ice.
Parnell found him playing poker in his field tent in CC-A's
main bivouac on the outskirts of Sidi bou Zid.

The small desert town was merely a collection of flat
sandstone buildings lit by flickering kerosene lanterns.
To the south and west of it were elements of the First Armored Regiment with their M-3 Stuarts and M-4 Shermans
in shallow revetments under camo netting.

The other officers in Theile's tent gave Red a silent up-
down. They all wore coats since the tent was freezing
despite two small gasoline heaters. It reeked of fumes, wet
canvas, and male crotch. Theile swore quietly and tossed
his cards down. Wordlessly, he rose and went outside. Parnell followed.

"You all look familiar, Lieutenant," Theile said. He
had a soft, honey-smooth southern accent. They walked

around the tent and climbed into a three-quarter-ton ammo carrier. "Detroit Lions, wasn't it?"

"Yes."

Theile chuckled without humor. "I lost a few bucks on you, fella." He started the engine and they drove slowly through the bivouac. Bird and the rest of the team followed in Dunmore's jeep, both vehicles using tiny blue headlights that cast faint, sapphirine auras into the fog.

The rain had stopped and there were patches of moonlight now. The fog percolated off the ground like fumes from dry ice. They passed rows of dark tents and antiaircraft emplacements. Nearby, to the east, loomed the ridges of the Eastern Dorsals etched with moon-glow.

The supply bunker was located underground, its walls made of newly poured cement and timbering. The air was crisp and rife with the smell of Cosmoline and pinewood. Red drew his weapons and ammunition along with a winter mackinaw, D-rations, chocolate bars, extra canteens of water, lensatic compasses, binoculars, watch cap, dust goggles, and a walkie-talkie.

The small portable radio ran on newly issued cadmium batteries and transmitted over in-between frequencies. All his messages would be nonverbal. Instead, he would use the walkie-talkie's transmit-listen switch to send click sequences that referred to specific code phrases. The phrases were on a plastic card taped to the radio case. Theile had assigned him the ominous code name Little Big Horn or LBH in Morse code.

While the rest of the team outfitted, he and Theile returned to the captain's tent. Theile shooed the other poker players out, pushed aside the cards and leather-cased field telephones, and spread out a map. It was a crude field map, five miles to the inch, which showed the present deployments of American units both in the Western and Eastern Dorsals and out in the flat country between.

Parnell studied it, focusing his attention on the Eastern Dorsal. The range contained seven main passes along its two hundred miles of mountainous terrain. They were Pichon, Fondouk, Faid, Maknassy/Sened Station, and El Guettar in the far south.

Theile pointed out Sidi bou Zid, which sat four miles southwest of the Faid Pass. "Our sector extends from Djebel Lessouda five miles north to Bir el Afey twenty miles southwest of us. To the west, it pivots at Sbeitla. Right here and here on these two mountaintops, Djebel Lessouda and Djebel Garet Hadid, are our infantry and artillery. First Armored's on Lessouda and the one-sixty-eighth Regimental Combat Team's on Hadid."

He moved the map slightly to highlight the ground east of the mountains. "This here's all floodplain, right out to the sea. About seventy miles. Basically it's as flat as a goddamned pool table with maybe a few scattered rock upcroppings. It's crisscrossed by drainage wadis and there are several small farming villages where the natives mostly live underground. When the Faid pass road leaves the mountains, it shoots straight for Sfax on the coast. About twenty miles out it junctions with two other roads. One goes north to Kairouan, the other south to Maknassy."

He swept his finger along an invisible line five miles east of the junction. "Right along here runs a north-south shelving escarpment. Thirty, thirty-five feet deep but four miles long. Beyond that line is where we think the Krauts have assembly areas. That's your Primary Task Objective."

He returned to the mountains. "You'll cross through a small pass at the base of Garet Hadid. It's called Ain Rebaou, right here. Just a little pissant goat trail, actually." He looked at Parnell from under his eyebrows. "I suggest you clear through fast and silent. Them boys in the one-sixty-eighth are right above you and they ain't been told you're coming through. They're green and jumpy as hell. You make too much noise, you can bet your ass you'll get ordnance down on you right quick."

"What about German defense works on the plain?" Red asked.

"We're pretty sure nothing significant. That we can see, at least. Our ridge posts hear a lot of mechanized stuff moving around at night. By morning, nothing's there. Not even tracks. The few air recons we've gotten also show zero. Either the pricks are reconning during the night and vacating the area before daylight, or they're massing and then going to ground. We think it's the latter."

"Minefields?"

"I'm pretty sure it's clear for at least five miles out. Beyond that . . ." He shrugged. "There might be antipersonnel charges in some of the wadis, though. Watch yourselves."

He took a few more minutes to go over the mission specs and radio procedure. Parnell's transmissions would be constantly monitored by a CC-A listening post on Dejebel Lessouda. From there they'd come directly to Theile.

It was a few minutes after eleven o'clock when the captain drove them the two miles to the mouth of their crossing point. The night sky was clearer now, the cold in the air bone-deep. Theile had to drive very slowly through a mined antitank field at the foot of the mountains but he did it totally from memory.

At 2340 hours, Blue Team entered Ain Rebaou.

The peculiar thing about the tiny pass was its vacuumed silence, as if Time itself had been locked down in there for centuries. It was a mere seam in the mountain, only as wide as a camel's shoulders. Once they got deep inside, the walls became sheer, sandstone cliffs with dark streaks of feldspar and quartz and occassional tufts of

Sudan grass growing sideways. On the trail were clusters of Jericho rose, free-rooted like tumbleweeds. Their leaves saturated the night with the scent of cinnamon.

The men trotted slowly in single file with a broken cadence, Laguna the first on point, Parnell bringing up the rear. The trail went up and down and curved around boulders but was generally clear and sufficiently illuminated by moonlight, which reflected off the walls. Twenty-two minutes later, the cliffs began to separate and they found themselves among tumble-rock formations and, soon after, on flat ground dotted with isolated stands of cactus.

The whole plain was visible now, a vast treeless prairie in moonlight with only tiny dotlets of light here and there to mark farmers' dwellings. Far out, the coastline was totally dark since all seaside towns were under Axis blackout watch. Only a silvery ribbon of ocean showed along the eastern horizon.

Exiting the crossing, Parnell set up a normal patrol overwatch formation with Bird now on point, Kimball and Weesay on his flanks, himself in the center with Cowboy, Smoker, and Horse to his rear, everybody's weapons still on safety but with rounds in their chambers.

They set off at a brisk trot toward the Faid Pass road. Once on it, they'd head due east since Red wanted to be ten miles out and under cover by 0430 hours.

# Twenty-one

Captain von Bekker stood at rigid attention and felt his neck reddening with a mounting sense of aggrieved impatience. He had been standing there for a full ten minutes. It was now 5:30 in the morning.

The room, a luxurious suite in the Hotel el-Menema on the outskirts of the holy city of Kairouan, was warm. Particularly so to him after his abominable ride from Sfax in an open military *Ladungwagen,* the only transport he had been able to grab on such short notice. Earlier that evening, he'd been rudely awakened by an orderly and told to appear before General von Arnim by midnight.

Despite daily requests to see the general, Gerd had been ignored for an entire month. He was desperate to explain to von Arnim the specific reasons for the humiliating debacle in the desert in which he had lost over half his command and nearly all his vehicles and guns.

It was totally due to the cowardice and incompetence of his men, he wanted to inform von Arnim. Especially that *arschloch,* Stracher, who had deliberately avoided informing him of all tactical exigencies and then had openly defied him by ordering a withdrawal of the force before their assault could be carried through. He would most certainly see to it that that man was stripped of his uniform and shot.

From the corner of his eye, he watched as the general dressed in his lavishly tiled bathroom, resplendent in field-gray Sturartillerie tunic and red-striped cavalry breeches tucked into glistening black top boots. With him was his orderly, a swarthy, Slavic-looking *Oberstleutnant*.

At last the general emerged, striding forth, his boots making whispery leather sounds in the silence. The orderly left, closing the door without a sound. Taking no notice of Bekker, Von Arnim moved to the window and gazed out. Stretching beyond the broad Avenue el-Moez ibn Badis, which ran by the hotel, was a large open ground now filled with elements of the Tenth Panzer, dark steel objects in the foggy dawn light.

At last, he turned and surveyed Gerd loweringly. A minute passed. Another. The faint sounds of machinery came through the window overlaid with the nasal voice of a muezzin calling the faithful to the first morning prayer.

Bekker could bear it no longer. He said, "Herr General, I would like to explain the incident at Ghoraffa. May I stand relaxed?"

"No," von Arnim barked.

"But it was not my fault, sir. You must understand. My men fled when we were struck unexpectedly by a force I was not told was present."

The general's eyes narrowed, glinting. "Fled?"

"Yes, sir. After we were taken from the rear, the men panicked. They had no steel, they turned like frightened women. My entire attack lost its integrity. When I attempted to recover, Leutnant Stracher countermanded my orders. He is a coward and—"

"Silence!" von Arnim roared suddenly. In three quick paces, he was standing directly in front of Gerd, eyes blazing, one cheek aquiver. "You dare insult fine German soldiers and a splendid young officer?" He seemed too outraged to continue. Instead, he hissed contemptuously through his teeth and moved away.

Bekker had thought he would strike him and had actually drawn back, his face drained, his head throbbing with sudden, shocked indignation. "Sir, I must protest—"

"I said be silent."

Von Arnim paced agitatedly about the room as the muezzin's call gently faded away. Once he paused beside an ornate desk of rosewood, distractedly picked up a riding crop. He studied the leather loop at its end. He said, "This is not a Bavarian salon, Bekker." He had pointedly left out the von before Gerd's name. "We are no longer playing at war with fencing sabers. You apparently have been unable to make this progression. Instead, you've proven yourself unfit to wear the uniform of a German soldier."

Gerd's face went stiff. His heart pounded.

Von Arnim returned to the window, looked out. Daylight was stronger now, with it came a thickening of the fog. "It's only for the sake of your family I'm not having you shot. Although I have no doubt they would prefer it." He swung around. "Instead, you are to accompany me when I meet with Rommel at El Ayoun. I'm reassigning you to the generalfeldmarschall's personal bodyguard." His eyes filled with a dark mockery. "You may go and be an insult to *his* command."

Bekker's response was almost a shout: "Sir, I formally request to be returned to my squadron."

"Denied." Von Arnim slashed the riding crop against his thigh. It sounded like a baseball smacking into a pillow. "Get out of my sight. I abhor the stench of cowardice before breakfast."

Trembling with rage and shame, Bekker withdrew.

\* \* \*

Last night, Parnell had sensed that somebody else was with them up on the rocky mound, a feeling in his belly. The seventy-foot-high mound on which he was hiding covered about two acres, its surfaces smoothed into curves by the wind with piles of tumble rock rimming its base.

He, Cowboy, and Smoker had come up onto it in the predawn darkness, feeling their way with their boots until they crossed a goat trail and followed it to a shallow wind-formed hollow that contained several caves deep enough to shelter them.

He had chosen one while Fountain and Wineberg took another farther downslope. His cave was deep enough for him to stretch out. Crawling in in the darkness, he'd worried about snakes and finally had to switch on his tiny vest light to check. It merely contained scattered piles of rock-hard goat turds and the remains of old campfires.

Exhausted, he'd slept until the sun woke him as it rose out of the sea. He immediately began glassing the landscape to the east. It lay out there purple and silver orange with nothing moving except hawks scouting the wadis.

He suddenly heard the tinkle of metal and the murmur of voices from somewhere above him. Someone was coming down the trail. He eased his Thompson up onto his thigh. Boots knocked against rocks and then a man sighed and began to softly sing a German tune. It was a Kraut soldier relieving himself.

There actually was an enemy outpost on the top of the rock, Parnell realized with a jolt. He held himself absolutely still. The man was so close he could actually smell his feces. After several long minutes, the soldier went back up the trail. Parnell cursed. Now they'd be forced to remain in their caves until dark.

As the sun climbed higher, the plain began to define

itself in clearer tones. Irrigation ditches and flood wadis were everywhere, forming a complex patchwork of straight lines and angles. Large sections of land were under tillage and the scattered farming villages looked like tiny, isolated oases. The rest of the flat country was covered in deep grass and cacti clusters.

He could faintly make out the escarpment line Theile had mentioned. Beyond it, there seemed to be a lot of ground activity now, dark objects moving along a ragged front of at least a mile in length. Dust clouds lifted from it into the sky, looking dark brown against the fresh new sunlight. To the south were more dust clouds.

He picked up his walkie-talkie, thumbed the volume down, and began tapping the transmit-listen key. But to his own ear, its clicks were too loud. He stuck it under his mackinaw and tapped out his ID code, paused, then sent a coded message: *heavy activity twenty miles east and south of Faid . . . possible armor assembly area.* He sent it twice, then switched off and took up his binoculars again.

His stomach felt tight. Something was in the wind.

A mile to the north, Weesay Laguna lay under a smoke tree beside a deep wadi. Next to him was stretched Kaamanui, binoculars to his eyes as he glassed a small farming village three hundred yards off. There were crop fields between them and the village. The fields were winter-fallow now, containing only wild esparto grass.

The village itself looked like a prairie dog town filled with holes and mounds of dirt where its residents lived underground. There were a few date palms and fig trees but the only human structures visible were a tiny white mosque and a triple-storied grain silo as shapeless as a child's mud hill with palm trunks stuck into its sides for steps and a tiny straw shack on the top.

Weesay shifted his belly. He was already sweating in his tanker's mackinaw, which was now topped by a heavy desert-colored poncho. Earlier, they'd sighted the tracks of motorized vehicles and motorcycles in the roads and fields around the village, the steep angle of the rising sun throwing them sharply into shadow. Now they were completely invisible.

Native cooking fires had started soon after first light, the earth seeping smoke. Men and young boys in long gowns came out of the ground leading camels and small flocks of black and white sheep, which they herded southward. Soon black-veiled women began hauling big stone jugs of water from the village's single well.

*"Maldito,"* Wessay hissed angrily. "I got bugs in my fuckin' clothes, meng."

"What can I say?" Kaamanui chuckled. "They like chili meat, *tipo.*"

"How come they don' like Samoan meat?"

"Too dark."

Laguna snorted.

The increasing discomfort of the heat made him recall the coolness of the previous night as the patrol moved along the Faid-Sfax road, everybody's boots hitting the ground in unison to keep good time and the sky completely clear with its stars big as bullet holes showing hot light beyond. The road was wide and gravel-covered except where they crossed flood wadis, and there it narrowed to the crossings of stone and gravel. Fog trapped down in the ravines looked like gray whipped cream.

Parnell had halted them outside the village and split the patrol. He sent Wyatt and Kimball a mile to the north, Weesay and Horse toward the village, while he, Fountain, and Smoker veered south and headed for the rock mound. The thing looked like the back of a huge white whale surfaced on a moonlit sea. From it, Red figured he'd be able to observe the entire eastern escarpment once the sun rose.

A bug skittered over Weesay's right testicle. It felt to him like the tip of a feather. He swore, started to say something. But Sol suddenly leaned into his binoculars and growled, "Watch it."

Weesay instantly lifted his head to scan the village. He spotted something. A figure had just stepped out of the silo's straw shack, a man. He squinted hard at him. The man was dressed in a brown tunic and breeches. It was a German soldier.

*Oh, yeah,* Weesay thought, *artillery spotters. . . .*

It was dusk now and the light was like a blue glow inside Parnell's cave. He had just come up out of sleep in a flash, abruptly awake as if he had stepped from hot to cold. He lay with the side of his face in cave dust, fine as baking soda, listening. Only the sound of wind, hissing through crevices.

Finally he sat up and picked up his binoculars. He looked to the east but couldn't see much in the dim light, only scattered dust swirls kicked up by the rising wind. *Well,* he thought, *at least they'll have decent cover on tonight's march.* That was good. He intended to push everyone hard. He was determined to reach the escarpment before dawn and get a good solid look at what was going on down below its rim.

Through most of the day he had watched the plain. A lot of movement and activity continued. After the encounter with the soldier, he'd heard nothing more from the German outpost above him. Then at one o'clock in the afternoon, a pair of American Lockheed P38F Lightnings appeared, hugging the earth and headed east, obviously looking to get surveillence photos. As he watched, they were engaged by six enemy aircraft. Both Americans were promptly shot down. One exploded into a ball of orange flame from which came a chute. But it was on fire and had plummeted disjointedly to the earth.

He flicked on his vest light, checked his watch: 6:39. Darkness was nearly here. It was time to move. He gathered his gear and crawled out into a hot wind.

At 2310 hours, a small convoy of three American M-13 half-tracks and a Chevrolet staff car rumbled to a dust-blown stop before CC-A's headquarters tent in Sidi bou Zid. Aboard the armored vehicles was a platoon of specially trained cavalry troopers. From the staff car stepped General Dwight D. Eisenhower and his chief deputy commander, Colonel Red Akers. Both officers disappeared into the tent.

Ike had started his inspection tour with the First Infantry Division, which held the northernmost part of the American sector in the Eastern Dorsal. He then went on to General Fredendall's II Corps headquarters in Tebessa.

At both locations he had been shocked and disgusted. He learned that Fredendall, timidly hiding his entire headquarters underground, had never once visited his own frontline troops, and had actually been deploying his forces solely by map and radio. That, coupled with General Anderson's constant interference, had created an extremely dangerous situation.

Determined to get a handle on it, Eisenhower decided to inspect *every* frontline unit, no matter how long it took him. Thus far, he'd also seen and spoken to the men and commanders of the Thirty-fourth Infantry and First Armored Divisions, which occupied positions from Sbeitla to Gafsa in the south. He found the entire area extremely susceptible to attack. By the time he reached Sidi bou Zid, he was in an ass-kicking mood.

Wordlessly, he studied CC-A's tactical deployment map while junior officers stood nervously about and the unit's commander, Brigadier General Raymond McQuillin, pointed out his own force dispositions. Finally, Ike leaned forward, his face and eyes hard, his high forehead gleaming in the light.

"This will *not* do," he said with barely suppressed rage. "You've got untrained troops in key positions, for God's sake. Here and here. And Waters's units on Lessouda and Drake's on Hadid would be useless if the Germans broke through the Faid and engaged you on flat ground. They're even too far apart to support each other."

Utterly dismayed, he turned and strode outside. Aker and McQuillin followed. Ike stood looking up at the great dark mass of the Eastern Dorsal, its ridges framed against the stars and the moonlight. The gusty wind made the tent tremble and groan and fluttered the collars of his short jacket.

Without turning, he said to McQuillin, "The American people will take a helluva lot from me. But *this* crap they would never tolerate." He turned, glowering. "Your defenses are totally unacceptable, General. By oh-six-hundred tomorrow, you will receive new disposition orders. Be ready to execute them immediately."

Without another word, he pivoted, strode to his staff car, and climbed in. It immediately sped away with the half-tracks rumbling after it into the night.

Unfortunately, his new orders were already too late. . . .


The wind smelled sour as if it had passed over fields of molding manure. It blew hot and hard, dust particles and small pebbles colliding against Blue Team's clothing, pinging off their storm goggles. It was 3:25 in the morning.

They were still on the Sfax road, making even better time than last night, a steady trot, Bird again on point, the others formed out a bit tighter so as to keep each other within hearing distance in the dust and wind.

Twice Parnell had called short halts to rest and figure their positions using star azimuths, the stars overhead still visible through the blowing dust. He calculated they were about four miles from the plain's main escarpment.

Suddenly, he heard Bird give the halt whistle. Everyone stopped, went to a knee. A few seconds later, Wyatt came running out of the darkness. "Somethin's comin', Lieutenant." He spoke over the wind. "I'm gettin' heavy ground vibrations. Feels like armor."

Red immediately ordered the team off the road, out into open plain. Completely dispersed, they went to earth. The grass felt warm from the wind. Parnell and Bird lay next to each other. "I've heard dogs howling for the last hour," Parnell said.

Wyatt nodded. "The ground shakes're spookin' hell outta the farm animals." He paused, rolling spittal through his teeth. He spat. "I don't like the looks of this, Lieutenant."

Soon they could hear motors clearly, the rapid, steely clanking of tractor treads. Hooded headlights appeared, a single pair coming through the dust, their soft blue glow making the particles sparkle.

Abruptly, a German armored car hurtled past, throwing stones. Directly behind it was a half-track, so close its headlights illuminated the after slope of the AC ahead of it. A second armored car blew out of the darkness and then another AC, all of them going at least fifty miles an hour. Gradually, their noise got sucked back into the moaning of the wind.

Red checked his watch: 3:37. He leaned close to Bird. "You spot the ensign on the back of those ACs?"

Wyatt nodded. "Eagles and oak clusters. That's Luft-waffe."

"Those bastards're forward air spotters." He looked back toward the east, felt his groin grip up. Whatever this was, it was looking to be big.

He slapped Bird's shoulder. "I'm going to radio Theile. Reform the men. We're still trying for that escarpment. But tell them to keep a sharp lookout." Bird scurried off.

Thirty-one minutes later, all hell broke lose.

# Twenty-two

At precisely 0408 hours of 14 February 1943, Valentine's Day, a heavy German artillery barrage opened against American positions on the Eastern Dorsal at the Faid and Maizila passes, big 155mm and 175mm field howitzers firing from emplacements beyond the eastern escarpment.

Soon after, while the barrage continued and their movement was hidden by the dust storm, crack elements of von Arnim's Tenth and Twenty-first Panzer Divisions hurled themselves at the passes in an offensive attack code-named *Fruehlingswind* or Spring Wind. Spearheading the assault were the huge Mark VI Tigers of the 591st Tiger Detachment. Behind them on echelon flank came the Mark IIIs and IVs of the Seventh and Eighty-sixth Panzer Grenadier regiments. Last were half-tracks and APCs crammed with mobile infantry regiments, and finally field artillery units.

As dawn slowly tinted the mountain peaks, the Tigers were nearing both passes. Suddenly the artillery barrage ceased. But the attack was immediately picked up by night-capable Stukas, which began dive-bombing U.S. ridge positions and the plain surrounding Sidi bou Zid.

Second Corp's defensive line in the Easterns rapidly began to crumble. Within two hours of the massive assault, Allied units were already executing a withdrawal. The Germans crossed through both passes and quickly took Sidi bou Zid, thereby cutting off the American units on Djebel Lassouda and Djebel Garet Hadid.

In the south, Rommel, at first enraged by von Arnim's unexpected strike, which had actually been scheduled for 18 February, quickly recognized a tactical opportunity. He instantly ordered attacks against American forces in Gafsa and sent strong recon and parachute infantry units twenty miles north to the key Allied airfields at Feriana and Thelepte.

Over the next three days, the massive Allied retreat degenerated into a rout. Mile after mile of exhausted, bedraggled infantrymen, trucks, mobile guns, hospital vans, engineering carriers, and armor fled toward the Sbiba and Kasserine passes of the Western Dorsal. Behind them, they left burning towns and dynamited supply dumps, burnt-out tanks and dead men. Thousands of U.S and British stragglers, cut off from their units, desperately tried to regain their lines, evading German patrols hunting them with dogs.

For Blue Team, the lightning shock of that black, windswept predawn attack had hit them like a hurricane. . . .

The barrage sounded like a clap of rolling thunder, very close, the individual muzzle explosions separated by nanoseconds, coming from left to right like sequenced fuses going off so rapidly they created a single roaring in the wind. The heavy shells whinnied and hissed overhead.

Parnell's first thought was: *We're closer to the escarpment than I figured.* His second thought: *Armor's coming! We've got to get the hell away from this road.*

Bird appeared through the dust, skidded in on one knee. Right behind him was Kaamanui. The three men huddled for a moment, shouting at each other, leaning close. The ground shook with concussion waves.

"We have to move," Red called out. "To the right. Move to the right. Follow me."

The two sergeants disappeared into the dusty gloom. Parnell twisted, saw a trooper nearby. It was Wineberg. He slapped his leg. Smoker instantly rose, grinning, his dust goggles looking like an insect's eyes. *Crazy bastard,* Red thought.

He paused, felt his body pumping hard. In a few seconds, the entire team came up, dark shapes. He pushed to his feet, turned, and ran to the right, down the slight embankment, sprinting through knee-high grass. He reached an irrigation ditch, checked it. It was too shallow. He ran on, directly into the wind now.

They were into a fallow field, the ground hard-packed. He paused, listening. He heard engines revving, the distinctive clanking of tank treads. *Oh, Jesus!* He started off again, came to another, deeper ditch. It was two feet deep with pebbles in the bottom. *Too wide, too wide.* The earth began to shake more violently.

Red lights appeared in the murk. They seemed to be coming straight at him. "Down! Down!" he screamed and hurled himself into the ditch, pressed his body down as hard as he could into the pebbles.

Twenty feet to his right an enormous black shape rushed out of the darkness. He watched it flash past, felt the heat of its exhaust, smelled the sharp odor of oil and hot metal sweeping past in the wind. He lifted his head higher, was aware of his heart racing, aware of a wild, delirious fear that struck him high in the stomach like an electric shock.

More red lights came, bursting into visibilty, twin dots, this time no distortion, bearing down on him in full throttle. He felt the wind buffet off its broad metal front.

Moving on instinct and terror, he spun his body so that he was lying across the ditch, facing the approaching monster.

The tank passed directly over him, the rumbling, slamming clangor of its treads so close, *right there!* its black underbelly passing so swiftly, so near above his face that the storm wind was blocked for an instant. Then it was gone, past him, its stern lights swallowed by the darkness.

He heard other tanks crossing in the storm. Then a sudden lull. He crawled back along the ditch, reached a man. He shoved his face close to him, shouted, "You okay?" The man nodded. It was Kimball. He moved on, going over churned-up areas in the ditch, the dirt formed into tread impressions.

Everyone was all right. He reached Bird. "That was the assault wave," Red yelled. "The next one's gonna hit us real quick. We better move."

Wyatt squinted his eyes behind the goggles. "I think we'd best stay where we're at, Lieutenant. We leave this ditch, they could catch us out in the grass."

Parnell pulled back his lips. Bird was right. There was no way of knowing the actual width of the assault front, whether or not they'd be able to get beyond it before the next wave. If the tanks caught them in grass, they wouldn't be able to see the bastards coming. *Too risky, too risky.*

"All right, we'll stay put till the armor's past. Come with me." He and Bird went back up the ditch, informing each man to hold ground, keep a sharp eye, let the goddamned things pass over them. It was scary shit but workable. Then they waited tensely, blood pounding in their ears.

Five minutes later, the second wave of tanks moved through them, these blowing past with even greater speed, their engines a higher pitch, Mark IIIs and IVs, bounding forward all around them. Everybody hunkered down, stretched along the ditch, jerking and dodging from side to side, anticipating, like rats in a hole.

Parnell peered desperately out into the blowing dust. The fear was back, tight as a strap around his chest, with it visions of himself, the others, going under treads, ground into— He forced them away. *Watch, watch.*

Time seemed to fold over on itself and come back around at them, as if they were trapped in a dark cage that tilted up and over, up and over. Engines revved on different levels, different distances, and the metallic clanking cracked through the wind.

At last, they too were gone, leaving only the endless thunder of the guns. Parnell waited. He looked up. Beyond the mist of the dust storm the stars shone with a softer, less-sparkly gleam, the sky now sheening over with the first, faint fusion of dawn.

He stood up, hollering, and headed off down the ditch once more, running, knowing that they had to find solid cover before daylight.


The old Tunisian stood beside a palm tree, his hooded kaffiyeh pure white. It whipped against his body. He stared as Parnell came running out of the darkness straight toward him, but did not seem afraid.

Minutes earlier, the team had reached a weir made of stones with a rusty metal gate. The ditch beyond it was deeper. Grass grew along its edges and smaller feeder ditchs branched off. Dogs began barking nearby and Red realized they were near a village.

The artillery barrage ceased abruptly, like the shutting of a door. In the sudden half silence the frantic howling of the dogs was clear now, with it the roar of machinery far away, distant explosions.

Gray light melted through the dust. Other sounds came like the keenings of the wind, but higher, sharper. They suddenly reminded Red of the eerie cries of mountain lions in the Colorado Rockies. But he knew these sounds were coming from German Stukas dive-bombing Allied positions to the west.

Parnell finally saw the Tunisian and stopped short, swung up his Thompson. Sol came up behind him. The old man stared at them both. Nobody moved. Finally, Parnell waved at him. *"Ami,"* he yelled. *"Ami."*

The Tunisian came slowly along the edge of the ditch. He was tall, angular, and moved with a cautious grace. He said something in French. Red shook his head, twisted the lapel of his mackinaw to show the small American flag patch sewn inside. *"Americaine,"* he shouted above the noise. *"Americaine."*

The old man's expression changed from suspicion to surprise and then delight. He grinned, bowing, his hands crossed before his face, palms out, a sign of friendship. *"Ah, oui, Americaine,"* he cried. *"Presidon' Roos'velt et Tom Mix."*

Red chuckled. "Yeah, *Tom Mix.*" He tapped his fingers against his mouth. *"Anglais?* You speak *Anglais?"*

The man shook his head. His grin went away. He grimly swept his arms wide. *"Les Allemandes et Italiennes sont partout, mon ami,"* he said. *"Son tres dangereux!"* He indicated that Parnell should follow him. *"Allez, allez, sil vous plait. Depeche toi!"*

"Watch it, Lieutenant," Kaamanui said. "We don't know we can trust these fucking A-rabs."

Red considered. It was almost dawn. He knew he had to gamble. He turned, called to the man behind Sol. It was Smoker, who came up quickly. To Kaamanui he said, "If we ain't back in five minutes, head south and find

cover. After dark, try to get back to our lines. We'll follow if we can."

Sol hesitated a moment, then nodded. "Right, Lieutenant."

Red and Wineberg followed the Tunisian along the
ditch. A hundred yards on they left it and crossed a section of knee-high grass. Date palms merged out of the
dust. The wind seemed to be slackening now. In the lulls
between gusts they could hear the faraway clamor of a
big battle.

They crossed a road and went along a narrow pathway,
the two Americans going alertly, weapons ready. A
square hole appeared beside the path. It had a ramp that
led down into a sunken courtyard which contained a
small fig tree and several tall, white jars like Greek amphorae. A blue door in one wall of the courtyard led into
an underground dwelling.

They passed a second sunken courtyard, then a third.
This one the Tunisian went down into. He paused at the
door, looking back, and then went inside. They followed,
entering a large room. It was very neat with an arched
whitewashed ceiling made of bricks. The air smelled of
olive branch smoke and animal dung.

Several doorways led to other rooms. The floor was
packed dirt, and cooking utensils and bottles were hung
on the walls. Two wooden bed frames with palm leaf
straw and blankets stood near a small fireplace. The light
came from three bronze oil lamps.

The Tunisian lowered himself swiftly to the floor, sat
there cross-legged, inviting them to do the same. He offered earthen cups of a dark tea with small blocks of raw
sugar. The tea was thick and smelled like cloves. From
somewhere hidden, they could hear the grumbling
belches of camels, a goat's bleat as the old man started
talking, rapidly, waving his arms. His face looked angry.

After a moment, Smoker dipped his head. "You gettin' any of this, Lieutenant?"

"Some. But not enough."

He was thinking: *Maybe we can use this old boy. But how do I communicate with him?* He wondered if anyone in the team spoke French. He didn't know. *Wait a minute, maybe college-boy Kimball might.* "Get the others here," he told Wineberg. "Post guards on the trails and send Kimball down."

The Virginian *did* know some French, a few words and phrases a French nanny had taught him in between romps in her bed when he was in prep school. Still, he and the Tunisian had to struggle along, Kimball using gestures and pidgin French.

After a few minutes, he turned to Parnell. "His name's Ajim bin Zarzi, Lieutenant. He's a Matmata sheik, a local big shot. Hates the Germans and Italians. Something about his crops and slaughtered animals. He says he was a soldier, some outfit called the Zlass horsemen."

"What do you think? Can we trust him?"

Kimball studied the Tunisian. "I think so, sir. In fact, I kind of like the old bastard. He's got a way, you know?"

"Find out if he'll help us get back to our lines."

Kimball asked, speaking slowly, repeating, making the Tunisian talk slowly, too. "He says yes. He can take us as far as the mountain ridges, him and his brother. But they won't go any further. The other plain's run by another tribe. The Jaghbab. He says he can disguise us as desert hunters."

"When can we leave?"

Kimball asked Zarzi. "Dawn," he translated.

"Tell him to get ready."

Dawn pushed out the darkness as gradually as the fade-in of a movie, the dust still blowing but visibility advancing steadily. Zarzi sent one of his women to fetch his brother. She hurried away like a shadow in a black-and-white *bakhnouq* shawl.

The team refilled their canteens from one of the water amphorae and soon the old man's brother arrived. He was a younger version of Ajim. His name was Banju. He brought keffiyehs for each of them. They too were white and made of coarse cotton that smelled of male body odor.

The men pulled them on over their uniforms and then darkened their faces and hands with mud. Ajim passed out dark glasses to those with light-colored eyes. Dark glasses were worn by most desert men. Meanwhile, Banju brought up their camels. There were seven in all, narrow-legged Arabians, beige-colored with single humps. They growled and spat.

As more solid light came, the small caravan set out, moving in single file with Ajim in the lead. He carried a long flintlock rifle with silver scrolling on the barrel and a flyswatter to prod his camel. The animals wore colorful blanket-saddles and tasseled reins and they trudged along slowly with a double gait. The wind had stopped completely. Soon, swarms of large black flies lifted off the ground to torment the men.

All day they headed south. Around them moved endless enemy columns headed toward the mountains, long lines of supply trucks and artillery caissons and infantry in personnel carriers. The sounds of battle went on for hours and finally tapered off by ten in the morning. But the German Stukas continued working the flat country between the two ranges.

At dusk another fierce battle erupted, apparently an Allied counterattack. But it ended quickly. Soon after, Ajim called a halt. They were now midway between the

Maizila and Maknassy passes, he told Kimball, about ten
miles east of the mountains.

Night came on swiftly while they ate: goat jerky and
blocks of pungent cheese. Overhead, the stars looked
cold and there was a half-moon. Then they mounted
again and turned toward the Eastern Dorsal, moving at
a gallop now.

It took two hours to reach the lower slopes. Above them
loomed high ridges as barren as gigantic sand dunes.
Along the mountain base were heaps of residual boulders
that appeared like old gravestones in the moonlight.

From here on the younger Banju guided them while
old Ajim remained with the animals. Parnell wanted to
give him something for risking his life but he had nothing to spare. Ajim seemed to understand and simply
wished them well. They took off their kaffiyehs and followed Banju up through the tumble rock.

The moon made shadows as stark as ink drawings.
Higher and higher they went along narrow trails, Banju as
agile as a goat. They passed through narrow defiles that
smelled of phosphates and across sloped, open ground
dotted with twenty-foot cacti and patches of foxtail brush.

The night grew colder and their lungs stung gently
from the menthol-like bite of the frosty air. Twice artillery
barrages started up, the heavy booming of 155mm howitzers and the sharper, high-velocity cracks of German
88mms.

By one o'clock in the morning, they had reached a
point two hundred yards below the main ridge. Up here
were thin stands of conifer, the air spiked with the sharp
scent of pine. Banju silently pointed out a faded trail that
continued upslope. Then, wordlessly, he turned and
headed back, darting like a ghost among the rocks.

Parnell and Bird went up alone and lay down on the
east side of the crest to survey the western plain far

below. It was alive with lights and movement, the controlled activity of a victorious army.

Red glassed the long sweep of it. He saw resting tank crews and heavy Panzerjagers or tank hunters, reserve troop formations, and vast assemblies of supply units and artillery batteries beyond Sidi bou Zid, all the way to Sbeitla and down to Bir el Afey. Scattered out on the plain were small fires from still-burning tanks and battle gear.

He could only stare in disbelief. How could things have changed so quickly? Beside him, Bird said nothing. He simply turned his head aside and spat. It was comment enough. Red felt a sharp, hollow sense of despair. *No time for that,* he cautioned himself. He tapped Wyatt's arm and they walked back down the slope where the others gathered around them.

"It looks like the Krauts control the whole plain," he said grimly. "No telling where our own lines are. If there are any left. I'd think probably back near the Westerns. That's sixty miles away." He scanned their dark, solemn faces. "For now, we wait. Get as much sleep as you can. When we move, we're going to do it fast."

He sent them farther down the ridge to set up their patrol base in a stand of pines. While Bird assigned rotating two-man security teams, Parnell returned to the ridge and took the first watch.

# Twenty-three

*Generalfeldmarschall* Erwin Rommel was livid. He paced about, snapped harshly at his senior staff officers. He was at his forward field headquarters on the heights above Gafsa. It was now nearly 9:00 in the morning. He had just returned from an inspection of his Fifth Light Regiment and Third Reconnaissance Battle Group, which had advanced beyond Gafsa and was now heading north toward the big Allied depot town of Feriana.

Although the Desert Fox might have overlooked von Arnim's jumping the gun on their agreement to mount a coordinated attack on the eighteenth, he could not tolerate the arrogant fool's continued refusal to release elements of the Tenth and Twenty-first Panzers to him. He considered it an unforgivably grave strategic error that would create a loss of precious momentum in the attack.

Since von Arnim's initial thrust had been so astoundingly successful, Rommel had ordered that they continue the attack. He wanted to push the Allies completely back through the Western Dorsal and then all the way to Bone on the Algerian coast. From there, German forces could strike at the vulnerable rear of the British Fifth Army and easily shove it into the sea.

When von Arnim refused to cooperate, Rommel was stunned. How could his cocommander be capable of such *blodheit*, such blind idiocy? His own instincts and that mysterious thing his men called his *fingerspitzenge-fuhl,* which meant a deep sense for the battlefield recoiled at such wasted opportunity. Still, for now, all he could do was wait until Kesselring interceded.

At precisely 0913 hours, into this heated atmosphere strode Captain Gerd von Bekker. The huge HQ tent was filled with officers and map and sand tables, field telephones, power units, and portable *feldfernschriebers* or teletypes. Everyone moved about with intense energy. At the moment, Rommel, in his signature high-peaked field cap with desert goggles up on its visor, was poring over a collection of air recon photos.

Bekker stood around not knowing whom to approach. His uniform was disheveled and smelled of garlic and rotten wine. For the last two days he'd been desperately trying to reach Rommel's sector, having missed him in Kairouan. Then von Arnim had abandoned him there. He'd finally managed to catch a ride with a company of grimy Italian service troops who had wandered aimlessly along the coast while they devoured purloined garlic sausages and putrid wine.

He finally decided to approach a colonel seated at a folding table. He braced, clicked his heels sharply. "Captain Gerd von Bekker reporting as personally ordered by General-Oberst von Arnim, sir."

The colonel's head jerked up. He was built like a tree trunk and was deeply tanned, his hair made white blond by the sun. He gave Gerd a frigid up-down. "Personal orders?"

"Yes, sir."

"To what purpose?"

"Reassignment to the feldmarschall's bodyguard."

The colonel continued to stare. Then his eyes went suddenly narrow. He grunted. "Von Bekker, is it?"

"Yes, sir."

"I see. Wait outside."

Bekker stood between the tents. The sky was thickly overcast and there was an icy fog across the plain. Occasionally, a surge of rain rattled against the tents and the numerous command cars and half-tracks parked among them. An artillery barrage was going somewhere beyond Gafsa. The muzzle flashes glittered and shimmied in the fog.

He had to wait twenty minutes. At last, an orderly summoned him. He hurried to the entrance of the HQ tent and stepped through. His uniform dripped onto the wooden floor. Rommel was still studying maps and photos with several of his senior officers. Gerd inhaled deeply and approached, paused behind the field marshal at rigid attention.

He waited. Everyone around the table ignored him. Long minutes passed. He began to sweat, feeling humiliated. Abruptly, Rommel broke off reading maps, turned, and walked past him to the tent's entrance. He stood looking out at the rain.

Confused, Bekker followed him.

Rommel didn't say anything. Finally, he chuckled to himself and remarked, "Von Arnim plays a prank on me, eh?"

"Sir?"

Rommel turned his head. He had dark, steady eyes, a thin mouth. "Why did it happen?"

Gerd could not look into his eyes. Instead, he fixed his focus between them. "I don't understand, sir."

"Ghoraffa."

The words went into Bekker like a sliver of ice. *He knows, he knows. What can I say? Lie?* No! You did not lie to *this* man. "I was inexperienced and made a fatal error, sir," he blurted. "I allowed my rear to become exposed."

"Fatal, indeed," Rommel said coldly. "Now you come here. Why?"

"I wish the opportunity to regain my honor, Herr *Feldmarschall.*"

Rommel stared. Time seemed to pause. Gerd heard all the surrounding sounds coming separately at him. Yet he was aware only of Rommel's narrow, clean face. A single droplet of perspiration slid down his chest.

"That is *your* motive, Captain," the field marshal said at last. "I'm certain von Arnim's is quite different." He flicked his hand. "So be it. You may remain. I will, of course, expect you to prove him wrong."

Bekker felt a rush of pure pleasure and relief. "Thank you, Herr *Feldmarschall.* I—" But Rommel had already moved briskly past him, dismissing him in both mind and presence.


Blue Team had awakened to an icy rain. The drops that filtered down through the thin pines formed a delicate mist. The entire plain to the west was covered in a blanket of fog like a white sea in which the faraway ridges of the Westerns looked gray-colored like round-topped islands, floating.

On their ridge, Parnell conferred with Bird and Kaamanui. "I'm considering splitting up. Twos and threes. We'd have better odds that some of us'd get through. Thoughts?"

Wyatt squeezed his eyes together. A muscle gripped and eased under the thick leatheryness of his jawline. "We'd lose maximum firepower, Lieutenant."

"Yes."

"We was trained to operate as a unit. I say we do jes' that."

Red turned to Kaamanui. "Horse?"

"I go along with Wyatt, Lieutenant. We all make it, or we all don't."

Parnell smiled. "That's what I figured you'd say. I agree completely." He looked up at the sky and sighed. "If we're lucky, maybe this overcast'll hold up. As cold as it is, the fog'll return as soon as it gets dark." He rose. "Let everybody get a few more hours of sleep. We'll start working our way down to the lower slopes around noon."

The two sergeants nodded, stood up, and moved back down to the trees.

Laguna lay with his head against bare rock, sandstone that smelled vaguely familiar. Like wet chicken feed? Yeah, he remembered now: kid-time in L.A. and his uncle Luis, who lived in El Cajon and who raised chickens, with his *piojosa* house always smelling of bird shit and souring chicken feed. Just like this rock. . . .

They had heard the small German patrol a half hour before anybody actually saw its men slowly toiling up the slope, five soldiers in dirty tropical grays and soup-pot helments carrying wooden boxes strapped to their backs. It was an artillery spotter crew up here to set up a ranging post.

Parnell had decided to set up an ambush, then use the German weapons and uniforms to get through the enemy lines. He chose a perfect site for it, a narrow defile that broached out onto flat rocky ground where the Krauts would have to enter the killing zone one at a time.

The team had been deployed in complete silence, Red giving his commands by hand signal. Each man moved with quick precision, Sol and Smoker downslope as security with the main assault force up higher, hidden along the trailside. Parnell was the last man out. The moment he jumped the point man, that would signal the others to strike.

It had rained most of the morning, the air cold and wet. Weesay knew he'd have to be careful with the ground so slippery. They'd be using only knives on this one, no gunfire unless absolutely necessary since it was likely other German patrols were in the area.

He inhaled, let his breath out slowly, heard the pumping of his heart through his skull bone. It was transferred to the rock. He shifted his Thompson across his back and rolled the handle of his knife, seating it in his palm for the tenth time.

It felt good and heavy, not like those punk-ass, featherweight switchblades he'd carried back in the States. He chuckled at that memory: Tenth Avenue Weesay Laguna, Kid-Zorro, the big-balled killer *cuchillero,* the knife-fighter. What a fucking laugh.

The first German emerged from the defile, wearily trudging against the grade. An MP-40 machine pistol was slung over his shoulder along with his cargo box. The wood was darkened by the rain. Laguna felt his entire muscle structure tighten and a surge of heat riffled into his bloodstream.

Another soldier appeared, then a third and a fourth. Weesay's eyes bored into the crease in the rock that was the defile's outlet. The next man out would be his target. He came, short, stocky, his box large and heavy-looking. His head was down as he gazed sullenly at the ground.

There was a quick movement up the trail. Parnell was attacking. In the periphery of Laguna's vision, he saw other movements, heard a shout, and then he himself was springing forward, up out of his hiding place. His man's head jerked up, swiveled sharply toward him. The German's mouth and eyes flew open and he instinctively dodged to the side, his right hand frantically groping for his weapon. Instead of a machine pistol, it was a Karabiner 98-K rifle.

Weesay plowed into him, felt the edge of the box jam into his chest. He thrust his knife at the man but missed, the Kraut dodging to the side, yelling something. His eyes were terrified. Laguna's momentum carried them both to the ground, grappling. The Kraut was very strong. Even though restricted by the box on his back, he managed to throw Weesay away. Both instantly twisted around and leaped back to their feet.

The German pulled a boot knife, long and stiletto-bladed. They circled each other in a deadly, silence-pounding choreography. Another part of Weesay's mind heard harsh yelling, the distinctive scuffles and deep gruntings of other men in close combat.

The German feinted clumsily and then charged, slashing his blade across from right to left. It ripped through Laguna's tunic. But Weesay had anticipated the move, was already lowered enough to come in under the man's thrust. He lunged up and in, ramming his own blade deep into the German's groin. The man let loose a wild scream and fell heavily forward into him.

Weesay heard his own voice bellowing, was unaware of what he was saying. He withdrew his knife, felt a surge of blood follow it, lifted the tip slightly, and shoved it in again, upward slightly, shoulder weight behind it. The blade went deep into the German soldier's chest under the breastbone.

Instantly, he became dead weight. Laguna dropped to one knee. He was panting heavily. He glanced up the trail. All the German soldiers were down. They looked like fallen condors. Above each crouched a team member, his eyes blazing with adrenaline.

At the top of the trail, Parnell began stripping his man, loosening the box on his back, taking the machine pistol and cartridge harness and tunic. The others were doing the same. Weesay got his soldier's harness and jacket off. They were sticky with blood as warm as fresh urine. The dead man's eyes stared upward without substance. Holding the tunic and rifle, he grabbed up the man's helmet and headed up the trail.

Silently the assault force withdrew, each man moving in sequence up into a grove of pines. There Parnell halted them and whistled. Downslope, Kaamanui and Wineberg instantly rose out of the rocks and came jogging up the trail. They stepped around the boxes and the bloody, half-clothed corpses with a dark indifference. Rejoined, the team melted off into the trees just as a fresh deluge of rain swept into the higher branches.

By dusk they had worked their way down to the lower slopes of the mountains, the low ground now filled with patches of daisies and desert poppies, which the rains had brought forth. Earlier, at midafternoon, they had seen a tremendous explosion out on the plain near Sbeitla, forty miles away. Great geysers of blue and then red fire and black smoke had erupted skyward with the roar of it rolling across the earth. They knew it was probably American sapper teams destroying fuel and munition stores before retreating.

The rain had hounded them most of the day but by evening there was a break. The sky cleared, leaving only long tendrils of storm cloud along the western horizon that looked red and yellow at first but then slowly deepened in color until they were the gray indigo of twilight. The moon was already up.

They waited an hour, until a shallow, ground-hugging fog had formed across the plains. Parnell and four others donned the German uniforms. Red's had the gray-black sleeve chevrons of the squad's leader, a *stabsgefreuter* or corporal.

He shot a quick azimuth, fixed it between the towns of Sidi bou Zid and Bir el Afey. Then they started out at double time, him in the lead. The others also in Kraut dress formed a guard unit with their Thompsons slung on their harnesses as if they were captured booty. The two without uniforms were in the middle like prisoners. Initially, the fog had come only to their knees. Yet as they got farther and farther out onto the plain, it had risen until it blotted out everything except the hazy, lopsided moon.

Soon, they passed a German unit and then another. The Krauts were very close and made all sorts of noises, engines, the metallic rumbles of tracks, surges of talk, and laughter. Even the odor of cooking food came. And as always, the rumble of artillery was constant but directionless.

They reached the site of a battle, the ground littered with debris: twisted shrapnel and shell cases, gutted tanks and armored cars, strewn papers, clothing, signal wire, and black shell holes. The air reeked of creosote and burned tires and death. They came upon two dead American bodies that the German mortuary teams had missed. Both were burnt into black hulks like charcoal statues, only their combat boots recognizable.

Hour after hour, mile after mile, they went, stopping only for security halts and to scrape off the thick clay mud that clung to their boots. The moon rose higher and higher until it was directly overhead. Its light created blue and white rainbows in the fog. Just before midnight, they ran into trouble.

A voice suddenly challenged from the darkness, *"Stoppen! Wer ist das?"* Everyone froze. *"Stoppen!"* the voice called again. Then: *"Otto, bist du es?"*

A different voice, farther out, called back, *"Nien. Ich stehense heir."*

A moment of silence. Then a frantic *"Pas auf! Amerikaners!"*

The burst of a German machine gun was like a chain of lightning cracks. Bullets slammed through the air about forty yards to the south of the team. Instantly, everyone took off, running hard toward the north. The machine gun paused for a moment. The faster chatter of machine pistols came, then the MG again, the Germans laying down probing fire in quarter arcs.

Again it stopped. Parnell and his men continued running for a few seconds longer before going to ground, using the gunners momentary loss of hearing to extend their distance. Once more the guns opened up. This time the arc fire was very close. It stopped and they sprinted another thirty yards before dropping. The third fusillade sent bullets sizzling just overhead, tracers burning hot orange lines through the fog.

By sprinting and dropping, they managed to work their way farther and farther from the German outpost. Its firing continued sporadically for a while but gradually tapered off and finally stopped completely. But they could still hear voices calling back and forth.

Parnell found himself alone. The rest of the team had scattered to decrease the likelihood of hits. Now he listened tensely. Deep in his ears he still heard the guns. He was beside a thicket of smoke trees. He quickly removed his gloves. The air was wet and cold, like the fumes off a freezer. Snapping his forefinger into his other palm, he made a sharp, snapping sound. Three snaps, pause, three more.

There was an answering snap from a few yards out, another from the left. Then, one by one, his men materialized out of the fog, homing to him. He checked them in. Nobody had been shot. He quickly took a compass reading and they headed out again, moving in a tight, silent line, each man keeping the one ahead in sight.

By two in the morning the overcast had returned, swallowing the moon. They came to a salt flat, a *chott*. Here the ground was completely shrubless, flat as a floor and pounded hard by the rain. The salt crystals crunched under their boots like broken glass.

Then they heard the dogs.

Everyone halted immediately. From far off came the faint sound of barking, excited yelps, the animals coursing, searching for spoor. A single whistle riffled through the wet, foggy stillness.

*Shit,* Red thought, *our luck's just run out.* On such flat, featureless ground, he knew the dogs would find them quickly.

He swiveled his head, this way, that, trying to tell the direction of the cries while he hastily considered what they'd do. Run? They *might* reach cover of some kind. No, that was foolish. The *chott* could extend for miles. Then what? He could think of only one other thing. They'd have to fight the animals, kill them before their handlers could come up.

He softly called to Bird. When Wyatt came up, he asked, "You know anything about trail dogs?"

"Yeah, Lieutenant. When I was a kid, we used to run hounds for bear and coon."

"How many you figure are out there? Can you tell?"

Bird listened for a moment, his head tilted. "I'd say five, maybe six." Suddenly, one animal let loose a single, rising howl. It sounded as if the dog had been hurt. Instantly the others joined in until there was a full chorus. Germans started shouting. Bird grunted. "They jes' cut our back trail."

All the men peered nervously out into the fog, their hackles rising with the ancient primeval fear of the marauding pack. Parnell said, "What'll the handlers do now? Release 'em?"

Bird nodded. "They'll likely let 'em run us to ground and then come in."

"How far back will they be by the time the dogs reach us?"

"Judgin' from the baying, I'd figure maybe a couple hundred yards."

"Are these big dogs?"

"Sounds like it, prob'ly shepherds or Dobermans. If they are, they're gonna be mean sons a bitches. They'll come right at us."

Red nodded. "Okay, everybody deploy across the trail. Keep low. Wrap your jackets around one arm, use it like a shield. Kill with your knife so we don't expose our position. When we've taken out the dogs, start firing. Traverse the back trail for at least a hundred and fifty yards out."

He lowered himself to one knee, listened to the men taking their positions, salt crunching under their boots, and heard the soft rap of safety studs on the MP-40s clicking off.


Wineberg was at the end of the line, on the left. He knelt there, unconsciously hissing through his teeth. He hated dogs. Rotten sons a bitches. Once on a road gang in Yellow Point, Louisiana, guards had sicced a big Airedale on him. Just for taking a leak without permission. The animal was powerful and fast and bit the hell out of him before the guards called him off. Smoker had fought back and that angered them so they flogged him with an oil-stiffened rope. *Sons a bitches!*

The dogs were very close now and had fallen into an intense silence. Only the chirpy tinkling of their harnesses and the quick, flicking rush of their padded feet on the hard salt were audible as they closed.

Kimball, on Smoker's right, felt knotted up inside. He was caught in a vivid childhood memory. He'd owned two German shepherds back then, black ones named Molly J and Mr. Mozart. God, how he'd loved those two dogs. Now he squeezed the haft of his knife and listened and was repulsed by what he was about to do.

A dog was suddenly there, exploding soundlessly out of the fog. He threw his arm up. The animal clamped its teeth down onto the rolled jacket. He felt the pure power of its jaws tighten against his arm. The animal's full weight hurled him backward and down. He threw his arms around it and they rolled together. The dog growled and clawed at him. Kimball could actually taste its breath. He worked his knife hand free, pulled it back, and then shoved the blade upward. The animal screamed as he stabbed it again and again, vaguely aware of other combats going on along the line, animals shreiking, men growling, and cursing and heaving as if they lifted heavy weights.

His dog suddenly began to fall away from him. Its teeth tore free of his tunic. Kimball rolled over and came to one knee. He could smell a thick musky odor like skunk. His legs shook. A few feet away, the dog whimpered. It was a black German shepherd.

A machine pistol opened up on his right followed by two others. Then everyone was firing. For a moment, he lost direction. Fixing on the sounds of the outgoing rounds, he twisted his MP-40 to the side and opened up, spraying along the back trail. Answering gunfire came and bullets whipped and skidded across the salt.

Thirty seconds later everything abruptly ceased. The smell of cordite drifted around him. He inhaled and felt something small and hard slam into his helmet. It made a loud, metallic ping. There were more impacts. It was beginning to hail. He rose. A shadow loomed up beside him, Parnell.

"Form up, form up," Red snapped and instantly disappeared back into the fog.

Kimball heard Smoker cursing closeby. He glanced down at the dog. It tried to lift its head. He bent and touched it. It was trembling. He drew his underarm pistol, flicked off the safety, and shot the animal in the head. He felt like weeping.

A minute later, they moved out.


Three hours earlier, sentries from the U.S. Thirty-fourth Infantry Division, posted on the heights above the Kasserine pass in the Western Dorsal, had detected movement on the eastern slopes, the scrape of boots, the soft tinkle of gear. They had also noticed a sudden increase of movement down on the adjacent plain. . . .

After roiling in frustration for nearly thirty critical hours, Rommel had finally gotten what he wanted. Feldmarschall Kesselring had made a quick flight from Rome to meet both his field commanders. Afterward, he ordered von Arnim to release the units from his Tenth and Twenty-first Panzers, which Rommel had requested. Moreover, he informed von Arnim that the Desert Fox was now *Oberbefehishaber Heeresgruppe* Afrika, commander-in-chief of all North African forces.

The designated units were immediately rushed south

to assembly areas four miles east of the major Western Dorsal passes of Sbiba and Kasserine, where they linked with Rommel's DAK Angriffsgruppe Nord and his Fifteenth Panzer Division. Together, they would attack both passes and, once through, would continue on to Tebessa and then north to the Mediterranean.

Since the first, crushing attack of the fourteenth, the Allied forces had been steadily retreating west across the bloody flatland between the two ranges. They were in total disorder, endless streams of retreating, decimated units that had at last funneled back through the passes of the Westerns into the momentary safety beyond. Now brigade and regimental commanders were trying desperately to regroup.

Although stunned by the debacle, Eisenhower had moved quickly, shoving massive reinforcements into the Allied positions along the Western Dorsal. To do this, he'd been forced to use raw reserves, many of whom were newly arrived from the States without combat experience or adequate training.

In the predawn hours of 17 February, amid bursting signal flares and a driving hail storm, the Germans struck. Von Arnim attacked the Sbiba pass while Rommel threw his desert-hardened veterans, now strongly reinforced, into the Kasserine and the El Ma el Abiod pass farther south.

Rommel's force blew through their designated passes with little opposition and burst out onto the western slopes. But there they ran head-on into a hurricane of fire from a quickly assembled U.S. defense force of infantry, field artillery, tank destroyers, and combat engineering units.

A short but vicious fight ensued. The German thrust was momentarily stopped and the assault companies hurriedly withdrew back into the pass under the cover of a smoke barrage.

Regrouping, they immediately struck again and were once more driven back.

All through the long, frozen day, the two contending forces went at each other in savage tank engagements and deadly artillery duels. Still, under almost continuous air attack, the American front gradually started to weaken. Gaps appeared in the contact zones through which German armor and infantry rushed.

By nightfall, the entire Allied defensive line began to disintergrate completely. . . .

# Twenty-four

It was two hours before dawn when they reached the edge of the salt and went up onto slightly rising ground, folds, and wadis with scattered patches of desert grass and cactus. The hail continued intermittently, the little ice pellets coming straight down to sting their hands and shoulders. But the fog had thinned and was now only a three-foot-deep layer over the ground.

Above it, the visibility was clear and the atmosphere carried sounds a long way. There was an endless stream of lights several miles to the north and from it came the periodic clatter of moving armor, the whine of trucks.

Parnell called a halt. The men flopped down wearily, strung out in a shallow wadi. The distant thunder and flashes from another battle came from the northern Westerns. But everyone was too exhausted to watch. Instead, they lay motionless, their clothes stinking of the dried dog blood, which had hardened in the cold.

Red was stretched in a patch of prickly grass that was strewn with hailstones like diamond chips. He felt them beneath him melting from his body's warmth. His fatigue was like a black smoke enveloping him. He thought he'd close his eyes for a moment. Instead, he dropped into sleep.

It seemed to pass in a single breath. He shifted himself petulantly, not wanting it to fade. As he did, light came faintly through his eyelids. He popped them open. The fog was saturated with a gray brilliance. His whole body went tense as he listened, trying to identify things. All he could pick up were the faraway sounds of battle and trucks still moving somewhere.

Then it hit him. The light was from the dawn. He sat up, rubbed his eyes, his gloves stiff against his lids. He glanced down at his watch, saw it was 5:41. Stiffly, he pushed himself to his feet and his upper body cleared through the fog layer.

His heart jolted. Less than thirty yards away was an Italian M-13/40 tank. Instantly, he dropped back to the ground. But in that fleeting instant, he had spotted others parked out beyond it, all motionless and silent, only their dark brown turrets and hulls showing above the ground fog. They'd stumbled into an Italian tank assembly area.

There was the soft scuff of boots. He whirled. Fountain suddenly appeared. "Lieutenant," Cowboy whispered, "we got trouble. Tanks. Bird sent me to get you, sir."

"Can you see how many there are?"

"We counted thirty-one." He sucked saliva. "Damn, this fog lifts, we're settin' out here like nekked jaybirds."

Now they began to hear the tank crewmen talking, murmurs and laughter, the rattle of mess kits. Red cautiously lifted his head for a quick scan. He ducked back. "They're parked in echelon. We're on the outside of the last row."

He forced his thoughts to slow down. *Focus,* he told himself. Distractedly he rolled a hailstone between his fingers, felt it melt away to a grain of sand. "Get Wyatt," he said quietly. Cowboy scurried off.

A moment later, Bird came up. By then, Parnell had decided what they were going to do. Before he could speak, a bugle suddenly broke the dawn stillness, tinny, lifting in a series of rapid, choppy notes and then repeating. A few seconds later came the slam of tank hatches and engines starting up, diesels clacking loudly as they came up into operating heat.

He pulled Bird close. "We'll commandeer the last tank in line," he whispered tightly. "The one at the south end. He's back far enough so they won't see us. I'll jump him first, get the hatch open. As soon as it's up, the rest of you come on."

Wyatt nodded, crawled off.

There was a loud pop overhead and a soft orange glow filtered down through the fog. A signal flare, sizzling two hundred feet above them. Gears immediately began grinding, snapping into drivelines, and engines wound up. There were the grating cracks and squeals of moving treads and the ground trembled slightly as the entire tank formation began to move forward.

The one closest to Parnell rumbled past him, just feet away. Diesel fumes drifted over him. He lifted his head enough to see it. Like the others, it had neither commander's hatch nor side viewing ports, which meant none could detect anything behind it unless it turned completely around.

As it drew away, he jumped up and started after it, running along the wadi for a few yards and then up onto higher ground, his upper body in plain view now. He heard the other men coming up behind him.

He quickly drew abreast of it. The turret was swiveling back and forth as the Italian gunner checked out his turning motors. The small tank was armed with a narrow-barreled 47mm cannon and one 8mm machine gun in a steel hump on the right side of its hull. A single crew hatch was on the closer side with strapped-down ammo cases and tool chests. The hull metal was streaked with rust.

The whole formation was rapidly picking up speed. Parnell broke into a full sprint, angling toward his target. Wadi grass slapped at his legs and boots. He came up along its side, its treads gouging up clumps of grass and mud. He took hold of its mounting ladder and hauled himself aboard.

The hull rocked and shook. He glanced ahead at the rest of the formation. None were slowing. Bracing his feet, he began pounding on the hatch with the butt of his machine pistol, shouting the only complete German phrase he knew. It had been taught to him back at Colorado U by a hulking tackle named Brofonosky: *"Verdammte Scheisse! Jetzt is mir der praser geplatzt."* It meant: *Goddammit, my rubber just broke!*

The hatch opened a crack and a suspicious Italian face peered out. Red pointed at his German collar insignia, motioned for him to open the hatch wider. The soldier turned his head, said something to another crewman. Parnell reached in, took hold of the Italian's coveralls, and bodily pulled him through the hatch. With the same motion, he hurled him over the side. Then, whirling, he lunged through the hatchway.

Just above his head was the cannon gunner, staring openmouthed. Below sat the driver and the machine gunner. Red put his weapon on them. "Stop!" he yelled. The machine gunner instantly raised his hands and the driver slammed down hard on the brakes. The tank came to a jolting halt. Red pulled himself completely through the hatch. There were hollow thuds on the outside of the hull as the rest of the team climbed aboard. Red pulled the cannon man down, shoved him through the hatch. Then the other gunner. The driver started to follow but Parnell stopped him, pointed back at his seat. The man sat down again.

The rest of the team came in one at a time. Two of

them had the coveralls they'd stripped off the crewmen. It was cramped in the small tank, everybody cursing and squirming around, trying not to knock themselves against steel edges. The armored vehicle was old and stank of rusted steel and overheated oil. There was no radio gear visible. Kaamanui was the last man in. He leaned out and pulled the hatch shut.

Parnell patted the driver's shoulder and pointed ahead. The Italian throttled up and they surged forward, hurrying to catch up to the rest of the formation.

"Anybody know how to operate one of these things?" Red yelled.

From up in the cannon seat, Wineberg called back, "I used to skin an old D-Eight cat on a construction job up in Idaho once, Lieutenant."

"Then get on down here. Watch how the Wop drives it so you can take over." Smoker wiggled down and squatted behind the driver's seat. The Italian gave him a frightened look.

The tank company was moving across the plain at a moderate pace, angling toward the northwest. It didn't take Wineberg long to figure out how to handle the vehicle. They stopped long enough for him to take the controls and then they booted off the driver, the man stripped of his jumper but grinning with relief as they left him, accelerating away to regain their position in the formation.

The sun came out and quickly burned off the fog, and the inside of the tank got uncomfortably hot, the heat compounded by the putrid stink of the dried dog blood on their uniforms.

By midmorning, they were near the east-west highway that ran from Sbeitla to Sidi bou Zid and on to the Kasserine. It was jammed with an endless stream of vehicles:

trucks, engineering drays, kitchen units, and medical lorries, all the support equipage of an army on the offensive.

Suddenly, a yellow flare skewered into the air over the lead Italian tank. Immediately the other vehicles began to close in, keying on it and forming up into a column. Smoker pulled close to the tank directly in front. They were still the last one in line.

The column ran parallel to the highway for about a half hour. Then it halted suddenly as a lone German military policeman on a motorcycle come racing out to meet it. He pulled up beside the lead tank, spoke to its officer for a moment, then sped back.

There was another flare and the column moved forward, executing an echelon movement to the right so that they were diagonally facing the highway. By the time they reached it, several policemen had already stopped the flow of traffic to let them enter the line.

For the next four hours, the traffic continually bunched and halted. Yet they were continually drawing closer and closer to the Western Dorsal Mountains.

Parnell, squatted down beside Smoker, glassed them through the viewing slit. He could see the wide notch of the Kasserine pass. It appeared like the cut of a gigantic ax into the main ridge. Its approaches were packed with armored vehicles, and Allied artillery rounds occasionally dropped among them, flashing bursts of light and fans of smoke.

Around 11:00 in the morning, there was a sudden, concerted surge in the waiting vehicles at the pass, the bigger tanks and then the smaller ones and the destroyers and half-tracks all forming up and dashing forward in precise ranks and Vs. The leading elements quickly disappeared from view, and clouds of black smoke began fuming out of the pass. Twenty minutes later, the lead elements of the attack came back out again but now their precise formations were scattered and ragged.

At 2:00 in the afternoon, the traffic was halted for the sixth time. The air was so hot and foul in their tank that Parnell finally allowed them to crack the hatch. At that moment, a column of German tank-destroyers roared past along the side of the highway. They were brand-new vehicles and looked lethally sleek, their long gun barrels bobbing gently as they hurtled over the uneven ground.

Soon after, more military policemen came and waved everybody off the road so a line of ambulances and mobile infantry trucks could pass, headed toward the coast. Wounded men lay on the truck beds with medics in bloody coveralls and white helmets working on them. In the bright sun their blood looked shockingly red.

They were still stationary by late afternoon, the sun already down below the high ridges of the Westerns five miles away. Then at five o'clock, the Italian tank commander either lost his patience or was ordered to move. He quickly pulled off the highway and headed west, running beside it as the German tank destroyers had done. One by one, his company followed in column behind him.

They all raced along, headed into the lengthening shadows. Soon the land began to rise, forming into ever deeper folds and cascade hillocks. That was what Parnell had been waiting for. He knew they had to leave the company soon or they'd be discovered when it reached an assembly area in the foothills.

After studying the surrounding ground through the viewing slit for a few minutes, he slapped Smoker's shoulder and pointed to the left. Wineberg immediately jacked the tank hard over and they plunged across country, away from the road.

The area they entered was like a maze, full of false valleys. Several times they ran into dead ends and had to backtrack. Parnell began worrying about fuel. Would they have enough to reach where he hoped to go? He'd decided to head for the Bou Chebka pass, which lay ten miles due south. It was several miles wide and would afford them a better chance of slipping through the German lines. Once beyond it, they could go either west to Tebessa or north to Thala.

It was night when they finally broke out of the cascade hills and reentered the plain. Two miles ahead lay the north-south Feriana/Kasserine Highway. It was filled with traffic lights all the way back to Feriana. He cursed. In order to reach the Bou Chebka, they'd have to cross it.

Luckily, their crossing went smoothly. Laguna, in one of the Italian tanker's coveralls, ran ahead and boldly stopped the traffic with a red guidon flashlight. Trucks came to a squealing halt and, while the German drivers watched and swore, the small Italian M-13/40 tank bounded over the road, paused just long enough to pick up Weesay, and then sped off into the darkness.

They ran out of fuel a little before ten o'clock that night. Everybody sat, quietly disgusted. Then they gathered gear, climbed down, formed up in patrol order, and marched away. Soon the little Italian tank was far behind, looking forlorn and alone on the vast moonlit plain.

The night was freezing cold and Parnell set a brisk pace due west. Twenty-five minutes later they entered the pass itself on its northern side. To their right were scattered pinnacles and domes and cubes of tumble rock that looked like ivory ruins in the now intermittent moonlight. An overcast had been rapidly moving in from the sea, tendrils of cloud scudding across the face of the moon like cotton cording.

The land was utterly remote, empty and silent except for the always-present distant rumble of artillery. By one o'clock they had cleared through the pass. Parnell called a halt. The men hunkered down and ate the last of their D-ration chocolates.

Since there was no visible battle activity toward Tebessa, Red chose to head for Thala where there was obviously still a battle line. The overcast thickened until it completely blotted out the moon. They edged away from the tumble rock so as to remain on level ground. Everyone was bone weary, trudging doggedly along, trying to remain awake.

"Halt! Who goes there?" The voice shot out of the darkness.

Everybody froze. Then slowly, soundlessly, each man lowered himself and lay out on the ground. They could see indistinct movement ahead, to their left. Parnell shifted his head, trying to isolate sounds, position them. Were these Germans or Americans?

A horrible thought struck him. He and some of the others were still in Kraut uniforms. If this was an Allied unit, they could be shot as infiltrators by their own side. He frantically tried to think of what to do. Call out the patrol's code name that Captain Theile had assigned them, Little Big Horn? No. It wouldn't mean anything to whoever was out there.

"Advance and be goddamned recognized," the voice called.

There was more movement, the faint shifting of weight on boot soles, the metallic clink of machine-gun belts. Red saw a shadow move across the faint pale surface of a nearby boulder. More shadows loomed.

He inhaled and lifted his head. "We're Americans," he

shouted. There was dead silence, which continued unbroken for several tense minutes. He felt his body jumping with adrenaline. "Goddammit," he shouted again. "We're Americans."

A light suddenly illuminated the ground a few feet ahead of him. Its beam swept forward, back over him, and then went out. More sounds came. A few seconds later a different voice ordered, "Leave your weapons on the ground. Stand up and get them fucking hands in the air."

He obeyed, heard the others do the same. Shadows moved beside him. A flashlight lit up Sergeant Bird's face just ahead of him. The same voice said, "Who the hell are you assholes?"

"A recon patrol from Combat Command A," Bird answered quietly.

The light went out. Hands began searching Parnell's body. "Hey, these guys got broke-down Thompsons," someone said. Another said, "That's booty, goddammit. We oughta shoot the fuckers right here."

The man who had questioned Bird said, "Back off, there." The searching hands stopped and a tiny vest light came on. It made an orange dot in the darkness. The same voice said, "All right, move it. Follow the light."

They went past dark gun emplacements. It began to rain, sudden and hard. After a few minutes, they were halted beside a slit trench in a cluster of cacti. There was a tarp cover over it, a second tarp hanging as a blackout curtain.

The soldier with Parnell went down and slipped under the tarp. He didn't come back for several minutes. When he did, he shoved Red forward. "Go on down."

An American captain in a GI mackinaw and watch cap pulled over his ears was seated on a wooden plank quietly smoking a cigar. On another board beside him was a field telephone, a map, and a hurricane lantern. Overhead, the rain slammed loudly against the canvas and the trench stank of kerosene fumes and cigar smoke. Red squatted down.

The captain said, "You Parnell?"

"Yes, sir."

He nodded. "Colonel Dikkson just vouched for you, Lieutenant." He voice carried no interest. "He figured you all were long dead."

"We've been out since the fourteenth."

The captain nodded again and introduced himself. His name was Joseph Procaccio, CO of I Company, Second Battalion, Sixteenth Infantry Regiment. He didn't offer his hand.

"What's happened since we left?" Red asked.

"The long and the short of it is we got our asses stomped."

"How bad?"

"Bad as she gets." Procaccio spoke in a monotone, like a man with too much alcohol in him, which had irretrievably dulled all his emotions. "It ain't over yet."

"What's the present situation?"

The captain took the cigar from his mouth, spat, put it back in. "The Krauts busted through the Kasserine last night. Carved out a fair-sized salient on this side." He snorted. "They went through our combat teams and task forces like shit through a goose."

Red stared at the lantern flame. It danced and hissed. "What's your strength status?"

"Crappy. There's us and some Senegalese troops covering our Bou Chebka flank. Reports say First Armor and some Frenchies have moved in artillery a couple miles west of us. I hope so. The Jerrys're gonna hit us again, sure as you're born. Right through that El Ma el Abiod pass. They're just waiting for dawn."

"Can we hold them?"

"Not with what we've got now." He puffed on the cigar for a moment. It had gone out. He took out a Zippo lighter, relit it, and blew smoke out the side of his mouth. "Second Corps's trying to bring in reinforcements. Personally, I think we're fucked."

Parnell stared at him. There was nothing to say.

Procaccio said, "You and your men grab some chow. Get whatever sleep you can. You'll be going on the line soon. As of now, you're attatched to my company."

"Yes, sir." Red started to rise.

"And get that goddamn Kraut uniform off before somebody shoots you in the ass."

"Yes, sir," Parnell repeated. He climbed back up into the freezing rain.

# Twenty-five

Captain Procaccio had called it slightly wrong. Rommel didn't wait for dawn. Instead, he struck at three minutes after four in the morning, sending his Tenth Panzer against the El Ma el Abiod while von Arnim hit Sbiba.

The Sbiba attack was stopped by units of the British Sixth Armoured and the Second Battalion of the Fifth Leicestershire Regiment in a three-hour, muzzle-to-muzzle tank battle. At the last minute, mobile artillery batteries of the U.S. Twenty-sixth Brigade arrived to lay down concentrated fire, which drove the Germans back through the pass.

Meanwhile, the forward assault companies of Rommel's attack had made a fatal error. They got lost in the darkness and rain and completely missed the approaches to the El Ma el Abiod. They found themselves at a dead end in a secondary valley. Desperately trying to recover offensive momentum, Rommel immediately ordered the force to turn southwest and cross through the northern side of the Bou Chebka pass.

By then, dawn had arrived, leaving the assaulting armor out in open, flat country where they were immediately brought under withering fire by hastily coordinated Allied artillery and tank destroyer units backed by the Stark Force, which had been rushed in from the coast, eight hundred miles away. Half the German armor was quickly destroyed and the remnants of the Tenth Panzer withdrew back through the Bou Chebka.

For the first time in his career, Rommel now hesitated. His instincts told him the lunge for Tebessa and the sea was no longer possible. The Axis forces had lost the initiative. His intelligence reports also showed the Allies were pouring everything they had into the area, including massive new air support.

But far more ominous to him was the approach of the British Eighth Army in his rear. Montgomery's forward elements had already been sighted west and south of Medenine, the main Allied strongpoint twenty miles southeast of the Mareth Line on the coastal plain.

So, at 1000 hours that morning he ordered his extended forces to go over to the defensive. Executing a fighting withdrawal all along its front, the Axis units retreated from the Western Dorsal Mountains and continued eastward until they reached the southern passes of the Easterns. . . .

*7 March 1943*

With its siren still wailing, the lead vehicle in a column of six half-tracks skidded to a stop in front of the El Maknes Hotel in the ancient desert town of Tebessa, Algeria. The hotel functioned as a false entrance to the American II Corps's headquarters located totally underground behind it.

General George Patton, chromed helmet and ivory-handled pistols glistening in the cold, bright sunlight, dismounted and looked about. He was here from Gibraltar to relieve II Corps's present commander, General Fredendall, whom Ike had pulled out following the Kasserine debacle.

General Omar Bradley drove up in a jeep. He had also just arrived from Gibraltar to be deputy corps commander and Ike's personal liaison in North Africa. He and Patton warmly greeted each other.

Patton turned to study the El Maknes. "Where in hell are these goddamned Fredendall rat holes I've heard about?"

"Out back, George."

"Where is the son of a bitch?"

"He decided to leave earlier this morning. Felt it would be more discreet."

Patton snorted with disgust. "Either he's nuts or he's scared shitless." He swung back to give the town a narrow-eyed scan. Abruptly he started off, striding. Bradley and Patton's adjutant, Colonel Al Stiller, fell in step.

They went along what once had been a wide boulevard. Now it was covered with garbage, burnt-out vehicles, and tumbled buildings. Veiled women and ragged children poked among the ruins while details of disheveled, unshaven American soldiers lethargically cleared debris.

Bradley studied them, his round, midwestern face sad. "These boys are badly demoralized, George. They took one helluva whipping."

"They were beaten long before Rommel hit 'em, Brad," Patton barked. "That dumb British son of a bitch Anderson had them scattered from hell to breakfast. And they were being commanded by cavalry officers who fight their wars from goddamned holes in the ground. The poor bastards didn't have a chance."

He paused long enough to whirl on Stiller. "Put demo teams on those rat holes. Right now. Unless we're under direct attack, every goddamned officer and EM in this outfit will function aboveground. And they're going to do it in Class-As. I want to see visible results by seventeen-hundred-hours today."

"Yes, sir." Stiller scribbled in his notepad. Bradley smiled.

They passed through a garden. Roman ruins showed among the date palms. Patton bent down, knocked a gloved finger against the edge of a partially buried chunk of marble.

"Here's where real soldiers fought," he said quietly.

"That really isn't a fair comparison, George."

"Oh, yes, it is. You know why? Because our poor bastards haven't learned the first lesson of war yet. You don't win the goddamned things on the defensive. You win them by attacking and attacking. And when you're too tired to continue, you attack again. I intend to teach them that lesson. Then I'm going to stomp hell out of Rommel, that Kraut son of a bitch. And I'm going to do it with *these* men. "

"You don't have much time. These units will be back on the line very soon. Maybe within days."

"I'll have 'em ready."

"How?"

"By making the sons a bitches more afraid of me than they are of the goddamned Nazis," he said.


On the previous day, the Germans had launched a massive spoiling attack, code-named Operation Capri, against Montgomery's Eighth Army at Medenine just south of the Mareth Line. Frontal in nature, it was ordered by Kesselring, despite Rommel's vehement protests. It was doomed from the start.

Twice the German Tenth, Fifteenth, and Twenty-first Panzer Divisions of DAK, supported by mobile infantry and artillery using the new *Nebelwerfers,* deadly 155mm rocket launchers, struck the British lines across open plain. They got decimated, regrouped, and were decimated again.

Although Patton would not know it until 18 March, this was Rommel's last battle in North Africa. Sick and disheartened by so many lost opportunities and by the moronic decisions made in Rome and Berlin, he soon returned to Germany and left the remainder of the African campaign to Kesselring and von Arnim. . . .

*14 March, 1943*

The cliff was there, in the yellow light of a quarter moon. Solid, immovable. Sergeant Bird clung to it with an intimate tenacity, his fingers feeling gently across the rock face. They touched something, another rock bollard that protruded from the solidness of the cliff's pitch.

He gripped it like a baseball and shifted his weight, pulled himself upward. Now he could see a narrow ledge above and to his right, a dim two-inch shadow like a knife wound in the stone. Planting the edge of his rubber-soled jump boot on it, he slowly went higher.

He could feel the warm rebound of his breath off the rock, even and steady. The thing itself was cold through his gloves. He paused and cut his head back to look up at the sky. The stars were as infinite as molecules, the moon a butter-colored scimitar. Twenty feet below him, his safety line jigging enough to make the snap links tinkle, labored Weesay Laguna, who now called up, "For chrissake, Wyatt, move you ass faster. I'm fuckin' freezin' down here."

Bird chuckled and explored further. One by one he found more wedges and crevices and tiny chimneys in the stone face as he went higher. The sweat under his clothing felt like greasy oil while the weight of his gear, which included a slung Thompson, spare clip bandoliers, grenades, and gelignite pouches, kept pulling him downward and back, forcing the muscles in his shoulders and arms to constantly counterbalance.

He and Weesay, along with eighteen other two-man teams, were practicing free climbs near the Bou Chebka pass. This one rose two hundred feet above a gradual slope of scree and scatter rock, curved like a shoehorn with its upper pitch nearly perpendicular. They'd climbed it once before but this was their first night ascent.

Over the last week, Patton had pushed everybody hard. That included Parnell and his men, who were now directly attatched to II Corps. He challenged and insulted them, imposed prison-gang discipline. He sent them on small, probing skirmishes to rebuild their self-confidence and fighting spirit. Slowly, methodically, the soldiers of the Corps began coming back, regaining their lost confidence. . . .


After Rommel's withdrawl from the Westerns, Blue Team, like so many other stragglers, had remained with the outfit that had found them. Then on 10 March, Dunmore ordered them to rejoin him. Two days later, he met with Parnell, Bird, and Kaamanui to sketch out their next mission.

Orders from Fifth Army Group had come down, he told them. Montgomery's Eighth Army was scheduled to strike the entire length of the Mareth Line on 16 March. Second Corps, much to Patton's raging disgust, had been given the job of protecting the British left flank by striking at Gafsa and the three main passes through the southern curve of the Eastern Dorsal, the El Quettar, Station de Sened, and Maknassy.

The assault on the Maknassy pass had been given to the First Armored Division, the Sixtieth Regimental

Combat Team from the Ninth Infantry Brigade, and Combat Commands C and A. Blue Team was specifically assigned a raiding mission, operating with a thirty-man unit from the 2/4th Prince of Wales Own Gurkha Rifles of the Fourth Indian Division under the command of a wiry *daffadar*-major, a sergeant-major named Dilbahadur Gurung.

Their objective was a German gun position located at the top of a half dome of rock that commanded a narrow point in the pass. Air recon photos showed it housed a battery of guns emplaced in standard German-type 685 casement bunkers, each nearly invulnerable to artillery fire and air strikes. This particular gun nest could lay down intense enfilading fire on the pass road and rail line fifteen hundred feet below it and had to be knocked out.

The western face of the position was a sheer cliff nearly two hundred feet high. On the reverse side was a service road and numerous machine-gun and watch posts. The original site had been constructed by the French in 1886 but the Germans had replaced the old French 10.5cm Benet-Mercie pit howitzers with tapered 88mm antitank cannons.

On Allied tactical field maps, the gun position was designated Hill 322. . . .

Bird again lifted his head to study the moon. He could see its continents and seas. It was the same moon from another place, another time, thousands of miles away. The memory rose, gently tugging him back into its own reality:

*Riding into Honolulu from Schofield Barracks on a Friday night, the cab a double-long that stank of dried vomit and disinfectant, the vehicle packed with other soldiers already half drunk on post beer and him with his half pint of Five Island Whiskey in his back pocket, the liquor raw enough to sear vocal cords but giving him a clean, comfortable feeling knowing it was back there. . . .*

Another rock bollard appeared directly over his head. He reached for it. . . .

*Watching that moon through the car window and feeling his stomach tighten with the old hunger, picturing the whores down at the Golden Palace off River Street, its old wainscoted walls and air stuffy and hot and saturated with the forever muskiness of pussy and Lysol, and the cracked, bubbling Brunswick juke-box athrob with Bob Wells and his Texas Playboys slamming out their shit-kicking two-step "Western Swing" while he waited his turn, the hunger so close to the surface now it made his mouth taste like copper pennies. . . .*

As Wyatt shifted his weight, the rock bollard broke off in his hand. Clawing frantically for another hold, he went backward. His boots cut at the rock face. And then he was in the air, shouting, "Fall! Fall!"

Moon-yellowed rock flashed past him as he went down headfirst. He heard himself cursing, more outraged than afraid. Suddenly, the line hooked to his harness's clip-ring went taut, humming softly. There was a second of give and then it went taut again. Bird's descent stopped. He swayed and swung back and forth, his waist and shoulders burning from the jolt.

Overhead, the safety rope made a faint white line in the moonlight. At the other end was Laguna, struggling with Bird's full weight and cursing in English and Mexican with a strained, hissing voice. He finally got himself rebalanced and began pulling Wyatt back up, hand-over-hand.

Quickly Bird got a new purchase on the rock face and recovered his own weight. The line went limp. As he passed Laguna on the way up, Weesay glared at him. "Holy Chris', *meng,*" he panted. "Chu fuck near tear my arms off."

Bird grinned and hooked his arm around the young man's neck. He didn't say anything. It wasn't necessary. Chuckling, he took the lead again.


The major had an odd smell, powdery like an old woman's dresser. His name was Ruppenthal, a minor officer on von Arnim's operations staff. He and Captain Bekker were in a staff car headed to the junction town of Bir Ali, midway between the Maknassy pass and the big coastal town of Sfax.

It was wet and freezing in the backseat of the little vehicle. Intermittent rain showers kept blowing in under the canvas top. The major had not spoken to Gerd since leaving the coast. Despite that, Bekker was in a good mood. He had just been given a reprieve.

His stint with Rommel's bodyguard had been disastrous. Downright humiliating, in fact. Everyone knew about his disgrace in the Algerian Desert. Fellow officers rarely spoke to him and the common soldiers, even the lowliest ones, obeyed his commands with open contempt in their eyes.

When Rommel left Africa for good, he'd taken his bodyguard with him. All except Bekker. Gerd knew von Arnim's hand had been in that decision; another insult for his old student. But then Ruppenthal had appeared with personal orders from the general. Bekker was actually being given a new command.

It took four hours to reach Bir Ali through the horrendous press of truck convoys and armor moving in from the coast. The town was blacked out and the flat ground on its outskirts was packed with German and Italian military units and vehicles that would soon be moving into defensive positions against Montgomery farther south.

They finally reached a command complex beside a parked company of tanks that bore the palm-tree-and-tiger ensigns of the Twenty-first Panzer. The driver stopped in front of a large field tent. Ruppenthal told Bekker to remain in the car and he went in alone.

Several minutes later he returned with a tall *hauptfeldwebel,* master sergeant, who wore the *richtkanonier* sleeve patch of the artillery. The sergeant mounted a motorcycle and they followed him to a fenced enclosure a quarter mile away. There were guards at the gates in greatcoats and woolen toques.

Inside the fence were lines of company tents. They went to the last line and the sergeant dismounted and entered the first one. Moments later soldiers began rushing out, pulling on clothing. They formed up in two lines just as it began to rain again.

Major Ruppenthal handed Bekker a flashlight. "Your command, Captain," he said stonily. "Would you care to inspect it?"

Gerd got out. With the master sergeant at his heels, he went along the front rank, passing his light over faces and uniforms. The men were disheveled and unshaven, fifty-seven in all. Except for the master sergeant and two *unterfeldwebels* or staff sergeants, none of the soldiers wore uniform insignias or unit designation patches.

Angrily he returned to the staff car. "What is this, Herr Major? These men are *schwarzchlaechters.*" The word, which meant black butchers, was military slang for stockade prisoners.

"Indeed."

"I am to command these?"

A cold smile touched Ruppenthal's lips. "Like you, they are being given the opportunity to regain their honor as soldiers of the Third Reich." He handed Gerd a large envelope. "Your orders, Captain. Tomorrow morning you and your command will be transported to the Maknassy pass. Specifically to an artillery position on a half dome of rock that commands the main road. You are to defend it to the last man. Is that clear?"

"But, I was expecting—"

"Is that *clear?*" the major shouted.

Bekker was taken aback. He gathered himself. "Yes, sir."

"One other point. Your entire position is mined. The keys to activate the demolitions are with your orders. Do not allow your position to be overrun. But if you fail to do this, the fuhrer will expect you to sacrifice yourselves so these guns can not be used by the enemy. Is *that* clear?"

Bekker felt his throat constrict. Then he braced stiffly. "Perfectly clear, sir. I thank the fuhrer for such an honor."

"*Heil* Hitler," the major said and drove away.

# Twenty-six

Although Patton had smouldered with indignation over being given a secondary role in the offensive, his attacks of the sixteenth through the eighteenth had gone with textbook perfection. Gafsa was taken by midday of the sixteenth, and the el Quettar and Station de Sened passes were occupied by the eighteenth.

Then the weather changed. Drenching spring rains turned the plain west of the Maknassy pass into a sea of mud in which everything got bogged down. He had to move up the Maknassy attack, scheduling it for 0430 hours, 22 March. For the last three days, his armor and infantry units had been slowly massing on the plain five miles west of the mountains in preparation. . . .

*21 March 1943*

At precisely 2113 hours, Parnell and the raider force boarded trucks in Gafsa to be taken to a demarcation point two miles west of the Maknassy foothills. All were dressed in black clothing, with their faces greased and their bodies loaded down with gear. Each man had the letter A taped across his back for identification during battle.

They sat quietly in the back of the trucks and stared at

the floor, bringing themselves to mental readiness for what lay ahead. The night air was near freezing. There had been rain periodically all through the day and into the early evening, and the ground was now deep with mud in which the trucks' tires skidded before gripping.

In the lead vehicle Parnell and Sergeant Major Gurung went over their battle plan one final time. The Nepalese sergeant's breath smelled of rum, a traditional part of the Gurkha prebattle ritual.

All the Gurkhas were small men with smooth skin and almond-shaped eyes. They were Kshatriyas, members of the warrior caste, and came from the Nepalese-Indian frontier. In addition to their standard weapons, each carried a traditional *kukri*, a long, curved knife shaped like a scimitar. These were veterans of two years of desert fighting and had lost half their batallion in Rommel's "cauldron" outside Tobruk.

At ten o'clock the trucks quietly passed through the Sixtieth Regimental Combat Team's assembly area. Its troops were already aboard trucks and APCs, hunkered down in panchos and under tarps, while they waited out the long night and the order to move into the attack.

A mile beyond the RCT's sector were the massed ranks of the First Armored Division, Grants and Shermans formed up in perfect attack separation along with tank destroyers and antitank caissons on their flanks. All were motionless and dark and silent in the night.

Two miles west of the foothills, they came upon a jeep parked in the road with its blue lights on. The trucks stopped and all the men dismounted as Parnell walked over to the jeep. Its driver was an American MP captain and with him was a tall, rangy Frenchman in a sheepskin jacket. He introduced him to Parnell.

His name was Pierre LeBlanc, an Algerian citizen who had run guns through the Easterns to anti-Vichy rebels in southern Tunisia. He knew these mountains intimately and would guide Parnell and his men through the German minefields and foothill outposts and directly to the face of Hill 322.

Red consulted with LeBlanc for a few moments, then formed up the men into two columns. A layer of fog had developed over the ground now and the night was eerily still, for once devoid of the rumble of distant artillery. It began to rain again, heavy drops slamming down into the men's faces. Parnell gave a signal whistle and the columns moved forward at double time.

Within thirty minutes, they reached the outer German minefields where LeBlanc halted. Small yellow ribbons had been staked into the mud earlier that evening by an American sapper team. He began moving among the ribbons, cautiously studying the ground.

Earlier, he had explained his procedure to Parnell. The Germans always wired and mined their approach fields in overlapping fan shapes, he told him. So once he could read the overall pattern of the sappers' ribbons, he'd be able to estimate mine-free seams through the field.

He finally signaled them to move again. The team formed into a single line directly behind him and he took them across the minefield, each man stepping gingerly into the footprints of the man ahead of him. With surprising speed, they reached the main pass road and crossed it two at a time to enter the foothills proper. They immediately found themselves in a maze of tiny arroyos that were calf-deep with rain runoff and filled with the hissing rush from hundreds of small waterfalls. Moving swiftly, they wound their way through and upward, slipping and sliding in the groundwater. Eventually they came to a long reach of open ground filled with standing rock and brush. Again, they dashed across in twos.

Once beyond it, they went down into another series of narrow, flooded gullies.

Occasionally, LeBlanc would stop the team and go ahead alone, returning a few minutes later to lead them past small, two-man enemy picket outposts that were always placed ahead of a German defensive line.

Soon, they began encountering larger German bunkers, first those of artillery spotters and finally the main line of machine-gun and mortar emplacements. They slipped by so close, they could actually hear the German soldiers talking and the static from their radio sets.

It was fifteen minutes after three in the morning when they finally traversed through a last draw with walls that went straight up and were water-polished and shaped like hanging drapes. At the other end of the draw was the sheer face of Hill 322.

Parnell checked his watch, winced. They were twenty minutes behind schedule. . . .

Two hundred feet directly above them, Captain Gerd von Bekker focused his binoculars and slowly scanned the Maknassy pass far below. Nothing visible was down there but rain and shadows.

He lifted slightly to study the darkness of the western plain beyond the foothills. For the last forty-eight hours, reports from advance spotter units said there had been an increase of Allied activity out there, particularly north of Gafsa. But he had been unable to see any such concentrations.

Gerd was on the viewing platform of his battery's range-plotting room, located directly above its four gun casements. The room was lit by soft blue light that cast the big Kommandogerat 36 range finder that sat before the room's narrow sighting port and its gun-director panel into blue-black shadow. Rain feathered through the open sighting port and the air was cold and smelled of instrument oil and wet leather.

He lowered the glasses, turned to look down at the three duty plot operators who were running a mock targeting drill. Periodically, they would call out elevation and traverse azimuths off the director panel. This data was automatically relayed by telephone line down to the slant-plane linkages mounted on each 88mm gun in the casements below.

Like the other *schwarzchlaechter*, these men had been trained in artillery units, primarily with the 999th Light Afrika Division. Before being imprisoned for various breaches of military discipline, they had fought against the British Eighth Army in Libya. As a result, their hands were familiar and quick with the equipment.

Although Bekker and his men had been at the battery site now for two days, Gerd hadn't yet accepted his circumstance. It was too insulting, too preposterous a thing to be absorbed. Isolated in an ancient French shit hole commanding a company of criminals? The absurdity of it mocked all his expectations and visions of a proper place in which to die for his fatherland.

Thus far, he had spent most of his waking hours prowling the cramped installation and putting his gun crews through endless firing drills. The site itself gave him little comfort. It was a grimy, three-level beehive with moisture-blackened walls, rusty metal, and low connecting tunnels that stank like Paris sewers.

Only the gun casements appeared new and renovated. Each contained two 88mm antitank guns. Electrically fired, they had wide traverse and elevation arcs and would be using high-explosive shells with impact fuses and ballistic caps that could penetrate ten-inch tank armor.

Fresh shells were brought up by a hoist from a powder magazine down on the third level. The guns had been cruciform-mounted so they could be retracted, allowing the double-steel firing doors to be closed against incoming barrage rounds.

Up on top of the rock dome, the old French drilling derricks were still standing, now merely rusted I-beams and cables. Two machine-gun pillboxes had been emplaced beside them, facing east to protect the position's reverse slope. Between the pits were twin trunk shafts and ladders that led directly down to the firing rooms.

Gerd left the platform and crossed the plotting room to the large steel door that led to his personal quarters. He swung it open, stepped through, and slammed it shut, the thing sounding like a safe. The inner lights automatically flicked on, showing a stone room as small as a prison cell, which contained a desk and chair, a bunk, toilet, and radio table.

He slammed down his field cap and dropped into the chair. On the desk was a lamp, a weathered briefcase, and a half-empty bottle of schnapps with a thick-bottom glass that had been left by the previous battery commander. He poured himself a drink and tossed it down clean. It tasted smoky.

Sighing, he opened his briefcase. Inside was the envelope containing the orders Ruppenthal had given him. He flipped it open and shook out the two demolition keys. They were gold-colored, slender as pencils, with the words HE-Ztx stamped on their heads. Both were on separate neck chains, one for him, the other for his senior NCO.

The demo system panel was located in the powder magazine. It was a brand-new red aluminum box with power conduits hidden in the wall. Its face contained two key slots. Each could activate the system of charges buried throughout the facility, which were set on a ten-minute delay. Once the keys were turned, a klaxon would sound to alert all battery personnel that they had exactly ten minutes to evacuate the site.

Bekker picked up both keys, thoughtfully rubbed them between his fingers. *The fuhrer will expect you to sacrifice yourselves.* Abruptly, he unbuttoned his tunic, pulled both key chains over his head, and settled them onto his chest. They felt icy. He rebuttoned the tunic, poured another drink, and stared at the opposite rock wall.

For two days Harrison Kimball had been having disturbing thoughts. They made him quiet and withdrawn. There had also been the recurrent memory of the funeral for his two-year-old baby sister, Joceyln Marie, who had died of pneumonia when he was seven: images of a dark mausoleum and a tiny white coffin drenched in red carnations. They kept coming at him from out of his past, so real he once thought he could actually smell the peppermint sweetness of the carnations.

But now his mind was fixed on the rock face four inches from his own. It was slick and wet, rain sliding down in streamlets. It smelled like wet chalk. He glanced to the right, then left. Scattered across the cliff with him was the rest of the team, laboring dark shadows. They weren't using safety lines this time, only pure free climbing. Above and to the far left he could see a soft blue glow from the firing windows of the German gun emplacements and the elongated sheen of protruding barrels.

Hill 322's cliff face turned out to be much easier than those they had trained on. This one had water fractures all over it, spiderweb cracks that offered easy hand- and footholds. Overhead, the stone face disappeared into darkness. So far, they had made a clean ascent.

He climbed on, his breath smoking in the air. Even inside the gloves, his fingers felt numb from cold and strain. His leg muscles quivered from the constant need to hold tightly against slippage. A spray of rain gently drifted against his cheek, as weightless as a girl's hair. He stopped. Had it smelled of carnations?

At that precise moment, the Allied preattack artillery barrage began, all at once. It was as if the distant plain had suddenly been electrified, forming massive short circuits like lightning webbing across the earth. Then the entire landscape and sky were thrown into brilliant near-daylight while the thunder of the guns rolled across the hills like pounding surf.

Within this roaring was detectable the smaller whirring rustles of incoming shells followed by their jolting impacts. The cliff shuddered against Kimball's chest. There was an abrupt pause in the firing as the Allied gunners readjusted range, and then it immediately commenced again, the great flush of light silhouetting the top of the mountain's mass.

He looked up. He was now about fifty feet from the top. As he watched, the shadows of the faster climbers reached it and quickly disappeared beyond the rim. He started climbing again, aware that the barrage seemed to be advancing slowly eastward. There was a definite increase of shell hits closer in and their roaring funneled hollowly to him through rocky defiles.

Several bullets suddenly slapped into the cliff wall, fire from German outposts downslope that had spotted the raiders in the barrage light. Kimball experienced a moment of overwhelming terror that made him feel sick and empty in his stomach. *God, oh, God!* his mind cried out.

And right then he knew, as certain as was his own breath, that he was going to die.

His body stalled, hanging there. Another bullet struck something directly above him, making a peculiar, absorbing thud. He glanced up. One of the raiders had been hit, the man curling over and then peeling back away from the rock. A moment later, he plummeted past Kimball, a dark flash.

That brought him surging out of his stupor. His heart raced wildly as he clambered up the rest of the way, quickly gaining the rim of the cliff, which formed a rounded stone lip. Flailing and grunting, he pulled himself over and crawled across flat ground that was covered with rock chips.

Parnell was crouched nearby, giving hand signals. All around him men moved, hunched over, their bodies in the flickering blasts looking like images in old newsreels. He got to his feet, ran with them toward the German pillbox. It had a new cement smell, and raw drill debris was scattered all around it. Cowboy and two Gurkhas were already there.

A brilliant burst of phosphorous exploded in the air far back over the foothills, flooding the top of the dome with eye-aching white light. In it, Kimball saw Fountain turn and frantically wave him down.

At the side of the pillbox a Gurkha trooper leaned out and tossed something through its gun slit. A moment later a grenade went off with a muffled bang as an orange tongue of fire blew through the slit. A moment later, a second blast sounded from the other pillbox.

Then everybody was moving again. Shadows darted past Kimball. He caught a peculiar sound, realized it was coming from the old derrick cables that were humming as they responded to the explosion vibrations.

He scurried toward the two trunk entrances and dropped to his knees beside the first. Both had already been pulled open, exposing dark, round holes and the tops of steel rungs. Parnell and Sergeant Gurung were peering down. Each pulled two grenades from their harnesses. Gurung glanced at Parnell. Red nodded. Together they pulled safety rings, the spoon levers snapping back, and dropped the grenades down into the shafts, then ducked back.

Twin geysers of fire and smoke blew out of the round holes heavy with the stench of sundered stone and cordite like burnt fireworks. Instantly, men began slipping down into the shafts one by one. Kimball felt someone slap his shoulder. It was Kaamanui, pointing. Instantly, he shoved forward to the first trunk opening, squatted, put his legs over the edge, felt for the rung, and started down. Smoke stung his eyes.

It was 3:44. . . .

Bekker had just finished his third drink when the Allied barrage started. The rush of it washed through the openings in the rock face and around his door as if it were coming from a movie in another building. The floor of his cell trembled.

Instantly, he was up, running for the door. He wrenched it open and started across the plotting room, bellowing, "Secure the firing doors. All crews up. Standby for counterfire." Shadows darted through the blue dimness as he vaulted the steps to the observation platform.

It was like intermittent sunlight out there, the mountains thrown into chiaroscuric profile. *They're coming,* his mind kept repeating. Adrenaline pulsed through his body like electricity, invested it with sudden hot energy. He heard, felt the huge firing doors sliding into lockdown below his feet.

Someone shouted, "Turn on the mains." A few seconds later, the overhead lights clicked on, buzzing.

Down on the plotting floor, men darted. Gerd saw his senior NCO lunge out of the stairwell that led down to the gun rooms and head toward the observation platform. His name was Bruno Hohne, broad-shouldered, scarred from ear to lip.

A muted explosion trembled down through the rock from somewhere overhead. Everyone glanced at the ceiling. Hohne paused below the foot of the platform, frowning with puzzlement. Bekker took a step back from the viewing window just as a second explosion shook the overhead. Like the other, it seemed odd, too soft. Had two small artillery rounds struck the top of the dome? he wondered.

Suddenly there were two simultaneous explosions directly above them that were much louder. He recognized the sound: grenades! As the vibrations riffled off, the throaty chatter of automatic weapons came, men yelling. In the plotting room everyone froze in position, stunned.

Hohne was the first to react. Shouting orders, he whirled and headed back toward the lower stairwell, grabbing a machine pistol as he passed the small arms rack beside the gun director. The plot operators, shaken from their shock by his movement and voice, began scrambling for their own weapons.

Bekker's mind remained immobilized for a fraction of a second longer as he watched his NCO disappear down the stairs, the other men following close behind. More frantic yells echoed through tunnelways. The sounds unlocked him. *They're here!* He plunged forward, racing down the platform steps, pulling out his side arm.

Parnell, the fourth to exit the bottom of the trunk shaft, landed into a maelstrom of fighting men: Germans in dirty gray tunics and black-clad raiders with the big As on their backs struggling and falling, punching and hacking at each other. Gun bursts resounded in the stone room, the clash of steel blades, bayonets against *kukris,* and the vicious, obscene grunts and curses and snuffles of men in hand-to-hand combat.

Thick gun and explosion smoke drifted against the overhead lights along with the noxious smell of expended gunpowder. Four men were already down, three Germans and a Gurkha. The head of one of the Germans had nearly been severed. Blood still pumped from the ghastly decapitation wound while the man's eyes continued blinking in startled surprise. His blood ran down into the old dynamite drill holes in the floor, making bright red lines in the gray stone.

Parnell charged into the battle, trying to isolate targets. A bullet went by him, sucking air and *whanging* off a wall. A German soldier suddenly rose above the breech lock of the first 88mm and fired at him with a revolver. He missed. Red killed him, then swung the muzzle of his Thompson around to fire again. He was savagely knocked to the floor by a second German.

They locked together. The German whinnied with desperate little bursts of breath. He punched Red in the neck and began clawing at his face. Parnell saw his short brown hair and sunburnt face for a fleeting moment and then he rammed his palm against the man's chin, snapping his head back. He drove his other fist into the German's throat. The soldier fell away but instantly started to come up again. Red shot him in the forehead, the bullet blowing a small black hole into his skull. He dropped.

A grenade went off on the other side of the casement, and rock slivers flew like chunks of glass. Parnell came to his feet, his ears ringing numbly. His entire body felt as if it were glowing, a familiar sensation, first contact, the fear and apprehensions evaporating in a second, leaving only the ferocious business of combat.

More explosions echoed from below them. Then the chaotic noise ceased directly around him. Men straightened up, rose from the floor. All were raiders, panting, their eyes glinting with a kind of insane brightness. Slowly, they began to prowl among the fallen. Out of nowhere, Kaamanui and Kimball appeared beside him. Red pointed at the stairwell. "Go after them! Don't let 'em bunch," he shouted. The two dove for the stairway and dropped out of sight. He turned, waved frantically at the remaining Gurkhas. "Down, down." They darted past him, headed for the stairs. He followed.


Smoker Wineberg was in his element. He'd been the first one out of the trunk shaft into the second gun casement, landing in the large dish-shaped hole Sergeant Gurung's grenades had blown in the floor. Their blast pressure had ripped out most of the overhead lighting and the room was in partial darkness like twilight, everything in dim, smoky silhouette.

He and four Gurkhas rushed across the room and were met with gunfire. A Gurkha went down, flailing backward. Smoker felt something strike his thigh. It created an odd feeling, as if his crazy bone had been hit. He ignored it and sprayed the far wall beyond the breeches of the twin 88mms.

A German counterrush formed and came on, shadows looming. And they were into it like a deadly barroom brawl. He bellowed and fired and punched and bit. *Kukri* blades snapped through the air around him, muffled pistol shots banged, men groaned and cursed.

Then there was sudden silence. It seemed so contrastingly still he thought he could actually hear the last, faint reverberations of the fighting being swallowed by the stony earth. An agonized moan came clearly, then a long sighing that tapered back into silence. He moved about, stepping among bodies. He found a Gurkha holding the stump of his left arm at the elbow. Another Gurkha came up, began to apply a tourniquet. Near the down stairwell, Gurung and Bird were rallying the men, shoving them down the steps.

Wineberg joined them. At the bottom of the stairs was a small hallway with a steel door at the opposite end. Two small lateral tunnels branched off the hall at right angles. A Gurkha had already climbed into one. Smoker hurried forward and crawled into the second. A Gurkha soldier came right behind him.

The tunnel was about twenty feet long with light at the other end. A sheet of corrugated iron formed the floor. The walls were covered with moss that stank like sour mud. He scurried to the end, paused to look out, and then dropped into another small room with a steel door that apparently led into one of the lower gun casements.

He placed two satchel charges against the door, one at the upper corner, the other below. He set the timers for thirty seconds and he and the Gurkha quickly took cover back in the tunnel. When the charges went off, the concussion hurled smoke and fire and flooring into it. He slid out of the crawl space and rushed the door.

It had been blown partially off its upper hinges. Smoker leaned against the wall and threw grenades through the crack between the door and sill, one after the other, five in all. The noise of the blasts shook the room, and the concussion pressures hurt his ears. Smoke flushed back through the cracks, the door's face thrumming and creaking like ship's timbers, the metal too hot to touch.

Finally he and the Gurka managed to pry it open enough so Wineberg could slip through. The room was filled with scorching smoke as thick as a fog and putrid with the stench of burning flesh. It was completely dark except for the light that came through the crack in the door.

Dimly, he saw dead bodies and parts of bodies lying all over the floor. Some were still burning. Then he heard Bird's faint voice shouting commands from the outer room. Automatic fire erupted from somewhere farther back. He turned and squeezed back through the shattered doorway.

# Twenty-seven

*0400 hours*

Throughout the vast assault force on the plain, the order from divisional HQ crackled through field telephones and radios in battalion and company CPs: *Execute preassault check. Zero minus three-zero minutes in effect and counting. . . .*

Twenty-two minutes earlier, crack Indian sapper teams borrowed from the British Eighth Army had moved into the German minefields, the artillery bombardment moving deeper into the foothills to give them access. Using electric disk detectors and bayonets, they quickly swept for mines and trip wires.

To mark out cleared, twenty-four-foot-wide lanes, they reeled out white tape and planted tiny, single-facing green lights along the edges. When they reached anti-tank ditchs, they blew wall charges to create temporary spans for the tanks and placed assault ladders against the sides for the advancing infantry units.

Now subtle movements rippled through the mass of waiting men and vehicles. Last-minute gear checks were made as stomachs tightened. There came the murmur of final prayers, the heavy metallic slam of big gun breeches, and the lighter, snapping chunk of rifle and machine-gun receivers. Engines started up, growled softly in idle while cylinders and engine blocks warmed in the cold night. . . .

Bekker's first kill had instantly changed him. Coming down the stairs to the fourth gun casement door, he'd seen a black-clad figure as short as a gnome lunge from explosion smoke. He fired at it. The bullet struck the man in the face, throwing tattered flesh and bone to the side. At that instant, something in him shifted. What had been pounding blood and a disjointed sense of confusion earlier now became a serenity. He even felt a moment of wild exhilaration.

Gun bursts continued making violent, echoing reverberations all around him, yet he strode forward calmly into the midst of his men battling against more black-clad raiders. A bullet richocheted off a wall near him. Rock slivers sliced across his cheek, stung like the flick of a fencing blade. He merely smiled and fired several times at shifting shadows, saw another man go down, and then realized with a rueful click of his tongue that he had actually shot one of his own soldiers. *No matter, no matter,* he thought gaily. *We will conquer in the end. We are Germans.*

The battle shifted, the pulse of its gunfire slowing for a moment. Sounds, trapped in the rock, came back, made the smoke-saturated air shimmer in visible waves. He stood still and solid, firing until his weapon was empty. Patiently, he jacked the spent clip out, took the spare one from his holster, popped it in, and jerked back the receiver.

Stabsfeldwebel Hohne rushed to his side, shouting, "*Kapitan,* they're overrunning us. We must fall back and regroup."

Gerd turned, looked at him. Such a pale, scarred face

and black fearless eyes, he mused. *Good man, this.* "Yes, of course," he said, nodding convivially as if Hohne had merely summoned him to mess. "Indeed, we must regroup."

They made a temporary stand in the kitchen and mess room, ten soldiers and Bekker. Moments later, several others appeared from the powder magazine below. They had an MG-34 light machine gun, its squad bipods extended, and several additional MP-40s with cans of fresh ammo.

Hurriedly they set up the MG near the door, offset at an angle to the sill, and began firing into the connecting corridor. The weapon's low, thick, rapid muzzle blasts bounded and rebounded back into the room.

There was an explosion just outside the hall door that sounded like a grenade. Almost instantly another went off, both pressure waves whomping in the air like one. The machine gun fired again, stopped, fired, stopped. Before its echoes died off, several men in black came hurtling through the door.

The Germans fired, their bullets gouging lines of holes against the far wall. Two raiders went down, writhing. Soon the others were driven back through the door. A vacuumed pause followed, which merely held the delicate little sound of a single spent shell spinning like a whirligig on the floor.

Another rush came with more vicious firing. This time the Germans had to fall back, fighting, stumbling, half falling down the stairs to the powder magazine. The last man to go down was Bekker, stepping lightly, almost strolling.

Then he caught the quick flash of a curved knife coming at him through the smoke. He sidestepped nimbly and shot its wielder in the chest, punching three perfect holes through the black cloth of his uniform. The rounds threw the raider backward. He crawled back and came at him again. This time Bekker killed the man, turned disdainfully, and descended the steps.

Laguna, Fountain, and a Gurkha named Sing Thapa lay atop dead and wounded bodies in the mess room. The gun smoke was thick as steam. Weesay threw a burst at the stairwell, his rounds richocheting off the wall, and his receiver locked back on empty. As he rammed in another clip, he suddenly felt the German beneath him move.

Weesay jerked back and lashed at him with the barrel of his Thompson. The muzzle caught the German in the forehead, knocked his head back. He lay there and began to weep, his blue eyes squinting with pain. Laguna reached over and took his weapon, hurled it against the side wall. Bypassing him, Weesay crab-walked to the edge of the stairwell.

Gunfire came from below sounding hollow, as if issuing from a barrel. Cowboy came up behind Weesay, who turned and glared at him. "Gimme a grenade," he bawled. "Gimme me a fuckin' grenade."

"I ain't got any left," Fountain said.

Now Sergeant Bird and Kimball came through the mess room door, crouched over. Both were bleeding from the face. They made their way to Laguna and Fountain. "What's your situation?" Wyatt growled.

"They're holed up down there," Cowboy said. "Six, maybe seven men, one officer." A sudden burst of MP-40 fire erupted from the lower room. Everybody hit the floor. Bullets *whanged* and screamed off walls.

"We gotta take 'em out before they set up, goddammit," Weesay hollered at Bird. "Who's got grenades?"

Wyatt shook his head. "Cain't use grenades. That's the

powder magazine. We set off ordnance, we gonna blow ourselves off this gawddamn mountain." He scowled, thoughtful, then twisted around, shouted, "Who's carryin' smoke?"

Several of the raiders had been supplied with small orange smoke grenades. If the raid proved successful in neutralizing the German battery, the grenades were to be used to signal the incoming armor. One of the Gurkhas crawled forward, pulling one from his harness. He tossed it to Bird. It was an aluminum tube seven inches long with an orange contact cap.

Wyatt gathered them into an assault position, a line with the men squatting, each man's chest on the back of the one in front of him. Kimball was nearest the stairwell so would be the first one going down.

Bird grabbed his arm. "Soon's you clear the overhead, lay in a high burst to hold 'em down," he said. "Then hit that damn floor. We'll be pickin' targets right behind you."

Kimball stared steadily back into Wyatt's eyes for a few seconds, then nodded.

Bird glanced around at the others. "Ever'body check your weapons for load." A single shot sounded from the powder magazine, followed by a loud shout in German. Bird drew back slightly, expecting another burst. It didn't come.

He leaned down and slammed the contact cap of the smoke grenade against the floor. There was a small, sharp bang inside like a miniature firecracker. The grenade began to hiss and sputter. He tossed it down the stairwell. A moment later, a billow of orange smoke drifted back up the stairs.

Wyatt slapped Kimball's shoulder. "Go!"

Kimball went.

\* \* \*

Thirty-three seconds earlier, NCO Hohne had confronted Bekker, his face grim, his eyes shadowed. The powder bunker was stone-cold and dark save for thin light from the stairwell. It was filled with ordnance crates, shell casings, oiled paper wrappings. Two men were kneeling near the stairwell, their panting breaths smoking.

"We are lost, *Kapitan,*" Hohne said calmly. "You must set the demolition charges."

Gerd whirled on him, stared, shocked. His mouth creased with contempt. He hissed, turned away. Hohne grabbed his arm, roughly pulled him back. "*Kapitan,* the enemy must not be allowed to—"

Bekker yelled into his face, "You dare touch me? Coward!"

Hohne's face muscled up. He lifted his machine pistol threateningly. "Give me the keys," he hissed.

Gerd's left hand touched his throat. Then he brought up his Luger and shot Hohne in the chest. The impact knocked the sergeant back against the wall. Looking startled, he silently slid down it until he was seated.

Bekker glared out at the other men in the half darkness. "I'll kill any man who surrenders," he bellowed.

Something came flying out of the weak light from the stairwell. It made a soft, tinny sound when it hit the floor. It was sizzling and dark fumes were shooting out crazily. The back pressure of the releasing gas skittered it up against a crate of 88mm shells. The two kneeling Germans instantly dove away as the entire room was quickly enveloped in a cloud of acrid orange smoke.

Plunging down the steps, Kimball reached up to locate the overhead doorsill of the powder magazine. There it was. He fired his Thompson, one-handedly, felt the familiar recoil. When he reached the bottom, he threw himself to the floor, landing on boards and against a wooden storage pallet.

The smoke stung his eyes. It smelled like used battery fluid. More gunfire erupted, Thompsons and Stens and then the rapid, burring *thrupps* of German MP-40s. Their explosions merged into a wild crescendo of ripping, echoing sound. Someone stepped on his ankle. He felt a body crumple to the floor beside him.

His head thundered. He rolled to his left until he came up against a wall. Behind him, the light from the stair glowed a murky orange like a jack-o'-lantern. It surged and fumed, making darting shadows. He blinked and blinked against the stinging smoke, and tears glided down his cheeks.

The firing stopped abruptly. Men called to each other. One was Bird's voice, another Weesay's. Then it became very still. Nothing moved. Slowly the smoke began to rise. Kimball came to a squat. He could see the base of the wall now. It was tar coated. He scooted to it as the smoke rose higher.

Seven or eight feet away, he saw the bottoms of a pair of boots. A German soldier was sitting against the other wall, crumpled over. Next to him was a German officer down on one knee, reloading his Luger. His hands angrily jacked a round into the chamber. He glanced up. For one brief, startled moment, the two men stared at each other.

Both fired.

Kimball felt the bullet go into his chest, the contours of the neat hole it made as it blew through bone and tissue and, spending, into his heart. A shock of unbelievable pain exploded in his chest. He fell to the side, hit the wall. Through slitted eyes, he saw the German officer down. Half the man's head had been blown away by his Thompson burst.

The pain spread like scalding water. He tried to breathe, couldn't. Something seemed to be blocking the air just under his breastbone. He thought, *OhJesusOh-Jesus!* His vision blurred and objects got fuzzy-edged and seemed to float away but then came back again. He saw the other German against the wall suddenly lurch forward. He watched as the man clawed at the dead officer's tunic and then ripped a chain from his neck.

His vision began to darken again. He willed his eyes to collect the light, the images. Distantly, he watched the German soldier slowly push himself to his feet, his tunic blood-drenched. The movement made the orange smoke swirl around him. Inching sideways, he reached for a small box that was affixed to the wall, fumbling with the object in his hand. It was a key. He held it to the box.

Kimball's head whirred up suddenly, as if he had just immersed it into icy rushing water. The pain rose to another unbearable peak. He groaned. His own voice sounded peculiar, too high. The tinted light deepened around him, then abruptly flared, throwing everything into a brilliant, silvery orange. Despite his pain, he chuckled with sudden excited recognition. The color of the light was exactly the same as he remembered seeing a long time ago on a Chesapeake beach just at sunrise where the air was sharp and cold and the sea and the sky burned in copperish splendor. . . .

A harsh sound punched through his dissolving consciousness. Staccato, metallic, clanging. *What the hell is that?* he wondered vaguely. *A klaxon, yeah. Silly thing.* He floated, sleepy now. The pain was drawing away. He felt clean air flood into his lungs. Sweet, sweet. It seemed to contain the heady fragrance of carnations. . . .

\* \* \*

Under two feet of cement directly below the powder magazine, a battery-operated master switch box clicked into life. From it ran a series of rubber-coated wires, also buried, which fed out to ten explosive caches, each with thirty sticks of high-velocity straight granular dynamite that had been hidden in trim holes throughout the installation.

Each payload, hooked to dual-composition caps of mercury fulminate, could be simultaneously detonated by a single electrical burst from the master box. The batteries for this burst were linked to a simple clock timer inside the box, which had been preset on a ten-minute delay.

Now the minute hand clicked off another two seconds, leaving exactly nine minutes, fifty-four seconds to detonation. . . .

### 0430 hours

When the Allied artillery barrage stopped, every gun going silent at the same moment, the night rang with its after sound as it quickly plunged back into darkness. Only scattered brush fires set off by the shelling and some burning enemy bunkers in the hills showed light. Then a single red flare arched upward, trailing sparks. It peaked and exploded into a bloom of shimmering, scarlet light. It seemed to hover, swinging.

The roaring started gently, first isolated engines winding up, merging into an increasing rumble, which rose louder and louder as eight hundred vehicles leaped forward, their exhausts blowing red-tinted smoke, their treads and wheels gouging and hurling mud as Patton's Maknassy force went on the attack.

A minute later a new sound came, carrying just under

the thunder. It seemed out of place, evocative of cadets on parade or Sunday afternoon band concerts. It came from mounted loudspeakers blasting out the crashing drum-and-brass strains of "Stars and Stripes Forever. . . ."

Parnell and Wineberg with three Gurkhas had been in the process of destroying the breeches and barrels of the 88mms when the klaxon sounded. They exchanged glances. What? Short circuit? A chill of foreboding riffled through Red's mind. Then the Allied artillery stopped, too, the muffled thunder of it there and then not. He glanced at his watch.

*Here they come,* he thought.

Forty seconds later, Bird, Fountain, and Laguna came into the room, shoving two German soldiers ahead of them. Weesay had Kimball's limp body slung over his shoulders. The Germans were dirty, their gray uniforms covered with sweat and blood. They looked terrified.

Parnell's eyes narrowed as he looked at Kimball. He glanced over at Wyatt. The sergeant's eyes were dark, opaque with a smouldering fire. He shook his head. *Oh, no,* Red thought.

Directly behind Parnell, Smoker suddenly cursed and stepped around him. He stared at the Virginian's pale face for a moment. "The sons a bitches," he said blackly. "The rotten fucking sons a bitches." Without warning, he whirled and slammed the butt of his Thompson across the face of one of the Germans. The man grunted and dropped to the floor. Wineberg stared menacingly down at him.

Bird said to Parnell, "We got trouble, Lieutenant."

"What?"

"Somebody set off what looks like a demo box in the powder room." He nodded at the two Germans, the one

Smoker had struck now uncoordinatedly trying to get up. "These boys like to went nuts when they heard the alarm. Throwed down their weapons an' started screamin' about bombs. I think the whole place's mined."

*Oh, shit!* Red thought. "Can you disarm it?"

"I tried to. Blew her clear off the wall." He shook his head. "I figure the charges're on a master delay system. Could be anywhere."

Parnell turned to the standing German soldier, pointed at the floor, the ceiling. *"Bombe? Bombe?"* he said. The soldier jabbered in German, waved his arms to simulate the action of explosions. "How long?" Parnell yelled into his face, pointed at his wristwatch. "How long before *bombe* go boom?" The German extended the fingers of both hands.

Ten minutes.

"Everybody out!" Red bawled at the top of his voice. "Bring up the wounded, topside. Now!" To Bird he said, "Take Cowboy and check every room for wounded. You find Sol and Gurung, send 'em to me here. Then get the hell out." They moved off.

He turned to Weesay. "Carry him up to the top and then see if the reverse slope's clear."

Laguna turned and headed for the trunk shaft, lumbering bowlegged from Kimball's weight.

Far below them in the master switch box, the timer's hands clicked off another two seconds. Time to detonation: eight minutes, forty-three seconds. . . .

Parnell was the last to leave the underground battery, everybody already up the trunk shafts, the men hurrying but silent, helping the wounded along the narrow ladder-ways. At last, satisfied no one alive was left behind, he started up too, going hard, pulling rungs three at a time.

He emerged into a landscape flooded with light. Hundreds of German flares were now drifting lazily across the sky. They illuminated the plain and mountains in an artificial, too-white brilliance in which objects and faces appeared washed of their color tones.

The air resounded with the sharp cracks of enemy counter-battery fire: 88mms and 105mm recoiless guns in forward antitank positions in the foothills taking on the approaching Allied tanks still a thousand yards out. There was also the whining rustle of heavier 150mm shells passing overhead from German support howitzers back on the eastern plain.

He pulled himself free of the shaft. The badly wounded men of his force lay in a line, three Gurkhas and Kimball. Parnell stared at it. *Goddammit,* he thought angrily. *I should take all our dead out.* A point of honor. But no, it was too late.

A few yards beyond the trunk shafts the captured Germans lay on their stomachs, fifteen or sixteen, guarded by two Gurkhas. Near the machine-gun pillboxes and old French derricks the rest of the team had already formed a defensive perimeter.

He looked down the reverse slope. Two hundred yards below, a full company of German soldiers was coming up the service road, advancing in spread platoon fashion, double-timing. He heard Sergeant Gurung holler something. Instantly, a fusillade from Thompsons and Stens exploded along the small perimeter. The approaching Germans hit the dirt. A momentary pause, and then return fire came in a blaze of bullets that whipped overhead, slamming solidly into the derrick beams and richocheting.

Red scurried to the closest pillbox. Gurung, three of his men, and Wineberg were hunkered down behind it. He leaned close to the Nepalese sergeant and shouted, "We can use the Kraut guns in the pillboxes."

Gurung shook his head no. "Both destroy-ed, sor."

"Then go get others from below. Ammo and satchel charges, too. Then we can start the wounded down the cliff face." The sergeant rose and hurried off.

Sol came over to Parnell, squatted against the back of the pillbox calmly slapping a fresh clip into his weapon. He charged it and looked at him. His chocolate skin appeared gray in the peculiar light.

Red's mind raced. He must stall for time. Time! Jesus, how much did they have left? He glanced at his watch: 4:34. He turned toward the German prisoners. They stared back at him, terrified, caught between death by gunfire or by massive demolition. *Just like us,* he thought, *all in the same goddamned fix.*

*Stall, stall.*

He abruptly began waving at the Germans. "Go down," he shouted at them through the gunfire. "Go on down."

The soldiers didn't move. Then, one by one, several rose to their feet, started off down the slope, looking over their shoulders. They began yelling to their comrades below and wildly waving their arms. The rest of the captured Germans slowly got up, some limping or helping each other, and staggered down the slope after them.

The fire from the approaching troops ceased immediately. Soldiers down there waved the others in, hurrying them on. Red watched them go. For a brief moment, the thought of surrendering crossed through his mind. But something in him recoiled vehemently. *No, goddammit,* he thought.

He turned, looked at his own men. They were quietly watching the captured Germans go down, their faces stony. He didn't see surrender in their eyes. That sent a surge of pride through him, the thing catching in his throat with almost aching intensity. He felt his head buzz with it.

*We're not done yet, you Kraut sons a bitches.* . . .

Time to detonation: Five minutes, fifty-three seconds. . . .

Sergeant Gurung and two Gurkhas brought up a single MG-42 machine gun with three ammo boxes containing several fifty-round metallic-link belts and three satchel charges that had already been mounted on the 88mm's barrels. They set the machine gun up inside the right-hand pillbox. The two Germans inside had been killed instantly by the grenades, their faces and chests looking like bloody rags.

Several spaced, hollowly metallic *whomps* sounded from downslope. Everybody hollered, "Mortar! Mortar!" and hit the ground. The rounds came in silently, just the tinny double click of their fuses before they struck. The explosions made the ground shudder and sent shrapnel and rock slivers knifing through the air.

In the riffling echos that followed, Parnell frantically waved the men back to the cliff's edge. "Everybody but the gunners start down. The strongest can carry the wounded. Move it, move it! Before they rake us again."

Men turned, started running for the lip of the cliff. He turned to Kaamanui. "Take 'em all down. Me and Bird'll cover you. Leave Kimball. I want to bring him down myself."

Sol nodded. He signaled the others. They moved away. As they did, four more mortar rounds came in. The explosions left another humming-ringing stillness through which rocks and dirt rained down.

Red watched the men singly and in twos disappear over the cliff rim. He lifted his eyes. Far out on the plain, still lit as bright as day, he saw the Allied attack coming: the lighter, faster M-3 Grants on point, the heavier M-4 Shermans following, their ACs and antitank destroyers out on the flanks, all the ranks of vehicles stretching across the plain in parade ground separation, their guns twinkling like sharp glints of sunlight, their exhaust smoke foaming up and back with explosions of black smoke laced with fire now appearing among them, some getting struck dead-on, disappearing in orange balls of fire. . . .

Time to detonation: four minutes, thirty-one seconds. . . .

Down the slope, the captured Germans had reached their own line. Instantly, a furious volley erupted, enfilading the entire dome. Gurung opened up with the Kraut machine gun. Several German soldiers had advanced beyond their front, shouting taunts and firing as they came up. Four were hit and tumbled back down. The fusillade intensified. Two more mortar impacts came.

Parnell and Bird, curled into tight balls, held on while the chaos of flying shrapnel and rock slivers slashed the air all around them. Then, gradually, the firing slowed, only scattered shots now as the Germans reloaded.

Red slapped Wyatt's back. "Let's go." He partially rose, called to Gurung and his belt man. The Nepalese sergeant waved acknowledgment through the small rear door of the pillbox, turned back momentarily to give one last burst.

Bird reached the edge of the cliff first with Parnell right behind. Smoke and rock dust, stinking of spent explosive, drifted in layers. As Red reached the edge, he heard two sharp double clicks and instantly threw himself to the ground. Both mortar rounds went off simultaneously, their concussion wave roaring over him to numb his ears. After it passed, he lifted his head and saw that they had blown the German pilbox, Gurung, and his belt man to pieces.

Three minutes, forty-four seconds. . . .


Harrison Kimball's face lay in repose, a faintly puzzled expression on it. Bird had already started down. Parnell lifted Kimball's body, tried to settle it across his shoulders. He couldn't quite manage it, its dead weight constantly shifting bonelessly without solidity. More enfilading fire slashed across the dome and then two more mortar rounds came in. They struck back near the derricks.

Red came up into a crouch. He sudied Kimball's body for a moment, trying to solve its weight distribution problem. It occurred to him that he could use his harness. He quickly slipped out of it, looped the shoulder straps around Kimball's wrists, and hauled them tight.

Then, bodily lifting the corpse, he ducked under its outstretched arms and fitted the belt part of the harness down over his head. It pulled tightly against his throat. He moved a step, another. *Good,* he thought, *it'll work.* He peered over the edge, down the face of the cliff. It was like a sheet of chalky white in the light from the flares with his men scattered across it.

Lying on his belly with Kimball full-length on his back, Parnell eased himself over the edge, feeling for protrusions with his boot tips. He found one. Releasing the edge, he shifted his weight. Instantly the harness belt snapped harder against his throat, gagging him, and he felt himself being pulled back and off the face of the rock. He instantly flexed his throat muscles against the belt and willed his body's strength to counter the corpse's weight. Slowly, he regained his equilibrium. He started down. In the sharp light, rock knobs and cracks formed dark shadows on the rock. Down, down he went, muscles starting to strain, burning. He ignored them, continued descending.

He'd gone ten feet, then fifteen, and finally passed a firing door twenty-five feet from the top. He was panting heavily now, his heart struggling deep inside him. His throat stung. He paused to rest a moment, then sucked in a deep breath and started down once more.

He passed forty feet . . . fifty . . .

Suddenly bullets stitched a path of holes just above his head, coming from an enemy outpost far down the slope. Another burst came. He heard the unmistakable thud of lead slamming into human flesh. A man hollered, the sound of it dropping away. *Oh, Christ,* he thought wildly, *we're like rats on a goddamned wall!* He pressed his forehead against the stone and waited for the firing to ease off.

There were more bursts, but then came the throaty, drumming chatter of Thompsons as the first men to reach bottom opened on the German outpost. He started down again. Sixty feet . . . seventy . . . He was moving rapidly now, everything in him burning, aching, his body dropping recklessly, chancing quick rock knobs, creases.

He felt it starting, in his fingertips, a faint shimmer in the rock like a deep shifting of its layers. He instantly stopped and hugged the stone face with every ounce of strength he could draw from his muscles.

Two seconds later, the entire top of Hill 322 blew into the sky. . . .

# Epilogue

The stunning victories of Patton in the southern Easterns and Montgomery along the Mareth Line marked the beginning of the end for the Axis in North Africa. Forced as it was into a completely defensive war, its total collapse was only a matter of time. But six weeks of bloody fighting remained before that occurred.

With the end now clearly in sight, however, Roosevelt decided to let the ultimate defeat of German and Italian forces fall to the British. It was only fair; it was they who had spent three years in ceaseless combat. He ordered Eisenhower to begin a gradual pullback of U.S. units.

Some Americans would still be involved, such as Patton's II Corps and the U.S. First Infantry Division, which were shifted to the north to begin a spring offensive aimed at Bizerte. In Central Tunisia, Anderson's Fifth Army began a drive for Tunis, while Montgomery's Eighth Army pushed in from the south.

On 6 May, the Tunis defenders surrendered the city. The following day, Patton's forces reached the Mediterranean twelve miles from Bizerte, which was then fully occupied on 9 May. Now only von Arnim's DAK forces remained in the south.

They were doomed. Rommel's once powerful *Deutsches Africa Korps* had shrunk to a mere shadow of itself. It had only eight tanks left, its troops with no more than a two days' supply of ammunition, fuel, and food. The skies over Tunisia, once controlled by Axis aircraft, were now completely in Allied hands.

On the morning of 13 May, von Arnim sent his staff officers to Montgomery's headquarters to negotiate a surrender. According to the agreements between Roosevelt and Churchill at Casablanca in January, the only surrender had to be unconditional. Von Arnim accepted. Late that afternoon, he ordered all remaining German and Italian forces to lay down their arms.

The campaign for North Africa was over.

*Algiers, Algeria*
*3 April 1943*

The hospital had once been a Foreign Legion barracks, high on a lush, flowered hill. Beautiful four-story buildings of albumen-white sandstone, exquisite lawns, and date palms and flower beds of bougainvillea and hibiscus. The day was bright but chilled by a breeze off the Mediterranean.

Colonel Dunmore and Parnell sat on a stone bench beside a rock statue of Captain Gerard Clissold, a nineteenth-century Legion hero. Red wore his maroon patient's robe and had a week's stubble on his cheeks. A few feet away, buff-colored sparrows busily hunted insects between the walkway stones.

This was the colonel's third visit. He'd first come to the hospital to greet Red and his men when they were brought in two days after the raid on Hill 322. That operation had been costly: nine dead, eighteen wounded, some gravely. But except for Kimball's death, Blue Team had suffered only minor wounds.

Following their descent of the dome's rock face, Parnell had withdrawn his men into the maze of arroyos near the base of the cliff. In such good defiladed ground, they were able to hold against sporadic attacks until picked up by forward units of the Sixtieth Regimental Combat Team. Meanwhile, it took only three hours for Patton's First Division to force the Maknassy pass and debouch its armor out onto the eastern plain.

Dunmore offered Red a cigarette, lit it. For a moment, the two men smoked quietly. Finally, Dunmore asked, "So, John, how are you feeling today?"

"Fine, sir." Parnell had changed. He seemed quieter, more watchful, now carried the calm but hardened look of the combat vet.

"The men?"

"The same. A bit restless."

Dunmore chuckled. "Yes, I expect so." He took a deep drag, expelled the smoke upward. "I spoke with Patton yesterday. He's damned proud of you boys."

Red nodded without comment.

"Which brings me to some other good news." Smiling, Dunmore retrieved a small metal box from his briefcase and handed it over. Inside were seven shoulder patches, each bearing the black profile of a Mohawk warrior on a field of sky blue. Across the top of the patches were the words RECON FORCE, and on the bottom the single word MOHAWKER. The letters were sewn in red.

Parnell chuckled. "We finally made it, eh?"

"As of yesterday. The Mohawkers are now an official unit of the United States Army. In the AD logs we're listed as ASF dash IO dash One designate MOHs. Helluva title, isn't it?"

"Sounds good."

"Actually, we're the army's first small, completely independent tactical force. In its entire history. What do you think about that?"

"Always nice to be first in something."

"It gets better. Blue Team's also the first such unit to win a battle commendation and ribbon. Patton intends to personally make the presentation."

Parnell looked at him. "He's coming here?"

"Yes, tomorrow. Remember, he's got a share in this, too."

Red looked at the patches again, mere bits of cloth. A year ago such things would have been meaningless to him, merely military insignias. Now they seemed profound, beyond price. For a moment, Kimball's face came to him. *Pity he isn't here to receive his,* he thought.

Dunmore took a last drag, then field-stripped his cigarette butt. "Are the men fit enough to go back into training?"

"Yes."

"Good. We've a new mission for you."

Parnell glanced up.

"Three days from now, you'll be flown to Cairo," Dunmore went on. "More specifically to the SecOp division of the Office of Strategic Services. A Major Steve Heaton will meet you there. OSS is going to run you through a three-week crash course on operating with in-country partisans. Ground familiarity, language, the whole bit. Then it's back to Falmouth, England, for retraining in new weaponry and amphibious assault techniques. Torch showed us a lot of things we were doing wrong."

"But we're one man short, Colonel."

"Only until tomorrow. I've reassigned a man from Yellow Team to replace Kimball. His name's Pfc Angelo Cappacelli. He's familiar with where you're going. He grew up there as a child and speaks the language fluently."

Three women passed along the walk. One was an American lieutenant in olive-drab fatigues. The others were native nurses in white uniforms and Islamic *hijab* shawls. The lieutenant gave Dunmore a snappy salute.

Red waited until they were out of earshot. "What's our jump-off date?"

"The main show's set to begin at oh-five-hundred on ten July. Your team will go active forty-eight hours earlier. I'll have your completed MTO by the time you get to England."

"What is the main show, Colonel?"

"The invasion of Sicily," Dunmore said.

Presenting . . .

A sample chapter from Charles Ryan's
next exciting Recon Force thriller

*Thunderbolt*

Coming from Pinnacle in 2004

# One

*Egadi Islands*
*8 July 1943*
*2118 hours*

The eighty-foot Elco PT boat slowed as it drew within sight of Isole Marettimo, the outermost of the three small Egadi Islands located forty miles off the coast of Sicily. It lay out there, the long, jagged ridges of its Mount Falcone black shadows resting on the moonlit sea.

The PT had made good time, skimming across what had started as a calm sea from its secret base on Cape Bon, Tunisia, her three big-bore Hall-Scott gasoline engines screaming, her props cutting a white wake in the ocean. The boat's skipper, a navy lieutenant named Broadhouse, had held to a northerly heading for half the trip to avoid German picket subs prowling the waters off the southern coast of Sicily.

With him up on the the conning deck was Lieutenant John 'Red' Parnell, leader of a small insertion force which would be put ashore on Marettimo. The force consisted of seven men, designated Blue Team, which was part of an elite company of specially-trained soldiers called the Mohawkers who conducted clandestine operations behind enemy lines.

Beyond Marettimo, the other Egadi islands, Levanzo

and Favignana, were lost in the larger shadow mass of Sicily, itself completely dark under Geman blackout. But to the east, the eleven-thousand-foot high open volcano pit of Mount Etna cast a soft orange glow up into the night sky.

Lieutenant Parnell was a broad-shouldered man, six-three, linear-muscled with crew-cut red-blond hair and a wide, athletic face which possessed high cheekbones, a remnant of Sioux Indian blood his mother had passed on to him. Now as he scanned the ocean ahead, Broadhouse abruptly came off the throttles and the roar of the engines died away. Instantly the deck tilted sharply forward as the drag from the ocean surface began drawing against the boat's hull.

The Skipper said, "Best get your men ready, Parnell. We'll be making our run-in in about fifteen minutes." He glanced toward the southeastern horizon. "Damn it, I don't like those cloud banks out there. They're moving faster than forecast."

"That gonna be a problem?" Red asked.

"It's chopped up the surface already. I don't like working shallows in chop. Besides, the wind effect could also mess up the water in those caves."

Red looked eastward and for the first time during the trip felt that pre-mission tension starting in him. It was an energy that wasn't really like energy at all, rather more a stillness or silence that actually held the real energy tethered.

He turned and went aft along the fire barrier to the forward hatch of the midhouse and knocked on it with the back of his fist. A moment later, it swung open. He quickly slipped down the ladder into the dark mess compartment as the hatch closed behind him. Someone flicked on a red battle lantern.

"Everybody up," he snapped. "We'll be closing in fifteen."

Instantly his men came to their feet and began gathering gear from off the mess table and deck. The room was stuffy with cigarette smoke and smelled of weapon oil and fresh paint.

Some of their equipment had been tightly wrapped in water proof oil cloth. There were Thompson submachine guns with spare clips taped to their stocks, handguns in shoulder holsters, demolition packs and timers, rolls of wire, underwater flashlights, and a long, folding steel auger with a roller bit and two extensions. One of the packs also contained several deflated goat bladders and diving goggles.

Loaded, they trooped up to the main deck and hurried past the PT's torpedo tubes to assemble beside a large rubber raft strapped to the deck just aft the bow. Besides Parnell, the team consisted of Master Sergeant Wyatt Bird, Staff Sergeant Sol Kaamanui, Corporal Billy Fountain, and Pfcs Weesay Laguna, Smoker Wineberg, and Angelo Cappacelli, a new replacement. All except Cappacelli were veterans of North Africa.

One other man would be accompanying them ashore, a short but heavy-boned Sicilian with deeply tanned skin and tattoos on his thick forearms. His name was Marcuzzo Vassallo, a *tuffatori* or lobster diver, and would act as their guide. All the men wore swimming trunks, tennis shoes and black t-shirts.

Moving slowly now, the PT rolled gently in the increasing chop from the approaching storm which shattered the surface into millions of dancing moonlit spangles. They cleared past Point Mugnone, the northern tip of Marettimo, and continued beyond Point Tiora before turning south, holding a mile off shore.

A few dim lights were scattered along the coast, kerosene lanterns from small fishing villages. But back toward Sicily there were dozens of tiny flickering orange lights bobbing on the ocean, tuna fishermen working the huge schools as they headed north after breeding off the African coast.

Lieutenant Broadhouse came forward. "We're at the shallows," he told Parnell. "I'll need your lobster diver to get us through the outer channel. Who's going to translate?"

Red sent Cappacelli. Although the entire team had gone through a crash course in Italian at the OSS, the Office of Strategic Services, in Cairo before the mission so they could work with Italian partisans, the Sicilians spoke a rapid, heavily-accented dialect that was extremely difficult to understand. Although Angelo had been raised in New York and San Francisco, he had been born in Sicily.

With engines idling, they passed through a series of reef channels and entered a small bay. Rocky gullies and wash trenches came directly down to a narrow rim of beach. As they neared it, the higher ridges began to emerge, tufa cliffs and jagged hogbacks silhouetted against the sky. To the left on a two-hundred-foot-high headland stood the dark outer wall of a seventeenth-century Capuchin monastery called *Il Posare de Nerovento*, the Place of the Black Wind.

The monastery's monks had been famous throughout the Mediterranean as embalmers, preserving the bodies of hundreds of wealthy Sicilian and Italian aristocrats, which were still in catacombs under the main building. After Mussolini seized power in 1925, he had converted the monastery into a prison for political dissidents and members of the Mafia whom he had sworn to crush.

Blue Team's mission was to rescue two still held there, a powerful *capo-di-capo*, or chief of chiefs, named Don Vincenzo Caprano and his brother Santegelo. . . .

* * *

High above them, Don Vincenzo was not asleep. Instead, he lay on his filthy straw bunk and gazed stone-faced at the dark ceiling of his cell. He waited with the motionless, primitive patience of a leopard at a water hole.

Suddenly, a small light played for a moment through the steel grating of his cell door. Then came a soft whisper, a man speaking in hill-country Sicilian: "Your lordship, the time approaches."

Don Vincenzo instantly rose to his feet. He wasn't a big man yet he bore an unmistakable aura of power. His face was round, jowly even, his hair thick and black and, unlike the other prisoners, uncut since even here fear of him prevented the guards from touching his person. He had a heavy, unkept mustache and beard, and his eyes, even in the dim light, were carbon black and cast a cold, lethal glint of pent-up violence.

He stood at the door. "You have it?"

"Yes." The man out in the corridor passed a revolver and a box of cartridges through the grating. The revolver was a 10.4 mm Bodeo with a ring on its grip.

"Santegelo?"

"Yes, your lordship. He too is prepared."

The night was silent save for the vague murmurs of sleeping men in the cells lining the inner wall of the corridor. It was cobblestoned and perpetually wet. Each day the prisoners emptied their slop buckets into the corridor which was then washed down with strong hoses. The stench of excrement and disinfectant lingered in the air.

The man who had brought the weapon was a soldier-guard named Ermenio Silone, a Sicilian from the town of Valdibella who had been drafted into the Italian army. Like all Sicilians, he despised mainland Italians, who considered anyone from Sicily an ignorant peasant to be treated no better than a dog.

The guard asked permission to leave. Don Vino dismissed him with a jerk of his head and returned to his bunk. He sat examining the revolver, felt its weight, and then loaded the cylinder. He didn't like handguns, they were too imperfect for killing. He had killed many men in his life, always with a knife or a *lupara*, a sawed-off shotgun. You knew a man's death was certain with these.

At last, he lay down again. He held the gun on his chest and stared at the ceiling, waiting.


The team gathered on the beach below the prison. The PT had retreated through the reef and was now anchored about a mile offshore, nearly invisible with its blue-and-white hull merging into the pattern of whitecaps.

Parnell huddled with Bird, Laguna, and Fountain, going over their orders and synchronizing watches. They were to climb up to the approaches of the prison and lay numerous small demo charges along its outer wall. Then, at precisely 0200 hours, these would be detonated, each blast followed by a thirty-second pause. Hopefully, the explosions would create a large enough diversion to allow the incursion team into the prison from below.

As the three disappeared into the rocks, Vassallo led the others along the beach to a rocky alcove with a high back wall. The water was deep but glowed with moonlight. Beyond the alcove wall lay a vast labyrinth of marine caves. But in order to reach them, the team would have to swim underwater for about a hundred yards.

Parnell quickly broke out the goggles and goat bladders and passed them out. The goggles had wooden eyepieces and leather tie thongs. With their gear strapped to their backs and bladders blown full of air, they slipped one by one into the water and went under with Vassallo leading the way.

The water was warm and clear, the shafts of moonlight shimmering, forming a distinct shadow line near the wall. Red flicked on his flashlight as did Vassallo, their beams playing against the face of the rock. It was pockmarked, the color of solidified lava. Its face was flat and partially covered with seaweed that swayed gently in the current.

He trailed the Sicilian down, feeling the upward pull of his goat bladder. Ten feet, twenty. His ears began to ache. Forty feet, then fifty. He saw the bottom of the rock face which ended three feet above a sandy floor, which was merely an indistinct blur of gray-white.

He saw Vassallo disappear under the wall and followed, then found the diver squatting on the sand beyond the opening, pointing ahead and up. Parnell's lungs were beginning to ache with oxygen need but he knew he couldn't yet breathe from the bladder. At this depth, the pressure would prevent his lungs from expanding.

He shone his light on the backside of the wall, the thing sloping sharply upward. Vassallo pushed off the bottom and went past him, headed up. He stayed close behind him. Twenty seconds later, the Sicilian drew up, floating. He pointed at Red's bladder and made signs for him to breathe. Although the overhead was still submerged, they had reached a shallow enough depth to let their lungs work again.

First releasing air, he unwound the nipple of his bladder, stuck it into his mouth and sucked in. The bladder air was warm and tasted the way rawhide smelled. Breathing evenly, he waited for the others to come up.

Sol Kaamanui was the first, rocketing by sleek as a seal; the one-time hardhat diver with the Corps of Engineers

was in his element now. Next came Cappacelli, and finally Smoker Wineberg, who shook his head at Parnell,
his eyes glaring behind his goggles.

It took them ten minutes to reach an open pool, Red
coming up last with everybody already sitting on the rim,
panting. Wineberg, his taut, wiry boxer's muscles showing clenaly through his wet T-shirt, spat disgustedly.
"This suckin' on goat guts is *bullshit*. I fuck near *drowned*
down there."

The air in the cave was dank and cold and held the
odor of spawning fish. Water drained slowly from the
walls. Each day at high tide the entire labyrinth of caves
was completely inundated by the ocean. Calcite stalag-
mites rose from the floor like stacks of rust-colored
artichokes, and there were veins of obsidian locked in
the rock, which sparkled like black glass whenever the
flashlights hit them.

The men quickly unsheathed their weapons and moved
out, going in line with Vassallo in the lead. He was intimately familiar with the cave system, having explored it
many times during lobster-hunting dives.

Parnell checked his watch and hissed. They were
falling farther and farther behind schedule. . . .

A woman's voice suddenly cried out, moaned, then
dropped, sliding down into an urgent Sicilian obscenity.

Instantly, Bird, Laguna, and Fountain dropped to the
ground. They were on the lower prison approach road,
about seventy-five yards away from the front of the main
building, rising huge and stone-dark and looking like a
fort.

They lay absolutely motionless, listening hard. Another
cry came, then a man's voice, incoherent. Bird lifted his
head. Wild grass lined the road, about two feet tall. Off to

the right were olive and orange groves long gone to seed, the citrus trees skeletal like blackjack oaks. Now came a riffle of laughter, female and throaty.

He signaled the others to remain and crawled off through the grass. The blades were thick, dry as fall hay. He reached the edge of a small gully and looked down the slope. There, clear in a pool of moonlight, were a man and woman fornicating on a blanket.

"God *damn!*" Wyatt said softly.

The man was naked from the waist down, the woman's legs wrapped around his back. His buttocks glowed white as he thrust steadily back and forth. One of his collar insignias glinted suddenly, indicating that he was a soldier, up here with either his sweetheart or a whore from the nearby village.

Wyatt returned to the road to wave the others in, and tell them they *had* to see this. They all crawled back to the gully. Laguna swore and laciviously sucked spittal through his teeth. "That god damn *hijo de puta,*" he murmured. "Poundin' pussy on guard mount?"

After a few moments, Bird tapped his shoulder and they returned to the road. Cowboy chortled. "Wait'll them charges go off, *chico,*" he whispered to Weesay. "If he's still stickin' her, that ole gal's gonna clamp up on him an' flat squeeze his dick off." They both got to giggling until Wyatt gave them the cutthroat sign.

They continued up the road, doing leapfrog dashes and going to ground. At last they reached a flat, sandy area directly in front of the prison's main gate. The gate itself was made of weathered wooden cross beams bound with iron bars.

They lay in the grass to check everything out. There were no guard towers along the wall and no visible lights. The entire place had the medieval look of a Norman keep. Dozens of seagulls were perched along the top of the rampart and occasionally one would lift off and hover on the wind. It had turned gusty over the last half hour and the air held the warm, moist odor of storm.

Finally they left the grass and worked their way to the left corner of the structure. There were jagged cliffs on this side sloping down to the beach. The wall was fashioned out of rough-cut sandstone and was heavily coated with bird guano. They could see the PT out beyond the reef, a vague block of white lines, stationary and oddly out of synch with the rest of the whitecaps.

Bird said, "Y'all take the gate, Weesay. Cowboy, you got this corner. I'll lay the bayside. Remember, thirty-second intervals on the fuses. Anybody spots you, duck and withdraw without firing. And watch out for that wop stud comin' back in."

Laguna spat. "That prick, I like to shoot him."

A twisting blast of wind lifted sand against their faces. Wyatt checked his watch, the luminous little dials indicating 11:31. "Okay, let's do it," he said, and shoved to his feet.

Down in the caves, they were lost, with the continually up-sloping walls and narrow, water-worn passages all starting to look alike. Vassallo was agitated, cursing, saying in Sicilian, "I *know* it was here. Look, look, this place. To God I swear it."

Parnell glared at him. "I think maybe there never *was* a plate, *l'amico,*" he said in Italian.

"*Che? Che?*" the diver cried excitedly. "This what you think?" He shook his head stubbornly. "*This* the place. Hey, I do not hold the knife by the blade."

Red turned to Cappacelli. "What the hell does that mean?"

"You've insulted him, Lieutenant," Angelo snapped.

Cappacelli always had a hint of cockiness in his tone, even when speaking to officers. He was of medium height and compactly built with tightly curled black hair and a broad, thick-skinned face. Although a trained Mohawker, he hadn't seen any combat yet and was not completely accepted by the others. "The knife phrase means he doesn't lie," he said.

"God damn it," Red hissed. "That means the son of a bitch really *is* lost."

For the last forty-five minutes they'd followed the diver all over hell searching for a brass plug plate he claimed he'd seen many times. According to OSS pre-mission research, an Egyptian archeologist named Massar had actually placed such a marker in 1920, after drilling into the cave system from the catacombs. To prevent the tomb area from being flooded, he had put in the plug and then backfilled the ten-foot drill hole with cement.

In order to break into the catacombs, Parnell intended to drill a blast hole beside the cement seal, going in at least eight feet before placing charges. With the noise of their detonations covered by those from Wyatt and his men, they would enter the catacombs, quickly locate and retrieve the Caprano brothers, and then withdraw through the cave system.

But now they had a major glitch added to the potential ones which were already a part of the mission. What if the marker plate had somehow disappeared since Vassallo last saw it, the thing washed away or stolen? Without it, there was no way to tell where the caves came closest to the tomb area. Or what if the catacomb wall was thicker than ten feet, and they weren't able to drill deep enough to blow through?

Red kept looking at his watch, trying to mentally will it to slow down. It was almost midnight already. That left them only a three-hour window in which to drill and

blast, locate the two *mafiosi,* and then get back through
the cave system before the tide flooded it. According to
oceanographic forecasts, the tide would begin peaking
by 0300 hours. If they weren't clear by then, they'd be
trapped between the impassable caves and the roused
Italian prison detachment.

Sol came up. "Maybe the guy's just disoriented, Lieutenant. OSS was pretty strong the plate'd *be* here."

Red nodded. "All right, we'll give her one more sweep.
Everybody spread out but stay within light distance."

Parnell moved off along a drift to the right, the walls
lined with jagged strips of anthracite. Unconsciously,
he began really examining the stone surfaces. He had a
degree in mining engineering from the University of
Colorado and now his geological curiosity kicked in.

He realized the walls were made of tightly compacted
sandstone and shale, pinkish in color. It was called
Graywacke sandstone. Interspersed with the main matrix
were feldspar and quartz, along with a skeleton of silica.
Precisely like the Old Red Sandstone of the ocean bottom during the Devonian Age. That turned him cold.
This kind of rock was going to be a bitch to drill through.

Someone shouted, "Here, over here! I found the
sumbitch."

The auger bit kept overheating, smoking-hot all the
way back and up through the men's gloves as they
worked the crossbar. Parnell instructed them to drill on
a down slant so they could pour water to cool the bit and
shaft. Each time they did, a burst of steam blew back out
the drill hole.

It was three feet to the right of the archeologist's cement plug. The continual emersion in salt water had
turned the brass plate a dull green and seaweed dangled

.ms. The inscription was barely readable. It
*by dr hafazah massar 9:22:1920.*

was gruelling. Everybody was pouring sweat,
s, even Vassallo, until their arms and shoul-
ıumb. It was now 1:34 A.M. Thus far, they'd
four feet into the rock.

rdered Cappacelli and the diver back to one
pools to get sand to tamp the drill hole be-
red. When they returned, Angelo told him,
's rising back there, Lieutenant. I think that
ɛ is already shoving more surface water into
ıan usual."

ıch has it risen since we came in?"
naybe two."

ﬁed to figure. They'd already used up an hour
o get just four feet into the stone, with at least
ɔre to go before reaching a point close enough
the catacomb side to punch through—if the
ɛd wall really was ten feet thick.

ɛd Sol over. "This is getting dicey," he told him.
"We better double up on the explosives. If it makes too
much noise, so be it. Can you boost that shaped charge?"

Kaamanui nodded. "Yeah. I can use one of the extension caps." He shrugged. "We could still hit soft stone."

"I don't think so. This rock's braze strata, tight as shit.
I'll tell you the truth, Horse. I'm not sure we got *enough*
charge to blow through at all." He looked into the big
Samoan's always-placid brown eyes. "And once that tidal
flood comes in full, we've got a problem."

"Yeah," Sol said calmly.

They drilled on.


Bird and Fountain sat in the sand in fading moon
shadow. High overhead, a thickening cloud cover was

damping the moon's intensity. In the bay, the PT had edged itself back through the surf line. It looked dark and sinister sitting out there.

All the explosive charges around the monastery had been set and timed. Everything was still quiet in the prison. They hadn't even seen the wop lover. Now the three men relaxed, that part of their task over. But inside they were still tuned tightly with the continual over-alertness of an operation in progress.

Laguna had idly wandered down to the water's edge, crabs clicking among the rocks. Here and there the tide had deposited tiny dotlets of phosphorescence. When he returned, he had one on the tip of his forefinger, the thing glowing a bright green like a speck of radium.

"Hey, check this," he said, holding up the finger. "Ain't that pretty? I wonder what it is."

"A crustacean," Wyatt said.

"A what?"

"A crustacean, a tiny crab. The things float round in the ocean. Back in Hawaii they shine pure blue." Bird had once served with the old Twenty-fifth Infantry Tropical Lightning Division in Honolulu. Deadpan, he said, "Them little bastards is poisonous as hell, boy. You get their juice in your blood, we gonna have to cut off your finger. Maybe your whole goddamn arm."

Weesay stared. "You shittin' me?"

"Hell, no."

"Aw, fuck!" he blurted, then dropped to his knee and began furiously dragging his hand through the sand Bird exchanged grins with Cowboy.

Laguna glanced up and saw their faces. He stopped, glaring at them. "Assholes," he croaked, then sat back in the sand and spat angrily.

Bird's grin faded. He looked out at the ocean, the tide visibly higher now, then swung his gaze back to the monastery and down along the rocky slope, scanning all the way to the beach, figuring possible attack lanes and firing positions.

Cowboy said, "What kind of weapons you figure they got, Sarge?"

"Probably just rifles and sidearms," Wyatt answered. "They ain't set up to defend nothing from the outside, just keep them poor ass bastards on the inside." He glanced at his watch, cupping a hand over it so the dials would show brightly. 1:41. Their charges would start going off in nineteen minutes.

He eased himself to his feet. "All right, let's get the raft out and then set up security positions." He lifted his chin, indicating the north wall of the monastery. "I figure them wops'll come down that main beach trail. We can set up firebase on boths sides of that ridge. The one that looks like a tit?"

They moved off along the beach to where they'd hidden the raft back in the rocks.

The drill bit was in a little past eight feet, two more feet of solid stone between it and the catacomb wall. Everybody was getting antsy about the incoming tide, the water already mid-way up their calves. Even Vassallo was shooting frowns toward Parnell.

After his final stint on the crossbar, Red had gone back to have a look at their entry pool. He had a difficult time finding it, the water now covering the entire chamber, its surface rising and dropping as if it were breathing, and the flashlight shimmering on it because of the stronger incoming surge.

He checked his watch. In sixteen minutes, Wyatt's charges would go off. He experienced a moment of claustrophobia, like a rat trapped in a drainpipe with someone about to open the flood gates all the way.

When he got back to the drilling face, he told Kaamanui, "Start loading the hole now. We got about twelve minutes." For a moment, he knelt to examine the jury-rigged shaped charge.

Sol had added one of the auger extensions to the original explosive canister. Inside the canister was a copper cone that would channel the full charge into a single point, creating a focus of highest pressure. By adding the hollow extension sleeve, he'd been able to double the charge.

They quickly extracted the drill and doused down the shaft. Then Kaamanui wired up the shaped charge and shoved it down into the hole, making certain it didn't butt directly up against the bottom. Next he laid in the string of three three-stick packs of DuPont Hi-Vee straight-granular dynamite and tamped sand around them until the hole was filled. All the charges had electrical blasting cap igniters and were wire-linked to a battery-and-plunger detonator.

Five minutes to two . . .

Parenll began placing his men into their assault positions, first Smoker, then Cappacelli and Vassallo, the three smallest men, with Sol and himself going in last. They checked their weapons, the soft metallic clicks of actuators flipping into full auto, safeties coming off. The Sicilian diver stood looking dumbly at the lieutenant. He finally understood what the American was ordering him to do and instantly began shaking his head and jabbering at Angelo.

"Goddammit, what the hell's he yelling about?" Red shouted at Cappacelli.

Angelo was arguing with Vassallo and waving his arms. He swore and turned to Parnell. "The guy says he ain't going in there. It's a place of the dead and nobody told him he would have to go in."

"Then get him the hell out of the line."

Angelo translated. Vassallo crept off.

One minute . . .

They waited. The air in the labyrinth had changed subtly as fresh ocean water was being flushed into the caverns. The suck and hiss of it filled the silence, intensified the passage of the seconds.

They didn't hear Bird's crew's first explosion but felt it, a soft tremor in the floor and through the walls. Two seconds later another explosion came and Parnell thought: *Somebody's timer screwed up.* He looked up the line, everyone's heads turned, watching him. Seconds snapped past. Another tremor came, this one stronger. It made the surface water riffle.

Red yelled, "Fire in the hole!" and rammed down the plunger of the detonator.

# ABOUT THE AUTHOR

Charles Ryan served in the United States Air Force, as a senior airman and munitions system specialist in the armament section of the 199th Fighter Squadron based at Hickam AFB, Honolulu. He attended the Universities of Hawaii and Washington, and has worked at numerous occupations, including judo instructor, commercial pilot, and salvage diver. He's written for newspapers in Honolulu and San Francisco and magazines, as well as being the author of six novels. Ryan currently lives in northern California.

## THE CODE NAME SERIES BY
# WILLIAM W. JOHNSTONE

__**Code Name: Payback**
0-7860-1085-1                           **$5.99**US/**$7.99**CAN


__**Code Name: Survival**
0-7860-1151-3                           **$5.99**US/**$7.99**CAN


__**Code Name: Death**
0-7860-1327-3                           **$5.99**US/**$7.99**CAN


__**Code Name: Coldfire**
0-7860-1328-1                           **$5.99**US/**$7.99**CAN


__**Code Name: Quickstrike**
0-7860-1151-3                           **$5.99**US/**$7.99**CAN


## *Available Wherever Books Are Sold!*

Visit our website at **www.kensingtonbooks.com**

# THE MOUNTAIN MAN SERIES BY
# WILLIAM W. JOHNSTONE